How *to* Ruin a Wedding

PRAISE FOR *HOW TO RUIN A WEDDING*

"Undeniably funny. Sexy. A fresh new take on fake dating. *How to Ruin a Wedding* delivers everything I want in a rom-com. With messy characters that feel as real as you and me, sizzling chemistry, and the perfect amount of forced proximity, Elba Luz gripped me from the very first line and had me speeding through the pages well into the night. I love this book, and you don't want to miss it!"

—Riss M. Neilson, *USA Today* bestselling author

"Irresistible from the very first page, *How to Ruin a Wedding* charms its way through revenge, secrets, complex families, redemption, and the love waiting for us on the other side of heartbreak. An effortlessly funny and steamy novel that will leave readers feral for whatever Elba Luz writes next!"

—Julian Winters, *USA Today* bestselling author of *Last First Kiss*

"Charming, funny, and devastatingly romantic, this is an instant classic that you need on your shelf. Beloved tropes are made fresh by the sizzling chemistry between Anders and Lucy, the two iconic characters that anchor this sexy and satisfying love story. I can't wait to see what Elba Luz writes next!"

—Kamilah Cole, *USA Today* and national indie bestselling author of *An Arcane Inheritance*

How to Ruin a Wedding

A NOVEL

Elba Luz

MINDY'S BOOK STUDIO

This is a work of fiction. Names, characters, organizations, places, events, and incidents are either products of the author's imagination or are used fictitiously.

Published by Mindy's Book Studio, New York

www.apub.com

EU product safety contact:
Amazon Media EU S. à r.l.
38, avenue John F. Kennedy, L-1855 Luxembourg
amazonpublishing-gpsr@amazon.com

ISBN-13: 9781662543043 (hardcover)
ISBN-13: 9781662539145 (paperback)
ISBN-13: 9781662537684 (digital)

Cover design by Emily Mahar
Cover image: © pe-art, © Veleri, © xamtiw / Getty; © G artist / Shutterstock

Printed in the United States of America

First Edition

For those who always feel a step behind—a late bloomer still blooms.

A NOTE FROM MINDY KALING

Okay, fellow romantics, can we talk about something? Have you ever been at a wedding—like, sitting there in your uncomfortable dress watching two people exchange vows—and thought, "Wait, NO. This is all wrong. She's supposed to be with someone else!" Just me? Well, if you've ever had that very specific fantasy (or just a hesitation about a couple's nuptials), then *How to Ruin a Wedding* is basically required reading.

This book is an absolute delight. I'm talking laughing out loud on public transportation, swooning so hard you need to fan yourself, and maybe shedding a tear or two.

So here's the premise: Lucy is a professional wedding wrecker. Yes, that's her actual job! She gets hired by this guy Anders to stop his sister's wedding, but then, as she's infiltrating the wedding party like some kind of romantic spy, she starts falling for Anders himself.

What I love most about this book is that it's not just funny. It's also about belonging, self-worth, and figuring out your place in the world when you feel like everything is falling apart. Lucy sees herself as this perpetual screw-up, and watching her realize she's actually worthy of love and happiness is oh-so relatable. Also, the chemistry between Lucy and Anders is ELECTRIC.

I think what really gets me is how this book reminds us that sometimes our messiest, most chaotic moments are actually leading us exactly where we need to be.

1.

Face down, ass up, under a canopy of overgrown bushes in an unkempt corner of the Keos Resort is not how I envisioned spending my Saturday morning.

Sure, I've ended up in this position before—usually by choice and on a mattress rather than a patch of itchy, probably poison-ivy-infested grass. This is, pathetically, more action than I've had in months.

This secluded clearing is far from the manicured perfection of the main grounds. Hidden, quiet. The kind of place where people go when they don't want to be seen—people like the couple currently sitting on a weather-worn bench beneath a stone archway, framed by climbing vines and wildflowers. I spy them through the dense shrubbery. The woman leans so close that her dark hair veils the man's shoulder, and their legs tangle with each other.

I'm crouched below the benches, hidden, itchy, and crawling toward what may or may not be the most devastating evidence of infidelity I've ever captured.

I know who they are. And I know what this looks like.

James—the groom-to-be. Sammy—his best friend. And if Jennie's gut is right, his not-so-secret lover.

Jennie, my newest client, has labeled them "the Birds." Not because they're sweet or whimsical, but because they call each other Sparrow and Finch—the same names as the doomed lovers in James's favorite French war film. A film his fiancée, Eliza, never finished because she thought it was boring. But Sammy? Sammy knows every line by heart.

You can't fake that kind of intimacy. And Jennie knows it.

She wrote to me just a week ago, her message panicked and personal: Eliza's about to marry the wrong person. James is in love with someone else—Sammy. I've seen it in the way they look at each other when they think no one's watching. I tried to tell her, but she thinks I'm jealous. Please, I need proof. You're my Hail Mary.

So here I am, hiding in the bushes like a creeper.

I inch forward, knees bruising against the ground, phone angled up for the best shot I can manage. The blue satin of my dress is definitely not camo—it practically glows against the underbrush—but I've shoved myself under enough tangled greenery to be mostly hidden.

A branch snaps near my shoulder, sharp against skin. I bite back a curse.

I can hear murmuring, but nothing solid enough to form words. And though I would kill my fiancé if he was wrapped around a woman the way James is right now, they could still claim to just be the best of friends.

Got to get closer.

Slowly, so I don't make too much of a rustle, I inch forward under the line of bushes, army crawling my way closer to my quarry. A light tingling crawls around the back of my neck, but I refrain from the instinct to jolt away or make any sudden movements. I'm sure most of these bugs are harmless—and really, I'd do anything for a paycheck, even risk a skin rash in the most sensitive of areas.

Wedding wrecking isn't exactly glamorous, but it's a job. And five months after my landlord pounded on my door for rent, I've learned dignity doesn't pay the bills. At this point, I'd look into selling my plasma—well, I have looked, just haven't quite worked up the nerve to actually go through with it yet.

I pause once I reach the final bench, and gain a better vantage point of James and Sammy. My cheek presses against the ground as I angle my phone up and start recording.

"We're just friends," Sammy says, her nose nearly touching James's. "We always have been."

James shuts his eyes like he's in physical pain. "Just friends," he repeats, like a prayer. "We don't work any other way?" The last part is framed like a question, a plea. I zoom in, holding my breath as a tickle develops in my throat.

"That was the last time." Sammy pulls her face back, but her hands grip his thighs and travel up until they reach his crotch.

Jennie, your instincts are so *on point.*

"We tried before, and—"

"And we almost ruined a good thing." Sammy pulls away.

James grabs the back of her head before she can establish a distance between them. My heart pounds in my chest. I steady my hands to ensure the camera doesn't shake.

"Wait," he says, his eyes on her mouth. "Just one more time."

"Finch," Sammy says, breathless.

"Tonight, while everyone is in bed. Come to my room. I'll be alone," James tells her. "I need this. I need you."

This is good. A planned meetup. More opportunity to get evidence. I'd already knocked on James's and Sammy's hotel doors earlier—feigned confusion, pretended I'd taken a wrong turn—but no one answered. They weren't at brunch either; the bachelor party was off getting hammered at one of the bars, blissfully oblivious. The bridal party was holed up at the spa. I even tried the obvious choreographed moves—asked the concierge with a smile, slipped the bartender a casual question while pretending to order another drink, and scanned the pool cabanas for anything suspicious—and still came up empty.

Sammy shuts her eyes, and their mouths gravitate toward each other.

Someone clears their throat. The Birds jerk away from each other, standing and placing themselves an arm's length away.

Luckily a new voice masks the sound of my curse.

"Excuse us for interrupting," a deep, amused voice says. "We thought this area would be unoccupied." I only catch the tip of his nose from my angle.

"You're not interrupting," James says, so smoothly I would have believed him if I hadn't witnessed what I did. There's no heat rolling off him, and he stands with slightly slumped shoulders, no worries within him.

My throat tickles again, and I clap a hand over my mouth before a cough escapes.

"Are you thinking about changing locations for your wedding?" another man's voice says from a body I can't see at this angle. "We're set for one of the ballrooms, but my future wife heard there was an *Alice in Wonderland*–esque plot of land and sent me to check it out."

Another sneeze attempts to ricochet out of me, so I press my hand hard to my mouth to muffle as much sound as possible, but it's still audible enough. James and Sammy glance my way, but the deeper voice says, "Ah, squirrels roaming around here. Not the best wedding guests."

The cheating couple's attention is drawn away from my hiding spot, and I'd breathe a sigh of relief if I didn't think it'd send me into another fit of sneezing.

"We heard the same," James says easily, "but it's not well maintained. We'll be off now. You two enjoy your day." He walks away without checking for Sammy, who follows close behind.

My nerves barely settle as the two men still remain.

"He's right," my unknowing savior tells his companion. "There's no way the staff can do enough maintenance here to be ready for tomorrow. Tell your fiancée she'll have to live out her wonderland dreams another way."

"Well, had to try," the other voice says.

The two walk off, and I wait as long as I can, nearly suffocating myself, measuring out enough time until they'll be too far to hear me.

Just as my throat feels as if it'll burst, I remove my hand, and a string of sneezes erupts from me.

Goddamn it, I must be allergic to something here. Great time to figure that out.

I wait until the sneezes slow, but something crawls along the back of my thigh, leaving a pinch of pain and heat in its trail. The sneezes rack my body as I free myself from under the bush of flowers. I mutter curses in between each one, pulling myself to a stand and straightening my dress.

For me, the video is enough. But will it be for Eliza and the people who align themselves with James? Jennie's hunch went ignored, chalked up to two close friends with a bond that is inexplicable to people outside the bubble.

When it comes to the ones we love, we often can't see what's right in front of our faces. A curse of feeling too much and loving too much is that your sense of logic halves itself.

If I'd learned that lesson earlier in life, I wouldn't have racked up two failed marriages, but that's a conversation for my therapist . . . whenever I can afford one again. I need to regroup.

A sharp pinch burns into my arm, and I swat at the insect that hitched a ride on my skin. I'll be finding welts, like the hives already spreading across my side, for days, but it's fine—temporary pain for something bigger.

Every job I take gets me closer to what I've been working toward for years: buying into Save a Paw, the shelter where I started volunteering as a teenager. The owner's retiring soon, and I've got a narrow window to come up with my share before he hands it off to someone else. I can't let that happen. I've pictured myself owning part of that place since I was sixteen. All these inconveniences will fade into forgotten memories soon.

First, I'll shower and lather myself in lotion to help with the itching. Then, I'll check the Excel grid and see where else there's an opportunity to catch the Birds—extra evidence wouldn't hurt. They're meeting at night, so that's something, but I'd like to have less risk involved. Something might happen that means they can't meet, or whatever evidence I gather won't be enough. I'll try to force as many interactions as I can before the day is up.

"Should I call security?" A voice brushes over my skin, and I yelp, whirling around.

My body stalls. I stand there in shock, half because his rough five o'clock shadow and dark, windswept hair seem so out of place in the delicate richness of where we are. This resort is like a slice of heaven, and he looks like he just sauntered his way through a storm.

The other half of me freezes to admire the height, the collection of muscles, and the eyes that seem simultaneously to be blue, green, or brown—their beautiful hazel a color I'd probably have tried to buy contacts to match a decade ago. He's not *overly* muscled, but not too lean either. Like he works out when he feels like it, but it's not a priority for him. His pale shirt is loose on him, aside from his biceps, where his sleeves seem to cling, rolled up to reveal veins and a Rolex.

And then I remember I just crawled out from under a bush. And his words sink in.

"And why would you do that?" I try to straighten myself out and make it seem like I'm not doing anything wrong. There's a chance he didn't see me unearth myself. I'm wandering around, just like him.

I get distracted by the dimple that appears as he speaks, when he points to me and then to my previous hiding spot. "I just assumed someone hiding under a bush isn't a guest at the resort." His Adam's apple bobs as he speaks, his finger back to pointing at me. "Your wig is falling off."

Shit.

I adjust the bundle of synthetic ginger curls atop my black hair as much as I can without a mirror. "Plenty of people wear wigs. Is that a problem for you?"

He raises a thick brow. "Not at all." I realize his voice is that of my savior from earlier. "Do you have an explanation for the first part of my question?"

I make a show of looking around. "Funny, I didn't hear any question marks."

He tilts his head, his full lips, with a sharply pointed Cupid's bow, pulling up. "They were more like statements, you're right. I just thought if I said them, you'd answer."

"Well, I'm not a mind reader. If you have a question, you should ask it."

I blink as the scent of mango and sandalwood encircles me. "Okay, stranger, why were you hiding under the bushes?"

"I don't know you. I don't have to tell you anything."

Amusement glimmers in his gaze, which travels up and down my body, and it takes all my self-control not to shift my weight or fidget. Usually, I have so much restraint over myself, but being caught like this is disorienting.

His thickly lashed eyes, the hazel that changes color depending on the way the light hits them, narrow on me. "You're right again." I'm sure he broke his nose during childhood, the way it crooks at an angle slightly. "But I saw you when I first walked through, and my curiosity is more than piqued."

I'm well aware the curiosity is more about my actions than me, but the way he says it, softer, sexier, sends ripples of awareness down my spine. Suddenly, I remember just how long it's been since I had sex, since I had a man speak to me with his gaze piercing me into place.

Just as suddenly, I realize what he said.

"If you saw me earlier, why didn't you say anything?" I cock my head to the side. "You knew it was me sneezing, not an animal."

"I'm no snitch," he says, and his smile is too infectious for me not to mirror.

"Well, I'm not a threat, stranger. No need to call security, and thanks for keeping my hiding place a secret." I step away, trying to make a break for it. He's already seen my real hair under the wig and already has too much attention on me when I'm supposed to maintain a semblance of anonymity while wedding wrecking. After a job, if you saw me again, you might recognize me vaguely, but you'd never be able to give an accurate description to an artist. Whether I'm contouring my face, sculpting a sharper shape from my soft features, paling out my tan complexion, covering my freckles, plopping colored contacts over my brown eyes, or wearing crooked glasses, I always put in effort to look far removed from my actual appearance.

There's only a slim chance someone will recognize me while ruining a relationship, but I prefer to make the margin even smaller. It's not something I want my own circle of vastly more successful marketing peers and honor-roll college graduates to know about. As much as it feels good helping, wedding wrecking's not supposed to be my forever career path; it's just something I stumbled into five months ago, right after I lost my job.

Even though my curiosity wants me to stick around a bit, it's better I skedaddle while I can.

He steps toward me. "I can't even get your name?"

"I'd only give you a fake one."

His chuckle is stormy and sexy, eliciting spots of warmth throughout my body, and the butterflies that have been long asleep flutter with anticipation. The way his appearance seems mysterious, but his eyes are alight with harmless mischief, is stimulating too many forgotten hormonal responses from me.

Love steals your logic, but lust steals your self-preservation.

"You're only making me want to know more," he says, his gaze traveling lazily up my body, and my legs actually buckle. All right, seriously, I've got to get out of here.

"Sorry," I say, placing much-needed space between us. "Someone's calling for me."

Another amused sound escapes his throat. "I don't hear anything."

"Coming!" I shout to the sky, and with no other options, I literally and metaphorically run away, as fast as my heels can take me.

When I make it back to my room—after showering and popping some Claritin—I remove the three missed notifications from Taina, who's house-sitting for me since I promised to check in on my neighbor's cat while she was away before I got this job.

I open my camera roll and pull up the video I threw out my dignity for to send to Jennie.

The Birds are in center view, angled slightly toward each other, as if they're in a romance poster. This could be it, what Jennie needs to save Eliza. I crank up the volume, hit play, and—

I rewind and try again.

I stare at the screen, the silence echoing in my skull.

My finger must have been on the speaker. The only noise is the occasional rustle of movement when I inch closer.

This isn't good enough. I can't send this to Jennie. It's basically a silent film.

I drop the phone on the bed and flop onto my back, staring up at the ceiling. It might have sea glass embedded in it. Or maybe I'm hallucinating from stress and Claritin.

A pounding begins to drum behind my eyes.

This job's already been harder than usual. The ruin is always simpler with time—it also allows me to infiltrate their bubbles more organically, instead of a last-minute insertion.

Some people want me to pretend I'm a long-lost lover. Others sneak me into the bridal (or bachelor) party to plant seeds of doubt into people's heads. Less risk, less reward for my bank account. Others—and this is mainly because of the false advertisement my sister, Taina, wrote on the website, claiming I have experience as a private detective—want me to dig around and see if their gut feelings about cheating partners are correct. My one requirement is that I only target couples I'm certain are bad for each other—this isn't about breaking up happy relationships.

Jennie's request came just a week ago. Extra charge for the timeline, sure—terrible for infiltration. No cover, no invitation, so I'm just another plus-one at someone else's wedding, poking around from the outside. Harder to get access, harder to find angles, harder to get proof.

Very little time to work with for a very big job. Regardless, I'm going to have to find that couple again tonight.

Get closer. Get cleaner footage.

With a long, dramatic sigh, I rub circles into my temples.

Some birthday weekend this has been—freshly twenty-eight, no real career, no real relationships, bug bites burning into my skin, and running around trying to prove someone's infidelity.

My parents would be so proud.

Wedding wrecking was supposed to be temporary. A weird little pit stop before I found another marketing job—preferably one that didn't involve a New York tech firm run by misogynistic man-children with god complexes and backhanded compliments that slowly crushed your will to live.

A job where I wouldn't have to worry about dress codes or about the way I speak. Or being assertive, but not too much, because you'll sound like a bitch. Taking exclamation points off emails because it's not professional, letting men think they're explaining a process to you that you already know how to do. Repeating the same marketing plan used for every campaign because the people in charge don't believe in thinking outside the box when they have a perfectly good, boring box already.

But that was five months ago. And I'm still here.

Every time I think I've hit rock bottom, the floor rips from under me and reveals another level.

When I first stumbled upon wedding wrecking, I told myself it would be just one time. That I was helping someone; that love, real love, should survive a little scrutiny. Then I did it again. And again. And suddenly, I stopped needing to lie to myself about why. Because the truth is, people don't get married for love. Not always. Not often.

People get married for so many reasons that have nothing to do with love. Money. Timing. Guilt. Social pressure. Because they're scared to be alone. Because their mom likes him. Because it looks good on paper. Because they're thirty-two and tired of dating apps. Because it's easier than breaking up and starting from scratch.

It's not that I don't believe in love. I do. I have so much love in me—it's kind of the problem.

That's why this job makes sense.

If love is real, if it's as rare and valuable as everyone says, then what I'm doing is a service. Stopping people who don't really feel it from walking down the aisle anyway. Making space for something truer to find them later.

Or at least keeping them from signing a contract with someone they're already lying to.

Or maybe I'm just trying to make myself feel better about blowing up other people's fairy tales, because mine didn't work out.

God, okay. That's enough of a spiral for one night.

Needing a distraction, I dial Taina. She answers on the third ring.

"Hey, Taina."

"Hey, Lucy."

Her tone sucks every drop of relaxation from my body. Taina never answers the phone without greeting me as a ho or bitch or both. She once called me Slut-bucket while I was in the break room at work.

My heart starts to pound and my brain surges forward with every possible devastating scenario. Losing both my parents left an ever-present fear that the universe will come and finish the job by taking Taina away. I have to remind myself that she's on the phone, so nothing could possibly be as earth shattering as that.

"What's wrong?"

"I left for a few hours to meet a friend," she begins. "Just a few hours! And then when I came back—well—I tried to stop him. I swear, I didn't even notice the eviction notice he'd taped on the door. I even offered to pay the rent, but I guess he doesn't trust you won't be late again. That bastard must have been waiting until both of us left the place."

Dread fills me, streaming from the pit of my stomach and spreading everywhere. "Taina, what are you talking about?"

"You've been evicted."

Time pauses, and my heartbeat does too. "I sent him half the payment! He was supposed to let me stay."

"I'm sorry."

This can't be right. He swore to me I could pay half now and the rest later. I rub my chest, and my heart starts to lose a steady rhythm. Maybe he just agreed to get what little out of me I had. *And you, a grown woman, were naive enough to fall for it.*

Taina says, "Whatever he didn't trash, I'm having sent to my place." Muffled, distant, she says to someone else, *"Fuck you; my husband will sue you for all you have, you absolute asshole. You're lucky I don't shove those keys down your wrinkled-ass throat, you lizard-looking bastard."*

God, I can't even bring myself to ask what she managed to keep. Everything, *everything* in there was from our parents. I didn't get rid of a single thing after their death. Almost everything they ever owned is in storage or in Taina's basement, but the rest, the best stuff, was in my apartment.

With me, so I could feel them every day. So it wouldn't feel like they were in an unreachable place. So I wouldn't be alone.

"It's a blessing in disguise," Taina says in my ear, focus back on me. "You'll be more secure with me, and we can see each other more. Your place was at risk of falling apart any moment anyway. This is exciting!" Again, muffled, to someone else. *"Fuck you."*

I love my little sister, but God I don't enjoy her voice very much right now. No way I would turn a miserable moment for her into a silver lining, not until she's had the proper time to process. It's been thirty seconds. I deserve at least sixty.

I turn off my phone. I close my eyes and try to breathe through my nose. Try to be calm. I hate being upset. Really, being sad is the worst. Your stomach feels raw and filled with rock salt and your eyes swell until keeping them open creates this headache, like a woodpecker is stuck behind them.

My hands grip my phone so hard I'm surprised it doesn't crack. I take another breath and it turns into a sob.

I pitch my phone to the other side of the room. It slams against the wall, and all I can think is, *How much is that going to cost?*

Damn it, damn it, damn it.

I rub my knuckles against my chest. Pressing as if it'll stop my heart from beating so damn erratic.

I should have asked Taina what she managed to save. Now I'll just think all the best stuff is gone. The Wall of Memories. Our family dog's ashes. Dad's favorite baseball glove. Mom's go-to pot for rice. I need it all. It's like glue linking me to them. A direct connection whenever I need them.

Evicted and jobless. But I can't think about that now . . . I have a wedding to wreck.

2.

Unlike a sprain that needs a cast or a cut that can use some Neosporin, emotional pain can't be cured with any over-the-counter remedy. But it can be dulled, if only temporarily, by regarding the bottom of a whiskey-filled glass. Repeatedly.

I've planted myself in a dimly lit bar in the farthest corner of the resort, handed over my card, which I'm sure will be declined soon, and taken a shot for every moment I think about my—no, not my—the apartment that once held my furniture, my most treasured items, empty.

Ah, another shot.

It doesn't even burn as it goes down. It tastes enough like water that I lift the glass to smell it, to make sure the heavily tattooed bartender hasn't decided to steal my emotional medicine from me. The scent of whiskey hits my nostrils, reminding me of my father sitting by our old coffee table, watching the game on a TV while I hovered nearby, ready to adjust the battered antenna every time the signal went out.

And that memory has me downing the rest of my glass.

I've lost track of how much I've drunk, but last time I looked at one of the flat screens hanging above the glossy mahogany bar, the teams on the screen were white jerseys versus blue ones. Now it's red versus yellow, and maybe a different sport? Football or fútbol?

I'm *very* buzzed. And there's a consistent feeling of a nail being hammered into the back of my eyes, sloppily pulled out, and hammered again. Maybe it's a migraine, maybe it's from all the drinking.

Maybe, I think as someone glides a glass of water over the countertop while heavily ringed fingers remove my empty glass, *I'm dehydrated.*

My head weighs approximately one hundred pounds, so turning it to the side takes extra effort.

There's amusement in those familiar hazel eyes and concern in his furrowed brows as he meets my blurry gaze. The man takes a seat on the stool beside me.

"Stranger!" I say, patting his arm. I meant to tap him, but my hand squeezes his biceps to confirm—yes, they are as hard as they look. Nice.

If he cares at all about my assessment, he doesn't show it. "Good to see you didn't sprain an ankle sprinting away in those heels," he says in greeting.

My eyes widen, and my hand grips my hair—my real hair without the wig. Not that it matters anymore; clearly, he recognized me, and if he didn't, the whole *stranger* greeting from me gave it away.

"I was concerned," he says at my silence.

Unlike me, who needed a shower immediately after our first meeting, he's wearing the same outfit. I've opted for an oversized shirt and jeans meant for a more casual environment. Something that I didn't notice until now.

"I'm honored." *To be worried about by a beautiful stranger who doesn't even know my name.*

His dimple makes an appearance, a heavy shadow on his cheek under the ambient lighting, and I'm not sure if I kept that last part in my head. "*I'm* honored to have witnessed someone down a beer and three glasses of whiskey and still remain upright." He gestures to the glass of water. "For your accomplishment, I've brought you a gift." He pushes the water closer to me.

I hold a hand to my chest. "Wow, it's exactly what I wanted."

"I saved up all year for it," he says so earnestly, I laugh, and some of the misery I've been collecting oozes out of me.

I down the water in one go, then catch the eye of the bartender. He raises his brows, both questioning if I want another one and inquiring if I am still coherent enough to keep drinking. I hold up a finger, then look to my right. "Want a drink?"

He thinks about it, then gestures *two* toward the bartender.

"So," Stranger says, "what has you drinking the night away on your own?"

"So many things," I say as the bartender drops our glasses. I collect mine, clink a cheers to Stranger's before he even grips it, and take a sip. "My eviction, my inability to get a new *real* job, my dreams coming undone, and it wasn't a major concern until recently, but for some reason, speaking to you reminds me of my failure to maintain any semblance of a romantic relationship. So, in other words, completely hitting rock bottom."

"Oh."

I thought about my eviction again, so I pick up his glass and down half his drink. His eyes widen so comically that it yanks a laugh from me, but even I can hear the bitter aftershock trailing behind it. I point at him. "You asked a simple question, and I just dumped all my life problems on you. Has your curiosity dwindled?"

So slight I nearly miss it, his head cocks to the side. I only catch it because a stray, dark wave of hair falls over his forehead. He drinks, and my gaze catches on how his lips meet my lipstick print on the rim. "I still want to know your name."

My head spins like whatever holds my brain steady in my skull is starting to crumble. I blink until it dulls, but the drinks start catching up with me.

"Lucinda," I say, because people only refer to me as Lucy. Lucinda doesn't even feel like a real name at this point. *I'm so drunk my own fingertips don't feel properly attached to my body.*

"Lucinda," he repeats, and the name coming from him sounds sultry and delicate. "Is that your real name?"

"Maybe, maybe not." I gesture for a refill as the bartender walks by. "Yours?"

"Anders," he says. "You know, there are less liver-endangering ways to deal with hard times."

"Like what? Therapy?" I scoff, as if I can afford such a thing.

"Like going for a walk, sitting out in the sun, reading a book."

I slam my hand on the counter. "Did you just suggest exercise to make me feel better? *Torture?* The thing that killed John F. Kennedy?"

"I think you're mixing up your world leaders."

"Get out of my sight."

His low chuckle doesn't help my already tipsy balance. "Forgive me," he says. "I just thought you may regret this many drinks tomorrow morning."

"You always show this much concern over strangers?"

"Only the pretty ones who like to drink whiskey."

It should be impossible, both from my drunken state and my all-around wallowing, but a zing of awareness shoots between my thighs.

I wouldn't say he's *conventionally* handsome, not that boy-next-door lead from a rom-com. He has the tall, dark, and handsome thing, sure, but the lines on his face are a little more complex, like every tiny scar or slight smile line comes with a story attached. Neither boy next door nor bad boy, but on the border of both, which makes me study his crooked nose and the sharp angles of his face too long to be polite.

The bartender places a dish of truffle fries and steak tips before us.

"Fuel," Anders says, pushing the fries toward me. "I thought you might need something to settle all the whiskey."

I immediately shove a fry in my mouth, moaning at the taste of warm Parmesan and salt. Whoever invented fries, I hope they had a long, fulfilling life. "So, you must have been watching me a while to have ordered food for me."

He clears his throat. "I was paying for dinner when I saw you stumble to the bar."

Stumble. Because I've had three—wait, make that four—whiskeys here but raided the minibar in my room before deciding to make my misery everyone else's problem. With every sentence we exchange, I feel each sip I took in a wave of dizziness.

"It feels suspicious how nice you're being to me," I say; as my head grows heavy, I lean my elbow on the counter and hold my chin. "Twice now you've caught me in poor form, but you sit by me, drink with me, order me food. Are you trying to sleep with me?"

He blinks, his mouth opening and shutting as he thinks about what to say.

I shake my head. "If you are, I can't anyway. Not right now." Wow, the alcohol has effectively removed the little filter I have. "I'm too sensitive. I'll either fall in love with you on the spot or instantly burst into tears. Maybe another time."

He gives me a small, not quite happy, smile, maybe a little sympathetic. "You're going through a hard time," he says softly. "I'm not busy, so I thought I'd keep you company."

I'd tilt my head if it wasn't so heavy. "Not to be a pessimist, but people usually do things for reasons other than just being a good person."

"That is absolutely being a pessimist," he says, then sighs. "Maybe I have an ulterior motive."

"So you want to sleep with me?"

He gives me a smile. "Your honesty is attractive enough for that to be a future endeavor."

My body warms, particularly between my thighs. I cross them. "But that's not it," I say, not too drunk to miss that.

He nods. "I'm here for a wedding."

I raise my brow. "Is attending such a miserable experience that you'd rather keep the company of a woman you found beneath a bush?"

"You say it like it's a bad thing," he jokes, then adds, lightly on the tails of it, "It's my first love's wedding." I choke on my fry. "First and only, actually."

I hand him my refill as soon as the bartender places it by the fries.

"Thanks," he says, downing it in one single gulp. He drops the glass on the counter. "Have I earned the reason you were hiding beneath a bush?"

"What's your first love's name?"

"Anna."

Not Eliza, so I don't have to lie too much about why I'm here. But I wonder if Anders would enjoy me wrecking his first love's wedding.

Then, a thought clicks. "Wait, you went to check out that plot of land with your first love's *fiancé*?"

He nods. "Lucas is my best friend."

"Your best friend is marrying your first love?" I shout, a burst of energy sliding through me. I grip his face in my hands. "Why are you here? Why would you subject yourself to this kind of agony? Are you a masochist?"

He places a hand over mine. For a moment, I think he means to remove it, but instead, he presses my palm closer to his cheek. Does the caress of a stranger offer comfort he couldn't admit he needed? "It's complicated."

"Life really sucks sometimes, huh?"

He takes a deep breath, closes his eyes, and I have the urge to press my lips against their lids. "Yeah," he whispers.

I just learned his name minutes ago, but I feel such a magnetic pull toward him. I need to, at this very moment, smooth out the wrinkle between his brows. It doesn't seem like he wants to try to uncomplicate his situation for me, and I can't really blame him. He's already extended himself to be here, attending a wedding he doesn't seem to want to go to, confiding in an almost-complete stranger.

He's done two solids for me already and has this disarming charm that's effectively removed the pit of anxiety I can't ever snuff out when left alone with a man I don't know. Maybe it's the liquor stealing that security measure from me, but I felt fine with him when we were alone before.

Maybe the universe decided to place two miserable souls together, however briefly, to give them some respite from all the damage done to them.

"Okay, Anders, let's be sad together."

His smile returns and warmth sparks in my chest, like a reward for bringing it back out of him, though something tells me nobody has to work too hard to do so. "Do you think a pity party will help?"

"Yeah," I say, still holding his face. "Party is right there in the phrase. Let's suck out the sadness like venom from a snake bite. Once it's gone, we'll feel better." I use my chin to gesture to the other side of the room. "And then, we'll drink some more, play some darts, and make bad decisions."

He shows a set of perfect white teeth, his canines a little sharper and longer than the rest, which widens his smile. "Okay. Let's."

I pull away to think, but his hand reaches around my stool and pulls the chair closer to him, so my thighs are between his. I shake off the attraction that runs through me. I have to remind myself as I think of what to say: *I'm going to comfort him, not sleep with him.*

"Okay," I begin, "I have a really sad life, so mine might be long."

He slides a finger over my cheek and pulls a stray hair behind my ear. "I'm here however long you need."

Lucy, do not *fall in love with a man who shows you a simple act of kindness.*

"Okay, so from the beginning. I have never had anything that has been only mine," I tell him. "My parents died when I was a teenager, and I spent most of my life trying to take care of my little sister."

His gaze travels around my face, then focuses on my eyes, like a camera lens finding its subject.

"Growing up, I spent recesses in a corner alone, studying to get perfect grades to make my parents proud, so friends were nonexistent for a while. My parents died in a car crash on the way to the hospital because my mom was sick, cancer, and as much as I love an ironic twist, that messed me up for a bit. After that, raising Taina on my own was a whole other kind of hard—balancing grief and responsibility was confusing for a girl who didn't even know how taxes worked.

"At work, aside from one other woman, I was surrounded by men. I'd never be invited to the weekly team dinners, instead tasked with projects that ran well into the nights my coworkers drank through. I studied my lovers like exams and picked up their hobbies and passions like my own, so we'd have more to discuss. I'd cook their favorite meals, remember their coffee orders, listen to their burdens, and try to ease them or resolve them, and they still left."

A touch of embarrassment and a shred of worry lodges itself in my throat. It's too much to admit to a perfect stranger, but it's because he's a stranger that this feels like getting the poison out of my body to allow it to heal.

"It's hard to explain. It feels like I had this deposit of gold within me once, treasured and sought after, but someone has been in there carving out every remnant of it. Only flecks of it remain, it's not even worth mining. Not so valuable anymore."

At that, he reaches over and squeezes my hand, and it somehow feels like a hug around my heart.

"Want to know the most humiliating thing I'm doing now to get by?" I ask.

"Tell me."

I chew on my lip, just a brief moment of sense, trying to keep my mouth shut before the confession slips out. "Wedding wrecking."

He frowns, scratches his ear before saying, "Sorry, I think I misheard."

"I'm sure you didn't." I tap his arm. And when his eyes grow wide, I hold out my hand. "I'm not here to wreck Anna's wedding!"

I can see the emotions ranging over his face as he tries to process what I said until he ultimately stalls at a mix of confusion and sympathy. "Okay," he says, "how does someone even get into that . . . field?"

I snort at his attempt at being polite instead of questioning my sanity. "Accidentally?" I answer. "I mean, the entire job is made up. There is no frame of reference for me to follow. The idea was this cumulation of an alcohol-induced night, the luck of a loud, even drunker, groom-to-be begging his groomsmen to stop his impending wedding, and a projection of my own misery wishing someone had saved me from a doomed marriage, twice. And, of course, the cherry on top of the dirt-cake, it was the night I was fired from my job."

"All right," he interrupts me, curiosity currently winning his carousel of emotions, "you have to give more details than that. There's a big jump from overhearing a groom having cold feet to straight-up wedding wrecking."

I shove a couple of fries in my mouth before continuing. "The groom-to-be was *begging* for sympathy. His friends knew he liked men, knew the marriage was set up by his parents in denial, yet his buddies were encouraging him to go through with it. They said it was better to play into the facade than risk his parents disowning him—"

"Assholes."

"I know, right? They kept saying he could date anyone he wanted, secretly. The groom-to-be—and me, when I stumbled physically and metaphorically into their conversation—thought it was unfair to the bride-to-be and whoever would have to live in secret with him."

"He must have been happy for someone to take his side."

"He was." I go on, "Walter was his name, begged me to help him do something about it. Something that became more intriguing when he offered me all the money his parents sent him for a wedding present. I hadn't seen that many zeros since one of my late-night, wine-fueled Zillow binges, where I scroll through houses I'll never be able to afford."

Anders's chuckle brings a warmth to my chest that interrupts my train of thought before I continue.

"It was a sloppy mess. Crashing the rehearsal dinner, claiming I was in love with Walter and that we were running away together after a one-night stand. But at the end of the night, Walter said this way his family wouldn't come after him for his sexuality, not for a while, and he planned to travel the world until he was ready to face everyone again."

"Hearing it like this," Anders says, downing one of the shots I didn't even notice him order, "it makes you sound less like wrecking, more like *helping*."

I've always viewed wedding wrecking as helping, as saving people. Either from an incompatible marriage or a pairing like Eliza's, where cheating is involved. Preventing them from feeling this ache of loving someone who betrayed you in this final, unforgivable way. Where you recall all the small injustices over the course of your relationship, rereading every chapter between you, searching every transgression, trying to pinpoint exactly where it all went wrong. The swift fear of having all this love but losing the vessel to hold it, wondering where you'll put it now—if you have the ability to do that at all.

Still, I point out, "I can't help but notice a hidden *but* there."

"But," he goes on, "how do you decide to wreck a wedding? What if someone requests it, but they don't have good intentions? And where do you even find them?"

I shake my head. "I only agree to help with wrecking the wedding when the pairing would be genuinely harmful to either party." It was chaotic at first, but I had poured more and more energy into the idea until it ballooned into something that could stay up on its own.

"And my sister helps with the rest, making everything more streamlined," I explain, ignoring the gnawing embarrassment of having to rely on someone whom I spent a year trying to teach to tie her own shoes. "She used to code for work and fun. So, when I came to her with the idea, she built me a website offering wedding-wrecking services. A portal for people to reach me, explain their situation, vet them, and even run marketing to anyone searching key terms like *How to get someone to call off a wedding? Wedding ruining. Wedding Crasher. How can I leave my partner before my wedding? My son is marrying a gold digger; how do I convince him against it?* And so on.

"My clients can run through my application and choose a variety of methods. I'm here to make one of the most difficult decisions of their lives as easy as possible. I shoulder as much blame as I can, so that both parties can be left unscathed enough to move on."

Anders looks at me with surprise, but do I see a hint of admiration as well? "This is all more elaborate than I'd think such a niche job would be."

I smile. "Do you picture me with fake pregnancy bumps and shouting 'I object!' at weddings?"

His returning smile lets me know I'm not too far off. "I've been proven wrong. Still, it's hard for me to wrap my head around all these people hiring you."

"Turns out normal people turn to the internet for help instead of downing cheap wine and watching reruns of *New Girl* to fix their life problems. Go figure."

Each time he laughs, a tiny *ding* rings in my head like I got the answer to a trivia question correct.

"Still, pretty impressive you can make a living with this. Turn an idea into a business."

I snort. "Making a living is a stretch," I tell him. "Sure, I can charge a hefty amount for my services, which helps. Even if the average American can't afford flights and hotels and wedding planners, the people who *can* don't have any real sense of the economy for the working class. I charge to make up for the lack of opportunities."

At the surface of a memory, I grip his arm. "Once I worked on a wedding where, after a meeting, the groom sent me home with five hundred dollars for an Uber to take me just a few blocks away. When he saw my wide eyes, he asked if it wasn't enough and threw in an extra hundred. It's the rich that make you wonder why God left you to scrape by and earn your living while others got to eat four-dollar avocados every day."

Another laugh. Another *ding*.

"So if this isn't making a living, what are you going to do once the jobs run dry?" Anders asks.

"Before that happens, I should have saved enough for my real goal—I'm going to buy into this animal shelter I've cared about since I was a teenager. The owner's retiring soon, and if I don't come up with my share in time, someone else will take it. And that place means everything to me." I sigh dramatically. "The owner promised me I'd have time, but now he's retiring earlier than expected. I have a few months to come up with my share before someone else swoops in and crushes my soul."

"What happens if he ends up taking the other person's offer?"

"I walk into the ocean, never to be found."

He chuckles again.

At least I'm funny. Something positive to balance out the fact that I'm a twenty-eight-year-old two-time divorcée with no real job, or money.

"Right, you were married twice?" he asks.

I blink, but I'm sure I said that part in my head. "Yeah." I nod. "The first time, I was freshly seventeen and desperate to care for my little sister and give her a home. He was eighteen, which wasn't really an adult, but he had a job and an apartment, which was more than I had. So I married him, mistook security for love. He left me for one of his classmates, and, luckily, it got annulled because of my age."

"Seventeen is too young to have so much on your shoulders," Anders says so quietly I'm not sure he meant to say it aloud.

I shrug. "After that, I had a string of bad relationships until I got married again."

Anders asks, "What was that jerk like?"

It makes me smile. "Ah. This one hurt the most. During one of my visits to my sister at college, I met her TA. He was sweet and kind. I loved him, really, no naivete about it. He never hurt me, not till the end. Married me because we were two years in, and it was the next step given the time we'd spent together. A good guy. He would have stayed with me forever—unwillingly resented me for it, but he would have stayed. All while being in love with his coworker."

Anders moves a little closer. "What happened?"

"I gave him an out. I was too embarrassed to say I knew he didn't want me, so I let him catch me making out with one of his friends. You'd think someone wouldn't be relieved to find his wife hooking up with someone else, but he was. I hated him for it, a bit. I wish he'd just never married me, left me himself."

I wish someone had stepped in and told him that it wasn't right. Subconsciously, it's probably why I jumped on the chance to wreck a wedding. It's so much worse, being hurt by the person you love most rather than a stranger. I know so well what it's like to feel trapped in a place not good for either party.

"They both sound like assholes," Anders says, rubbing circles over my jeans. "I hope they're living mediocre lives. Nothing too horrendous, not life-threatening, but incredibly annoying. That they live dealing with a thousand inconveniences that make it impossible to have a good day."

A laugh tears out of me. "Like always stepping on a wet floor with socks on."

He nods solemnly. "And consistently hitting the corner of the dresser when they walk by."

"Paying for a commercial-less subscription and still getting commercials," I say.

"Always feeling like they have to sneeze but never being able to."

"Evil!" I say. We both laugh, and it feels like the last of the poison has seeped out of me.

Anders is a perfect stranger, yet weirdly it feels safe here, letting it all out. He doesn't know me well enough to judge me, so if he does, it won't hurt as bad. But the way he watches me, his gaze piercing and fully focused on me, like he has to make sure not to miss a single word, makes me believe he wouldn't judge me at all.

"So," I finish, "isn't my life so bleak?"

He smooths my hair, his hand moving until it's holding my cheek. "It sounds like you've had some hard times." I nod, a little embarrassment creeping its way up my neck. "And yet here you are, undefeated by it all. Able to smile, make jokes, and comfort a perfect stranger. Someone who dedicates her life to animals and her family. Life is bleak but you seem bright."

"Oh," I say, and though I felt steady this entire interaction, his words snap something inside me, and I burst into tears. "Sorry, oh God, sorry!"

I wipe them away, but he brings an arm around me, pulls me in so my forehead is on his chest, and rubs small circles on my back. Losing my parents has made me a lot more hungry for physical touch. I used to flinch at hugs, but I think it was because I was afraid to want them too much and feared not getting them. But when I lost them, I grew this anxiety from the fact that you never know if the hug you give someone will be your last.

But something about this hug, this gift from someone who owes me absolutely no comfort—and, in all honesty, if I had met him the way he met me, I might not have offered the same—envelopes me in this warmth that feels like basking in the sun on your favorite beach, the waves licking at your feet just as soon as the heat and humidity get to be too much.

When I finally stop crying, I pull away and slap my cheeks a couple of times with a laugh. "Wow, that really made me feel better." His answering smile tugs at my chest. "Your turn."

When he doesn't say anything, I say, "This is a safe space. You can vent. Or if you don't want to, that's fine too. There's always another whiskey."

He reaches for his glass, and I guess that's that.

Then he chugs it and says, "I was with Anna for ten years, since high school graduation, and in love with her since we were ten years old and she moved into the house next to mine in South Carolina." I still, trying to mimic how attentive he was to me. But I am drunk, and my gaze is a little glossy.

"I hated school, but it was everything to her, so I worked hard to get into the same high-ranking university. I majored in business, not because I liked it, but because I needed to make sure I could pull my weight when she became an attorney. I'd down Red Bulls and Monsters mixed with instant coffee crystals to stay up and study when she did so I could spend time with her. I moved across the country to be closer to her family, neglecting my own, when her mother got sick. I got a job at her father's firm, started making good money, and tried to be the perfect person for her."

"It sounds like you were," I can't help but say.

He rubs a thumb across my hand. "I wanted to be. She pushed me to be things I never thought I was. Everyone around me always thought I was an idiot—my father, my teachers—but Anna never did. She was the one who helped me learn to read when I was struggling and took me to her mother, who found out I was dyslexic. Changed my life. She saved up from her part-time job at a soft-serve shop during high school and bought me a car. Her family took me in like one of their own, and she made me feel like life could be worth living. She was the love of my life."

"But she's marrying your best friend," I say, harsher than I mean to. I'm just trying to figure out how someone who sounds so lovely would do such a thing after having a man so dedicated to her, and being so dedicated to said man, for most of their lives.

He winces, and I wish I'd shut my mouth. "Like I said, it's complicated."

No matter how much he props her up, I'm on his side. I don't know her, and while I absolutely don't know him either, I *kind* of do. In a way. First come, first serve for Lucy's Loyalty.

"I think marrying the best friend of someone you loved classifies you as a not-so-great person."

He smiles sadly. "People are complicated. Wonderful people do horrible things, and horrible people can have slivers of humanity. She was my love, but I wasn't hers. And that's my own fault. I betrayed her.

Led her on for years and years. She wanted a family, and I pretended to want the same." His Adam's apple bobbles. "I'm the not-so-great person. I was so scared of losing her, the family she surrounded me with, that I lied. Every moment I spent with her, every year I wasted her life, was a lie because I never planned on having a family. Never will. And so she left me."

Well, that's a shitty situation. Makes the whole best friend thing not as black and white. But he's right; wonderful people can do horrible things. We all make mistakes, and if we beat ourselves up too roughly, we don't get up to learn from them.

I hold out my hands in a hug formation. "Come here."

"I'm okay—"

I wrap my arms around him. His body stiffens for just a second, and then his shoulders slump. His hands snake around my waist, and I hear him let out a shaky breath. I want him to feel the same comfort I did when he held me, so I run my hands through his hair, rub circles on his back, and try to offer the warmth of a perfect day on my favorite beach.

A kinship has blossomed between us now that we've spilled our lives. I feel oddly close to Anders and, more oddly, somewhat protective too.

He doesn't pull away, so eventually, I do.

His cheeks have reddened, and he averts his gaze from mine. I find something about it so endearing that I reach over and slap my hand on his shoulder.

"Okay," I say, cheerfully, "we took the first step. Pity. We got it all out. Now let's—"

"Party?"

I hop off the stool and link my arm through his, my smile wide. "Until we can't see, think, or walk straight."

3.

It's been so long since I've been hungover, my first thought when I wake is *I'm dying.* This wonderful thought continues as I rip the sheets off my body, dash to the bathroom, and hurl into the cool toilet.

By the fourth time, I'm sure I've thrown up something important. Some vital organ has to be missing at this point. Holding my breath, I flush, then lie on the floor. *Yes.* It's the only thing that slows the salsa-dancing walls. I could stay like this forever, on the cold tile.

There's this nagging in my skull, like I'm forgetting important things.

Goddamn it, what exactly *happened* last night? I look down, and I'm in a giant white button-up that is absolutely not mine, my bare legs spotted with bruises.

I can't remember *anything.*

My stomach somersaults violently.

Far, far in the distance, the echo of my phone ringing reaches me. I groan, my nose pressing so hard against the floor I can smell the lingering bleach. There's a desperate need in me to remain horizontal, but I force myself to crawl out and make it to bed.

I should be grateful I'm even alive at this point. I should have been extra careful knowing where I was, what I'm here for.

My eyes shut as I make a snow angel in the thousand-thread-count sheets, feeling around for my phone.

I find it, bring it to my face. Missed call from Taina. No big deal. My fingers scroll to the other missed calls: an unsaved number. That one logged over a dozen missed calls.

The time reads 2:00 p.m., and suddenly, sense rushes into me.

Two fucking p.m., as in, half an hour till Eliza's wedding.

Damn it, damn it, damn it.

God fucking damn it.

I try to hop off the bed, but my legs tangle in the sheets, and I face-plant on the floor with a *smack*. But adrenaline is pumping through me now, and like a guided missile, I'm in the shower scrubbing every ounce of alcohol from me. In fifteen minutes, I'm clean, teeth brushed, and basic mascara and blush on.

Damn it, I can't find my contacts or my backup glasses. My eyesight isn't *too* horrendous, but I can't make out faces unless they're directly across from me, and lights become long stripes that ruin my field of vision.

But I can't take another minute to look for them, mainly because without them, I can't see well enough to find them. I must have been well and truly drunk because I usually leave them right beside me.

My hands frantically search through my duffel, and I pluck out a blond wig and shove it over my head. I don't have time to secure it with pins and clips as I normally do, so I pull it down as much as I can, then dig within my bag until I feel a thin wire, and I excitedly pull up the item.

They aren't my prescription glasses, but these are oversized round ones that make my eyes look cartoonish. I put them on and try to think. The plan failed, but I'm resourceful.

Resourceful enough to stop a wedding from happening in less than an hour? Remains to be seen.

I yank on a tiny blue dress I stole from Taina and grab my heels before dashing out the door. What the hell is wrong with me? How could I have drunk so much that the entire night is just a dark blur? This is my only source of income, for God's sake. I let my personal business get in the way of this job, let my misery from the eviction drive me to drink, to make my pity party a priority.

Something about the words *pity party* scratches at my skull, but I have to keep it moving.

All right, it's time for a wedding-wrecking Hail Mary. I'll create mass chaos and confusion and claim I'm a mistress. I've only had to do this once, and it was the first wedding I ruined, and it ended with me thrown over the priest's shoulder as I was dragged away, but at least it worked. A last resort. Something that can be disproved but disruptive enough to delay the wedding. Hopefully, it will be long enough to gain more time and really find proof of infidelity.

When I get on the elevator, I put on my heels and recall the hotel layout from memory. At least I wasn't an idiot every day of my life; I'd already studied the hotel map, the venue attached to the back, and the gardens beyond.

God, if everything works out, I promise never to drink again. I know I said that after Taina's wedding, and after my first divorce, and *that time I bought a $20,000-winning scratch ticket and lost it while buying myself a celebratory layer cake at the grocery store, but I really mean it this time.*

I make it to the first floor, and repeat the mantra while mad dashing through the lobby. It's not a confusing layout; this place is just so damn big I'm out of breath by the time I make it to the hallway with the reception rooms.

Of course, it's massive here too. I crane my neck up to see the stretch of ceiling, this one painted like the sky scattered with clouds, heavenly. My vision starts to tilt, and I shake it off. I should have drunk some water before leaving, but the wedding will be starting—

Shit, now.

I sprint to the room with the double doors on one side. Eliza isn't waiting there, which means everyone is already inside the ballroom at the end of the corridor. I could be too late. If I am, no big deal. I'll find a window to fling myself out of.

My heels are on the brink of shattering as they slam against the polished marble. I almost collide with the oversized doors as I grip the golden knobs. I pull and they move, just too damn slow. I have to use my foot as leverage on one door and yank the other to slide between them, my curves getting squashed as I tumble through the opening. I catch myself before my face meets the floor.

A few people in the back row, resting on chairs so heavily covered in flowers it looks like they're sitting on top of a garden, spot me.

Eliza is under the arch of roses, her husband is looking down at her, and the pastor is reading from his book. I'm not too late. They're not pronounced yet. Not yet.

I pick myself up from the floor and scream, "I object!"

Now *everyone* is facing me. All at once, heads turn. I can actually hear the collective shuffle of bodies. People gasp, some clutch their jewelry. My skin heats from it all, or maybe it's the lingering hangover, but I'm too deep now.

I jog forward, objecting again.

Nobody moves as I rush toward the arch. I mean, how many times does a wedding get objected to? I can't blame them. They're probably in shock.

I grab James by his tie and yank his face to mine. "You told me you'd marry *me*!" I shout, hearing the collective gasp from the unwillingly but fully immersed audience. "How could you do this to me?"

"What the hell is this?" James asks, his voice shaking.

The pastor's hand reaches out. "Now, what is going on?"

James slaps my hand away from him. "Who the hell are you?"

"Who the hell am I?" My voice climbs even more. "I'm the *mother* of your unborn child!"

The gasps turn into shouts, buzzes of conversations. James jerks around, denying this, calling me crazy, but nobody is listening to him. Especially not when tears start spilling down my cheeks, and I hold my stomach dramatically. The last part is definitely not an act. A few more minutes of excitement and I might throw up again.

When nobody listens to him, his eyes narrow in on me. He grabs my shoulders tightly.

His nails pierce my skin.

"Get off me!"

When I try to wiggle out of his grip, he shoves me. I fall back into the arch, and the metal and my back collide like two cymbals banging against each other. My bones rattle as I land on my ass, sending the pain reverberating up my back.

The arch tips slowly. I reach up and grab the back of Eliza's dress, yanking her away from it as it falls over.

Right into the pastor.

Oh, I'm going to *hell.*

That has got to be a major sin. Injuring a pastor? Not as forgivable as the many offenses I've already accrued.

I hurriedly right myself, grabbing an edge of the arch and lifting. But the man isn't the only thing tipping over.

The pastor falls back on a wall of delicately placed candles. Glass shatters, and most of the flames flicker out, except for some that join with another and another until a gathering of light grows at the center of it all.

Fire first, pastor later.

I rush forward without thinking, reaching the flame with nothing to smother it with. I have enough sense not to use my hands but not enough sense to keep from blowing on it as if it'll snuff out the flame.

When I stomp on the fire with the bottom of my shoe, a shard of glass pierces through it and carves a tiny home into my foot.

I shout, instinctively jumping away, but I lose balance and fall back—*toward* all the broken glass.

Arms grip my hips, pulling me back from the potential damage.

My savior yanks off his long blazer as he passes me, smacking it over the flame until it's smothered. Once it is, he turns on his heel, and I freeze.

This close, nose to nose, my vision is good enough to make out a face. It's the man from the garden.

Flashes of memory blink through my head in rapid clicks. Giggling as Anders pulled me away from making water angels in a fountain out in the gardens. Tossing french fries into each other's mouths from way too far a distance to ever make it. Getting a piggyback ride through the halls. Fingers cupping my chin as Anders held a bottle of water to my dry lips.

"Anders!" I say at the same time he says, "Lucinda!"

Even with my haphazardly-put-together disguise, he recognized me.

My throat desperately needs a gallon of water. I tear my attention off him, and several people lift the arch while someone pulls the pastor up.

Most everyone is on their feet now, and it sounds like the beginning of a concert, with all the chatter and buzzing of movement. Anticipation is pounding through the bottoms of their shoes, causing the floor to shiver.

James is shouting at Eliza, gesturing toward me, screaming that he has no idea who I am. Eliza turns to face me, pulling up her dress and stomping over.

The veil catches around her face, and she yanks it away and snaps, "Who *are* you?"

With the veil and my lack of sight, I didn't see her well enough, but this close, her features become clear. Her nose isn't supposed to be as straight and pointed as it is right now. It's supposed to be rounded, and lower. And her skin should be riddled with enough freckles, no amount of foundation could cover them all, unlike the tan, clear skin I see. Her lips should be thinner, her jaw rounder, not full and sharp.

I never understood the phrase *time stood still.* Not for my two weddings, not when Taina got married and I walked her down the aisle, and not when I got my first client. Not until right now, when I realize this *isn't* the best friend of the woman I ran the background check on. This bride isn't Eliza.

I slap my hand to my mouth.

My thoughts all come too quickly yet too slowly. If I stop pressing my hand against my mouth, bile will spill from it.

How could this have happened? I'm sure this was the time for Eliza's wedding. I triple checked the times and dates.

A shadow pours over me.

"Lucinda, what's going on?" Anders asks, and somehow, he seems less accusatory and more concerned with my well-being. "You said this wasn't the wedding."

I swallow down a lump of bile. Every word that comes out stutters into something incoherent. I wonder if I can begin speaking Spanish and pretend I don't understand a thing. Sure, they heard me speak fluent English already, but I can gaslight over fifty people. I've done it before.

The bride takes another step toward me. I move back into Anders's body.

He waves a hand in my face. "Lucinda?"

Is it too late to pass out and hope everyone just leaves me to die?

"Oh my God," I whisper, removing my hand from my mouth, speaking to the bride. "I'm so sorry. I don't know your fiancé, this is—I'm just—" How the hell do you explain something like this? There are no words. I want to find the nearest body of water and fling myself into it. "I'm sorry."

As fast as my feet will take me, I sprint down the aisle, ignoring all the stares and the shouts. My bad foot half drags as I push through the double doors. The other doorway is wide open when I make it to the opposite side of the hall.

People file out, smiling, chatting, forming two lines.

Eliza and her *husband* walk through them, hand in hand. As I approach them, I can see that Jennie is dragging behind, a tight smile on her face as she follows the couple. Because I went to the wrong hall, and I didn't stop her best friend's doomed-to-fail marriage.

Oh God.

I keep moving until I'm at the end of one of the lines. James high-fives and fist-bumps the people as he goes, like a football player getting praised after a touchdown. Eliza presses kisses on cheeks, nods along the way, but coldly. Like the royals greeting people they consider peasants. Not like the great Princess Diana.

Then Jennie spots me.

Her green gown glides behind her, making her appear to float as she approaches. Her blond hair is pinned in a delicate bun, pearls like the ones sewed on to her gown clipped all around it. She looks absolutely stunning.

In the same way they described Lucifer as being the most beautiful angel.

She removes her hand from her husband's arm, wraps her arms around me, and presses her mouth so close to my ear she's kissing it as she speaks.

"I *hate* you."

Well, shit.

Jennie didn't give me a single break, even after I met her in her hotel room while the rest of the wedding celebrated at the reception. I could barely hear after the first minute, when her screaming popped my eardrum. I didn't say a word. Only sat there and listened to her disappointment, her reminder that her best friend would have to suffer from this doomed marriage.

There's no defense here. She came to me for help, and I failed her. Failed *Eliza*. I remember the hope and joy of getting married—despite nerves and hidden reservations. That feeling of something being *wrong*, and the swift, heavier obligation that if you had gotten that far, you had to stick it out. And the other feeling, too, of loving someone and them being in love with someone else.

Like my second marriage. I bet Eliza has had the same conversations with herself I had. *He's just friendly with her. They've been friends for years. You'll look crazy if you bring it up. You'll be* humiliated *if it turns out to be true—and it can't be true if you avoid it.*

Even now, years later, there is this missing fragment in my chest, permanently shattered from heartbreak. It doesn't matter how much time passes, it only eases the pain, but the scars remain. This haunted feeling that I'm irreparably flawed.

And now Eliza will have to feel that way too. I couldn't help her, like nobody could help me.

I had no time to pack, and with the lack of time and proper eyewear, I'm sure I've forgotten something in the rush of leaving. Even though most of my meeting with Jennie is a blur, I got the gist of it. Not getting paid. I ruined Jennie's best friend's life.

She got me the worst seat in economy—though I'm lucky she paid for a seat at all—set me up with a thirteen-hour, two-stop flight from the tiny island in the Caribbean back to Taina, and threatened to call security if I stayed on the premises any longer.

On the flight, I try to sleep, but the seat won't recline, and some kid won't stop kicking the back of it like I'm the one who forgot his gaming console back at the hotel. All this misery, and I don't even get the comfort of nearing home.

Because there is no home to go to.

Even if there is comfort in the safety of Taina's support, it's tainted by questions I don't want to answer. Faces I don't want to see. And dreams falling further out of reach.

4.

It's difficult to say what's weighing my body down the most.

It could be the jet lag, the delayed and congested subway car that added four hours to my travel time, the bruises spotting my skin, or just my overall misery about my failure and bleak life options and cramping that I'm sure means my period is coming.

All those factors are kicking my ass, but the worst uppercut to the gut is the bright smile my sister has as she lets herself into the back entrance of her guest suite, where I'm moping on the couch. My little sister, younger by five years, drops a tray of desserts on the marble, crescent-shaped coffee table.

It takes extra effort to meet her gaze as she plops down on the opposite love seat.

"You're in desperate need of a face mask." She tucks some of her highlighted curls away from her golden face, sculpted by the gods—and Michelle Rajan, the best aesthetician in Connecticut. "I made a thousand pastries for you to try."

"Thanks."

Taina looks around. "You haven't unpacked. It looks like you've melted into the couch."

"It's been just a couple of days, Taina."

"You never let me rot in bed more than two days in a row."

"And I'm regretful for that at this moment."

"I'm one hundred percent sure that's not true."

Perceptive little brat.

"Sadness doesn't look too good on you," she continues.

The insult is enough to combat my lack of desire to do anything more than lifting a finger. "Everything looks good on me."

She stands, her blue baby-doll dress clinging to her curves as she saunters over and tosses my legs off the couch so she can sit directly beside me. It forces me to maneuver myself upright.

"Mathew is away for work, and I was bored." She taps my leg. "So I thought I'd see what my pretty, sad sister was up to."

"Well, I applied for more jobs and was rejected within hours. A new record, really."

"Who rejected you? Give me a company name," she says, smiling—her murderous one where she thinks if she looks sweet enough, nobody knows her intentions, but a threat glistens in her heavily mascaraed gaze. The phrase *if looks could kill* doesn't apply to Taina. Taina *will* kill. Taina, despite my best efforts, has a criminal record.

Not for murder, but I wouldn't put it past her.

Neither of us is exactly the best law-abiding citizen, but when I was the head of the household, I did *try* to be a good influence. Not too much cursing, thinking before speaking, counting to ten before letting anger get the best of me—though it got the best of me more often than I liked. But Taina has always had a fiery temperament that I had to constantly smother, and I, quite literally, had to bail her out of jail. Twice. Though the men she clawed at the nightclubs did deserve it for trying to cop a feel.

Especially since Taina's anemia was so bad when she was younger. I'm convinced the more her blood pressure rose, the more frequently her fainting spells occurred. Having a calmer reaction to stressful environments would be helpful for everyone involved.

I close my eyes, and somehow even that hurts. "No hacking into company websites."

Her gaze narrows. "You can't tell me what to do." Then, her gaze softens. "Well, okay, you can. You can tell me things, and *I'll* do it. And if *I* tell you to do things, then *you* can do it too."

"Taina." I pinch the bridge of my nose, too tired to have this argument again. "I'm not moving in with you and your husband."

"Oh, please," Taina says, gesturing to the space around us. "This is your own floor. A private entrance, kitchen, and bath; it's like your own apartment."

Of course, this was Taina's motive for coming here with treats and a smile. Offering the comfort of her $3.4 million Connecticut mansion. Since I started the Wreck a Wedding business five months ago, she's been hounding me to move in with her.

Granted, I have also called her numerous times complaining about a faulty sink, a leaking shower, moldy walls—so this request has been a long time coming. But I *chose* my old apartment knowing it wasn't the best. It was the lowest rate I could get in New York a short distance from my old job. I could have gotten something better, but I wanted to save as much as I was able.

My dad always preached about how much better it was to live below your means—to always have a little extra stashed away for emergencies, like hospital bills or unexpected expenses. We saw that firsthand with Mom's illness. Saving wasn't just about being responsible; it was about survival.

Still, I've gotten better at allowing the people around me to care for me when they can. I wouldn't deny Taina's help if it were about anything else. If I needed a shoulder to lean on while whining about a date gone wrong, or help with an essay for my online university courses because I can never remember where an apostrophe is supposed to live, or company while cleaning up crap and dirt from the animal shelter. For anything else, I have no problem taking Taina's often-extended hand.

Money is an entirely different story. A story I've yet to tell Taina, and am not sure I ever will—for her sake. "I'm looking for another place," I get out, trying to ignore the sudden pinch in my chest.

"You lived in the equivalent of a dumpster. Actually, worse than that, dumpsters have roofs. You had a collection of holes vaguely connected by twenty-seven coats of paint. And you couldn't even afford that. How will you afford anything back in the city?"

I jerk back, then soften my posture. I know Taina doesn't mean it maliciously. It's just, when she has a goal, she will do anything to reach it. She's driven like that. Her current goal? Keeping me in the safety of her home.

I completely understand because, for most of my life, my thoughts were all just fragments broken from my singular purpose: *Take care of my sister.*

When we were kids, and our parents gave up dinner so we could split a bowl of Avena, I would give her my share. I worked multiple jobs and did under-the-table work at a bar to get her through college. Stole clothes from rich neighborhoods' trash so she would have brand names in class when the other kids would sneer at a knockoff. At my lowest, I "borrowed" books and supplies she needed from department stores.

And now her bank account looks like a phone number, while mine looks like the receipt for a hamburger.

"I just need to get through the slow season. Or actually get a call back for an interview somewhere. I've started applying outside of the city."

These past months have felt like a yearlong slow season. It's not like I can hang around wedding venues and hand out flyers. I don't have a large pool of clients to draw from.

"What you need is help," Taina says, softening. "The job market sucks right now and—"

"And after I was fired, I destroyed my supervisor's desk and had to be escorted out of the building," I finish for her.

That day is still fresh in my mind. My condescending, aging prick of a supervisor sat me down, called me the name of the only other woman in the department, and asked me to wear looser clothes because I was distracting my peers. If I was going to continue to dress that way, I was basically "asking for it."

Taina was ready to sue the second I got fired—Mathew's a lawyer, and she practically had the paperwork drafted before I'd even made it home.

But buried in the mountain of new-hire paperwork I signed on my first day was a clause that waived my right to sue the company. I didn't catch it. I was too busy feeling grateful—after years of juggling part-time jobs, night classes, and overdue bills, I would've signed a napkin if it came with health insurance and a 401(k).

"I'm sure they've warned every firm in the tristate about me. My resume is too impressive not even to get a callback."

And yet, given the chance, I'd for sure say yes if they offered me my position back in the field rather than the high-risk, low-opportunity, anxiety-inducing trade of wedding wrecking.

I've always been happier with the ability to keep a roof over my head. And when you try to live without it, you find that money does indeed buy happiness—something achievable with a stable, salaried job like my marketing role at a New York City tech firm.

"Clearly not impressive enough," Taina points out.

"How I wish I shipped you off to military school to learn some manners."

"Sorry." Taina salutes. "Clearly, it's not impressive enough, *sir*."

I reel my arm back, ready to slap her. She dodges me, sticks out her tongue, then grabs my phone from the coffee table, flips it over, and points to a Polaroid photo tucked beneath the clear case—my pit bull terrier gleefully demolishing my couch.

My heart lurches at the loss of her, still fresh even though it's been a year. I've always thought photos held an impossible responsibility, carrying the weight of memory even if the people in them are gone. It keeps the moment alive, anyway.

"If you won't officially move in with me," Taina says, "or let me commit murder, let me help pay for your share of Save a Paw."

Anxiety bites at me when she mentions the animal shelter.

Save a Paw is my real dream, not this wedding-wrecking mess I'm in. A haven for dogs that provides services for homeless animals, like vet care and any necessary surgeries, nurturing and caring for them, and trying to house them where they can get all the love and care they deserve.

Since I was sixteen, the owner had promised me that once he retired, he'd sell the business to me. I was supposed to have years more time to be able to buy it from him. But a couple months ago, Joshua told me his wife wanted him to retire earlier, spend the rest of their years traveling the world, so he'd come to me first, like he promised. Save a Paw could be mine for $30,000.

I'd been putting aside small amounts for years and had already saved up $10,000 for it. I'm nowhere near the other $20,000. When I told him that, he said his wife gave him a year to get his affairs in order, therefore, *I* had a year (now three months left) to buy it off him.

A stressful fact made more anxiety inducing when he informed me that his partner, the other shareholder, already had someone interested in buying.

In a cruel and genius way, Taina goes into my photos app and starts playing videos of Storm and me. "Think of all the Stormys that need you to keep the business thriving. What would have happened to her if you hadn't found her?" she asks, knowing damn well she probably would have *died*. "Don't you remember? How much pain she was in?"

Of course I do. How could I not? My dog was my everything. "Don't be cruel," I tell her.

"I'm just saying, Storm helped you realize your passion in life. Animals. You can't let the shelter go to some Wall Street, high-water, cufflink-wearing asshole."

I rub my palms against my eyes. "I'm pretty sure it's a former veterinarian wanting to take over." But she's right, Storm had helped me.

In every aspect of my life. In every relationship, platonic or otherwise. It doesn't matter how hard I work at being a good friend, an amazing girlfriend, or an incredible employee; it's like I was specially created to be an extra in every main character's life. It doesn't matter how much I bend and twist and break to become a priority for the people around me, I'm always just an afterthought.

The first time I'd ever been needed was on my sixteenth birthday. My parents forgot—understandably—since Taina had the flu so horrendously, she had to be taken to the hospital, and I dragged myself on a ten-mile walk, hoping that each step would feel less miserable than the last.

And then I saw a dog limping across a road, under the drizzle becoming rain. Its leg buckled halfway through, and it dropped as the headlights of a car poured closer and closer toward it. Without thinking, I ran out, hands up, screaming for the car to stop. It swerved, barely avoiding us, but the near-death hardly shook me.

The poor silver thing was whining, its hind leg bent at a grotesque angle. Its eyes were blue and wide with pain, and they held such a familiar kind of heartache that I wrapped it up in my arms. A pit bull. Fifty pounds of dog that I somehow managed to drag to the nearest shelter.

Save a Paw—I'll never forget walking through the building.

It was all a blur. The staff took the dog from me, questioning things I had few answers for, taking her away for hours, and returning with a declaration that she was recovering from surgery, but her leg had been purposely broken.

I spent the rest of the night waiting for any updates. I cried when they carried the wounded dog and placed her within a large cage at the shelter. When I wouldn't leave, the employees let me enter the room and lie with the dog to ease her cries as she tried to sleep through the pain. Each time she woke, her eyes met mine, like she was checking to make sure I was still there. Only when she confirmed it did she let herself drift back off to sleep.

She needed me.

It was work convincing my parents to let me adopt her, but once I brought in the tears, they couldn't deny me. I buried her name tag and called her Storm, for the night I found her. Finally, I was a first choice.

Storm needed me, but I needed her more. We spent every day together; our walks got me outside and kept me healthy, and her company as I read or watched TV or studied or slept kept me sane.

She was my best friend and I was hers, but I often thought about the other cries I'd heard. The other animals crying out for love and having nobody reach out.

So our walks took us back to the shelter, where Storm made friends, and I volunteered to pass the time. I helped shower the dogs, distracted them when they were getting their shots, cleaned up the kennels, and worked out potential adoptions to see if families really *wanted* and *could* care for a pet.

Save a Paw is *mine*.

"This wedding wrecking isn't sustainable," Taina says, pulling me from the memories. "I've been tracking the click-through on all the ads I've been running, hits on the site. It's tanking. And the job market *does* suck."

Anxiety bites at me when she says it. "I know, but it's only temporary. Once I save up for my share, I can start working on how to make the shelter financially sustainable. Make enough for it, and me, and then, no more wedding wrecking."

Taina raises an eyebrow. "And how do you plan to do that? Bake sales?" When I open my mouth, she holds out a hand. "Just kidding, don't be mad. I know you've been playing around with ideas, but you still haven't told me *exactly* how you plan to get any revenue for it."

Eager to remind my little sister I am a capable adult, I tell her, "Multiple ways."

"Keeping me in suspense here?"

I smile. "I want to restructure it. Keep the mission side nonprofit—adoptions, hospital costs, rescue costs—but add a couple for-profit arms. The first, a boutique dog-grooming service in the front—spa treatments, high-end. Think about a sauna for dogs. People spend *so* much on their pets."

She nods slowly, eyebrows coming together like her own wheels are turning—probably designing me a website in her head as I speak.

"Second—dog merch. Collars, leashes, raincoats, safe nail polish, whatever. All branded. Profits go back into the shelter."

"And the third?" she asks, taking out her phone and typing what I assume are notes.

"Dog parties."

She pauses. "Huh?"

"Birthday parties. Engagement shoots for couples and their dogs. It's a real market. I've done the research. I already know how to market emotionally charged events—weddings, breakups. Same psychology. Just rebranded for dogs instead of people. I've been building an email list from the weddings I've worked. Brides, grooms, jilted exes with rich friends. They owe me—and my silence. A few of them are already interested in sponsoring fundraisers."

Taina whistles. "You lost me a bit with the dog birthdays, but the rest I can get behind."

"Tough crowd," I say, "but, Taina, don't worry too much about me. I can do this. I'm good at getting people to care. And I'm really good at getting them to pay attention. I'm good at most things, when I put the effort in."

"I know you are," she says, her eyes narrowing, "so let me just expedite the process. Let me invest in you."

I peek over at her. We're the same height and nearly twins, but she's without freckles, and her face is sharper where mine is rounded. She is all I have, and I would do anything for her.

Except this.

It's for her own good. Her own marriage. She doesn't know *I* know about the dozen couples' therapy sessions she and her husband went through because she forced them to move from Vermont to Connecticut to be closer to me, and took money out of their joint account to pay off my student debt without me knowing. That she skipped a major trip—the first real vacation Mathew had planned for them in years—because it conflicted with my birthday.

But I do. Because Mathew told me. In a plea and a threat that let me know *I* was a rift between them, widening and ruining the one marriage I would never want to wreck. He didn't yell. He didn't demand. He just made a point. In that soft, careful way someone from HR would use when they want to sound reasonable while firing someone.

He never said go away forever. But it was in the way he thanked me when I missed a date Taina invited me to, or a networking event his job was running and Taina wanted me to join—like I'd done something good. Like I'd taken a step back on purpose.

It's about Mathew watching every time she chooses me—and quietly resenting her for it. How he's on his very last straw, and Taina thinks there are dozens left.

At first, I thought Mathew was too rough, his love too conditional. But then the doubt crept in—what do I really know about love? After all the failed attempts I've seen and lived through, and watching so many couples around me who seem to get by without it, maybe love isn't the grand thing I once believed. My experience with wedding wrecking should have made me immune to romance by now, yet here I am, still trying to unravel what love looks like, trying to decipher how something could look so vastly different depending on who wears it.

So, no, I can't take her money; I can't cross that line again. If I do, I'll ruin my sister's marriage. Taina told me every time they make it through a fight, she feels closer than ever to him. Feels convinced that she chose the right person: someone that she can confront anything with and make it to the other side.

"No." I press a kiss to her cheek. I grab my laptop from the carpet. "I'm going to convince my landlord to give me my apartment back. Maybe bring up the several building code violations as a blackmailing point."

I mean, I *should* have gotten a discount from that crumbling building. It would help tremendously, seeing as I have no way of paying at the moment. It's not like I'm *dead* broke, but I definitely don't have back-rent amounts of money.

Even the thought of going into my savings makes me nauseous—partly because that's for Save a Paw, sure, but the *most* stressful fact of it all is that the money is locked away in a CD savings account.

I pitched damn near all of my paycheck into it, putting aside just enough for rent and noodles. I thought for sure I'd never need to pull from that money. I've always made do with very little; it made sense to continue to live that way. I signed the contract, locking myself into a three-year agreement without access to the funds. The penalty for drawing before then is six months' interest. I'd lose nearly all I've gained just like that.

It would be like starting from scratch. Not an option. Not even a thought.

"Oh my God," Taina mutters. "You're too good for my money?"

If Taina had stuck to her tech career, I'm sure she would have acquired a nice lifestyle herself, regardless of whether she had met her renowned attorney husband. She just accelerated the process by marrying a well-off man with two properties, a strictly Prada-filled closet, and a penchant for making sisters-in-law feel guilty for existing.

"I can't take your money," I say, wishing I could, at least, *some* of it. "I can figure things out on my own. I always have. I believe in myself, and honestly, each time you try to convince me to accept your help, it feels like you don't."

That's the worst of all. Taina used to need me for everything, and now the most she'll ask for is for me to remember to text her back. To go from someone who wasn't just constantly needed but *good* at helping others to someone who can't even pay their bills on time feels like karmic punishment from a past life where I kicked puppies and children or something.

Her face turns pink. "Well. That's not my intention. But still, stop trying to run out. Consider this a temporary respite. Stay here as long as you need. The door is always open."

The door, in reality, is glued shut.

I start up my laptop, the only thing I own that's brand new. I begin drafting an email to my old landlord, knowing in my gut it won't get me anywhere, then shoot a text to my favorite employee at Save a Paw.

Sadness doesn't look good on me, no, but it's hard not to wrap it around me in this house I don't belong in and with a sister who should be asking for advice instead of giving it.

I need space to breathe, so I send my email, gather what I need, and head out.

5.

Water sprays all around me, clinging to my already drenched T-shirt and soaked sweats. Stick, the golden Labrador standing against the wall, has been dodging the showerhead every time I aim it in her direction.

Two days in a row I've come to Save a Paw to escape the house that's entirely safe and somehow feels close to collapsing on me every moment I'm there. Here, despite the confined space and constant noise, I'm more comfortable than ever. Stick let me lather her with the anti-itch conditioner, was cute enough to press her nose over mine, and dropped a paw over my leg once I gave her a nice ten-minute massage to let the ingredients soak in, tricking me into thinking she was complacent. Now my mouth is full of shampoo, aloe, and a liberal helping of dog hair.

I place the showerhead beside me, cross my legs, and hold Stick's wide-eyed gaze. "All right, sweetheart," I tell her as firmly as I can, given that she's just a cute bundle of gold fur and love. "This is for your own good. Do you think keeping that conditioner in is going to help you? Trust me, I've done it, and my hair fell out. It's no leave-in. You will regret it and need bangs."

She whines, her head lowering.

"Look, the faster you let me rinse you off, the faster I can dry you. Wouldn't it be so nice to strut through the dog park with a fresh mane? Don't you want to be the envy of all the other dogs? It's up to you."

Stick sighs, and it's not that I think she fully understands me, but at least I've bored her into a tentative submission. She stiffens when I bring the showerhead over but doesn't jump around or run to the glass wall overlooking the reception area where Ted, my favorite staff member, gives me an encouraging thumbs-up.

We give it another go, and Stick heroically only fights me one more time before we finish off in the corner of the room, where I use the blower to dry *both* of us off. As a reward, I bring her to the back of the shelter to join the other dogs running around the spacious play area featuring fake grass and walls painted with sky and clouds, creating the illusion of being outside. Sometimes when I'm here, I turn on high-speed fans to make it feel windy.

My shoes squelch with every step I take to Ted, who has a head of hair not too far off from Stick's, and brown eyes that are always warm and welcoming.

He salutes me as I approach him. "Thank you for your service."

"At ease." I play along, scanning the board behind him with heartfelt photos of Save a Paw's furry residents pinned by colorful tacks, looking their absolute sweetest to encourage the people entering to adopt, volunteer, donate, or all three.

My gaze snags on a photo of Storm in the upper right corner, smiling under a pink raincoat. Grief pins another tack into my chest as I go around the desk and grab it.

Knowing the way Taina's brain works, she probably opted to save more practical items during my eviction, like furniture, electronics, and cookware. The sentimental items would be last on her priority list, so I pocket the photo in case the boxes I still haven't finished unpacking at her house don't have a single framed photo within them.

When I turn, Ted's insistent clicking on the desktop catches my attention. Before he can exit the screen, I recognize the format of a resume. Unsurprising, since I'd only edited and reformatted fifty-seven of them over the past three months.

Guilt frames his widening eyes. "It's just a backup plan. I know you'll take over this place soon."

"You'll leave if I don't?"

"I like Joshua, I like you, but if you guys are gone, my dad's been meaning for me to join his auto shop for a while now." He shakes his head. "But I know you'll buy your share."

I place a hand on his shoulder. "This is smart. Be smart."

"I'm trying," he says, his gaze averting to my wet shoes. "How is that going, by the way? Think you'll be able to take over soon?"

I'm doing everything possible, but I'm barely above water. But I'll manage. Of course I will.

The words are there, ready to reassure, but I think about the hopeful ping of each email notification I've received this past year, followed swiftly by the crushing words of rejection. It's a painful and somewhat degrading process I wouldn't want Ted or any of the staff here to go through.

I reach over and grab the desktop's mouse. "Let me help you buff your CV."

I can't tell if Ted's sigh is one of relief or disappointment.

Save a Paw is on the border between New York and Connecticut, so it takes me two hours to get to Taina's place and, after pulling her Lexus into the drive-up garage, about five seconds to want to go all the way back.

Mathew's Porsche is parked outside. Taina's at Pilates, so I will be left alone with the man who has said only seven sentences to me since I moved in a week ago. It's always the same: *We're* so *happy to take care of you.* Only when Taina is around.

I get out and shut the door so lightly that it doesn't lock. Hopefully, Mathew's had a full day of helping rich people to get richer and is napping on the edge of their cloud couch in loafers that he refuses to take off even when in the house.

Instead of going in the front door, I circle the country home that sits on five meticulously manicured acres. My feet sink into the soft grass as I move past the pristine landscaping Taina helped arrange, white and yellow flowers dotting the bushes, until I reach a single curved white door at the back.

Taina was right, I think, as I let myself in. Under different circumstances, being here could give me the illusion of having my own place.

It's nothing I'd pick out on my own. A pale cushioned couch facing a curved flat screen. Sterling-silver cookware on the stainless steel stovetop in the wraparound kitchen overlooking the living room and the all-white bedding set in the corner. Neat. Tidy. Colorless.

Way nicer than my New York apartment.

If only there weren't this chunk of unwelcomeness lodged behind my rib cage the moment I walk into the house. Even as I shove my shoes off at the door, then throw myself onto the couch and sink into its luxury, the feeling thickens until my chest pinches with the pain of it.

With all its faults, my apartment was my sanctuary. The insistent drip of the kitchen sink was a sound that became a song that lulled me into relaxation, away from whatever the day outside the crooked, double-locked doors weighed on me. A place similar to our childhood home; a place my heart put loose roots into.

The memory of the sound, the *tap*, *tap*, *tap*, plays in my head. It's enough to lull my body into a state of comfort that brings my heavy eyes to a close.

On the cusp of sleep, the door slams.

Mathew walks in, loafers on, to loom over me. It's the first time we've been alone together in seven days. I knew the moment would come but foolishly prayed I could somehow avoid it if I worked around his long hours.

He doesn't speak. He crosses his arms, the sleeves of his blazer tight against his biceps. It must be a power move he does to assert dominance over his clients.

A sliver of pettiness makes me want to remain silent, to see if I can get him to break first, but it's hard to be petty when I'm living rent free in his house.

"Mathew," I greet him. Not Matt. Math*ew*. No nicknames allowed. I learned that the very first time we met, and he shook my hand as if we'd just closed a multi-million-dollar deal.

"Have you been applying to jobs?" he asks, his tone clipped, final, as if he *doesn't* want me to answer his question. His default tone when speaking to anyone other than Taina.

"I have been," I respond, wanting to fold into myself. "Now and for months."

He sucks his teeth. "That scene you pulled at work was foolish. Word gets around. Now what? There's only so many jobs *you* qualify for."

"And what jobs do I qualify for?"

"Jobs that won't pay you enough to move out of here fast enough."

"Fast enough? Don't you want me gone yesterday?"

"If you know, you shouldn't have moved in."

"I'm not moving in." My voice is a tiny thing now. "This is just until I find a new place."

I hate feeling myself becoming smaller under his scrutiny. It feels like he's shoved me in front of a studio audience ready to laugh at a moment's notice, planted a spotlight over me, and is waiting for me to say something that's as pathetic and stupid as he believes I am.

It's humiliating, trying to reach for my pride and finding only shame in its place. There's no place for it here, no shield I can grab to defend myself from his condescending glare. I have no place to go, no jobs lined up, and a maxed-out credit card. I can't say anything for fear of pissing him off. I have to let him speak to me in whatever demeaning way he wants to.

It's hard to believe that this is the man Taina would keep me up at night talking my ear off about, with tales of all the romance and charm he radiated. The way he speaks to me makes me think I've warped all those stories.

Surely he couldn't be the man who made customized playlists and burned them onto CDs (Who even has CD players anymore?), or named a star after her, or brought flowers for her on every single date they had, or painted her nails?

Under his continuous glare, I add, “I’m trying my best.”

“Clearly, that’s not enough.”

Heat builds beneath my eyes from the growing embarrassment flooding through me. “What more can I do if my best isn’t enough?”

At the sound of my voice cracking, Mathew pinches the bridge of his nose with manicured fingers. The way he’s smoothed his ashy hair back allows me to see every line of disappointment and irritation framing his square face.

“Don’t make me out to be the bad guy here. You’re the one who lost your job. Now I have to pick up the pieces.”

“I’m trying to pick up my own pieces.”

“I don’t mean *yours*.” He yanks his hands from his face. “I mean Taina’s. You know those nightmares she used to have? The ones of you and your family in the car, a crash, and then she crawls and crawls to find you? They’re back. Every night, she screams awake or keeps herself up until she’s exhausted so she doesn’t even risk having them. Two years straight, she didn’t have a single one. Now they’re back.”

My vision grows spotty as panic slides down my throat.

Of course I know the nightmares. Before Mathew, I was the one who had to lull Taina back to sleep or spend hours consoling her, reassuring her I was fine, we were fine, and everything was fine.

I wasn’t in the car crash that killed my parents; neither was Taina. But since they died, like me but worse, Taina has had this paranoia that *I* would be next, a worry she’d deny during the day and cry about in the middle of the night. She told me how real the dreams felt, how she felt every piece of shattered glass sinking into her knees as she crawled from the flipped car, following a blood trail she knew was mine, screaming for me over and over, and I would never appear.

Stress made them come more frequently, or whenever *I* was going through something. A breakup, a divorce, a job loss. Anytime my life felt like it was scrambling, it was as if Taina synchronized with my emotions and they became hers, but worse.

"I didn't know," I whisper.

"Of course you didn't, because she's *my* wife. *I'm* the one who has to deal with anything you throw her way. You couldn't just keep your problems, your problems." His voice tinges with disgust. "When I signed my marriage certificate, it only had Taina's name attached. I didn't sign up to become a caretaker too."

I try to swallow, but there's no moisture in my throat. "I'm sorry."

He blows out a breath. "I'm sure you are, but that doesn't mean anything to me. Already she's talking about going away, taking you on a trip to get your mind off the consequences of your own goddamn actions. It's happening all over again. You take up all her time, use up *my* money, and I have to grin and bear it because Taina can't handle seeing her *older* sister in trouble."

He says the word *older* with a laugh, and it feels like a jab in my stomach.

"I won't let her go on a trip," I say, but the words come out fast and jumbled like the syllables are nervously tripping on themselves. "I'm going to get a job. I'm going to move out. I'll find something to do for now, during the day, the night, whenever you want some alone time. I'll be invisible."

"You'd be invisible to me already if not for Taina," he snaps, his patronizing control finally cracking. "I'm not dealing with this again. I won't figure out how to fix the rift in my marriage. I'll give you three months to get out—three months only. If you're not out, you—" He shakes himself and takes a fortifying breath. "You *and* Taina can leave."

I've always considered myself a brave person. Not that I'm not easily frightened of things, but because no matter how fearful I am, it never deters me from doing what I need to do. But now a knot of fear in my chest tangles itself into a bond so tight it feels like it's a permanent addition to the organs that keep my body functioning.

I cannot ruin my sister's marriage for a plethora of reasons, mainly because I love her more than anything in this world. Another reason is that Taina cannot be alone. She clings to people. Not in an overbearing way—in a quiet, secretive way. Because she's so wonderful, so giving and charming and funny, people don't realize when she's formed a permanent place by their side.

But she only does so when she's fully in love.

Taina has had many boyfriends, many "almosts" and "could have beens," but she'd told me she was in love with Mathew the first night she met him. She knew they were perfect for each other. She's pretty sure our parents made a deal in heaven and sent Mathew to earth to take care of her.

I can't be the cause of her divorce. I don't want to even imagine how she'd react. But of course she'd resent me; she wouldn't be able to stop herself. Right?

It's one thing to feel not good enough for anyone else, but to know that my own sister might see me that way after ruining something she's wanted for so long—fear burrows in my chest. That would kill me.

"I'll be out in three months," I tell him. "I swear."

No matter what, I won't set foot in this house again, even if I have nowhere to go.

He gives me one final look. "I hope so." Then leaves.

At the sound of the door slamming shut, I press my palms into my eye sockets. I almost laugh. Whenever I *think* I've hit rock bottom, there's another pitfall to tumble into.

It used to be that, despite accumulating my fair share of misfortunes, I'd always thought I had a weird, pitiful sort of luck. I lost my parents, but Taina was supposed to be in the car with them the day they died—she got sick and stayed home with me—so I got to keep my sister. Whenever I thought I wouldn't make rent while getting Taina through school, some good Samaritan left me a large enough tip to cover expenses. When I ran out of food stamps, the local shelter would host a food drive where I could pack up two weeks' worth of groceries.

No matter how bad things got, somehow, barely hanging on, I could pull through.

This time, it looks like my luck has finally dried up. What else am I supposed to do? I've already applied to jobs I'm overqualified for and underqualified for, and the money I have saved up was meant to buy my share to save the dog shelter.

Since I got Storm, it's been my dream. I've just had too many responsibilities to really work toward it.

Do I have to give it up?

Should I give it up? I haven't saved enough yet, anyway. I could use that money to move out and cover rent for a couple of months as I continue to get rejection after rejection, before I get evicted again.

Why can't I be lucky? Not pitiful lucky, actually *lucky, with my own happily ever after?*

I bury my face in the cushion and scream.

The muffled noise tears my throat as I release it, trying to let go of this choking bundle of emotions lodged within it. I only stop when I feel my phone vibrating in my back pocket.

I snatch it from my jeans to answer on the fifth ring. "Hello?"

"Lucinda?"

I sit up so fast that the room spins. "Hello?" I say again, checking the screen, but I don't have the number saved as a contact. "Who is this?" But my subconscious recognizes the voice now that time has passed and I'm completely sober.

"Ah," he says into the speaker. "You didn't save my number. Understandable since we were supposed to be perfect strangers, but I saved yours, sorry." When I don't say anything, he adds, "It's Anders."

"I know," I say, then slap my forehead. "I mean, hi. Well. Why are you calling me?"

I haven't thought too much about him because I've been preoccupied with my glaring unemployment, eviction, and the brother-in-law who hates me. The last time I saw him was when I ruined the wrong wedding.

His first love's wedding.

Oh shit. I hadn't thought of *that* detail in particular. Is he happy with me? Angry that I wrecked the special moment between two people he still weirdly cares about? Confused by me? All of the above?

His answering chuckle, even muffled by a phone speaker, sends a quick zing of awareness down my spine. "How are you? When I tried looking for you after the almost-wedding, I heard you already left."

How are you? This was not the first question I thought he'd ask me—not that I thought he'd ask me anything. I never thought we'd have another interaction in my life.

I've already trauma dumped on him once and don't think it's why he's calling me now, so I go with, "I'm fine."

"You live in New York, right? That's what you told me," he says, and he means *You may or may not have given me the wrong name, and you wrecked a wedding, and you have a track record of being a complete weirdo, so I'm not sure if you were telling the truth about your place of residence.*

But I don't feel like admitting that I now live with my little sister, so I tell him, "Yes."

"Perfect. I'm in the city for work this week, our offices are based here, and I was hoping we could grab coffee."

"Why?"

I don't mean to sound so short, but I'm too confused about him reaching out and on the tail end of misery from speaking with Mathew to think of anything other than single-word responses.

He only chuckles again. "I'd like to see you. Talk. And, honestly, I have something to ask."

"You can ask me now," I point out, trying not to sound like I was screaming into the couch cushion only moments ago.

"I'd rather do it in person."

Curiosity tickles my spine straight. Though I only remember bits and pieces of our night together, the small bundles of memories among the black spots are all pleasant. He was charming and never creepy, comforting but not too soft.

And, of course, whenever our hands brushed or our shoulders knocked into each other as we stumbled around the hotel in search of snacks, an arrow of heat shot between my legs.

My fingers dance along my lap. I could say no, but there's no real reason to, just like there's no reason to say yes. But an excuse to get out of the house seems more appealing than flinching at the creak of every footstep I hear whenever Mathew walks along the kitchen floor above.

It'll take me another two hours to get back into the city, but at least the drive will help me clear my head. Or, if I want to drink, I can take the train.

"Make it dinner tonight, and I'll say yes."

"Dinner," he repeats without hesitation, "tonight, so say yes."

"Yes."

6.

Anders sent over the restaurant and time without being asked, so I didn't have to wonder if my linen pants and sleeveless top were appropriate attire for the dimly lit bistro stuffed between high-rise buildings downtown.

He sits at a table in a far corner, overlooking the other diners clinking glasses and laughing while a slightly too loud indie-folk playlist surrounds us.

I walk over and plant myself in front of him with a polite smile. "Anders."

"Lucinda," he greets warmly, and heat spreads at the tips of my ears.

"You can call me Lucy," I offer as I hang my tote on the chair.

"I like Lucinda."

I tilt my head and gaze at him. His hair is perfectly tousled, his light-brown button-up somehow makes the flecks of gold in his eyes glow a little brighter at the center of their pools of green, and he's missing the slight five o'clock shadow that was present when we first met.

When I don't say anything, he adds, "You look beautiful. Your hair is nice too. Different."

"Ah." I twirl one of the bouncy curls reflectively. I didn't have enough time after my shower to straighten it. "I usually wear it flat."

"Both styles look good on you."

Wow. Three compliments back-to-back in the span of thirty seconds. Is he making good on his *future endeavor* promise? Or is he sweet-talking me into whatever favor he needs? I have no idea what *I* could possibly do for him.

The waitress arrives for our drink order, and Anders asks for a flight of their best wines for us to try.

"Okay," I say when she leaves, "I am so incredibly confused by you reaching out that I'm not sure what I'm supposed to say right now. If you can get straight to the point so I don't have to keep scrambling to try and figure that out, I'd appreciate it."

His dimples appear. When he opens his mouth, I hold up my finger. "Actually, if this is going to be a stressful and/or confrontational conversation, do I still get dinner out of this? I'm starving."

His small smile becomes a full-blown one. "I guarantee you can have dinner, no matter where the conversation leads. Dessert included."

"Phenomenal."

The waitress leaves two flights of mini wineglasses and asks for our order. Anders asks for a steak and then points to the menu laid out in front of me. "The vegan burger is supposedly very good."

My eyebrows quirk. "Did I tell you I was vegetarian?"

"Do you not remember?"

I sigh and order the burger. When the waitress leaves, I grab one of the glasses and down the dry wine like a shot. "I don't remember much of that night," I confess, grabbing the next glass over. "I'm not sure of everything I rambled about to you. I only remember the beginning of the evening, not the end."

"I see. Well, you didn't say or do anything embarrassing, if that helps."

I snort. "Sweet of you to lie, but I know myself, and that is absolutely what happened."

"Not to me."

I narrow my eyes at his sincere expression and bring the glass to my lips. His gaze briefly flickers to where my mouth presses against the glass before reaching my eyes again, and my cheeks flush.

"Did we sleep together?" I blurt out. I'm sure we didn't. I'm sure I would remember *that*—my body would, anyway—but I need confirmation. Just in case. To be sure. "I woke up with a shirt that wasn't mine."

"I walked you to your room, and we ended the night." He tilts his head in debate about whether to add the next part. Then, "You said you wanted it because I smelled nice, so I gave it to you before leaving."

The way he frames it lets me know he's politely omitting a more dramatic scene, one where I said something a lot more sexual, or, worse, yanked it off him before he gently turned me down.

He doesn't sound like he's lying about nothing happening, but drunk me is a little more adventurous—and shameless—than sober me. "Be honest, did I make a move on you?"

"If you did, it would have been more than welcome."

Which is a polite way of saying yes. I groan and rub my hand over my face, freezing when I remember I layered on mascara. I already acted insane around him; I don't need to look the part too.

"Why are you sitting here with me and not running away? You have at least five reasons to."

"I don't want to." He grabs a napkin. He then reaches over and cups my cheek in one hand, wiping the cloth over my skin with the other. I blink as he pulls away, spotting the black mascara staining the cloth as he places it on the table and continues, "And I need a favor."

I frown at him. "I bet you get yourself into constant misunderstandings."

His brows bunch together, pulling down a scar at the side of his right eyebrow. "What do you mean?"

I gesture to the napkin. "You're very affectionate," I point out, but affectionate doesn't seem like the right word. *Charming*, maybe, but it doesn't encompass what I mean to say, either. "I can tell you don't mean to be, that you're just doing things in the moment, but it only makes you more endearing. You probably think you pass as friendly, but other people might believe you're looking for more than that."

His gaze latches onto me. I can't quite read the emotion in it. It's a little darker than the easy warmth that seems to fill it most of the time. "I know exactly what I'm doing."

I'm not entirely sure what he means by that, but for some reason, tiny circles of heat sear through my skin as he looks at me. I shift in my seat and take a fortifying sip of wine. "Anyway, what favor could *I* possibly do for you?"

"When you wrecked my friend's wedding," he begins casually, as if we're talking about the weather, "I tried to find you but you left pretty soon after."

I want to shrink inside myself for a moment, to become so small he forgets I ever walked into the restaurant, but his words don't have any judgment in them. It's enough to let me push aside the pulse of embarrassment vibrating under my skin and actually listen to his words.

"For a blissful moment," I say, "I forgot I told you what I do."

"Nothing wrong with trying to make a living."

I hold up a hand. My pitch is a little too high not to hint at some mortification. "This is not to *make* a living but *for* a living. It's not my life's goal or anything. I stumbled into it, and one day, I'll stumble out of it."

Hopefully.

"Right, because you want to buy Save a Paw."

What didn't *I tell him?*

The bar is so low for men that Anders remembering this one detail sends a fluttering to the pit of my stomach. "Yeah, among other things."

"I'd like to hire you."

My hand stills on the glass pressed against my lips. Nothing about this conversation is going in any direction I predicted it to. "You're engaged?" Being hung up on his first love marrying his best friend didn't make it seem so.

"No, I'm not. It'd be for my sister's wedding."

My eyes widen. "Your sister?"

"You think less of me for it?"

"No." I cross my arms against my chest. "It's just, you didn't seem the meddling type. You sat back and didn't object to your first love and best friend getting married, but you're inserting yourself into your sister's relationship?"

He flinches, and guilt slices into me. I quickly add, "I'm sorry. That came out harsh. I'm just trying to better understand." And, since the floor is open. "Did they set a new date? Your friend and ex?"

"It's okay," he says, sitting back, but there's still a bit of tension in his shoulders. "They got married the next day. They'd reserved one of the halls for another night of celebration, so it didn't stop them. Only made for some interesting speeches from the guests."

Knowing I starred in those speeches isn't too embarrassing. Aside from Anders, none of them know me, and it doesn't seem like Anders told them anything. One day I'll just be some deranged, faceless woman they tell stories about.

I down the final wineglass. "This is unexpected."

The waitress comes over and drops our plates, pausing our conversation a moment before I ask her for another flight of wine, which earns me a chuckle from Anders.

"I'll let you eat before I overwhelm you with information," he says as I stare at the plate of burger and truffle fries.

"I can multitask." I pop a salty fry in my mouth. "But before you waste your time—no offense, really—you should know that I am very expensive."

He raises a brow. "And?"

I shuffle through the hazy and blacked-out files in my brain and pull out the folder of our first hour together when we participated in the official *Get to Know You Handbook* of asking: *What do you do? Where are you from? Do you have siblings? Do you think the moon landing was fake? Want to get so drunk we forget our names?* "You're a graphic designer, aren't you? I'm sure you make a decent living, but my clientele is usually the annoyingly rich who couldn't tell you the price of milk if you asked."

He looks at the ceiling and chews on his bottom lip like *he* is shuffling through our night's files together. When he finds what he's looking for, Anders brings his gaze back down and catches me staring at his bottom lip. "You need twenty thousand to buy your share of the shelter. I can pay you that."

My eyes widen. "Excuse me?"

"Do you want more? Tell me a price."

I drop my next fry onto the plate and hold up my hands. "Wait, wait, wait. You're telling me you have twenty thousand dollars to spare? Are you a thief in the night? What exactly is it that you do?" I'll have Taina vet his funds first thing, though he doesn't seem like a liar.

"I'm not sure if I should take your shock about my wealth as an insult or not." He leans back. "You must have been more drunk that I thought, seeing as we had this conversation before. But I own a share of Lightshop—"

"The search engine?"

"Yes." He nods, casually, like having stock in the second most used search engine in America behind good old Google is no big deal. "Through pure luck of knowing Lucas, meeting him in college. His family created it. He gave me a share one Christmas, before it became as big as it did."

"That explains affording a stay at the most expensive venue on the planet," I say, mostly to myself in awe.

"That makes me more than enough, but I still do design on the side—mostly book covers."

"A joy to be able to work for fun and not for survival." I blow out a breath. "I didn't mean that bitterly," I get out quickly. "I mean, not at *you*, specifically. Just in general. I am bitter. But bitter toward, say, the universe itself. Does that make sense? I'm rambling, let's move on."

His chuckle is low and light as it reaches me. "So, will you consider my offer?"

"I have to," I say. Maybe I should be embarrassed about how easily I agree, but the truth is I need the money desperately. That, and ever since I failed at wrecking Eliza's wedding, I've had this wedge of guilt lodged in my throat. I know exactly the heartache she's inevitably going to suffer through. This could be a chance to redeem myself and clear my conscience of the failure.

"Okay." I take a glass from his wine flight. "Tell me your reason."

"Long story short, she and her fiancé will never work out."

"And short story long?"

He chuckles, then sighs. "There's so much wrong with the pairing. My sister is just twenty-three, way too young to get married. She's only just legally been allowed to drink. Now she's choosing who she wants to be with forever?"

He shakes his head. "My sister is flighty. I love her, but she's never fully grounded. She loves someone, something, for batches of time, and then moves on to new things, to new people. They've only been engaged for a few weeks and wanted to have a shotgun wedding, but my aunt threatened to disown her if she didn't plan an event the family could celebrate, so now we have some time. This is her fourth engagement, but it's the only one that's made it to actual wedding-planning stage, and I need it to end there."

I cock my head. "Do you think it's possible this wedding is developing further because they are a better pairing than her past lovers?"

I muffle my laugh when the word *lovers* makes him shudder. "No, not at all. I know the guy, John. I used to be his roommate in college, and we were really close. He's quiet, nerdy, introverted. He never knew how to stand up for himself and was constantly taken advantage of by anyone who asked him for things. He was constantly broke, and if he did manage to save anything from his part-time jobs, he'd get scammed out of it all over again."

I feel my brows pull together. "Your best friend married your first love, and your sister is going to marry your college roommate." I blow out a whistle. "That seems difficult."

He rubs the back of his neck. "You're not wrong. And maybe that's part of it; maybe I'm scared that if this doesn't work out, I'll lose another friend. I don't have too many to spare."

"It almost sounds like you want to ruin the wedding for him."

"It's for both of them, really. My sister will break his heart, and he won't recover. But that doesn't matter if she's the one doing the breaking. Whenever my sister dumps someone, she falls into this deep depression. She's devastated that she didn't find the one. She spends months in the dark; she doesn't eat or sleep. When you meet her, she seems so bright, and she is, but when she isn't, it's dark. If she makes it to marriage and has to get divorced instead of a simple breakup, I don't think she'll recover. No matter how much I talk to her about it, she just pushes me away."

I place my hands on my lap and let out a sigh. "I know all too well about the mistake of marriage at a young age." I close my eyes, trying to smother the emotion clogging my throat. I was younger than his sister, but being young hadn't made it easier to jump back into dating. If anything, it felt even harder to get back out there.

"So you accept?"

I chew on my bottom lip. Of course, I *have* to accept. I have nothing lined up, Save a Paw is at risk, Mathew is threatening to divorce my sister, and I have no place to live. I should say yes and move on, but something within me tugs to gamble for *more*. (This kind of behavior is precisely why I can't go within a hundred feet of a casino.)

"I'm going to take advantage of you by asking this, but how much more *can* you spend?"

He cocks his head to the side and a single wave of hair lands on his brow as he smirks. "Why? You want to empty out my bank account?"

"What you're offering will help me with the shelter, but if I got more, I could hurry and get my own place again."

His smirk slowly turns over. "That's right, you got evicted, didn't you?"

Some of the pity-party kinship from our first meeting spreads through my chest, and I'm surprised to realize him knowing this about me isn't as embarrassing as it should be.

When I nod, he crosses his arms against his chest. "You've had it rough."

I purse my lips. "Yes, which is why you should upgrade the flight to a full-blown bottle of wine for me."

Just in time, the waitress comes over to check on us. Anders cancels my second flight and orders a bottle, and I help myself to a handful of fries. Anders lets me get in a few bites of my burger—as good as promised—before speaking again.

"You tell me how much you need, and I'll give it to you."

His voice is so confident and final and warm, and I have to swallow the sudden moisture in my throat. "Then I'll accept. I'll do it. I'll need a *lot* more information and a cover. We'll talk more details as it gets closer. Do you think anyone will recognize me from the wedding?"

He shakes his head. "The only thing anyone remembers is the pastor falling over and the almost fire."

With perfect timing, the waitress drops off the bottle of wine and fills my glass. "You recognized me," I point out, something I meant to do earlier.

"I did," he answers, "and as for cover, be my girlfriend. You can stay at my place—I have an extra room—so it'll be easier to bring you around, and you can be my plus-one for any events." He lets out a long breath. "And my aunt will stop worrying I'm spiraling after the wedding."

It's an easy cover and will give me plenty of access to insider information. But my focus catches on the tail end of his words. I would think worrying about a grown man being lonely would be the mother's responsibility.

I bring the wineglass to my lips. "Have *you* been having it rough since I last saw you?"

"Not anymore," he says, his hot gaze pinning me in place.

Not frozen, as I am, the wine slides down the glass to my mouth. I nearly spill it over myself as I drop the glass back on the table and lick the remnants from my lips.

Anders, no napkin in hand, reaches over the table and swipes his thumb beneath my bottom lip, catching stray beads of wine I missed. My stomach fizzes, like a bottle of champagne popped open within it.

"Some ground rules." I jerk back, forcing my hands flat on the table as my cheeks burn. "You can't do that."

"Do what?"

"Anything remotely kind: holding the door open for me, a hand on my back leading me somewhere, looking at me for more than five seconds at a time, pulling my hair behind my ears, wiping crumbs from my mouth, physical touch." It's a warning I've never had to give a client before, but sirens go off in my head now, telling me lines have to be drawn. Anders feels dangerously charming.

He leans over the table, breaching the little space I gave myself, as if he is showing metaphorically and physically that the sloppy lines I've drawn don't matter too much to him. "Why not?"

"I'll fall in love with you," I say, surprised when humor, not horror, fills Anders's eyes. "I'm in a delicate phase in my life where the smallest acts of kindness feel like declarations of love. And my bar is so low you'd have to scrape it off the floor. I'm pretty sure I'm already halfway in love with you, and I barely know you."

It's better to lay it all out like this, be honest, to avoid any mishaps and broken hearts—mine, of course. With all that's happening in my life, I'm not sure I can trust that my emotions are sane and not overreactions as I deal with turmoil.

"I'll keep that in mind." He smiles, and the shadows of his dimples, combined with the heat and sparkle of humor in his gaze, make my heart stutter.

Uh-oh. I press my hand against my chest. *Might be too late.*

7.

Taina frowns at me from the edge of the mattress as I hold up a yellow sundress that I'm not sure will fit after the ten pounds I unintentionally lost courtesy of all my stress. It's only been a day since I met with Anders, and I'm not leaving for his hometown until the end of the week, but I couldn't wait to pack. And I wanted Mathew to see my suitcases and ease up on the stick he willingly has perpetually shoved up his ass.

I can add a belt, so I fold it and drop it into the oversized suitcase open on the pale wooden floors. Taina organized all my clothing while I was away, so I rifle through the drawers of the white dresser to find some shorts for the humid South Carolina spring.

With each item I pick and pack, Taina's gaze burns hotter and hotter on my skin.

At first, I ignore her because the more I sort through my stuff, the more I realize Taina managed to salvage nearly everything I would have wanted.

The clothes, the charger cords, the books with my dad's notes scribbled in the margins, the ratty throw blanket I used to fall asleep under that my mom hand sewed for me—she got it. Most of it. More than anyone else would have.

And yeah, some things didn't make it. The little items. The ones I never pointed out, never shared the weight of. Like the sticky notes my dad used to leave all over my room, each one marked with a tiny smiley face—slips I eventually gathered up and tucked together beneath my jewelry box. Or that mug with the chipped rim that only mattered because I spent all day worrying my mom would ground me for it, only for her to laugh at the way it made the clay look like it was bitten. Taina couldn't have known, and I didn't give her a reason to ask.

She saved what she could.

When my cheeks start to burn, I sigh and face her. "What do you want to say?"

"Oh, can I speak now?"

I look around at an invisible audience. "At what point did I say you couldn't?"

"Every time I talk, you shut me down."

"If that's the case, pick a different topic of conversation."

Taina groans and stomps her feet like she did whenever I told her she had to stop eating twenty Flintstones-vitamin gummies in one sitting. The memory fills me with a nostalgic warmth—something I assume mothers feel when they look at their children.

"I don't see why you're so against me going with you," Taina starts for the fifth time. "I *love* South Carolina. I want to go to the beach to tan, eat melting sorbets, and read till I fall asleep with sand in my hair."

"I'm going for work," I tell her. Again. "And you're going because you're unnecessarily worried about me. I told you. I. Am. Fine."

"The more you say it, the more I don't believe it," she says.

"The more you don't believe it, the more I wish I had sent you off to a distant aunt."

"You don't even know this guy."

I go back to picking out clothes. "I don't know any of the people I work with." Though strangely, it feels like I do know Anders. At least, I know him a lot more than any other client, since he's the first person to request me *after* spending time together.

"Yeah, but you're *staying* with him. Shouldn't he put you up in a hotel?"

"I looked up his place." I gather three pairs of jean shorts and shove them in the suitcase. "There is plenty of space, and it's by the beach. It'll be nice." I give her a look. "And you've already vetted him."

"Anders Kennedy—graduated from Belhaven University, phone number 843-555-4458, email anders kennedy reads at gmail dot com, no priors, a speeding ticket when he was seventeen that fell off his record. Listed as a donor to the American Library Association. Single."

I chuckle. "I'm surprised you don't know his social."

"Two-four-seven-two—"

"Taina!"

"What?" She crosses her arms. "I'm nothing if not thorough. And, okay, *fine*, I *am* worried about you. You're going through a lot, and I know you hate that I know you are, and you wish you could quietly deal with your problems and make it so I think you're happy and healthy and financially stable because you know my anxiety gives me nightmares. So what? Is it a *crime* to care about your sister now? Lock me up."

I let out half a sigh and a laugh, then approach Taina and place my hands on her shoulders. "No, my dearest, prettiest, funniest, nosiest little sister, it is not. I love you, so look at me and listen when I say I am fine." Taina and I rarely have any miscommunications, because we overcommunicate. We leave no room *not* to tell the other how we feel. We always want the other to be happy. Even when we're mad, we have a rule to let it out, say we love each other before bed, no matter how hard it is to get out. So dealing with all her worry feels less overwhelming and more of a comfort. *No matter how bad life sucks, I have a sister who loves me unconditionally.* "I feel better than I have in a while. Trust me. And your anxiety is only going to make mine flare up. We can't both be worried all the time."

Taina rolls her eyes, and looks to the side, but not anywhere near me. "If I can't go, then you have to share your location with me. And text me updates. And eat good, big meals. And lock your door at night—I'm talking chair under the handle, knife by the bedside. And sleep with Anders if the opportunity arises."

There's always a burst of love and pain whenever Taina's protective side makes an appearance. What a gift it is to be loved so deeply you can *feel* each panicked beat of someone else's heart pounding for you. And what an embarrassingly crushing feeling to know that—despite living most of my life trying to get Taina to view me as someone resourceful, dependable, the person you come to with any and all problems, the woman with countless bandages at the ready, pockets full of pep talks, a constant, unbreakable, figure—she still sees me as someone to protect for all I try to hide.

I pinch her cheek. "First you didn't want me to stay with him, but now you want me to sleep with him."

"You think I didn't see his photo?" She whistles. "I'm anxious, but I'm only a woman. No better than a man, really."

I laugh, then shove her to the side. "Just help me close this suitcase."

During my two-hour flight, Anders and I exchanged over a hundred messages. If I'm going to show up as the girlfriend he's allegedly been dating for four months, we need to be completely on the same page—timeline, backstory, favorite sandwich.

I've started jotting down Anders-related facts in the journal Taina gave me to help keep track of the weddings I've crashed. It's now doing double duty as a relationship study guide. I figure I should know at least the basics in case someone brings it up or I need to casually drop a detail without inventing a whole new life for him.

And yes, if we've been together that long, you'd think I would've been at the wedding two weeks ago. Reasonable assumption. Anders has fielded these suspicions by telling his family that he "wasn't ready for everyone to meet me yet" and wanted to be sure things were serious. Which is very noble and romantic—now that I've been called in to fake it.

- Favorite color: Green
- Favorite movie: Anything with Will Smith
- Favorite team: Eagles
- Broke his arm trying to climb a tree to save a bird nest from falling when he was 11
- A night person
- Likes "anything but country" music
- Has traveled to seven countries
- No allergies
- Wanted to be an astronaut growing up, realized he needed to be good at math, immediately moved on
- 30 years old
- No mention of parents, only Aunt Bethany
- Has a best friend since childhood, Lucas, who was the one who told him to climb the tree to save the nest

When I land, exhaustion adds weight to my bones, and I drag myself from the plane out the winding path of bars and restaurants to baggage claim. It's a little after 3:00 p.m., but I barely slept the night before, after spending most of the evening reconvincing Taina not to come with me.

The more anxious she got, the more worried *I* got, and our late night has added five-pound dumbbells to my eyelids as I try to stay awake while I wait for the conveyor belt to bring my borrowed luggage.

I blink, and I'm not sure how many minutes have passed. One moment, there was silence as I and the other passengers stood around, and the next, the belt was moving and packed with suitcases.

It's easy to spot the lime-green case hidden under an oversized black one. I drop my matching carry-on on the tiled floor and move toward it.

Nobody comes to retrieve the stray bag, so I try to shove it off, but it's too heavy. I suck my teeth and shove my palms on the rough canvas, and it budges, but not enough. I keep trying, but the belt moves it whenever I almost get it off, and I lose momentum.

Frustration sprints through my blood, and I brace my foot against it, finally managing to knock it over. I reach for the handle of my own bag and get it halfway off when someone pushes it back onto the belt.

A man dressed in a full camo tracksuit shoves himself directly in front of me. "The hell you get off kicking my luggage?"

I let out a sigh as *another* body shoves itself between us. So close, I jerk back and get a full view of Anders, in pale-washed jeans and a white shirt rolled at the sleeves, leaning over and gripping my luggage handle with one hand and the black luggage with his other.

The veins in his arms and the muscles in his biceps constrict as he lifts them both off the belt and puts them on their wheels.

Anders turns and faces me. "Any other luggage?"

His unexpected appearance steals my ability to speak, so I shake my head. Camo points his finger over Anders's shoulder at me. "Hey, are you listening to me?"

Anders half turns, a polite smile on his face. "Your suitcase is right there."

"Yeah, I can see; I'm not *blind*. I'm asking why the hell she kicked it."

With the way his reddened eyes are bulging out of his head, you'd think I kicked him instead. I might. If his voice gets any louder. I wouldn't beat him in a fight; he's even taller than Anders, but I would do some damage and run to safety after.

"It was in the way," Anders goes on, less polite though a smile still pulls at his lips as he turns around to face the man. "And now you are too. We'd appreciate it if you wouldn't mind ending the scene you're trying to make."

We. The word shouldn't stir the teenager-worthy crush my weak heart decided to develop over Anders. Next thing you know, I'll be lying in bed, kicking my feet up, writing our names together in tiny bubble hearts.

"Listen, asshole—"

Anders places his hand on the man's shoulder and says something I can't hear from where I stand. Whatever it is makes the man frown, half puzzled, half shocked, but completely silenced.

Anders turns back to me with a warm smile as he reaches for my suitcase again. "Let's go," he says, walking toward the carry-on I dropped and slinging it on his shoulder. My bones forget how to function for a few moments before I hurry after him.

"What did you say to him?" I ask as I try to grab my carry-on from him.

"A secret." He winks at me. *Did you charm him or threaten him or both?*

He grabs my hand I'm aiming toward my carry-on and guides it toward the side of my jeans. The warmth of his large palm presses against my hand as he places it inside my pocket before pulling his away.

"You know I was wrong, though. I *did* kick his luggage."

"He should have moved it," he says.

"I should have been patient," I say.

"And he should have been understanding."

A laugh rumbles through me. "I think we both know the truth here."

"Maybe," he says as the automatic doors slide open for us, "but I'm team Lucinda, right or wrong."

Heat slides down my body. I look sidelong at him while we walk to the airport garage.

"I'm thirty minutes early," I say as we cross the roadway, turn signals blinking, cars honking, people chatting, and guards yelling at people not to park for more than literally five seconds at a time. "How early did you get here?"

"I was tracking your flight, so I knew you'd be landing."

"Of course you were," I mutter.

He shoots out his arm, and my chest bumps into it. Better his body than the metal doors I nearly walked into. When I right myself, we walk to the elevator, and he presses the top button. He whistles softly as we wait.

A bundle of voices joins us in one wave of loud noise just as the elevator doors open. Funnily, it's a bachelorette party. One girl has a **BRIDE** banner draped across her white minidress, and all the other girls, in pink miniskirts, stumble over each other as one—the maid of honor, probably—leads the charge.

"All right, ladies," she says as Anders walks in first. "There will be no stopping, no breaks, straight to the bar, and we will not sleep until *tomorrow*."

They all cheer, and I swear they don't even *see* me. Like the most beautiful NFL football team made of perfectly curled hair and six-inch stilettoes, they charge into the elevator. I'm tackled by their bodies and herded in like a sheep.

Anders looks up from dropping my carry-on on my suitcase and reaches out to me as I try to avoid being trampled.

He catches me and pulls me into his chest. The girls shuffle in. The scent of vanilla and tequila engulfs us as the doors shut, and everyone squishes against each other like sardines in a can.

His arms snake around my waist. I grip the fabric of his shirt as we're pressed up against the back wall of the tiny box.

"Guys, there are *other* people here," the girl right beside us says.

"Who wants shots?" someone else asks.

The brunette beside us gives me an apologetic smile as a body shoves me so close to Anders that there is scientifically no way we can be any closer without merging into one person.

My blood hums. I look up and catch Anders's jaw clenching. I try to move so I'm not making him too uncomfortable.

My hands slide up his chest, and his pulse quickens beneath my palm. I move my legs, but Anders must have the same thought because he adjusts himself, too, and I end up with his thigh between both of mine.

Heat, blazing and fast, flares between my thighs. The shock of it makes a needy whimper bundle at the base of my throat. He hardens against me and I freeze. The way my heartbeat pounds in my ears and the shot of need throbbing at my crotch steals my breath. The slightest movement will wrench the moan from my lips.

Anders clears his throat. I press my forehead against his chest and hold my breath.

An insane, irrational, idiotic brain cell *screams* at me to move. To learn how it would feel to free myself of the tension simmering under my skin. To place just the slightest pressure where my currently pulsing center begs for it.

I start counting backward from ten. The lack of free space is the reason for my nipples tightening and straining against the fabric of my shirt, and simultaneously, the only reason Anders can't see my body's reaction to him, to *us*.

A *bing* echoes around us. The girls shuffle out. As soon as cool air swirls behind me, I push myself off Anders and whirl around so fast my vision blurs.

I'm out of the elevator in half a second, crossing arms against my chest, trying to hide my nipples. Anders moves past me, pulling my luggage behind him.

"I'm just up here," he says tightly as he leads. Veins peek through the skin of his hand as he grips my suitcase.

"Right."

My stomach is doing Olympic-worthy gymnastics while I continue to count backward and forward, trying to lower my blood pressure to an acceptable rate. We pause at what I *think* is a Jeep, but the back is a bit bigger than the Wranglers I've seen before.

He pops open the trunk and lifts up my bag with an ease that undoes whatever minuscule cooling-off progress I managed to achieve. If I were connected to a monitor in the hospital, the staff would assume I was having a stroke.

I swallow and keep my legs far apart to prevent the slightest bit of friction.

Anders walks toward the passenger side and opens the door. I can't hold back my groan. When I reach him, he smiles. I grab his hand, remove it from the handle, shut the door, and then open it again.

My finger points accusingly at him. "I told you not to do this."

He chuckles a low rumble that brings a victorious blush to my cheeks. "I never said I wouldn't."

I'll keep that in mind is what he said.

Anders moves behind me, sliding his hand down the small of my back. I feel every one of his fingers burning there, leaving a perfect trace of his palm as he guides me into the vehicle.

I nearly throw myself in to get away.

He shuts the door, and I have to fight the urge to lock him out. Enough that my fingers lie on top of the button by the time he lets himself in the driver's side.

"So," he says as he starts the engine, "how tired are you?"

Eager to focus on anything other than the shock of want coursing through me, I answer, "Not at all."

"Okay," he says, "then if you're up for it, want to meet my family?"

My eyes widen, and the heat within me cools into sheets of icy nerves. "Right now?"

He casts an apologetic look my way before turning to reverse out of the spot. "My very adorable, very nosy preteen cousin overheard me talking about picking you up from the airport. A fact she kept to herself for all of thirty seconds before my sister knew, then my aunt, and so they are all at my aunt's place, dying to meet you."

I *am* tired. And I didn't think I'd have to be on so quickly after touching down. I barely have had time to memorize all of Anders's fun facts. I definitely don't know anything too personal if anyone asks.

"We don't have to," Anders says at my silence.

I shake my head. "Yes, we do. It's the whole reason I'm here." And being overpaid for. Frankly, if Anders asked me to lick the floor of a gym locker room, I'd do so. "I just haven't picked out a disguise, or a name, or a backstory."

"The red wig and crooked nose." Anders cocks his head to the side as he pulls up the memory of me beneath a bush. "It's smart, but do you need one for this?"

"I always do."

"We're in an entirely different state, and you'll be here a while, so it'll be a hassle to keep it up. I'd rather remember *actual* things about you than made-up ones. Just be Lucinda."

I open my mouth to tell him he shouldn't remember things about me. That I'll be a fleeting memory in his life, and three months from now, maybe even sooner, we won't see each other again. But some mangled emotions I can't patch up enough to fully understand stop me.

My body turns to face him as he drives. My gaze scans his profile, sharp and defined, aside from his eyes. Tiny creases mark the skin around them, a symbol of years and years of laughter.

Usually, the people I work with want nothing to do with me once the job is done—understandably so. Maybe I'm so used to it that it's a reflex to reject the thought of someone doing something different. Would it be so bad not to be a complete stranger to Anders?

"Okay," I say automatically. "Let's go."

His hand reaches over and squeezes my knee.

Uh-oh, my heart warns again. *Are you sure about this?*

8.

After a look in the rearview mirror and a muttered curse at Anders, I demanded he pull over so I could grab my makeup bag. It's now sitting on my lap, and I pat concealer under my eyes as he pulls off the highway. He reaches over and presses his finger on the side of the vanity mirror, where LED lights surround the glass.

"Wow, I can see every single pore on my face. Turn it back off."

His laugh is warm and echoes, or it does in my head, anyway. "You don't—"

"If the next words out of your mouth are something along the lines of *you don't need makeup*, then swallow them."

He raises a hand from the wheel. "Note taken."

After some silence, I speak, "Can I ask you something?"

"Of course," he says.

I swipe gloss over my lips, then drop it back into my bag, zipping it shut. "Why are you paying me so much?" He'd agreed to double what I needed to buy my share of Save a Paw, simply because I asked. "I mean, you know I've been evicted, and I'm unemployed, so really, you could have paid very little, and I might have agreed."

"I have the money. You need the money. Why would I say no?"

"Because my pricing is unreasonable?"

His head tilts slightly to the side—a habit I'm noticing he does whenever he takes a few extra seconds to think before answering. "But your reasoning is not."

I squint my eyes, but I can see nothing in his face that seems like an ulterior motive or a lie. He answers everything I ask, not vaguely either, yet I still feel more questions take root after he does.

"You seem pretty steady, so I can't imagine why your aunt would have to worry about your spiraling," I say without thinking, but Anders doesn't tell me if the statement crosses any boundaries.

Instead, he shrugs. "My aunt says I keep my emotions in my bones. That no matter what I'm feeling, I don't let it show or let it out. It just merges with my body and becomes part of my foundation—she's worried for the day it crumbles. What'll be left behind."

"Are you? Worried, I mean."

"I'm not sure. I feel fine, more often than not."

I purse my lips and watch a man walking two large dogs on the sidewalk as we drive. I have to know, seeing as I'm meeting with his family, but it still feels like trespassing into Anders's private, meticulously locked corridors when I ask, "Where are your parents?"

"My biological mom? Somewhere in the world, traveling, maybe remembering to send a postcard from wherever her free spirit pulls her. My dad and stepmother are here in South Carolina. My father's an executive director at a law firm; my stepmother doesn't work."

"You talk about your aunt as if she's more maternal than them."

He rolls his shoulders. "She practically raised me. My mom was my father's mistress, so my being born caused a lot of problems. For my mom, who never wanted kids, and for my dad, for obvious reasons. My mom kept me because she figured my father would send her money to keep her away. She was right."

"That's horrible." I can't keep the horror from my voice. "I'm sorry."

My resentment at the loss of my parents is entirely directed at the universe, and my love for them remains this great, beautiful thing. So much less burdensome than it must feel to be entirely, voluntarily left behind the way Anders was, without ever feeling the love a parent should give.

"Don't be sorry. My aunt is the greatest person. I've lacked nothing in my life."

There seems to be no underlying grief behind the words, but I can't imagine it being true unless Anders is far more emotionally resilient than most, or he truly has just accepted his mom abandoning him. I'm not sure what's sadder.

"They're still assholes," I mumble and earn a low chuckle from Anders.

"So, anything else I should know about you? Something your family will expect me to be aware of?"

He shakes his head. "We went over the basics already, but nothing is pressing. Don't worry about that; they're easily charmed by compliments and gifts. Just try and get to know them, especially Val."

I blow out a breath and nod. I needed that, the reminder of what I'm here for. It's not about getting to know him, though my brain keeps forming questions that branch off endlessly. No matter how sweet Anders is, his sister is also his priority. I need to focus.

"Right, so I'm going to impress them all. Charm them into letting me in on the wedding planning and get invited as a participant."

"Anything I can do to help?" he asks.

"Not yet. I have to figure out what kind of wedding your sister's is."

"What 'kind' of wedding?"

I nod. "Each wedding, the ones that need wrecking, falls into one of three categories: Because of Family, Because of Opportunity, or Because of Delusion." I explain, "There are smaller umbrellas, too, that couples can fall under. Usually, it's Trust, Lust, or Rust. Trust, there's infidelity. Lust, you only said yes because you had rose-tinted glasses, or you're in love with someone else. Rust, the love got stale, and you're staying together out of obligation and duty. Once I figure out that, I can decide how to ruin it."

"Wow." He whistles. "I know you said this isn't what you want to do forever, but you seem to know a lot about such a niche gig in the short amount of time you've been doing it."

"If you're going to do a job, do it right," I say, echoing one of my father's many mottoes.

He grins. "A true professional."

There's a long stretch of silence, and I catch myself watching Anders more closely than I probably should. Part of me wonders if I'm genuinely curious about him—or if it's just the shallowness of finding him so attractive that I want to know what's really underneath.

My curiosity buzzes too loudly to stay quiet any longer. I tilt my head and ask, "An inappropriate question, maybe—but do you believe in it?"

He lifts a brow. "In what?"

"Love," I answer. "You've had some pretty crappy experiences with it, and it seems too many examples of it haven't surrounded you—romantically, of course."

He exhales, looking past me for a second like he's thinking about how honest he wants to be. "I used to, so it exists, maybe." He huffs a short laugh—no bitterness, just distance, like he's not even talking about himself. "More like, love exists, but it's not built to last."

"That's cynical," I point out.

Another smile. "Maybe so. I think love is more fragile than people want to admit. And way more common. People fall into it all the time. It's staying in it that seems impossible. I loved Anna, but now that love is gone, it's something affectionate, but not as intense anymore."

I nod slowly. "I'll downgrade you from cynic to skeptical."

"Still feels like the same meaning."

"Skeptical sounds less harsh."

He nods. "Thanks, then." Another beat of silence. "And you?"

I'm saved from answering as the car rolls to a stop in front of a two-story home surrounded by a deck filled with furniture, rocking chairs, benches, and couches, like it's the main living room. And curved windows with no curtains to let in every bit of sunshine the sky offers.

Nerves circle the pit of my stomach as a lanky girl comes barreling down the porch toward the car. Before I can say anything, she yanks Anders's door open.

"Uncle Anders!"

"Little Olive!" Anders jumps down and sweeps this preteen into his arms. I let myself out and wait until they make it around the Jeep, Olive riding piggyback with a wide grin matching Anders's. They're technically cousins, but Anders mentioned she refers to him as "uncle" and Valerie as "aunt" because of the age difference and how they've helped raise her since she was a baby. Olive's dad is not around, a one-night stand that didn't want a kid.

She hops off and places her hands on her hips, looks me up and down with a full-blown assessment before speaking. "Pretty, and smells like peaches even though you just got off a plane, two pluses. Do you like dogs or cats?"

"Dogs."

She crosses her arms, covered in colorful friendship bracelets running their length. "If you had one superpower, what would it be?"

"Teleportation."

"Who wins in a fight: Iron Man or Thor?"

I smirk at the interrogation. "Verbally: Iron Man. Physically: Thor."

"What's the best sauce to dip fries in?"

"Ice cream."

"Do you think nine is too young for a phone?"

"All right." Anders ruffles Olive's light-brown hair, blond in spots because of the beaming sun. "Introduce yourself like a normal human being, please."

"Mom says 'normal' is a man-made construct that I shouldn't have to abide by."

Anders half laughs, half sighs. "Olive."

Olive rolls her big, hazel eyes framed with blue mascara—the only thing about her I can attach to Anders. She holds out a hand for me to shake. "I'm Olive; it's nice to meet you. You seem cool enough. For now."

I shake her hand, firmly, each of her fingernails painted a different color. "I'm Lucy, and you seem cool too. For now."

She smirks, then wraps an arm around me, leading me to the front door. "How'd you know about the ice-cream thing?"

"My little sister has asked for that combination almost every week of her life."

"So cool."

Olive leads us through the home, so many frames pinned along the walls that it takes me a moment to spot the sliver of gold paint behind them. I trip over someone's boot as we walk through the living area to the kitchen, overlooking emerald couches and chairs, dozens of colorfully patterned rugs, and candles surrounding us in warm cinnamon and vanilla scents.

A woman in a flour- and grease-stained red apron that matches the bright red shade of her silky hair approaches us, then punches Anders's arm. He feigns pain before Bethany wraps him in a hug. "I haven't seen you in *months*. Who the hell do you think you are?"

Anders pulls away, his clothes stealing some of Bethany's flour. "It's been a single month."

"Wow, and now you're claiming I don't know how to count? I hope your guest has more manners than you."

Bethany turns to me then, and I get the full view of pale, glowing skin, so good I honestly can't tell if it's skin care or makeup, and a sharp, heavily defined Cupid's-bow smile not unlike Anders's. The only sign of her age is the wrinkles by her eyes and nose, made more pronounced when she smiles at me. "Lucinda."

"Please, call me Lucy," I say, hand outstretched, "and I promise I am filled with abundant manners. I can say thank you in seven different languages."

A joyous laugh erupts out of her as she tackles me into a hug. "Thank you for coming. I know you're right from the airport."

Anders wraps an arm around me, pulling me against him so my back is tucked into his chest. "If I had known *you* were cooking, I would have stopped at a diner so my poor girlfriend could have something edible after her trip."

The warmth of his body behind me feels comforting enough, and it almost tricks me into thinking it's real. But it's all an act, one I'd have no problem falling into in any other situation. I have to view this as a job, because it is, and that doesn't change just because Anders is beautiful and sweet and way too affectionate for his own good.

"Don't worry." A voice comes from behind as a woman so strikingly beautiful I actually gasp enters with oversized brown bags on both her slim arms. She drops them on the circular island and brushes her hands together. "I brought Vinnie's."

"Did you get calamari?" Olive pipes up from the couch she threw herself on.

"Obviously." Valerie pops a hand on her hip, stopping just out of arm's reach. The silky white top clinging to her petite frame is something I swear Taina tried to sneak into my luggage, and her curled, layered hair could be one of those pictures you look up as a reference for your own hair stylist who can never get it right. "So, you're the secret girlfriend."

"Not so secret anymore," I say.

She snorts, her tiny nose wrinkling as her green eyes land on Anders. "Hard launching your girlfriend right after your ex-girlfriend's wedding. You sure you're not spiraling?"

Anders pulls away and reaches for Valerie in a full hug. "Is that sibling concern I hear?"

Valerie makes a disgusted noise before wiggling out and walking toward me, scanning me up and down, then twisting my hair in her fingers. Her once-over is a lot more focused and x-ray-like than Olive's. "Cute, if a bit understated." Her sharp nails poke at the side of my face. "Ever heard of microneedling?"

"Nope." I reach over and press a finger to the side of her face. "But if it can get me looking a fraction of how pretty you are, I'm more than willing to try."

She lightly slaps my shoulder. "Shut up," she says, her grin filling her heart-shaped face. "Do you mean it?"

"Absolutely," I say, and it helps because I genuinely do. "You look like you're a freshman. Maybe I misheard Anders. Are you sure you're not a student?"

Valerie tucks her hair behind her ears, two diamond studs hanging on the lobes. "Yeah, right. As a proud nepo baby, I wouldn't step foot into a nonmandatory school. I'd rather wear something off the rack for a year straight." She presses her finger to my nose. "But I did *technically* go to Clemson if you count all the times I was invited to sorority parties and found myself in the back seat of my favorite tight end's car."

I can't help but laugh and then feel my brows furrow. Anders did go to college, had a job, and didn't give off any nepotism vibes. Though he quickly agreed to my pricing without so much as blinking, like he had a lifetime without financial worries.

Anders and I trade glances, and I wonder if he can see the question in my eyes before he looks away. I bring my focus back to Valerie. "I was more of a quarterback girl myself. Something about the star quality."

She nudges me. "Oh, taste."

Bethany grabs Valerie's arm. "Come help set the table."

"Ugh, manual labor? You have a perfectly capable teenager lounging around to help."

Bethany flicks Valerie between her brows. "The *pre*teen over there has more manners and is more helpful than you have been your entire life."

"Excuse me, I'm the one who got us real food so we don't have to eat your penitentiary home-cooked meals."

Valerie's scream lasts the entire time Bethany pinches her ear and drags her to help.

Anders's arm makes its way around my shoulders again. "You know I was the quarterback in my elementary school gym class."

"Of course I know; my soul did. It's a prerequisite to dating me."

"Anders," Bethany calls, "come grab the good plates. I can't reach them."

Anders kisses the side of my head before helping, and sirens go off in my skull. I need to keep my head straight. *It's pretend; it's just for show; keep it together.* I'd be an idiot to romanticize anything done within the confines of my time here. Any relationship-esque actions taken by Anders are strictly to keep up our ruse—he's probably not giving any of it a second thought.

Given what happened to him and his first love, his perspective on his sister's relationship, and his parents, I can't help but wonder if his affection is so easy to display because there is no pressure on it?

I thought I believed in love—but maybe not as heavily as I used to. Maybe it's less this grand, all-consuming thing, and more something smaller now. Or some people simply go through life without a lasting version of it, and I might be one of them.

I doubt he'd be interested, but he'd do amazingly as a wedding wrecker, a pretend boyfriend, an actor, all of the above.

My mouth opens to offer help, when I catch sight of a gold frame surrounding a young boy holding a clear bag with a goldfish swimming within. I walk over to it and grin at Anders's smile, spotted with missing teeth.

Beside that is a younger Bethany holding an even smaller Anders by the leg and a Valerie on her back, nearly choking her in her tiny arms.

"Cute," I can't help but say.

A hand settles at the small of my back, its warmth pressing into the inch of skin my raised shirt reveals. "Ready to eat?" Anders whispers to me, his lips brushing my ear.

Surely he doesn't mean to ask the question as gravelly as he does, eliciting more heat throughout my body. But I burn up all the same, clear my throat, and remind myself it's an act, and I'm not an amateur.

I chew on my lip and tell myself to tighten the hell up as Anders leads me to a long mahogany table, pulls out a chair, and takes the one beside me. Valerie takes the spot across from me, Olive facing Anders, and Bethany at the head.

"This is so lovely." I gesture to the table, the Italian takeout still in its to-go boxes, and what I *think* is meat loaf, or lasagna, or casserole that must be Bethany's doing, along with burnt pieces of bread and a salad covered in Parmesan shreds. "Thank you for having me."

"Thank you for coming," Bethany says, waving a hand. "Go on, fill your plate. Since you're vegetarian, I made shepherd's pie—mushroom for the beef." She looks over at the burnt dish and sighs. "But if you want to eat some pasta, I can't blame you."

"That's shepherd's pie?" Valerie starts filling her plate with calamari, stealing the tongs from Olive. "I thought that was a gathering of the neighbor's three-day-old bird food."

I lean over, grab the ladle, and fill my plate with the homemade dish, ignoring the bread. I take a forkful and raise it to my mouth, when Valerie holds out a hand.

"Oh my God," Valerie says. "Do you have a death wish?"

Even Bethany winces. "This is a big moment for me, for us, for Anders. We've only met one girl before, so I felt it was right to make a meal, but my hands are meant for gardening, riding horses, and pressing the buttons on a microwave. You really don't have to."

Guilt pries its way into my side at that. Even though Anders asked me to do this, being here and lying to these people feels a little too . . . personal.

Maybe my other jobs felt more clinical because of my lack of connection to clients, and I've only pretended to be a fake girlfriend once. But Anders's family thinks I will be a staple in his life, and Bethany made a meal for my diet, and Olive keeps looking at me with wide, curious eyes, making my chest tighten.

"You cooked it, so I'll eat it." I place the forkful in my mouth and swallow it down. It tastes like charcoal, rubber, and salty potatoes. I don't flinch as I take another bite, this time strategically mixing it with the salad.

"Olive, close your eyes. I think we might be witnessing a death," Valerie whispers.

"Awesome," Olive says.

"It's really not that bad," I say. "Trust me, I've had worse." Or, often enough, nothing at all.

Anders puts a hand on my knee, and when I face him, his eyes are warm and soft, with just the slightest touch of heat glistening in them, so the skin behind my ears begins to warm.

"Well," Bethany says, with a wide smile, "your parents raised you very polite."

At that, Anders squeezes my thigh. The touch isn't fake this time but for comfort. I squeeze him back: *I'm okay.*

"So, Valerie," I begin as everyone starts digging into their own plates—Anders, too, is eating the burnt pie—"how is the wedding planning? Anders says you'll be walking down the aisle in three months."

She frowns, pointing her knife toward Anders. "I'm sure that's not all he said. Usually, any conversation that starts with 'wedding' ends with 'don't get married, you idiot.'"

"I have *never* called you that," Anders says, aghast.

"No, you only say that it's *foolish* for me to. I can read between the lines."

"You're one of the smartest, wittiest people I know," Anders tells his sister. "There are no lines to read between."

"Oh, shut up—"

"And there's no need to worry about me disapproving anymore," Anders interrupts. "Lucinda here has convinced me to let it go, that I should let you make your own decisions and support you along the way. I won't try to talk you out of it anymore."

"Shut up!" Valerie drops her knife and snatches my hand across the table. "I love you, you're amazing. Can I call you my sister-in-law? I'm going to call you my sister-in-law. What are you doing tomorrow? I'm scoping out venues. You have to come."

"Sure," I say. "I can tag along. If you don't mind."

Valerie shoots up. "Do you like wine? Let's drink wine." She scurries off to the kitchen.

"If you can convince Uncle Anders to leave Valerie alone," Olive begins, "can you convince Mom to buy me a phone?"

"Hush," Bethany tells her while Valerie comes over with a glass for me. "So, Lucinda—"

"Lucy, please."

"Lucy," Bethany says, "Anders tells us you work in a publishing house in New York. How is that going for you? The travel you guys must do to see each other has to be taking a toll on you."

This is the cover story Anders told me he gave to his family. We met at a book launch, I was marketing the title, and he did the cover for it. After we made small talk, we couldn't stop thinking of each other. I place a hand on Anders's arm. "Not at all; every time we reunite, all the exhaustion leaves my body."

Valerie pours my wine. "Because I love you right now, I'm not going to mention how disgusting I find that statement."

"So, how often do you guys get to see each other?" Bethany asks.

"Every two weeks," Anders answers. "We take turns visiting each other."

"John travels a lot for work, right?" I ask Valerie as she moves back to her seat, wineglass in hand. "As a management consultant. Is he going to settle down for a bit after the wedding?"

"We have a week in Croatia for the honeymoon before he has to travel again."

"That's lovely," I say, sitting up straight, taking a sip of wine. "So, I've been dying to know how you two met? How did you know he was the one? Anders has been stingy with the details. All I know is they were best friends in college."

Valerie sips her wine and smiles. "Okay, so it's actually crazy. I'm all about signs, you know? They're everywhere, but most people overlook them or brush them off as coincidences, déjà vu—but not me. I'm not so good at reading them, but I have this psychic I go to, and she has guided my life since I was twelve."

Anders sighs, and Bethany asks Olive to pass her the wine.

"Boo to both of you," Valerie says at the reactions. "Anyway, my psychic has always said four is my number. I always check the time and see fours, I ranked four hundred and forty-fourth in school, four times is all it takes for me to ask someone for something and they give it."

Anders wraps his fingers around mine holding the wineglass. He lifts our hands toward his mouth and drinks, the bottom of his lip pressing against my pointer finger on the glass, sending a lining of fireworks in the pit of my stomach into a violent show. My throat dries as he places the remaining wine on the table and pulls away.

"So, I'm in this relationship with this guy for four months, and we break up on the fourth of April. Then, I ran into John on the fourteenth floor at this party, and we hit it off. We hook up that night—"

"Valerie!"

Valerie pokes Olive's ear. "Erase that from your memory. Anyway, John was born April fourth, and it felt like fate. My psychic said that my thread of destiny has been pulling me toward him my whole life."

"Right," I say, ignoring Olive's snickering. "That sure is something. So, do you still go to this psychic?" I ask, an idea forming in my brain.

If Valerie is into signs, the universe, and fate, I could try to warp their relationship from her perspective. Taina went through a yearlong astrology phase and spent every other sentence scolding me with "That's so Aquarius of you." I'm sure she can give some insight.

"Ugh," Valerie groans, throwing her head back. "She died last year. So sad, for sure. But, like, I'm so lost without her. The last thing she told me was to cling to my love, so I haven't found someone to replace her. I need to get this feeling, you know? To know who the right fit is."

"Really?" I say, pulling my phone from my pocket and checking the time. I stretch out my words so they come out slow, almost slurred. "That's. So. Interesting."

I feel Anders's eyes on me as I go on. "So. Special."

The time changes, and I clap my hands. "I know someone." Valerie's eyes widen. "My sister is similar to you. Studied astrology in school and everything," I lie. "She sees someone regularly, and you know what? My sister lives an *amazing* life. Her girl travels. I can give you her information."

"Oh my God!" Valerie shoots up again. "Really? That'd be perfect. I have been searching for someone to no end." Subtly, I push my phone closer to her side of the table. Her eyes flicker toward it, and she snatches it up. "Oh my *God*." She holds out the phone for us to see. "Look at the time!"

"Four-forty-four," Anders reads with a smirk.

"A sign," I say.

I finish my wine, carefully avoiding where Anders placed his lips. Maybe I can get Valerie to back out of the wedding earlier than I thought with the help of a psychic who can show her all the red flags in her relationship. I've never tried it before, but somehow, I know this wedding will require a little more creativity than I'm used to.

Anders reaches over and swipes a stray bead of wine from my bottom lip.

Creativity and the willpower of a much better woman than I am.

9.

At first, the ride to Anders's place is bearable. But as time passes and we get closer to our destination, the air between us thickens into something like syrup—sweet, but hard to swallow an even breath.

The road to his house winds through hundreds of trees arching over the pavement like the top halves of hearts. It eventually spits us out into a wider clearing where the trees are taller, their branches too high to feel enveloping, and his house is tucked between thick bushes. Several warm lights glow from tiny old-school lanterns hung along the porch beams.

We get out at the same time, Anders heading to the back to grab my suitcases. He rolls his sleeves up and pulls them out. He doesn't even glance at my outstretched hand.

"Come," Anders says, gaze flicking from my face to the porch and back. "I'll give you the tour."

I follow him up the steps, my nerves doing cartwheels in the pit of my stomach.

He leads me past shiny wood floors and richly colored details—dark golds and greens against lighter woods. The ceilings are high, or maybe they just seem that way from all the books stacked in every corner, on every surface—the tables, the counter—even used as coasters for an unfinished wineglass on the coffee table. Not messy. Warm, comfortable, and attractively well maintained.

My mom always said that the way a man treats his home, his sanctuary, speaks volumes about how he'll end up treating you. But then again, she married my dad, who was the best guy around but could not fold a sheet for the life of him, and she loved him all the same.

To the left, at the end of the entry hallway, is a kitchen with dark cabinets and more books. To the right, the living room, with an oversized tan sectional and two blankets tossed over the back. Candles sit on books atop the side tables.

"Anything in the fridge is yours," Anders says, brushing past me. "Any room you want to hang out in—yours."

I press my hand on the couch, and the cushion is as soft as it looks. "And if I wanted to snoop in your room?"

"I'll leave the door open."

The cartwheels in my stomach upgrade to backflips.

Anders leads me farther into the house, pushing open a door in another hallway.

A king-size bed sits at the center, cushioned with several pillows and a pale blue comforter so plush I have to physically stop myself from face-planting into it. There's a little desk in the corner, another softly glowing light—all the lights are warm and golden here, no LEDs.

It's simple and intimate, and being in the space with Anders as he places my suitcase by the bed makes my heart trip over itself.

"This is so cozy," I say, scanning the room, trying not to notice how it still smells like him—sandalwood and citrus and warmth. A combination that only makes sense against Anders's skin.

Anders leans against the doorframe, arms crossed. "I like cozy. Not a fan of extra space with nothing in it."

"Did you do all the decorating yourself?"

"Yes," he says. Then, hesitantly, "Do you like it?"

I roll my eyes. "Of course I do, and of course you did. You have great taste. Do you have any flaws?"

"I can't parallel park."

I bark out a laugh and drop down on the bed, bouncing lightly on the mattress. "Tragic."

He smirks, then pushes off the doorframe and nods toward the kitchen. "Wine? Water? Do you need some time to settle in?"

The way he says wine—low, intimate, like a secret, delicately wrapped gift—makes my mouth go dry.

"Water." Better to keep my head on straight, especially with how my body heats the more time Anders and I spend in this room together.

He returns with two glasses, one dark, one transparent. He hands me the water, his knuckles brushing mine when I take it, and the heat burns through me, like a rubber band was pulled tight and snapped across the skin he touched.

"Okay," I say, trying to pretend I'm a normal, sane, not-at-all-horny woman. "I have some general ideas for interfering with the wedding, but I need to gather my thoughts, get more info, get on Valerie's good side."

He doesn't sit right away. He watches me for a moment, sipping his wine, something unreadable flickering behind his eyes. Then he walks over and takes the spot beside me.

"Let's hear those wedding types again," he says. "Lust, Trust, and Rust?"

"Right," I confirm. "Valerie's feels like a cross between lust and delusion. She met John during a rebound spiral and thinks the universe gave her a gift-wrapped husband."

"And she's big on signs," Anders adds. "Which is why you brought up the psychic. You don't actually know a psychic, do you?"

"No, of course not," I say, "but it's a good play to plan."

He sighs. "I feel a little guilty about this," he admits, "but I'm willing to feel anything if it means helping Val make the right choice about her future. I want her to be happy. And I don't think John can do that. Not forever."

"Well," I say, "then I'll do my job."

"You're more than just the job," he says, so quietly I almost miss it.

But I hear it. And, unfortunately, so does my heart.

I shift in my seat. "You're paying me to be here, Anders."

"I know."

There's a silence between us, charged and buzzing like static on skin. The kind that makes your body restless no matter how much you move. A constant thrum of nerves and heat.

He's too close.

The room is too quiet.

And it's been too damn long since I've been this attracted to someone—just his brushing my skin for half a second shoots arrows of heat and awareness between my thighs.

I jump to my feet. *Don't be an idiot. This is a job—he is your* boss. *Pull it together.* "I'm so tired. I have to get ready for bed before I pass out mid-conversation."

Anders doesn't press. He nods, then moves toward the door. He pauses there, one hand on the knob, the other in his pocket.

"If you need anything, get it. Or let me know, and I'll get it for you."

"Okay," I say.

Our eyes lock for a heartbeat too long.

"Okay," he repeats, breaking the spell.

Then he shuts the door, and I drop backward onto the bed, slapping a hand over my mouth, my pulse hammering in my throat.

Already, I'm getting lost in Anders's gaze, his warm words, his easy way—enough that it's becoming a distraction from my actual purpose here.

And it's only the first night.

10.

My first impression of Valerie was an intriguing combination of spoiled, self-aware, selfish—but with a dash of kindness and a hint of warmth. Those traits still rang true after six hours of venue scoping. However, with those characteristics in place, I thought she'd take more of a back seat in wedding planning, maybe hire a handler.

Now we're at our seventh venue of the day, sunlight still pouring over us in Valerie's convertible, the breeze tangling my hair into wavy knots. I'm convinced she's purposely wasting time. There is no venue for her. She only wants the marriage on paper, not a grand event—though even that feels off. Everything about her screams *Look at me; I know you want to, and I admire my admirers.*

And yet here we are, speed dating buildings. Had Bethany not pressured her into a wedding, a real one, Valerie would be out drinking wine and socializing with friends—so she has reminded me multiple times as we continue with our scouting. Is this some subconscious sabotage? Surely this modest art gallery the employee is leading us through isn't as good a fit as the others we visited. Valerie had hated each one more than the last.

Bed and breakfast? (Too homey. Meant for those "over the hill" and on their third marriage.)

Church? (Beautiful stained-glass windows, sure—but hard to get married in a place where she once hooked up with the priest's son.)

Garden? (One gnat flew in her face, and she turned us around.)

Boat? (If anyone got sick during the ceremony, she'd shove them overboard.)

Hotel? (Too pretentious.)

Beach? (Not pretentious enough.)

The employee stops by an arched opening. "I'll let you two wander. Do let any of the staff know if you have questions."

Valerie barely waits for her to finish before she marches into the first room, heels clattering on the floor. I hurry after her, my battered sneakers leaving less of an impressive echo.

"Didn't peg you for a lover of the arts."

She tosses her hair over her shoulder, revealing the top of her sleeveless dress. "Unfortunate as it is to admit any sibling worship when I turned out to be so amazing, Anders might have rubbed off on me."

"Your brother adores you," I say, pausing as she stops to view a landscape of a forest. "I think he'd like to hear that."

She rolls her eyes. "What he'd like to hear is that I'll call off this wedding and stop making him worry about my mental health every other day. God forbid a girl get sent to the psych unit once."

Whatever she sees on my face makes her bark out a laugh before narrowing her eyes.

"So," she says, "Anders didn't tell you about that."

Just how close are you really, then? is what I hear. It's treacherous—this balance of playing the doting girlfriend, the supportive friend, while having only read a chapter of Anders's story. If anyone skips ahead to a page I haven't reached, I'm lost trying to fill in the blanks.

"Unfortunate as it is to admit any sibling worship," I repeat, "his love for you is pretty evident in the way he talks about you—including what he doesn't share."

She stares at me for three seconds, then faces the painting again, though not before I catch a small smile.

"That's his fatal flaw, you know. He loves too hard." She snorts. "Maybe I shouldn't be saying that to you, but if you can't accept him for who he is, then you should leave."

There it is again, a snag of guilt pulling at my chest. What will Anders say when I'm gone? Will his family worry all he holds in his bones will crumble? Will they hate me for whatever lie he tells them about our separation?

Why do I care if they do?

I smother the guilt, but I can't stifle the building curiosity rising within me at the mere mention of Anders's name.

"Some people would say loving isn't a flaw at all."

"It is for Anders," she says, crossing her arms. "He does anything and everything for whoever he loves. Whatever's in his capabilities. He has this need to protect people, to care for them so they don't feel any pain. He doesn't realize that can be painful in itself."

That doesn't make any sense. Since when is trying to protect someone you care about a bad thing? As an older sibling, I know exactly what it's like—it's not even conscious; it's a reflex.

"You don't agree," she says when I don't respond. "But you're an older sibling, too, so you don't get it. But as a younger sister, nothing sucks more than feeling like everyone's waiting for you to crack. Like you're too fragile to make basic decisions. And worse, the guilt of always being a constant worry in their life. I mean, if I can get over losing the head cheerleader spot senior year to Mary Tambini despite her inability to do a basic handspring, I really can come back from anything."

"That's not how my sister feels," I snap, then immediately hold up my hands. "Sorry, that was aggressive. I mean, everyone is different, and from what I know about Anders, you're severely underestimating the way he views you. He doesn't think you're weak."

She groans, moving on to the next installation—a series of different-sized canvases with delicately painted bubbles stretching almost to the ceiling.

"This one is from a local artist. *Chasing Reflections.* It's one of Anders's favorites," she says, arms crossed. "Older siblings are so dense. I was just starting to like you for getting Anders to back off the wedding. Please don't bombard me with some lovey-dovey defense."

A good point to bring up. I shouldn't go against Anders in a way that'll raise flags, but I need to get on Valerie's good side. Earn her trust. Learn more about her relationship, figure out exactly where to poke, pull, twist, and pry, like she's my own personal Bop It! Securing a place in her inner circle is my top priority.

If she wants to have incorrect opinions about sibling relationships, that's her prerogative.

I press my hands together like I'm in prayer. "Forgive me for bombarding you with lovey-dovey interactions. Shall I equal things out with an insult?" When she raises a brow, I add, "I have never seen someone so terrible at parallel parking. Honest to God, I felt such secondhand embarrassment even though no one was around to see it."

She laughs. "You should've. There were probably wandering ghosts that pointed and laughed. If you've seen him try to reverse into a space, you'll know it can get even worse."

"How'd he even get his license?"

She leans in like we're coconspirators. "It took him five tries. And on the fifth, I'm pretty sure Aunt Bethany bribed the DMV examiner."

I grab her hands. "*Please* let me tease him about that."

"I'd love it if you did. It's one of the only things that riles him up."

At the image my brain conjures of the cool, collected, charming Anders being anything but, my lips pull into a smile.

"Gross," Valerie says, shoving me before continuing her journey through the gallery.

My phone buzzes in my pocket, and when I glance down and see Joshua's name, my stomach tightens.

"Hey, give me one sec?" I tell Valerie, already stepping away. "It's a work thing."

She shrugs and drifts toward a bright red canvas.

I answer the call, moving into a quieter corner near curvy, silhouette-shaped sculptures. "Hey, Joshua."

"Lucy," he says, upbeat but direct. "Just checking in. I wanted an update on how things are going on your end. You still on track for your buy?"

I force a smile he can't see. "Yes, thanks for asking. Sure am."

He hums, clearly not fully reassured. "That's good to hear. The other potential buyer reached out again this morning. He's ready to sign, and frankly, I can't hold him off much longer unless I know you're a sure thing."

I press a hand to my forehead. "I'm in, Joshua. I want this. I just need a little more time to get the rest of the funds together. But I've got a plan. I'll meet your deadline."

There's a beat of silence on his end. "All right. I just need to know where you stand, Lucy. I want this to be you. I know how bad you want it."

"I'm in. I promise," I say, too quickly.

"Okay," he says. "Let me know if anything changes."

The call ends, and I stand there for a second, heart hammering. I tuck my phone away, adjust my expression, and head back out into the gallery like this didn't send every wing of anxiety fluttering in my stomach.

If anything, this needs to get me focused even harder on the task at hand.

When I spot Valerie walking, I match her pace, watching her weave through the building. Sometimes she stops to admire a piece; other times, she barely spares a glance. As someone with the artistic capabilities of a newborn, everything looks confusingly beautiful. Some pieces are so abstract I can't even place what they are, and yet, my brain still simply thinks *pretty*.

"So," I say, "it's been half an hour, and you haven't said a single bad thing about this place. Is it special?"

"Well, it was the first gallery ever built in Charleston."

I roll my eyes. "I meant to you."

She tosses her hair. "Not really."

Her tone sounds normal, but her shoulders stiffen ever so slightly. She tilts her head away, and the act reminds me so much of Taina that a sense of homesickness strikes me square in the chest. I maneuver myself in front of her.

"Oh, it *is* special to you!"

"I guess."

"You have to spill now." I loop my arm through hers. So she feels less pressure, I keep my gaze on a portrait of a woman facing a lakeside cottage, painted with such detailed strokes it looks like a photograph. "Share it with the class."

"Is the class a private course or a public one?"

"It's whatever your heart desires." I hold up a pinkie.

She takes it in hers, and the ever-present guilt of this job sinks its claws into my stomach. Not only will I break every promise I make to her, but I'll be sharing everything with Anders as soon as I can.

"My first love took me here on our first date," she says, and I frown. I'm sure John is last on the list of Valerie's loves. "It was one of my favorite dates ever. I thought he was the first person to see me as more than some bratty little airhead—and I can be that—but I'm more. And Nick always had a way of bringing that out in me."

As soon as I feel my eyes widen, I blink until they're back to normal. I keep my voice smooth. "You want to get married here? Where your first love took you?"

"You think that's crazy?"

Even if I'm trying to impress her, Valerie seems to value honesty—and a bit of snark—so I don't mince words. "I don't think it's exactly sane."

She snorts. "Maybe that's why I think it's a good idea. I'm drawn to the crazy. And this is where I discovered true love exists."

"Don't you think getting married here will only remind you of your ex?"

She purses her lips. "Is that a bad thing?"

For Valerie to have such a strong impression of this place, it must mean a great deal, but it sounds like it's less about the place and more about the person who brought her here. Is this Nick someone she still harbors feelings for?

Has to be, for her to even consider this venue. I mean, I still can't enter the coffee shop my ex and I used to frequent—going so far as to walk two extra blocks to avoid it.

Those who are alive can haunt places just as much as those who are gone.

And it doesn't seem like Valerie minds this particular ghost.

"I'm not judging you, to be clear. But I don't understand. I'd like to."

She sighs. "This is getting too heavy. We're supposed to be having fun."

The change in her is quick. I know I won't get anything more out of her now, and if I push, it'll only make it harder later. I'll gather this and tuck it into a mental file.

I wrap my arm around her. "You're so right. And I bet the café upstairs has enough champagne that anything from this moment on is guaranteed to be fun."

"My treat." She squeezes my arm, and we race to the liquor.

11.

All the blood rushes to my head, and bile swiftly climbs my throat. The backs of my knees burn from the pain of the metal monkey bars I hang from, but I still dangle upside down for what feels like the tenth minute.

"I can't do this anymore," Valerie says beside me. She grips the bar with her hands and flips herself right side up. "I'm gonna be sick."

I follow suit, flipping myself over. My feet lack sober strength and can't absorb the impact of the jump—I hit the ground.

Valerie is not too sick to keep from pointing a finger my way and laughing as I groan, then laugh, then groan again. Wood shavings cling to my jeans and my back, and when Valerie reaches over to brush some off my skin, she falls on top of me.

Two drunk women fumbling around a playscape. Very mature. Very normal.

We giggle, trying to help each other up.

"I knew we should have stopped at six," Valerie says. "Your tolerance is crazy."

I shake my head—the world teeters—and I make a mental note to keep it as still as possible. "Your fault," I say, leading us to a bench overlooking the rest of the playground. "You said you could handle more than I can—and I can't stand losing. I lose a lot, but not for lack of trying."

After Valerie declared she wanted to host the wedding at the art gallery and demanded no follow-up questions, she ordered us a flight of shots. Somehow, it became a celebratory night, turned competition for who could take the most.

It didn't help that Valerie slipped a fifty under one of the glasses—a reward for whoever finished the row. I currently have the bill stuffed into my bra.

The art gallery kindly asked us to celebrate elsewhere, as they had a private viewing arriving. Both of us being unable to drive, we wandered a mile up the road and decided the playground was the perfect place to sober up.

Valerie pinches my cheek. "You're fun," she says, almost accusatory.

"Thanks?"

"Anders isn't some bore, but he's not one to join a drunken excursion. And he's always been tight lipped about whoever he's dating."

I thought he'd only dated Anna?

Valerie snorts and shoves my face away. "Please," she says. "You think he's only been with Anna?" Oh. So I must've voiced my annoying thoughts out loud. A drunk habit I need to snuff out. "Sure, she's the only girl he's ever loved, but he's been around. Trust me, I'm dating his college roommate. Anders has had many a fling."

I actively work to keep my face neutral at the mention of Anders with "many" anything.

"That's why I'm confused about you. I like you, but Anders mentioning you, then bringing you to meet us right after, when he doesn't even give us the names of the people he's seeing—what's really up with you two?"

My nerves ratchet up. Is it really so out of character for Anders to bring along someone he's dating? He seems to be the appropriate amount of private, not meticulously secretive, but not going out of his way to keep his love life entirely separate from his family.

But it's not like I could possibly know him better than them.

"Nothing," I say.

She narrows her eyes at my stomach. "You pregnant?"

"Hell no." I cover my belly. "I've just been helping myself to a few extra servings this week."

"Hired an Etsy witch and fed my brother a love potion?"

"Please listen to yourself and tell me if you sound sane."

She barks out a laugh. "See? You're funny? I never pictured Anders with someone funny. Or cool."

"What did you picture, then?"

"Not sure. Anna was reserved, really quiet unless you knew her. Not exactly someone you'd invite to an after-party, but she'd show up if you needed help setting up. Reliable. And boring."

"And I give off loud? Drunk? Unreliable?"

"Unpredictable," Valerie pitches in. "And my brother is anything but that. Not that I'm complaining. If you can help him have a little fun every now and then, that'd be nice."

Of course, being referred to as someone fun, enough so that it can bring joy to another person, welcomes warmth into my chest. But as swiftly as the warmth comes, guilt seeps into its place. Anders's family has easily welcomed me into the fold, without much effort from my part. That easy kindheartedness in them is something I see when I'm with Anders.

Would it come so easily to them if they knew I came here under false pretenses?

"Valerie." A male voice joins us. "This is absolutely not the corner store you said you'd be at."

A lanky man with large, circular wire glasses approaches. A mess of curls frames his heart-shaped face, which is covered in so many freckles you only catch tiny peeks at his pale skin. If Anders hadn't told me his age, I'd think he was twenty-one instead of thirty.

"John!" Valerie opens her arms wide, shoving me away in the process.

"This is exactly why I have you share your location," John says with a sigh. He glances at me, and his smile widens. "You must be Lucy."

I help Valerie up. "Nice to meet you," I reply politely, but my brain snags on his words. Is he forcing Valerie to share her location so he can track her? That seems controlling. Maybe it's not, but I find myself stuck on it.

With their age gap, someone—i.e., me—might find it suspicious. The typical story of an older man taking advantage of a younger woman, watching her every move, frowning upon drunken nights with friends, attempting to keep her all to himself.

Does Anders know about this?

"Likewise," he says, and I can't tell if he's stuffy or if his voice naturally has a nasally undertone. He holds out his hand, and I shake it.

Not too firm, a bit weak, and a teeny bit wet. My father always said you can tell a lot about someone by their handshake. I'm too drunk to figure John out, but I'm erring on the side of nervous.

We swap custody of Valerie, and she throws herself at him, mumbling something into his collared shirt. Whatever he mumbles back, he says it in an even quieter whisper, but his face pulls into a wrinkled frown.

He keeps both arms around her. "I wish we could talk properly, but I need to get this one home."

"Come on," Valerie shouts. "We'll drop you off at Anders's."

"I'm okay," I say. "It's a beautiful night out."

"It isn't safe for a girl to be alone at night." Valerie points to what I'm sure she thinks is me but is actually a set of swings.

"I know jujitsu," I lie.

"I don't know what that is," Valerie says.

"Picture something incredibly badass and unbeatable."

Her answer is a thumbs-down, so I add the lie, "Don't worry, I texted Anders, he's on the way."

The thumbs-down becomes a thumbs-up, words already beyond her. I wave them off, then make myself comfortable on one of the swings. Each push and pull makes the evening air cooler as I gain momentum. The more I move, the better I feel—as if I'm following the tipsy world instead of waddling through it.

As the night continues, the air begins to bite, and I ease my swinging. My eyes close, and for a moment, the world softens, and out of nowhere, my mom's voice floats through my mind—singing her favorite lullaby. One she learned from her mother, and one she made Taina and me memorize as soon as we could form words.

It's not often I remember specific moments like this. Maybe it's the silence. I've never been good with it. For so long, keeping busy was my armor. Work, school, caretaking, endless motion—it kept the grief locked away when I lost my parents. I had to be strong. Had to take care of Taina. No room for breaking down.

But now, with Taina grown and steady on her own, those quiet moments I once feared have more room to creep in. My life is still busy—new, but less frantic than when I was a young girl desperately trying to be an adult, less buzzing with constant motion. In these calmer spaces, the grief surfaces more often.

And, if I'm honest, the silence leaves too much room for self-reflection. A reminder of where I want to be and where I actually am. Still struggling, still single, still trying to find steady ground.

At least, filling these quiet moments with the soft echo of my mother's lullaby feels better than letting my mind wander to all the things I haven't fixed yet. At least here, wrapped in memory, the silence isn't empty.

"Lucinda." Anders's voice cuts through the song. For a moment, it feels like a dream, so I smile when I meet his concerned gaze. Only when his hands grasp my face do I jolt to reality.

"What's wrong? Are you hurt?"

"What are you doing here?"

His hand on me pulls me to a full stop, and the world shakes a bit like an aftershock. "Why are you here alone? It's midnight. You should have called me if you felt uncomfortable riding with Valerie and John. By the way, Valerie says if you're going to lie about asking me to get you, you could at least try to pretend to have been on the phone."

More perceptive than I thought, the drunk nepo baby. "I wasn't uncomfortable."

He pauses, then cocks his head slightly. "Then why didn't you come home?"

I'm going to need him to stay far away from referring to his place as *my* home. Trouble, this beautiful, unintentionally charming man is. Far too much of it. And I don't have the emotional capacity for it when my life is such a mess I'm confusing basic human concern for romantic gestures.

"My God, I need to get laid."

Anders blinks. Then blinks again. And again.

I shoot up, removing his hands from my face, nearly headbutting him. I step away, but it's not enough space. I move again, trying to widen the gap, but the slide behind me hits the backs of my knees and nearly tips me over.

He snakes his arms around me, tightening until our bodies press together like the pages of a book slammed shut. His hands take up so much space on my back, their warmth somehow seeping through the fabric and burning like hot coals.

To break the tension, I move my lips to thank him, but we're so close together I fear any movement will lead to our mouths pressing. And though my body begs for the touch, the warmth, for Anders in this moment—I fear if I start kissing him, I won't stop.

And those are too-real desires for a fake-dating situation.

With effort, I sneak my hands between us, pressing against his chest. A gentle push doesn't budge him.

His eyes flick between mine and my lips, like he's measuring the distance too.

I know I'm attractive—I'm not naive enough to think Anders doesn't find me so. Still, there are millions of attractive people in the world, and normal people can appreciate seeing one and keep it moving, they don't *do* anything about it.

But when I see Anders, my brain doesn't move on to the next thought, it only burns with the feeling of finding him so sexy it feels like the world might end if I can't have him inside me.

And it's the first time I've felt it in such an all-consuming wave. The attraction runs deep—visceral, bone deep, and between my legs.

Just my luck it's for the most unreadable, unattainable man I've ever met.

I push harder. It's not enough to move him, but he blinks, then pulls back, righting me to stand, before stepping away. My knees buckle, and he swoops in again, wrapping an arm around me.

"How much did you drink?" he asks, mistaking my shaky legs for drunkenness rather than lust. He leads me to the bench, sits me down, and leans in, fingers massaging through my hair, pulling out tiny strands. After the second pass, I notice wood chips under his nails before he flicks them away.

I chew my lip, gaze down. Each time he leans in, his scent orbits me, and the warmth from my cheeks spreads and spreads.

"Do you feel okay?" he asks.

"Why are you here on your own?" he asks.

"Are you upset with me?" he asks.

His fingers pause their exploration. "Are you on a silent strike?"

"No," I say. "I'm just trying not to embarrass myself."

His hands slide to my cheeks, thumbs pressing into the high points. "What are you talking about?"

"I know with how you met me, this silly little job, and my failure to actually do it right before—you may think I don't have any pride. But there's a sliver of it left. And there are only so many times I can be drunk in front of you before you start thinking I have a problem."

His brows furrow. "Don't speak for me," he says. Firm, not argumentative, but close. "The only thing I have a problem with is you being out after midnight, drunk and alone, not answering your phone. You're not from around here, you don't know anyone—you should've called me."

"You don't have to worry about me."

"I know that I don't," he says. "Is it a problem that I do?"

"I think we had this discussion when you took me out to dinner, and it feels like you're disregarding that."

"No. I believe I said, 'I'll keep that in mind.' And I have. And I don't think caring about your safety is as big a deal as you're making it out to be. You should expect basic human decency and concern from other people."

Something tightens in my chest.

It's not that I don't deserve it, but that I've gotten used to not expecting it. It's been a while since I've been in a real relationship, and the ones I was in before didn't offer much care. There was a turning point for me, a pivotal moment in my life's path of failed relationships and excessive self-deprecation, where I learned to view care from others as a luxury, not a bare-minimum act from another human being.

Right. Good. It's not a big deal to him. Just *human decency*. Which means it shouldn't be for me. Good. Great.

The warmth that enveloped me quickly cools off. Every time I think I'm getting mixed signals, Anders is quick to remind me that this is just how he is.

It's me and my eager little heart and imaginative mind that muddle things.

"Okay, then." I wave him off, removing his hands from my face. "I am drunk. I got drunk with your sister, and I think she really likes me."

"Of course she does," he says, settling beside me on the bench. "She cursed me out for leaving you out here on your own—despite me not knowing you were here at all."

I laugh. "Oh, she's so far gone."

"If"—he points a finger right at my nose—"you end up on some drunken excursion again, you call me. Okay?"

I press the tip of my finger to his. "Okay."

He leans his head back and takes a deep breath. "It is a nice night."

Nice enough that he pulls up the sleeves of his black top, and I know I should tear my gaze away a moment after I catch it snagging on the veins wrapped around his arms like knotted rope.

"She invited us on a double date," I say, since business is the only reason I'm here. "It's progress. And I think she likes me, but she's a little bit suspicious of me too. She doesn't know exactly why, but she knows I don't exactly fit with you."

"Says who?" Anders frowns.

I decide, right now, that every time Anders gives me a round of butterflies, I have to deflect and move on quickly. He sends them fluttering in the pit of my stomach too easily for me to maintain focus. Better to just breeze past every moment.

"We're going to some billiards place tomorrow. I didn't get much of a feel for John when he came to get Valerie—it was too quick—but I'd like to speak to him more when we meet." I lean in. "Would you make your girlfriend share her location with you?"

"Is she going on a trip?"

"No, just in general. To keep an eye on her."

"Well." He scratches his neck. "I'm not sure. I wouldn't think to ask for that unless I was worried she was going places she shouldn't be. And if I didn't trust her, I'd probably just want to separate before doing that."

Humming, I turn from him and face the moonlight. "I get that."

It takes a couple of extra seconds to pull up the sober parts of the day. "Do you know Nick?"

His eyes widen a fraction before returning to normal. "She told you about him?"

"Not really, no," I say, an idea playing in the back of my head—but I'm not able to pull it into a coherent thought yet. "She just brought him up, which I thought was a little strange, seeing as we were searching for her wedding venue."

I refrain from mentioning that it was her and Nick's first date or the initial moment she believed in the authenticity of love. I owe Anders a lot, but I also owe Valerie some respect—it's girl code.

It doesn't feel right sharing more intimate secrets she may want kept closer to her chest. I'm already planning to ruin her marriage; I don't need things getting out that could maximize the hurt she'll feel when it all falls through.

"This is what I meant," he says softly. "Valerie is all over the place. And wherever she decides to land—even if she knows it'll hurt—she latches herself to it anyway. After Nick . . ." He cuts himself off, then restarts. "That was a dark time for her. Maybe the worst. I've never known anyone more careless with their own heart."

"Do you think Valerie does love these men? John, and Nick, and anyone else? Or do you think she doesn't understand it?"

He opens his mouth, then shuts it. "I'm not exactly sure."

Then, after a few moments, he adds, "Did you love them? Your ex-husbands?"

I hold a hand to my chest like he landed a direct hit. "Thanks for the reminder of my two failed marriages."

"Sorry—"

"I'm kidding." I nudge him. "And sometimes I think, of course not, and other times I think, I must have." I shake my head. That doesn't make any sense. "You know what I think?"

"What do you think, Lucinda?" he asks, and the way he says my name disregards any vow I just made to keep from longing over him.

I peel my gaze from him. "I think people make *love* out to be this scary and weighted word—and sure, it can be—but love comes in many forms. It can be this lighthearted feeling, this sense of true contentment, like sitting out and basking in the sun for hours and listening to the sky breathe. It can be as small as the act of letting a bug out the slider door rather than killing it. It can be weighted and filled with baggage, but still feel warm—like loving people who hurt you as much as they make you laugh. And it can be this all-consuming desire to care for another person."

"So." I slap my hands on my knees. "Maybe Valerie does love John, and I loved my men, and love isn't so hard to feel as people make it out to be. But some people don't deserve that love, and sometimes it isn't enough to keep two people together—when so many people get away with hurting others because they know that love can save them. How horrible is it to keep hurting someone and let love be your shield from accountability for it?"

When he doesn't speak, the tips of my ears warm.

"I'm rambling now. Sorry. I don't mean to project. I'm not making much sense."

He reaches for my hand, bringing it over to hold it in his lap. "You make perfect sense."

Anders keeps his hand wrapped around mine, his thumb tracing small, hot circles into my skin, until my initial nerves settle and my heartbeat slows.

My eyes flutter, and my head becomes too heavy for my neck, so it rests on Anders's shoulder.

Neither of us complains, or moves, or speaks—as if any disruption to the peace will ruin this delicate, confusing comfort between us.

We stay like that for hours.

12.

"Well, well," Taina says into my ear, "look who finally decided to give attention to her worried, restless sister."

I pat my finishing powder into my face, speaking loud enough that my phone—buried under makeup brushes on the bathroom counter—picks up on it. "I have texted you over five times each day."

"Texting isn't the same; anyone can text. What if some freak stole your phone and was messaging me the whole time? How would I know it's you?"

"How do you know I don't have a gun to my head and my kidnapper isn't forcing me to speak with you right now?" I counter.

She pauses, then says, "I've already contacted the authorities. You'll never get away."

I snort. "My hero."

"Speaking of heroes," Taina says—and I can visualize the exact smirk on her pretty, nosy little face—"how's the sexy boy toy wandering around the house? Has he made any moves?"

"Now, Taina, why would the man paying me to ruin his sister's wedding make a move on me?"

"Because you're equally as sexy, and you're smart, and fun, and have a perky ass."

"It is very nice."

"Do you want to sleep with him?"

I shut my compact and start gathering all my stray items, shoving them into my makeup bag. "Sleep with who?"

"I'll kill you."

"Then I'm better off staying with my kidnapper." I take her off speaker and bring the phone to my cheek. "I'm not sleeping with Anders."

"Why?" she asks. "He's right there."

"I'll get too emotionally attached." I look over my shoulder, making sure the door is shut. "If I could sleep with him and be done, then I would—God, he is so beautiful."

"I knew it! You slut; you sexy little slut," she says, delighted. "What's wrong with getting emotionally attached? From what you've said, it's not like he's a bad person."

"Right," I say, looking in the full-length mirror, adjusting my hair's middle part. "But we live in entirely different states. He's technically my client, so if I sleep with him, that's way too messy. And once this is all over, realistically, what's going to happen? We're going to live happily ever after when his family finds out what I did?"

"Lucy, look at me right now."

"We're on the phone."

"Look at me in my soul eyes. I know you can feel me staring at you," she says. "Honestly, who cares? I think you've earned the right to be a little selfish. If you want to have sex with a man—regardless of the consequences or mess—then that's your God-given right as a woman. If God didn't want you to hook up with hot men, he wouldn't have made you so beautiful. You're actually going against your duty here."

"I can feel Dad getting upset with your blasphemous use of God's name right now."

"If he has a problem, why doesn't he put those dusty little bones together and come fight me, then?"

"Taina!"

"Am I wrong?"

"Yes," I say. "And okay, fine—if I'm honest, I'm pretty sure there is some sexual tension between us, but I also know that I'm so deprived of any romantic relationship, something casual feels incredibly more intense for me than it might for him."

"Here's an idea," Taina says in such a condescending tone I instantly try to tune her out. "Instead of wondering if it's as intense for him, why don't you just ask him?"

"Anyway," I say, not admitting that her words hold weight—or that the encouragement to explore Anders eases some of my jumbled thoughts—"on to vastly more important things: How are you?"

I can feel her rolling her eyes. "I'm fine. Bored. Mathew and I are having dinner tonight with some friends. In two weeks he'll be gone for a work trip. I'll be all by myself, then. If only there were someplace warm, someplace with beaches, someplace with someone whom I love so much and would love to tan with, that I could go visit . . ."

"Well, hope you find the place."

"Lucy," Taina snaps, "let me come visit."

"And stay where?"

"Don't worry," she says. "I wouldn't want to cockblock. I'd get a place nearby. Only see you when you're free."

I chew on the inside of my mouth. It would be nice to have Taina nearby. And if Mathew is going to be away anyway, he won't be able to say I'm taking Taina from him. As long as this trip is out of boredom, and not Taina coming to rescue her pathetic older sister, he shouldn't have a problem with it.

Somehow my gut tells me he'll find one anyway.

"I'll think about it," I promise. "I have to go now."

"Okay, I love you. Have safe sex—"

I hang up on her and exit the room.

Anders waits by the island in the kitchen, sipping from a mug that reads *Best Uncle Ever*.

"Sorry for the hold-up," I say, dropping my phone on the counter. "Did a life check with my sister."

He smiles at that, the dimples at the corners of his lips denting, and my heart speeds up.

"Tea?" he asks, gesturing to a second, plain mug on the counter.

I'm about to say no, because I've always believed tea is the equivalent of sewer water, but I see the steam rising from the cup and realize that he's already made me one.

"Thanks," I say, grabbing it with both hands, and before I can cop out, I bring it to my lips. It's exactly what I thought: hot, stagnant, and muddy. I lick my lips and nod, as if it's to my exact taste.

Anders reaches over and pulls it from my hands. "That was insultingly bad acting."

I bark out a laugh. "No, no, no!" I try to snatch it from him. "I love it so much."

"Yeah, right."

"It's my favorite drink of all time." I grab it and try to pull. "Just delicious."

He chuckles, and the sound feels like hundreds of feather tips tickling my skin.

"Get out of here."

"No, let me drink it."

He places his hand on my forehead and pushes gently. "You don't have to drink it because I made it. It just means more for me."

"Well"—I lean back—"if you're that thirsty . . ."

He gives a full-on laugh that lifts my mouth into a smile. "You're so generous."

When I wink at him, his smile mirrors mine.

"So." I clap my hands together. "Ready for our double date?"

"Whenever you are," he says. "Anything you need from me?"

"Just stand around and look pretty, as you do," I say. "This is going to be super simple. I want to get to know them, see if I can spot any cracks I can widen more. I think our best bet is to get Valerie to see she doesn't want this wedding. Even if it seems John may be easier to convert, I won't have much access to him to plant any seeds. Well, unless you want to take that on."

"Me?"

"Yeah, you two are close, aren't you? Roommates. Or has it been a bit rocky since the whole engagement? Actually, can we unpack this before we meet them?"

He places the mug down. "We were closer in college, and then he moved to California to be with his family for a couple of years. We stayed in touch—monthly catch-ups—and if I was ever out west, we'd meet up, and vice versa." He clears his throat. "When Anna and I broke up, he came for two weeks and helped me move out. Awkwardly stuck around and never knew exactly what to say."

"That was kind. Until, you know, he hooked up with your sister at some party."

He winces. "Apparently, they got together that day, broke up that first week, then they were back together the next, engaged at the end of the month."

"A shaky start. I wonder what it was that broke them up," I say, more to myself. Maybe it's something that can be broken again—especially if there's a part still fragile from the first time.

"Not sure. John and I really haven't spoken much since they announced they were getting married last month."

My phone vibrates, and I catch the screen lighting up from my peripheral vision.

"Will it be weird for you?"

Anders's gaze is on my phone after another vibration. Then he clears his throat, not looking at me when he says, "Maybe. This will be our first time meeting since."

"I'll do most of the talking," I reassure him. "So it won't be too bad."

He nods, his gaze still on my phone. He looks a little uncomfortable. I frown, fearing Taina has sent some text of encouragement with way too many details about what I should do to Anders. I snatch my phone from in front of him and peek at the screen.

Nothing from Taina—just several notifications of likes on my dating profile.

Anders busies himself by turning his back on me, cleaning the mugs. I approach his side, peeking up at him with a grin. He slightly turns his cheek, and something in me bursts like stray embers from a campfire.

What an interesting reaction.

"I'm guessing you saw those notifications," I say, leaning closer toward him until I pick up on his light, woody, fruity scent.

He clears his throat again.

I bring my hand toward his neck and press my thumb against the base of it. "You coming down with a cold?"

He stills, his hand freezes under the running water, but then he turns to meet my gaze. His eyes are warm—warming up the more we hold each other's stare, like a pot of honey on a stove, simmering, then boiling.

"I'm okay," he says gruffly.

Interesting.

"So," I say, giddiness flooding through my veins, "tomorrow night, I'm going to be out late. You don't have to wait up for me."

He drops the mug he's working on in the sink and faces me fully. "And where are you going?"

His left hand—still clutching the dishcloth—lands on his hip.

His face screams sexy, irritated man, but his body screams irritated, passive-aggressive housewife. The juxtaposition of it all makes me bury my face in my hands, smothering a cackle.

When I settle, remove my hands from my face, and catch his deepening scowl, the laughter takes over again. I pull open my profile on the app and hold out my phone to Anders.

He moves to shove it away. "I don't need to see—what is this?"

"Not me," I point out. The name on the page reads Ashley Palmer and features a beautiful blond I found on Pinterest who bears a striking resemblance to Valerie. "Just in case John is actively seeking the comfort of other women, I made a profile that's just his type. I've gotten a lot of attention, but nothing from John yet. He might not be a cheater, which would be the most obvious reason for a breakup."

"Oh," he says, his shoulders relaxing. "Oh. This is bait."

I nod. "Just trying to work every angle possible."

"You really think of everything."

"For some things." I narrow my eyes at him. "Others, not so much."

I'm not sure if it's some kind of game, or if we just like staring intently at each other, but we lock gazes—and somehow Anders's face inches closer to mine, or mine to his, or maybe we both just pull together like we're magnetized.

Regardless, some of my confusion about reciprocated attraction begins to clear up.

Even when Anders drops the dishcloth over my face, breaking the moment, the fog continues to dissipate. He's not voicing it, but he's annoyed at the thought of me going on a date. Now, whether that's because he thinks I should be focusing on the job or because he finds the idea of me going on a date romantically irritating—that's still up for debate.

For now, I try to take Taina's advice and not overthink. I laugh, toss the towel back at him, and head to the door.

"Hurry up—we don't want to be late for our date!"

13.

Seeing as how Anders and John have exchanged fewer than three words in thirty minutes, my promise to avoid an awkward night feels like false advertising. The two men greeted each other, led us to a booth overlooking the dozens of pool tables and a heavily populated curved bar, and haven't said a word since.

Valerie returns from the bar with a round of double shots for our table, and I refrain from thanking God outside my own thoughts.

"Here"—I push two of the wet glasses toward Anders—"loosen up."

Valerie downs one herself before snuggling up beside John, holding his glass to his lips. Anders scowls at them, and I grab his chin to do the same.

This earns me a frown. I give him a look that reads *You're not helping*. He returns one that reads *I'm at a bar with what used to be a close friend who's marrying my sister.* He wins the silent argument, but downs the shot anyway.

"Come on," Valerie says. "You're really not drinking?"

"No," I say. "My liver is on its last leg right now. I'll stick to water."

"Don't be a bore." Valerie pushes a shot at me.

Anders takes it and drinks it in a gulp. My gaze watches the way his Adam's apple bobbles, and something about the movement sends a jolt of heat between my legs. He peels the glass away, and leftover whiskey gathers at the side of his lips, slowly slipping down his chin.

Jesus Christ, Lucinda, you're like a dog in heat.

In a humiliating moment, my hands act of their own accord, lifting themselves to wipe away the droplet. I freeze, hand midair, as his gaze pins me in place.

Anders takes my thumb to his mouth and swipes the liquor from his skin. The act alone is enough to send my stomach into a frenzy. But then he pulls my thumb into his mouth and sucks the alcohol from my finger.

An arrow of heat shoots itself directly between my legs.

Unable to resist the instinctual urge to rub them together and relieve the heat building, I cross them, snatch my hand away from Anders, and direct my attention to John.

"So, sorry to be blunt, but as much as it makes Anders feel awkward, I'm so interested in you two." I smile between them. "I mean, John, you must have only seen Valerie in tiny moments between hanging with Anders. What was the moment you realized you had feelings for her?"

He pushes his glasses up the bridge of his nose, looking at Valerie for immediate assistance with what I would assume is a very basic question.

"We've always had these little moments the few times I was around when he was visiting Anders." Valerie speaks for him. "Questioning glances, tiny brushes, but I just thought he was my brother's cute friend, never made it a big deal. Then, when we saw each other at that party, I don't know, everything just *clicked.* We realized it could never work with anyone else because we were meant to be. There aren't words to explain it; you just *feel* it. We couldn't be apart. We couldn't, wouldn't, let anything come between us."

I face John. "What was coming between you two?"

"What wasn't?" Valerie answers again. "The obvious one is scowling right beside you."

In answer, Anders grabs a free glass and takes another shot.

"Like him, Aunt Bethany had a big problem with us. Thinks the age gap is too large, but it's not like I'm freshly eighteen years old and he's been waiting by the clock until I officially became legal. Is seven years really that bad?"

"It's a big gap," I admit, "but you are an adult."

"*Thank* you," she says pointedly, "and I can make my own decisions. Sleep with who I want to sleep with."

"Christ—" Anders mutters.

"John is the one who didn't want to pursue it. I'm the instigator. He kept pulling away from me, kept shutting me down because he was worried he'd ruin his friendship with Anders. But love is love, and it can't be contained."

"Are you still worried about that?" I ask John. "About how you and Anders can't even look at each other right now?"

"Lucinda—" Anders starts, and I wonder if I came off too strong. But really what I'm hearing is that, eventually, John *stopped* caring about Anders's feelings, and if so, fine, but what was it that made him stop?

"I guess," I say, trying to put together some missing pieces, "what I'm trying to ask is, why right now? Why have you decided Valerie is the one. What happened?"

"What is this, an interrogation?" Valerie asks.

"A friendly questionnaire," I assure her, but the way she doesn't speak for John leads me to believe that this is a question she, too, would like an answer to. "Am I making you uncomfortable?"

"No," John answers, his voice barely audible over the pounding of music and vibration of drunken conversations. "I just fell in love with her. I know it's fast, but we've been without each other for this long, we want to hurry up and spend the rest of our lives together." He looks toward Anders. "I'm sorry if it's come between us."

"It hasn't," Anders answers smoothly, and I can't tell if he's just saying that, or if he thinks they'll be okay in the future, once John and Valerie don't marry.

"This is bringing the vibe down," Valerie says. "We need more drinks."

"I'll get this round," I offer, trying to wiggle out of the booth, but Anders is in the corner seat, and I need him to move, or I'll have to shove my ass in his face to get out.

When I see his mischievous smirk, I shove him. "Get up," I say, the words caught in a laugh.

He moves out, takes my hand, and helps me up. "I'll go with you."

I place my hands on his shoulder and shove him back down. "I'm a big girl," I say, and he grabs my arm, pulling me toward him.

"Take my card," he says, and though half of me thinks the sound and feel of his words on the skin beneath my ear is more pleasurable than humanly possible, it's a little embarrassing he thinks I can't cover one round of shots.

I can't, but still. That's what credit cards are for—future me problems.

"I can handle it." I tap his cheek gently and head to the bar.

There's no real line anywhere, just pockets of people all trying to flag down the bartenders. After scanning the crowd, I set my sights on a man with cropped hair and a shirt nearly bursting at the seams around his biceps. I pull my white top lower, so my breasts—aided by my very best push up—nearly spill out.

This maneuver gets several men to offer me their spots, so it takes mere seconds for me to reach the sticky bar, and even less for my target bartender to ignore his other patrons and come to me.

"What can I get you, beautiful?" he says in a drawl.

"Three double shots of whiskey." I lean in, pressing my breasts together, fluttering my eyelashes.

"Keep looking at me like that, darling, and I couldn't possibly charge ya."

"Yeah." I reach over and run my nail up his arm. "Prove it."

He holds a hand over his heart before moving along, making my shots like a good, easy man.

Life is hard, but taking advantage of horny men is always easy.

He gives me a performance as he pours my shots, then places them across from me. "What's your name?" he asks, his gaze trained on my chest.

"Lucy."

"Lucy," he repeats, "and what's your number?"

I gather the drinks close to my chest. "You'll learn that when I get my second round." I wink at him and turn, nearly spilling all the drinks on my chest when I bump into Anders.

Before I have the chance to feel embarrassed by being caught in the act, he reaches to help hold the cups. "That," he says, "was—"

"Manipulative?" I offer.

"—magical," he counters, "and for some reason"—his hand lingers over mine as he takes the remaining drinks—"incredibly sexy."

It's not that I disagree—I *know* it was; it's why I got the free drinks. But in this moment, I know with full certainty that Anders is attracted to me. More than a general appreciation of acknowledging someone is just conventionally good looking.

But witnessing me charm another man, hike up my breasts, and flirt my way to a deal has made him look at me like he wants to devour me. And *God*, do I want to let him.

Which is exactly why I chose not to drink. I'm going to be clear headed. Focused on Valerie, my actual job, and not what sex-hungry Lucy wants. Though it pains me to, I move away from Anders and give him a friendly shove.

"Well, hope you enjoyed the show," I say as we weave through couples and rowdy groups. "Now that he sees me with you, he's not going to offer me another round."

"Do exactly what you did to him to me," he says as we reach the table, "I'll give you my bank account information."

I laugh so hard it shakes me, and I smack his arm enough some of the drinks spill before he can place them on the table, and we take our spots again.

"What's so funny?" Valerie asks as we rejoin. "I like to laugh."

"Lucinda charmed the bartender."

"Scammed," I say, though I appreciate the fluffed words. "I could have got several more rounds if *somebody* hadn't shown up."

Anders grabs my hand, presses a kiss at the center of it. "My deepest apologies."

It is so teenage-like, this night, the way Anders is pulling giggles from me every other minute. The way my cheeks are forcing themselves to keep from smiling. The way I keep catching him watching me, smiling too.

"Gross," Valerie says, "and cute." She scans the space behind us, so I turn to find where she's looking. "No more free drinks from that guy, but look for the redheaded woman. She owns the place and always gives me drinks on the house." As though the woman hears herself being talked about, she catches our gazes and waves. "I'll tell her to look out for you."

"Noted."

Anders wraps an arm around me, pulling me as close as possible beside him. Though I know he's playing it up for our lie, I can't help but notice the inches of distance between John and Valerie. I'm struggling to see the connection, the romance, and I can't tell if I'm biased by Anders's wish for them not to be together, or if there's something off about them in general.

"What's next for wedding planning?" I ask Valerie, knowing changing subjects is better in the long run. I don't want to make it obvious I'm prying. "Anything I can help with?"

Valerie groans, hitting her head on the cushion behind her. "Maybe. Probably." She takes a drink, her manicured nails gripping the glass, and downs it in one gulp. "My maid of honor, the bitch, is in the Peace Corps. Literally. She was supposed to be back this month to help plan, but she's stuck in Belize with these annoyingly cute kids that want her to stick around for their soccer tournament."

"So, she's a generous bitch," I say.

Valerie laughs. "Yeah, that's right. Generous to everyone but *me* right now. She had one little epiphany about wanting to be a better person after a night out, and now she's thousands of miles away. So rude."

"Well, I too am generous, if you need anything while she's away making the world better than how she found it."

Valerie narrows her eyes at me, then, at my chest. I blink, and she's completely over the table, and her hands are feeling my boobs, then my stomach, back to my chest.

All the thoughts written in my mind go blank, a dry-erase board washed clean.

"Christ, Valerie." Anders shoves her away, and my thoughts slowly write themselves back in my brain.

"Relax." She sits back in her seat. "I won't take your girlfriend." She wiggles her brows at me. "I could if I wanted, I bet, but you know, you and Cierra are around the same size. You're probably a little taller, but the proportions are almost the same."

"Then she must have a great ass too," I point out.

Valerie barks out another laugh. "Okay, please, come to the bridesmaid fitting coming up. Cierra wants me to pick out something for her. This way, I'll be able to see how the dresses would fit her body type."

"Just give me a time and place."

"You're the best," she says, and her eyes go wide and deerlike. "Ever since I met you. Who would have thought Anders would have such good taste?"

Anders tightens his grip around me, and I smother all the usual thoughts that float to the surface. The *This is fake, how will she feel when it comes to light?* And, most urgently, in neon flashing lights in the script of a business's flashing **CLOSED** sign: *Do not sleep with Anders.*

Instead, I ease up and lean into it all. For one night, I'll just have some fun. I've secured another place beside Valerie, and I'll continue to plant seeds and find cracks to slip in.

But—I grab my water—*I'm still going to be sober.* It's a lot safer that way.

We have more rounds of drinks, laugh, and even John opens up, albeit barely, to share some stories about Valerie. Whenever they ask us to do the same, I hurriedly press them for more, and they're all so drunk nobody seems to notice.

But then Valerie grows curious about me and my life, and it's easy to share the truth. To talk about busy but loving parents, and precious dogs, and a sister that feels like a soulmate, and I find that opening up to her, to Anders, feels *real*.

I've been worried how it'll affect the people I'm leaving when this is all over. Maybe . . . maybe I have to worry about myself.

Despite the new worry, the night passes quickly and lightly. Eventually, John whispers to Valerie, and she announces he has an early morning meeting, and they should get going. We say our goodbyes, and I turn to Anders.

"Should we head out?" I ask, my hands reaching into the pockets of his jeans. "I'll drive."

He places his hands over mine, pinning them there. "Not yet," he says, his gaze warm and focused. "I don't want this night to end."

"Why?" I say lightly. "You want to spend more time with me?"

It's a joke, at least to me, but Anders moves his hands to my wrist, his thumb caressing the skin there. "I do," he says, and there is no humor in the declaration.

Though his words elicit warmth throughout my body, I notice then that he's *drunk*. The sight of him, his eyes wide and pleading, and his lips just slightly pouted, is so incredibly endearing and a little pathetic—which somehow makes him even sexier.

"I don't know," I sing, holding out the possibility like a tease.

His hands move from my arm to the base of my neck. "Please?" he asks, his voice barely a whisper.

The sound of it, the sight of him, is like an enchantment. The word is out of me before I can think it. "Okay."

14.

"I'm telling you," I say as Anders hands me the cue stick he just chalked, "I am humiliatingly bad at pool."

"Nobody is bad at pool," he swears, placing all the balls in a triangle and centering them.

"Well, I can't wait to prove you wrong."

He smiles as he finishes setting up, then gestures for me to take the lead. "You know the rules, right?"

"I do," I mutter, "but it doesn't help." I break the balls—barely. The white one moves at a snail's pace, and the impact scatters them scarcely an inch from their original positions.

Anders coughs into his hand.

I point the cue stick at him. "Don't you dare laugh at me. I told you I was bad."

"Not laughing," he says, taking over my spot and moving so quickly I barely have time to prepare. He hits the white ball with a resounding smack, and two stripes slap into opposite pockets.

I lean on the side of the table. "This feels like a humiliation ritual."

He smiles. "I won't go again." He reaches for me, positioning me by the white ball. "Even if I get a stripe, I'll just hit it once. We'll go back and forth."

"Oh, so you want to prolong my suffering?"

"I believe in you," he says, rubbing a hand over the small of my back—and it's more of a distraction than encouragement.

"That makes one of us," I say, and I hit the ball at an angle that causes the stick to slip from my fingers.

When I turn to face him, he grips my cheeks. "No more frowning."

"This is my resting face."

"It most definitely isn't."

"You stare at my face enough to know if it isn't?"

At that, he spins me around to look at the table. His hands wrap around my waist, his fingers resting on my belly underneath the fabric of my shirt. Anders bends slightly and positions the stick in my hand. "First," he says, his lips brushing my ear as he speaks, like each vowel is a hidden kiss against the skin, "your body should face the direction of the cue." He uses his knee to bend me over more. "And you need to reposition your fingers. Only use your index and thumb to form a bridge for the cue to rest on. Gives you better control."

I swallow to combat my dry throat, trying to focus on his instructions, but his fingers caress mine, and he positions them so delicately around the stick. All I can focus on is the feel of his large palms on my flesh—think about how they would feel over more sensitive places.

"Practice," he whisper-kisses into my ear, moving me—and us—so that my fingers travel up the stick in a way that sends my imagination spiraling. "You don't have to strike it until you feel ready."

He's entirely too close and not at all close enough. Each time Anders gets near to me, physically and emotionally, my first instinct is to welcome it, welcome him into my life like I'm writing his name in damp sand. Then a wave of logic smacks into me, sweeping his name away before it can be permanently imprinted on my heart.

"You're"—I clear my throat—"very *near*. We don't have to play up the act."

He hums in my ear. "No acting here," he says softly, "but if you need a reason, Valerie's bartender friend keeps glancing our way."

"And why is that?" I can't help but ask. "One of your many flings?"

He chuckles, and the sound sends a dizzying warmth through me. "Don't be jealous."

"I'm *not*," I lie.

His lips lightly press into the skin below my ear. "Ready?"

I can only nod. When he moves away, I genuinely try to focus, but my grip is shaky without his guiding touch, and I miss the white ball entirely. I sigh, then face him again.

"You know, it's unhealthy of me, but I do better under pressure."

He cocks his head slightly. "Do you?"

"Want to make a bet?"

"You," he says, pressing the side of his cue stick to my chest, "want to make a bet against me?" He presses it to himself. "At pool?"

"Yes." I keep my chin up. "If you help me a bit more."

When he doesn't say anything, I breach the space between us. "The look you're giving says you don't think any amount of help will make a difference."

He grips my chin between his finger and thumb. "I just don't want to take advantage of you."

I most definitely want him to take advantage of me.

I know that thought remains in my head. Yet, the way Anders gives me a once-over makes me think he heard it loud and clear.

My fingers hook into his belt loop, and I pull him even closer. "Are we betting or what?"

"What would you like, Lucinda?"

"What are you willing to do, Anders?"

"Anything."

"Anything, then," I repeat. "Winner gets a wish. Anything is on the table."

"Deal."

"Deal."

I move to the table, bending over. I turn and glance at Anders, whom I catch admiring the view.

"Are you going to help me?"

He positions himself behind me at an almost respectable distance, leaning over with one hand around my stomach to steady me. His other hand reaches for mine, tightening my grip on the cue stick.

I arch my back, pressing it against his front. I already feel him there, as if he was waiting for me, but when I grind myself deeper against him, he hardens even more. He muffles his groan into my neck, his body pressing against my ass, gripping my stomach tighter—as if he needs to steady himself before losing his balance.

His reaction snuffs out any lingering doubt that this thing between us is one sided. And the way he reacts to me—instinctively, helplessly—fills me with an unfamiliar confidence that spreads along with the heat flooding my body. My heart pounds against my chest; I feel it beating in my eardrums.

It awakens a wildness I didn't even know existed within me.

"Sorry," I say sweetly, grinding against him once more before pulling away. I position myself incorrectly and ask, "Is this better?"

His hands move from my stomach downward, to just below the top of my skirt, as he pulls me back against him, pressing me against his body. He's so hard, and if he slipped a hand beneath my skirt—and I ache for him to—he'd find me wet, ready, and waiting.

Like an afterthought, he stills the pressure of his hands over my crotch and maneuvers us correctly. "Like this," he says, his breath raspy and dark.

I hit the ball, and it moves fast this time, but I miss every other one in sight. I turn into him, lifting the cue stick until it's pressed between my breasts. "You know, maybe a bet wasn't the best idea."

His gaze travels to my chest, so I lean in more, pulling at the fabric so it nearly slips from my breasts entirely. Anders tears his gaze away from my chest, then digs his fingers under the sides of my straps, lifting so the cotton covers the entirety of my nipples.

"I'm not taking the bet back."

I hum, my hands traveling up his chest. "Okay, then."

He swallows—I only know because his Adam's apple bobs—and peels himself away to take his shot. It's another point. If he keeps up this pace, the game will be over in minutes.

This time, I move around the table, away from him. From the angle I bend, he has a full bird's-eye view of my chest. Even without looking up, I feel the heat where his gaze scans every exposed area of skin.

I take a deep breath, hold it, then smack my cue into the white ball, which hits a red ball into a corner pocket. "Oh," I say, trying not to smirk. "I think I get it now."

When I lean over again, Anders places a hand on the table. "What are you doing?"

"Huh?" I say, then laugh. "Oh, no, it's my turn. You're the one who said you'd only go once after a hit. I never agreed."

I meet his gaze, and he catches on in seconds, lips pulling into a smile.

The next two minutes I spend smacking every ball I need into the pockets. I barely take a moment to position myself before moving on to the next shot. Only the eight ball remains.

I haven't looked up once since my first shot. Though Anders is watching me circle the table intently—especially when I bend over directly in front of him, sinking the eight ball.

Finished, I turn, lifting myself onto the edge of the table, and press a kiss to the space just below the tip of my cue stick. I drop it on the table behind me and tuck my hair behind my ear.

"Well," I say, "I think that's game."

I send a quick thank-you to the college ex-boyfriend who forced me to play beside him every Thursday night for seven months.

Anders crosses the small space between us, his knee separating my legs so his thigh presses against my crotch. I inch myself off the table, and the feel of his muscles against my center sends tiny fireworks exploding through my brain.

"You played me," he says, and of all things, it sounds like adoration.

"I did," I say, nails digging into the edge of the table to keep from climbing on Anders. "And I believe you said if I did exactly what I did to the bartender to you, you'd give me your bank account number. You can text it to me."

He throws his head back and laughs so freely that my heart is the one setting off tiny fireworks now. When he settles, he brings one hand to my neck, lifts until his thumb is under my chin.

"You are so incredibly beautiful," he whispers.

"I just scammed you for your bank info, and you're complimenting me?"

"I'd like to do far more than just that."

I suck in a breath. "Anders."

"Lucinda."

"You're drunk."

"And you're sober," he counters, his hand reaching under my skirt, pressing against the skin of my thigh, higher and higher until he reaches the curve of me. "But you still want me. Like I want you."

My pulse speeds up enough that I worry Anders is going to give me an actual heart attack. I press my hand against my chest, rubbing the skin there as if it'll slow the beating. "This is . . ." I struggle to speak as he moves his hands around to my ass, pulling me against his thigh so that my wet panties press against his leg. The relief and pleasure the pressure gives slips a moan out of my mouth before I can stop it. "Messy." I moan again as Anders's fingers dig into my skin, positioning me to ride his leg once more.

"It doesn't have to be," he says, leaning forward and flattening my body against his, moving in a hard, patterned rhythm.

"You're drunk." I feel the need to say it again, but the words are pathetic whimpers timed with every grind of our bodies. My center throbs, each pulse jolting through my entire body, desperate for more. "Let's revisit this when sober."

My vision grows hazy, tiny lights bursting at the sides, like lost planets trying to find the right orbit. It feels so good. My panties are drenched enough that Anders's jeans will be soaked through. But the thought of stopping feels impossible. I don't want to stop. I need to stop. I can't stop.

"Excuse me." A woman's voice jolts through the mind-blowing pleasure running through me. Anders barely pulls away; I turn my head to see the girl, wide eyed, in front of a man. "It's, um, our time slot at the table."

"Oh my God," I say, slamming my palms against Anders, who barely budges. I nearly fling myself off him. "Sorry, really sorry," I tell them, pulling my skirt down and rushing toward the exit as fast as my shaky legs will take me.

Mindless lust is what that was. Now I feel like someone dunked me under a bucket of ice water. Dummy. A horny, deprived dumbass is what I am.

"Lucinda!" Anders calls, grabbing my arm.

As he pulls me to a stop, I realize I've made it to the parking lot. "Give me the keys."

"Lucinda," he says again.

With the floodlights illuminating the area, my gaze catches on the damp patch I left on Anders's thigh. "Oh my God." I press my hands over my face. "I can't believe I just did that."

"We," Anders says. "That wasn't just you."

"I remained sober to have some self-control," I say into my hands. "This isn't appropriate. We're basically coworkers."

Anders pries my hands from my face and replaces them with his own. "There's nothing wrong with what we just did."

I open my mouth, then bite my tongue. Clearly, even sober, I can't act rationally around Anders.

"Stop that."

"Stop what?" I ask.

"Whatever thoughts you're having, wishing you could take it back."

"I don't want to take it back," I say without thinking. "I'm not some naive virgin, Anders. We're two consenting adults who, under any other circumstance, could hook up without a second thought. This—this is just messy. And sober Anders will agree with me. Drunk Anders—well, I don't even know who you are at this moment."

He chuckles, and the sound somehow eases the worry seeping into my bones. "Lucinda, I think you're overreacting," he says. "And for the record, when I'm sober, I'll want you just the same—I have since the day I met you."

"No!" I shout, making us both jump, then laugh. "No, I told you. You can't say things like that to me. Don't be romantic. Or sexy. Don't be anything. Just—just be quiet."

Anders brings his thumb up, tracing my bottom lip. "Let's do what you wanted before. You're too frantic right now. I don't want you to feel rushed or panicked. We can revisit this conversation."

"I wish you'd agreed to that before I dry-humped you on the freaking pool table."

"That was far from dry," he says, and my jaw drops open.

He presses a hand against his mouth so I won't see the shit-eating grin I'm sure is there.

"Shut up," I say. "Stop laughing!"

"Stop making me laugh."

"I'm not being funny," I say, but the laughter spills out anyway.

"Let's go home," he says.

I groan at the use of the word *home*. I am, already, in way too deep.

15.

Thank God Anders's second bedroom has its own bath—and that I left a bag of chips on the bedside table so I have something for breakfast. I haven't left the room since I woke up at five this morning.

My internal debate has ping-ponged among approaches for confronting Anders today. All of them make me want to scream into a pillow—which I have done several times already—and none of them feels right. Of course, that's because yesterday should never have happened.

I should have just been drunk. It's the oldest and easiest trick in the book. *I was drunk, my head wasn't on straight. I don't know how that happened.* Or, if I'd had an egregious amount of alcohol: *Morning. I feel horrible; what happened last night?*

Instead, I have to navigate the fact that I behaved that way completely sober.

To be fair, Anders is not entirely innocent in last night's events. I simply catalyzed his drunk and flirtatious behavior. Though "flirtatious" seems like an understatement for my spreading my legs in the middle of a crowded bar.

He's knocked twice, and each time I've flung myself onto the bed and pretended to be asleep. I have no doubt he heard the movement, particularly when I snagged my toe on the bed frame and cursed, but he hasn't forced me out yet.

Maybe I should let him take the lead in the conversation. He's the one paying me; he's the one who, though drunk, very obviously wanted to get me in his bed. It'll be best if he's sober now and says, *Though it would be plenty fun hooking up, with the current situation between us, it's best if we maintain whatever semblance of professionalism we can.*

Anders is a reasonable man. I'm sure that's the conclusion he's come to this morning. And if, for some reason, he hasn't, I have no issue taking the lead in the conversation. It's fine. I'm an adult. He's an adult. We're all adults.

Good, great, amazing.

Before I can talk myself out of it, I bullet out of the room and head straight for the sound of coffee brewing. As soon as I reach the kitchen, my body stalls and my mind empties like a TV unplugged from its outlet mid-show.

"Well, well," Bethany says, a cherry-patterned dress clinging to her body as she pours milk into a glass. "Look who finally woke up. How much did you have to drink last night?"

Olive, in a matching dress beside her, rushes toward me. She sniffs the air and frowns. "You smell pretty good."

As opposed to reeking of liquor, I assume. "Good morning to you too," I greet both of them.

Olive pokes my side. "We've been here for hours," she says, approaching Bethany again. "You missed watching *Iron Man* with us."

A hand slides over my back; Anders leans down in what will appear to them as a kiss on my cheek, but he says, "Sorry, they came without warning."

I refrain from jerking from his grasp in front of his family, but I pull away just slightly, and he frowns at the movement. I was hoping to snuff out this awkwardness the moment we spoke today, but I guess it'll have to wait.

When I move to walk away, Anders snakes his hand around my waist and pulls me toward him. I can't wiggle free without raising flags to his family, so I just smile and let him lead us to the counter.

Bethany pours a shot of espresso into a glass of iced milk, then pushes it my way. "Hear you're not a fan of tea."

I glance over at Anders. When did he tell Bethany about that? He just learned that fact, and it's not something necessary to share. Is he speaking about me to other people, just randomly?

"Thank you." I grab the iced coffee and drink; the flavor is much more bearable than anything you have to steep a bag of tea in. "What brings you here this morning?"

"Today is the Sunday market," Bethany says, pouring syrup into a different glass. "I thought you could join us for some girl time. We haven't had a chance to get you alone yet. You don't mind, do you?"

"Of course not," I say, pinching Anders. "You could have woken me once they got here. I'm sorry for holding you all up."

Anders brushes a stray wave behind my ear. "You just looked so peaceful, I didn't want to disturb you."

"Sweet." I glare at him when he squeezes me tighter to his side. "I can be ready in fifteen." I give Anders, in his oversized shirt and gray sweatpants—a painfully attractive boyfriend look—a frown. "Are you going like that?"

"I'm not going at all," he says, and I feel my eyes widen.

"What's the matter?" Bethany asks with a smirk. "Nervous to spend some time with us without a buffer?"

"Nope." I recover quickly. "I'm just nervous you'll fall in love with me and favor me over Anders. He'll be devastated."

Bethany cackles. "We'll see about that." She waves me off. "Go on, the market opens soon."

Anders lets me go, and I grip his arm and pull. He doesn't give me the grace of pretending to follow me like I'm urging him to.

"Can you help me reach something at the top of the closet?" I smile at him, yanking the bottom of his shirt.

"I left the stool there for you." He removes my hand and takes a glass from Bethany.

I narrow my eyes at him. Is he avoiding me? That's not one of the scenarios I played out in my spiral this morning. I'm not sure how to approach that. I could play along, act like nothing happened, and that way neither of us have to face last night.

An option, yet something about this is pissing me off.

I breathe in through my nose and force a smile before walking off. My routine is a fast movement of scrubbing my skin until it reddens under the shower, slapping makeup on my face, and slamming around every item I pick up.

Out of all the options to play at, Anders choosing to pretend yesterday didn't happen is the worst choice. Is he regretful? Sure, I am, but why is he? Is it because he agrees this is too messy, or am I some mistake he wishes to erase?

I shouldn't care, I don't want to care, and this flurry of emotions is exactly why I should have closed my goddamn legs in the first place.

When I walk out to the kitchen again, I make sure I appear pleasant, easygoing. The girls sit on the oversized couch, gazes glued to some cooking show.

I approach Anders on the gray love seat and sit on the arm, the bottom of my pale sundress inching up my thigh. He wraps his arm around me, so I fall on top of him. "You okay?" he asks on my arm, his lips moving against the skin there in his kissing-and-speaking method that sends a line of heat down my spine.

I tap his thigh and say to the girls, "I'm ready when you are."

Olive says, "Oh, you look so pretty."

The power of an angry hand patting-on an immaculate face. "Not as pretty as you."

"Yeah, right," she says, but she can't help but smile as she gets up.

"Perfect." Bethany stands. "Don't wait up—we're stealing your girl for the whole day."

"I'll bring you back a treat," Olive promises.

"You're the best," he answers.

When the girls head toward the front door, backs to us, I inch forward so that my dress hikes up. I arch and lift myself from Anders, giving him a half-second view of my pantie-less ass before the fabric falls back down.

He's up before I can blink, pulling me back toward him, grabbing my chin to face him. "Are you trying to drive me crazy?"

I narrow my eyes at him. No matter if he's pretending yesterday didn't happen, his body's reaction to me was not something he could control. If he's going to try to erase it from his memory without talking to me first, I'm going to make it as painful as possible for him.

It's completely hypocritical of me, but my pride as a woman is on the line, and I need the last laugh. Just for today, I'll be a tease. Tomorrow, I'll remember to be a professional, sane person.

I tap his chest lightly. "What are you talking about?"

He pulls my arm when I try to leave. "We'll talk once you're back."

"We don't have to revisit anything," I say, then pull away and join the girls, leaving Anders to think on that.

"I don't need it," I say, as Bethany holds up the thin, golden chain with a lily hanging on the thread.

"Then why do you keep staring at it?" she says.

An unexpected tag team, Olive pulls my hair into a ponytail, and Bethany clasps the chain around my neck. "It's perfect on you," she swears, spinning me toward the tiny mirror on the white-clothed table hosting dozens more delicate sets of jewelry.

The flower hangs at the center of my collarbones, and it's the perfect shade of gold that doesn't blend and dull against my tan skin. I finger the curves of it, admiring how lovely the detailing is.

"Lilies are my favorite flower," I share, twisting it in my fingers. "I used to try and fail to plant them in our tiny little garden."

"Well, you won't have to worry about killing this one," Bethany notes.

It really is perfect.

It's also over a hundred dollars, and I had to run and check my bank account just ten minutes ago when I bought a tiny cup of shaved ice for Olive.

"I'll think about it." I unclasp it from my neck and hand it over to the beautiful old woman behind the table.

"I guarantee it'll be gone by the end of the day," Bethany warns. "Made the mistake of missing out on the most beautiful set of diamond earrings here."

"I'll risk it," I say, pointing at a stand in the distance when I spot a giant sign on the side of it in the shape of a paw. "Mind if I take a peek at that stall?"

"Go on." She gestures. "I see a coffee stand with my name on it."

"I'll go with you." Olive loops her arm through mine.

We walked together through the park's many sidewalks, both pathways of concrete lined with vendors selling handmade art pieces, photography, soaps, and candles. We've stopped at almost every single one, and Olive—ordered to by Bethany—has bought at least a single item to "support local businesses" at each and accumulated enough bags we had to make a trip back to the van to shove them in the back.

There are several speakers playing different songs, and at the very end of the path we walk stands a fountain with a tiny waterfall, where several men perform a dance, and I know after one flip Bethany will shove bundles of cash at the hat sitting across from them.

We pause at the tent with the paw sign. A banner hangs on their table that reads **PAW PRINT BAKERY**. Two women sit behind the packaged treats for dogs and a couple of colorful collars.

But my gaze locks in on a woman around my age, with a round-shaped face and dark hair pinned up with colorful clips, sitting beside them, a way-too-thin black Lab lying by her feet. Olive and I approach them, and I go on my knees. "Who is this cutie?" I ask, holding back Olive when she reaches to pet the dog.

"Sora," the woman answers, reaching down and placing her hand in front of the Lab's eyes before petting his head. Sora leans into her hand. "We rescued him six months ago, the precious boy."

When Olive reaches out again, I grab her hand and ask, "Is he okay with strangers?"

The woman looks sad as she says, "Yes, but place your hand where he can see first. He's deaf, so you have to show him when you're going to pet him."

"You hear that?" I tell Olive, whose eyes are wide and filled with a familiar sympathetic gaze as she does exactly that.

While she gives Sora attention, I ask, "Are you putting him up for adoption?"

"He's been available for months," she says, her lips frowning even deeper. "He's a senior dog with a disability; it'll be difficult to find him a place."

"Poor baby." I go on my knees, let Sora see me before joining the petting spree. He turns on his back, revealing his stomach, and it makes my chest ache.

Exposing his belly this way to someone he's just met means he's way too friendly, leaving him vulnerable to attack, which is probably how he got the scar running under his chin.

"What will happen if nobody adopts him?" Olive asks, and the employee looks at me with wide eyes. We both know what usually happens, but I'm not sure if I'm the right person to show Olive how cruel the world is to animals without a home—and I'm not entirely sure if Sora is in the same danger as so many dogs tend to be.

"Well," says the employee, Dainese—I read the sticker tag on the side of her blue shirt—"we have these treats, the bone-shaped ones in that jar right there." She points to the container filled to the brim with them. "Each time someone buys one of those, we keep the funds for Sora. It helps us keep getting him more treats, and have the ability to keep him longer, take him for fun walks to the park and the beach."

Both Olive and I shoot up and say, "I'll buy some," at the same time.

Dainese chuckles, but her doe-eyed gaze is filled with gratitude as she stands and helps us with the treats. Sora remains lying on the tiny blanket, staring at all of us, and I have to tell myself I have no way to care for this dog, and I cannot reasonably bring him back to Anders's home.

But he has the cutest round dark eyes, and I see such pure gentleness in them that tears fill my eyes.

Dainese pulls out an individually wrapped treat. "They're five dollars each."

I'll probably overdraft for this, but I say, "I'll take ten."

When Olive reaches into her polka-dot wallet, I grab her hand. "Olive, get the big guns. Let's clear it out."

"You got it," she says, then sprints off in search of Bethany.

Dainese laughs as she runs my card. "I can spot a true dog lover a mile away, and you've got the heart of one."

I nod. "I volunteer at this shelter in New York every week. I love them so much."

She raises her brows. "Not from here?"

I shake my head. "Here for a couple of months."

Dainese reaches over and hands me a business card. "If you ever have the time to volunteer while you're visiting, I work at a tiny shelter by Folly. It's not much, but we love what we do, and there are never enough hands."

I pocket the card in the tiny bag I received from a vendor. "Will do."

Olive returns with Bethany in hand. "I got her."

"Oh." Bethany takes one look at Sora and hands over her black card. "We'll take it all."

"Thank you!" Dainese squeals.

"Leave the treats," Bethany says when Dainese reaches in the container. "Consider this a donation. Add a zero to whatever it is. Sell the rest if you can."

Dainese begins this stammer of gratitude, and though it has nothing to do with me personally, I hold Bethany's hand in mine and squeeze. "Thank you."

Bethany pokes my nose. "You softie."

We wrap it up here, and the employees scramble to put together a bag with human treats and a thank-you card for Bethany before we go.

"Now," Bethany says, "I've worked up an appetite. Let's get some food."

16.

I don't admit I've never had high tea before, but the way I examine each tiny sandwich and delicate pastry, I'm sure it's obvious to Bethany. But she only laughs at each declaration as everything I bite into becomes my next favorite food of all time.

I grab a stack of chocolate from the top of the three-tiered silver platter between us and make the same announcement.

"Lucy," Olive says as I take another bite. "Are they going to kill Sora if nobody adopts him?"

I choke on the cake, pounding on my chest while I cough it out. Olive shoves a glass of water toward me, too hard, and it spills on my dress. The water drenches my entire top, dripping over the skirt.

"Sorry!" Olive yells while Bethany shoots up and shoves a napkin all over me.

"It's okay," I say, taking the cloth and blotting my chest while Bethany flags down a waiter for me. "I was getting too hot anyway."

The waiter offers me plenty of napkins, and I wave off Bethany's aid. While I dry myself off, I answer, "It seems like Dainese really cared about Sora. I think she's going to take care of him as best as she can."

"So he will die?" Olive says simply, then turns to Bethany.

Bethany immediately holds up a hand. "No, you know I'm allergic."

"But *I'm* not."

"Good for you." Bethany squeezes Olive's cheeks. "But until you have your own place, you live under my—what I like to think are—pretty easygoing rules."

Olive scoffs. "I can't have a phone. I can't have a dog. It's like you *hate* me."

"If I hated you, darling, you'd be shipped off to some boarding school by now, but I like waking up to this pretty little face every morning."

"Stop it." She jerks away. "You're being so *selfish*."

"Me?" Bethany points to herself. "You want me to suffer every morning in my own house?"

"Who cares if you have a runny nose every now and then?"

"You cute little brat—"

"The shelter Sora is at is a no-kill," I interrupt, holding my hands out. "I'm planning on visiting Sora sometime this week. You can come with me and check on him." I look to Bethany. "If that's okay with you?"

"Please." Olive grips Bethany's arm.

"Of course. Now take back what you said."

Olive grins. "You're generous and pretty and smart."

Bethany laughs, then faces me. "Anders said you worked at a shelter when you could. I guess the love runs deep—and I understand that. You love dogs, and I'm a horsewoman myself. Ride every weekend at my favorite farm. Volunteer there, too, when they need a hand managing things."

Again with Anders speaking about me. Of course, it could be from Bethany just having a conversation with him like we're having one now. But the idea of him speaking about me without me around feels like we're real.

And we're absolutely not.

"It does," I say. "I've always wanted to run my own shelter."

"So I hear," Bethany says. "You know, there are *plenty* of opportunities here in Charleston. Lots of places to invest in, buildings to lease out."

"Are there?" I say, my words stretched out to hide my shock.

Bethany narrows her eyes at me. "So you want Anders to move to New York?"

Ah. She's worried I'm taking her nephew away. I should have picked up on that sooner and gone along with it. Now it'll look like I'm just trying to appease her.

"Not really," I say, going with as much of the truth as I can. "To be honest, the traveling hasn't taken a toll on us. Moving one place or the other isn't something we've discussed yet."

"I don't want Anders to move," Olive says. "He already travels a lot anyway."

"He talks about you so sweetly," I tell her. "I think he misses you just as much when he's away. You don't have to worry about him going anywhere anytime soon."

"Really?" Olive goes wide eyed.

"Really," I promise.

Bethany still has her gaze trained on me. "Would you be opposed to moving down here, if the conversation did come up?"

I rub my thumb across my bottom lip. "You know, I don't think living down here would be too bad. It's cozy but not too small town, but not overwhelming either. It's this perfect in-between where a fifteen-minute drive can get you out by the peace of the water or the buzz of a city."

"That's good to hear," Bethany says, "and I'm sorry to keep prying when you're obviously going through a religious experience each time you take a bite, but I'd love to be sure that you're serious about my Anders."

This was expected, of course. You can't position yourself as someone's partner, especially one who isn't known for showing his girlfriends off, and not expect them to have questions and suspicions.

Bethany goes on. "I'm sure he's told you a bit about his upbringing, but I consider Anders to be my son. He was my firstborn baby, and I know he seems like he's always put together, like he takes everything on the chin—I mean, he was the best man at his first love's wedding.

He'll never complain about a thing, but that doesn't mean he isn't hurt or angry or any negative emotion he likes to hide away."

She reaches over and grabs my hand in hers. "Ever since he was a kid, he's tried to be perfect. At first, I think he was worried I wouldn't want him since he wasn't technically mine, so he cooked and cleaned and barely made a sound because he thought if he was invisible, I wouldn't want to kick him out."

A habit created from fear. I recognize it. I know what it's like to live that way. And maybe that's why he feels so familiar, like someone who's been carrying too much for too long, just like me.

Imagining the child version of Anders feeling that way, running around trying to be perfect, filled with worries no child should have, makes my chest ache. Even in the short time I've been around him, I can see it clearly. Even when I've been unreasonable or overly emotional, he's just taken it in stride and maneuvered the conversation, easing my worry like it was second nature.

"You understand," Bethany says to me, "my worry that he'll be taken advantage of. I know he's this strong man, and he'd hate that I'm speaking this way about him. But you're something new, unfamiliar, and I want to make sure that this is real for you, because I guarantee it is to Anders."

You're wrong. So incredibly wrong, but of course, I cannot speak those words here to her. I wonder if she'll stay by Anders's side when he comes up with whatever breakup story after I finish up here. Or will she continue this quiet worry, unable to voice concerns to Anders directly, and building up anxiety?

I wish that I could be here to ease her worry when she does.

But that's impossible, and I shouldn't care about it anyway. But I do. I can't lie to myself about it. Already I care about Bethany, and Olive, and Valerie. Even if it's been a short time getting to know them, they've treated me well enough, and at the end of the day, they're just people who love their family members so deeply that it hurts.

And that's something I understand fully.

So I say something I know to be true, even if this thing between Anders and me is fake. Maybe not the attraction, but the real relationship, of course, is something that'll never happen.

I squeeze her hand. "I'm never going to hurt Anders."

"Thank you." She squeezes back. "Now, it's getting a little too heavy here. Olive, give it to Lucy."

"Huh?"

Olive dips her hand into a bag beside her, then drops a tiny white box in front of me.

"Open it," they say in unison when I freeze.

I do, and within it is the lily necklace I fell in love with at the market. My heart feels like it's been squeezed tightly, like a wet rag, and wrung dry. "No," I say. "You didn't have to get me this."

"I didn't have to, but I certainly wanted to," Bethany answers. "I wish you and my son a long and happy relationship."

Oh no. The guilt running through me intensifies, almost burns as the emotion passes through my body. It's not that I didn't think Anders's family would be excited to see him seemingly enjoying his time with someone new.

It just didn't occur to me that the possibility of them placing that happiness on me would make *me* happy too.

And I have no right to be.

Not just because this whole thing with Anders is a lie, though that's reason enough. But because sometimes, in a small voice, I question if down the line, I deserve a place beside anyone at all.

I've spent most of my life being the one who held everything together. My value was always tied to what I could do for someone else. That was my role: the responsible one, the strong one, the provider. And I was good at it.

But I've accomplished so little lately, at least by the standards I set for myself. I'm not sure I even have anything worth sharing with someone else, let alone this family who cares for each other deeply and easily and has no financial struggles of their own.

So when Bethany looks at me like I'm the kind of woman her son deserves, when Olive and Valerie smile at me like I belong here, it does something to me. Something warm and scary.

Because under different circumstances, I would want to accept their acceptance of me.

I want to believe that kindness like this could be meant for me, that I'm worth it, but what do I have to show for it? What about me is worthy of being loved when my life is such a mess? When *I'm* such a current mess.

I come up with nothing, and I shut the box gently.

17.

Bethany and Olive honk the horn as they drive off, leaving me alone when I reach the front door of Anders's place. I let myself in with the key he gave me, the necklace hanging around my neck, heavy as a weight, and head to the living room.

When he hears me approach, Anders attempts to get up from the long corner of the couch but stops midway, pressing his hand over his face. "You're back," he says, his voice strained.

My pace quickens, and I drop my gift bag on the coffee table and stand by him. "Are you okay?"

"Yes," he says, removing his hands from his face to reveal dark, thick bags under his eyes. His hair is soaked at the tips, as if he just took a shower, but when I see moisture at the center of his shirt and the sides of his brow, I realize it's sweat.

Immediately, I place my hand on his forehead and neck—he's burning.

"Oh my God." I grip his face in my hands. "You have a fever."

"It's not too bad," he says with a strained smile.

"Why didn't you tell me? I could have picked something up for you." I keep moving my hand around his face, looking for a cool spot, but he's hot everywhere.

"At first I thought maybe I was just hungover, but after a while, I just felt worse. I'm better now, I swear."

"Liar." I let him go and head to the fridge. After a quick scan of the shelves, I find there's nothing to aid with a fever. I scour through the cabinets next, when he appears beside me, laying a shaky hand on my arm.

"I'm fine, I promise. Tell me about your day?"

"You can barely stand straight," I say, and even I hear the anger in my voice. I'm not sure why that's the emotion choosing to appear, but it makes me move with purpose and speed. I grab his arm and drag him to his room.

"Lucinda," he says, his eyes barely open.

"Lie down." I shove him, and I know he's sick because he's usually a rock. At my force, he plops right onto the bed. "Have you eaten? Drunk? Taken any medicine?"

"I'm—"

"Say you're fine one more time and I'll choke you out, I swear to God."

He laughs, then coughs, and I rush to the kitchen to bring him a cup of water. When I'm back, he's leaning on the headboard. After he takes a few sips, I ask him again what he's had today.

"I can't keep anything down, so don't make me anything." He drops the glass on the bedside table. "And I took some pain medicine for the headaches."

"How long ago?"

He pauses, like he can't remember.

"I'm taking your car," I say, "and getting some things from the corner store. Do not tell me not to, and you better be in this exact same position when I get back or the choke out happens—and I promise you, I will do it."

"Yes, ma'am."

My time at the store is brief and efficient. With Taina being a sickly kid, I know exactly what to look for in each aisle and what mixtures of medicine combat all symptoms without causing negative reactions. Though my time in his car is confusing—there are way too many buttons, and everything looks a lot farther from the vehicle when you're inside, and there's a small scratch from a curb I'll have to apologize for later.

For now, I let myself back in and find Anders exactly how I left him.

"Good boy," I say, dropping one of my plastic bags on the bed. I pull out an energy drink for the electrolytes and start popping open the pills, gathering the mix in my palm. "Take this." I hold the pills and the drink toward him.

"I don't want to put you out," he says.

And all I can think of is little baby Anders, cleaning up after himself, making barely a sound, locking himself away in his room, fearful of being a bother.

"All I want is to make you feel better," I say, my brows pulling together.

He holds my gaze a moment, softening despite his rising fever, before taking the pills. How many times was he sick and suffered through it without the comfort of a loved one? Just lying in bed in pain, waiting for it to pass?

When he finishes, I take the bottle and leave it beside him. He grips my wrist. "Why do you look sad?"

I gaze down at his fingers on me, then lean in and wrap my arms around him in a tight hug. He stiffens, then eases, pulling me closer to him. And I think of Bethany saying he just goes with the flow, makes this easy-to-like version of himself, and I wonder if even this hug is that too. Just reacting to me for my comfort. Maybe he doesn't want to touch me at all, right now.

I pull away, and he brings his hands to my shoulders, his brows bunching. "What was that for? Was girls' day that torturous?"

"No," I answer, "it was perfect, and fun, and I want Bethany to adopt me." I press my finger against his chest. "The hug was for kid Anders."

"Excuse me?"

"You know," I say, "if I do anything you don't like, you can tell me. You don't have to appease me because you think it's the right thing to do. Tell me to leave you alone if you need to. And you should do that to anyone else too."

He gives me a little shake. "What are you talking about?"

I think the fever is making it hard for him to keep up.

"Lie down." I pull at his arm.

His gaze is trained on me, laser focused. Whatever he's thinking, I have no inkling, but he shifts and does as I say. I reach into the bag, snap the tiny ice pack I got, and place it on his head.

"I'm going to make you something that I promise you can keep down," I tell him. "Just wait here. If you fall asleep, that's okay—I can warm it up later."

His hand reaches for my wrist again, sliding down until he holds my palm in his clammy, hot hand. I brace myself for his opposition, but he watches me carefully again, and I wish I could figure out what's going on in his head.

"I'll be right back," I promise, and he lets me go.

I bring the bag with me to the kitchen, then get to work, moving around as quietly as I can while putting the food together. Each time I use a dish or utensil, I wash it so Anders doesn't see any mess if he slips out of the room.

I peel the yuca in my hand—no cutting board here—like I've done a hundred times before, the motion muscle memory from watching my mom do it when I was little. The kitchen fills slowly with the scent of sofrito sizzling in oil. I drop in the chunks of meat and vegetables and pour in water to let the sancocho stew in the pot.

My stomach keeps turning on itself as I stir the stew. I hate when people are sick. It's always a reminder, a trigger, watching Mom hunched over the toilet or the trash or the floor when she couldn't get to the bathroom fast enough. Watching her gave me this unreasonable anxiety—that anyone sick isn't just sick, but finally showing symptoms of some grave disease that had been hiding within them all along.

I made *myself* sick countless times taking care of Taina. I never showed her, but every day her anemia gave her a bad spell or she had any kind of virus, I would spend all night taking turns watching her breathe, then vomiting in the bathroom from fear.

Of course, Anders is just sick. A fever is normal. Nobody goes through life without it. Yet my chest tightens and releases like the claw in those rigged machines at an arcade—pinching closed over and over. It's been a while since I felt like this, but I quickly wipe away a tear when one slips, stirring the pot until it boils.

After the stew is cooked through, I pour it into a bowl and bring everything I need back to Anders. I pause at the doorway.

Now that he thinks he's on his own, his hand is over his eyes like they're pounding from pain, and he holds the ice pack to his neck. His lips turn down.

Anxiety gnaws at my organs.

My tiny container of medicine falls from my tray, and Anders jolts up, a strained smile on his face.

I try to do the same as I approach him. "This is sancocho," I explain. "It's a stew, a mix of veggies and broth. I used chicken for it—it'll be better on your stomach. Just try a little. Don't force yourself too much. But you do need something in you."

He motions to take it from me, then places it on his thighs. After gathering a spoonful of broth, he brings it up to his lips.

I grip his wrist, lean down, and blow when I spot the steam rising from the spoon. When I pull away, my cheeks heating up, he doesn't give me a funny look or call me dramatic—he just tastes it.

He sucks in a breath. I can't tell if it's relief for having something in his stomach or if he's trying not to get sick. Then, he takes another spoonful, and another, until just an ounce of anxiety stops eating my insides.

The bowl is halfway empty before he says, "I think I have to take a break."

I snatch it from him, dropping it on the tray so hard some broth splashes out and lands on my hand. I hiss, jerking away.

Anders grasps my palm, inspecting the skin. "Are you okay?" he says, filled with concern as if I've given myself a third-degree burn, as if he isn't the one with glassy eyes and a head drooping on his neck.

"Yes." I pull away, moving the tray to the bedside table, and grab my next potion.

I open the Vicks VapoRub and gather some on my finger. "Lie down?" I ask this time.

He opens his mouth, then stills when he sees whatever look of pathetic worry I have on my face, and does just that. I swipe the eucalyptus ointment on his forehead, then rub small circles at the base of his neck, moving down to the center of his chest.

"This is every Puerto Rican's medicine for whatever sickness you can possibly have," I say, trying to lighten the mood and explain while I'm lathering him up to smell like a human candy cane. "There's no science behind it, but I swear it never fails."

I sit on the bed and lay a hand by his feet. "I need to take off your socks for a moment." He does his head tilt, and the familiar sight eases another sliver of worry. "Please?"

He nods, and I remove the fabric. Then, I gather a hefty amount of Vicks and rub hard, small circles all over the bottom of his foot. Even when there's enough of it on his skin, I keep massaging. Anders's eyes flutter shut, and I keep going to give him respite from the fever until my thumbs cramp. After, I do the same to the other foot, then cover them with his socks.

"My mom always said this will suck up the fever," I explain. "All the sick will leave from your feet."

I rub the excess from my hand with a paper towel, gathering everything on the tray to remove. "I'll let you try to sleep." I grab the tray. "But I'll be right next door if you need me."

He takes my wrist again, his thumb running over my skin. "Lucinda," he says, his voice raspy and sleepy. "Why do you look so sad?" he asks again.

"Me?" I say, way too perky to be believable. "I think your fever is making you delirious."

When I try to pull away, he leans to me, wrapping his arms around my waist, and pulls me on the bed with him, my body over his.

Anders brings a shaky hand to my cheek. "I'm okay," he promises, though I didn't ask if he was. But in my head, in my heart, I keep worrying that he's not. But he doesn't know that.

"Of course you are," I say, and I'm not sure why my words come out shaky and unsure.

Just as I'm unsure why, humiliatingly, my eyes burn with unspilled tears.

"Of course I am," he says, using the little strength he has to position me beside him, my head tucked by his chest as his arm wraps around me, his other hand rubbing circles into my back.

"It's just a fever," he says into my hair, caressing me. "It'll pass quick. I'm completely okay."

"Okay," I repeat, nestling myself closer to him.

The more he traces circles into my back, the more the movement in my stomach settles, and my eyelids grow heavy. I know I should move, give him space, take care of him, but whenever I try to pull away, he tightens his hold on me until I give up, and murmurs small, soft reassurances that *he's* okay, but they feel like he's saying *I'm* okay.

Until all the worry in the pit of my stomach subsides completely.

18.

"Lucinda." Something hard and gentle shakes me. "Lucinda, it's me."

My eyes barely have the strength to open, and I wave the hands off me, pressing my face into my pillow. "No, thank you."

A chuckle, and then, "Having some good dreams?"

The previous night catches up to me in one swift moment. My eyes blink open, and Anders towers above me on the edge of the bed, his aftershave enveloping me. "Are you okay?" I get on my knees, pressing my hand to his neck, his head a little too out of reach at this angle. His skin is warm, but not at all hot.

He presses my hand in between both of his. "I'm a lot better, I promise." He smiles. "I think there's some residual fever in my feet, but that's about it."

My cheeks grow hot at the memory of massaging Vicks onto his heels.

"I have to go," he says while I try to think of what to say. "I would have let you sleep in more, but I didn't want you to wake up and me be gone."

"What time is it?" I ask. "Where are you going?"

"A little after seven," he answers. "Aunt Bethany is helping her farm owners with a horse that got out in the middle of the night. I'm going to bring Olive to her volleyball league for her."

"What a cool kid," I say, a yawn escaping me.

"I'll be a couple hours," he explains. "Go back to sleep."

"Okay," I say, shutting my eyes as if even speaking with him is exhausting. He lays me down, tucks me under the covers, and I wait until I hear the door click shut.

I open one eye, listen for the sound of the front door doing the same, and then I sit up, fully awake, and shove my face into the pillow and scream.

I slept with Anders.

Not sexually, not with his fever, but in the same bed, pressed against each other, cuddling without moving an inch away. Sleeping together without having sex somehow feels way more intimate.

I sit up. "No, no, it's not a big deal," I say aloud, like an insane person. "I just wanted to be close in case he needed me, and he wanted the same, in case he got sicker. Just being considerate."

That would be more believable if the whole dry humping on the pool table hadn't happened, but you know what, that's already in the past. Basically, a faded memory. Forgotten as vegetables at the back of the fridge you swore you'd incorporate into your meals.

These are all problems for future me. I'm not going to sit here and replay the events in my head until I'm crazy. Anders isn't even here to discuss them with, if I knew exactly how to discuss them at all.

I shoot up and get ready for the day, shower, change, lather myself in lotions.

The first part of the morning I spend scrubbing down Anders's house. I remove his sheets and stuff them in the washer, like it'll erase the memory of my body on them beside his. I organize his shelves, dusting where I can, wiping down glass, sweeping and mopping as if I'm getting paid extra for it.

By that afternoon, the skin around my nails is almost entirely missing. Anders is still out—swindled by Olive for an impromptu shopping spree—and my brain is hunting for something to do.

The bridesmaid fitting isn't till tomorrow, and I'm not getting any hits on the dating app, so I count it as a dead lead. With Anders busy, there's nothing I need to do at the moment, but every time I sit still, I think of his hands rubbing circles on my back.

I think of him sick with a fever, dealing with his own pain, and still spending his time trying to comfort me, and cannot for the life of me smother the way it makes my heart pound.

I shoot up and go to my room, snatching the business card from Dainese. Instead of sitting around thinking about Anders, wondering how he feels, if we're just getting lost in the act or if we care about each other, I decide to busy myself with something I love. Something that makes sense when everything else doesn't.

Without a car, it takes me an hour to walk to the tiny shelter, just at the end of the beach. The humidity has stuck to my skin like a second layer, but when I enter K9 Friends, the air conditioner soothes the gathering of sweat on my skin.

It's a modest place, tighter than Save a Paw, and the cages holding the animals don't give them much room to do anything other than stretch their legs. But they're all painted in blues and yellows—colors dogs can see—and filled with cozy bright blankets and toys, and with thick tablets in each one playing videos of birds chirping through trees. Dog TV.

There's nobody at the tiny computer desk in the far corner, but I spot a head of pin-straight hair by an open cage.

Dainese is inside, carefully brushing the hair of a tiny Yorkie, humming as she does. She's smiling, too, and she looks like she loves this dog as much as she loved Sora. A true dog lover, that's what she thought of me, and I see the same in her, hunched over, soothing after each brush.

It reminds me of the first time I held a stray—after Storm—in my arms and felt, for just a moment, like I was doing something right. Like I mattered. Because if a terrified animal could look at me like I was safety, like I could be trusted, then even at times when I didn't feel useful to anyone, it meant that someone—even a dog—needed me.

I remain silent until she finishes. She shuts the gate, then yelps when she spots me standing there.

There's a domino effect from the noise, and a majority of the dogs howl and bark to mirror her worry.

"It's you." Dainese's eyes go wide. "I didn't think you'd actually come."

"Lucy." I hold out a hand. "And should I be offended?"

She shakes it firmly, twice, then lets go. "No, sorry, it's just. So many people say they will, but life gets in the way a lot."

"Good thing for you I don't have a life."

She laughs, and I can see her shoulders relax. "Wow, come, let's talk outside until they settle."

I follow her out, back under the humid, cloudy sky. "I'm Dainese," she tells me in case I forgot, leading me to a small bench by the front door overlooking the stretch of beach. "My mom, Bibi, owns this place, but she's always busy helping my sister with her triplets, so it's usually just me."

My eyes widen. "God bless your sister."

"She certainly needs him to." She whistles.

"How many dogs do you take in?"

"We can fit ten but only have the funds to care for five. There's another shelter, Fur-Friends Sanctuary, on the opposite side of town, that we work with when we can, sending them dogs we can't board. They're lovely over there."

"And it's just you caring for the five?"

"Well, it used to be my mom, my sister, and me, but you know—"

"Triplets," I supply for her.

"Yeah, newborns too. We usually get college students volunteering for the summer, but this year has been a little sparse. Still, it's not too bad. Five is manageable."

"How long have you worked here?" I ask, and I appreciate that there's no awkwardness between us, no need for small talk. We immediately speak like we're already friends just having a catch-up.

"Since I was a kid," she explains. "My dad started this place, and I was always his little shadow. He passed a couple years ago, so my mom has taken over, but she's not really a hands-on person." She then asks, "You said you work at a shelter?"

"Yeah, back in New York. Boards about twenty dogs, which is great when you think about saving that many from the streets, but hard to give them all enough attention. Started volunteering when I was a teen."

"What made you want to?"

"Long story short, the most precious dog I rescued from the street, and I couldn't move on since." Short story long, working with dogs gave me something no job or relationship ever did—purpose.

"Ah, there's always the first." She gives me a gentle tap. "Well, I won't beat around the bush. If you're willing to help, I have two dogs to wash, and three of them are going to need some moral support when the vet techs get here to give them their vaccines. Though, today is a good day—one of them, Shelly, is getting adopted. But that'll take up some of my time. I don't mean to ask for help the first time you visit—"

"I'm in." I stand. "Use me as much as you can."

She joins me. "I don't have any money to offer, but my mom is coming in the afternoon to feed me donuts and matcha, and you're welcome to have your fill."

"Deal."

The only difference between here and Save a Paw is the space and equipment. Everything here is thoroughly used, from brushes to collars, and there's not a popular name brand in sight—at least, for the washes and grooming care—but the food is from the most reputable vet-tested brand. The team here tightens the wallet for smaller things, but food, the most important, doesn't seem to have a limit.

It's another thing I love most about this work—not just the dogs, but the people who care about them. The ones who make something out of almost nothing. Who don't get applause for it but keep showing up anyway.

Save a Paw is my dream; I built it with hopeful hands. A place where I could finally prove—to the world, and to myself—that I'm not a failure. That I have purpose. That I belong. That I can be a part of something that doesn't fall apart when life does. While we work, Dainese talks to fill up the space. As someone who was raised with the most talkative human alive (Taina), I'm no stranger to a constant stream of chitchat. I don't have to nod or grunt or display signs of listening (I am) because Dainese just assumes I'm keeping up.

Even when we move on from my laborious tasks—like trying to wash a hyperactive husky in a closet of a shower—Dainese barely changes tone.

She tells me Sora's story, of the loving home he had with an elderly couple who passed within weeks of each other, and how the displacement brought him here, and more.

She checks her athletic wristwatch and says, "The couple adopting should be here soon, perfect timing." She grabs a towel from beneath her desk drawer and tosses it to me. "Then we can eat."

"Sure," I say, approaching the Yorkie's cage. "Good luck, buddy, be good."

On the door, there is a paper taped up, reading **One month at shelter.** One month in, and already finding a home. It's amazing, and I'm so happy for the cutie, but I move to the end of the hall and spot Sora lying on his side, wide eyes looking up at me.

Six months at the shelter.

If I'm being honest with myself, I know he very likely won't be getting a new home. Senior dogs already have the least chance of getting adopted, second only to a dog with a disability. Combine them both, and Sora has no chance.

How many times has he lain here and watched another dog leave with a family?

I find Dainese at the desk, typing away. "Can I take Sora for a walk?"

She glances up, her sharp features softening. "I know, I feel bad too." She reads my mind. "Go ahead, it's muggy, but not hot, so he can stay out longer."

"I'll be back," I promise, and erase the image of running to an airport and bringing Sora to Taina's place with me.

I grab a stray ball and a harness for Sora and let myself into his cage. His tail does a single wag, like he smothered his excitement as soon as it built up. I get just one more wag when I wrap the collar around him and gently tug the leash toward the door, making sure I'm in his direct view.

He follows, and I maintain a slow enough pace he doesn't feel like we're rushing, but fast enough that he can feel free to be excited. I steal a bottle of water left on the windowsill in case he gets thirsty and head out.

We wander toward the back, descending a small hill leading directly to the sandy shores. It must be the weather, and the late-afternoon weekday, that has this side of the beach empty. Only our feet leave prints on the sand as we walk together.

Sora keeps watching the water, but I can't tell if it's with affection or fear. I scan the beach again, making sure we're truly alone, then unhook his leash. I pop off my shoes, toss them closer to the sand, then jog to the tide.

Sora watches me for a while, letting the cool water surround my feet then disappear. Like a game of double Dutch—hopping in place, waiting for the best moment—Sora waits until the tide pulls back, runs after it, then runs away when it comes for its turn of tag.

I join him, running forward and then away until my chest burns and reminds me the last time I ran a mile was a year ago. I settle for tossing the ball in the shallow water for him while I catch my breath.

When the ball is lost, he simply runs into the water. My heart pounds for a split second, waiting to see if he's able to swim, but it seems he's experienced enough, so I drop down and sit on the damp sand, just above the tide line.

I keep glancing up at Sora as I pull out my phone and type in "Mason Maguda"—the name of the man who offered to buy Joshua's share of Save a Paw.

Information I'm not supposed to have, but Taina knows how to dig, and I asked her to find it.

Unlike me, Mason comes from a long line of animal lovers. His family lives and breathes this stuff. Some are vet techs. Some, emergency surgeons. A couple are dog walkers and groomers. Mason himself owned a private veterinary practice for years and now, according to his website, wants to dedicate his life to helping as many dogs as possible.

There's a site called Vet-Vetter, where people post uncensored reviews—nothing filtered, nothing deleted. Every review under his name is glowing. Clients say he goes above and beyond. That there's no one better.

And here I am, sitting on a beach with sand between my toes, competing against someone who's actually qualified. A nepo baby with real credentials and multiple degrees directly related to animals.

It sucks. Not because he's a bad option—because he's a good one, a great one, actually.

Because even I have to admit—if it can't be me, he makes sense.

But I love Save a Paw. I know the dogs by name. I know the quirks of our plumbing system and how long it takes the heating to kick in in the back kennels. I forced myself under Joshua's wing, learned how to run payroll, fix the books, talk to donors, manage inventory—all of it. Not because it came naturally, but because I refused to let the dogs go without what they needed.

Mason may have the resume. But I have the heart.

And yeah, I know that sounds like the kind of thing you say when you don't have enough credentials to back yourself up. But it's true. I would die for animals.

If this doesn't work—if I can't save Valerie from this wedding disaster—I'll lose my shot at Save a Paw. I'll lose the only place that's ever felt like mine.

Like he heard me thinking of him, Anders's name appears on my screen.

I answer on the first ring.

"Hey."

"Hey," he says. "Where are you?"

I look at the time, and it's already four. "Long story, but I'm at a dog shelter."

"Dog shelter?" he repeats.

In the background, a loud, young, excited voice echoes, "Dog shelter?" There's a rustling of movement, and then, Olive has the phone. "Are you with Sora?"

"Hang on," I say, FaceTiming her.

She picks up immediately, and I turn the camera to Sora playing in the water. Olive squeals, then snaps, "You said you'd bring me!"

"I still can," I offer.

"Can we go now?"

"That's up to your uncle."

There's another rustling, and I take the camera off, bring the phone to my ear just as Anders is back on the line. "Will you send me your location?"

"Sure," I say, then ask, "How are you feeling?"

"Better, thank you for that."

My cheeks heat at the warmth in his words, and I hang up before I say something like *Thank you for existing.*

It takes them about twenty minutes to arrive, and when they do, Olive—dressed in the cutest strawberry-print matching set—takes off running toward the sand and promptly face-plants.

Anders immediately scoops her up, inspects her for injury, and murmurs a string of comforting words I can't quite make out. Whatever he says makes Olive's slumped shoulders slowly straighten.

The sight tugs at me with a strange mix of nostalgia and loss—feelings that catch me off guard. It shouldn't hurt, but it does. Watching them together reminds me of Taina and me—of the kind of closeness that fills you with burning warmth.

It's been a long time since I've had someone to comfort, or someone who looked to me like that—for safety, for softness. The absence hollows out my chest.

When they approach me, I plant a smile on my face and remind Olive that Sora is deaf, so she should try to let him see her first.

She agrees, then shoos me off to join him.

Anders approaches soon after, his white shirt rolled at the sleeves so almost every inch of his biceps is revealed. I give him a wave, he returns it with a smile, before standing beside me, overlooking Olive and Sora.

"Olive told me about Sora," Anders says. "Did you steal him?"

I chuckle, then sigh. "Just letting him out so he doesn't see another dog get a new family while he sleeps on his own again."

Anders places a hand on my lower back for comfort, and I lean into him. He moves so that his hand covers the side of my waist, and I'm tucked at his side as we watch the two play.

"Are you a dog person?" I tilt my chin to look up at him. "Or a cat one? Or anti-animal?"

"Not sure," he answers. "Aunt Bethany always had allergies, so we never had pets. Some of my friends had cats growing up, and I liked when they'd come around while I visited their house. Never really been around a dog."

"They're angels," I explain though he didn't ask. "They love you no matter what, even if you suck as a human being. It's why so many dogs get hurt. They're overly trusting, and it leads to them being attacked, and injured, and still they come back to us."

His features pinch together as he frowns and squeezes my cheeks. "You look so upset."

"A polite way to say *rough*, because I spent hours showering dogs, and smell like one too. Sorry to your shirt, you're going to reek in a minute."

He presses a kiss on my matted hair in answer, and it makes my stomach do a tiny dance.

"I'm sad to bring him back," I tell him. "That's the worst part of working with dogs. You can't take them all in, but you want to."

"How do you manage it?" he asks.

"Lots of crying, and wine, and more crying. Sometimes I sleep in the cages overnight. It's very dramatic."

He turns us, his hands entirely around my waist as he leans down to me. "You're an incredibly empathetic person."

My hands slip up his chest. "So are you."

He smiles, and moves closer, as if to press a kiss to my lips. I jerk back, fanning myself like the heat has suddenly become unbearable.

Since we met, it feels like my brain and heart have been playing this game of fact or fiction whenever we touch, or steal a glance, or speak. Is it real? Is he playing it up for an audience? Are we just getting lost in the act? Is he genuinely just charming, albeit dangerously flirtatious?

But I already know it's real—that's what makes it harder.

He's not playing anything up for an audience. He's genuine. Honest in a way that feels rare. He is a good man.

One who may be easy to take advantage of. And I'm not a good enough person to stop from grabbing his hand. "Remember our night playing pool?"

He coughs, then glances over my shoulder, back to me. "Yes, but maybe we should talk about that another time."

My cheeks heat as I shake my head. "No, not that part. The part when I scammed you and you bet a wish."

"Oh, yes." Then, again, I swear he can read my mind. He says, "Lucinda, I've never owned a dog before. I have no idea what I'm doing."

"I could help you"—I squeeze his hand—"and it'd be so much fun. You'll have a little running buddy. And company, so you'll never be lonely. And Sora is such a sweet thing. Dainese says he never barks, even when all the other dogs are getting rowdy. He's potty trained, and he only eats twice a day. He's deaf, so you have to make sure he sees you before you touch him, but he won't get violent, you just don't want to scare him."

"Lucinda." He removes his hands from mine and grips my cheeks. "Breathe."

"Can you promise to at least think about it?" I beg. "I can answer any questions you have while you do."

"I—"

Olive barrels into us, Sora close behind.

"Look," she says, jumping in front of Sora and tracing a circle with her pointer finger. Immediately, Sora plops down into a roll. Olive claps her hands. "He's so cute, how does he know to do that?"

I lean down, hold out my hand. Sora places his paw in it, letting me shake. Olive makes a delighted sound.

Sora moves from me, then circles the new face, his nose sniffing around Anders before rubbing his snout on the end of his jeans, then plopping down to lie beside him with a sigh.

Anders and I meet each other's gazes, his eyes wide and soft in a way I didn't have to manipulate. He leans down, lets Sora see his palm before giving him a head rub. Sora nuzzles into him, grateful, licking Anders's hand in thanks.

Olive rushes back toward the water in search of a lost flip-flop, and Anders continues to pet Sora. I sneakily snap a photo of the pair with plans to use it as ammo later.

He catches me, and sighs. "Is anyone interested in him?"

My heart races off. "Nobody. He's old and deaf, and nobody ever takes him out for walks," I say, though that last part is pulled right from my ass because I'm not sure it's true.

But Anders pouts, gives Sora another rub. "I travel so often—"

"There are plenty of dog-sitters," I say, gesturing to Olive in the shallow end, "and one willing preteen."

"Aunt Bethany would kill me if I brought a dog for a sleepover."

"We can stuff her with allergy pills."

He stands, and as if Sora's own heart is drawn to the hope, too, he follows Anders over to me. "I'll think about it," he says. I smile widely, and Anders holds up a finger. "I said *think*, Lucinda."

I hold up my hands. "I didn't say anything."

He taps the side of his head. "I heard it just the same."

"Well, can you hear this?" I ask, then lean over and press a kiss on his cheek.

But as I pull back, he grabs my arm—gently, but purposefully—and draws me back in. His lips land on mine, direct and certain, like this is something we do, like he's done it one hundred times, and he could land his lips on mine without having to aim.

For a second, I'm frozen. Everything about this feels startlingly real.

Him. And me. And this.

His mouth is warm. Familiar, somehow, like my many dreams and fantasies about the feel of his mouth on mine were memories instead of hopeless fabrications.

When he pulls back, I'm still blinking, heart stuttering. Then Sora yawns loudly and settles beside Anders, curling up directly on his shoes. Distracted, Anders looks down, sympathy pooling over his features, and he meets my gaze again. "I have a dog now, don't I?"

I hear what he says, but it feels like he's just reached into my chest and peeled the rib cage apart, grabbed hold of my heart and said, *I own this now.*

19.

Since Bethany is still helping out at the farm when we finish up with Sora, Olive comes back to Anders's place with us. We didn't mention Sora in front of her, in case Anders changed his mind. But I told Dainese he was considering—so he thinks, but I know after he struggled to close the cage on Sora for five minutes, he will agree—and she stuffed a tote bag full of information packets and forms and mochi donuts.

When we get inside, I lay out the rest of the pastries on a plate and reply to a dozen texts from Taina asking for life updates every hour. I feel a little guilty since we usually text throughout the day, so I send a detailed account—sans Anders—and pictures of Sora.

While Olive and I finish up the last of the donuts, Anders walks in from a short call.

"Aunt Bethany is staying by the farm, you're sleeping here," he tells Olive, then me, with an explanation. "It's a couple of hours away, and her astigmatism is bad at night. She'll be back in the morning."

Olive makes a victorious sound, then grips my arm. "Let's watch all the Marvel movies."

"Let's," Anders says, grabbing Olive's shoulders and pushing her in the direction of the hall, "take a shower before anything else."

She rolls her eyes. "I was in the ocean. The salt water already disinfected me."

"A creative approach," Anders says, "but not good enough. Shower."

Olive shakes a thumb down in Anders's face, the preteen equivalent of the middle finger, and I have to smother my laugh until she's out of the room.

Anders stands there, puzzled. "Did she just flip me off?"

The laugh escapes me. "I'm pretty sure."

"I used to be her favorite person." He grabs my hand, which is still holding half a donut, brings it to his mouth and takes a bite.

I use the edge of my thumb to wipe stray frosting from his lip. "I'm sure you're still at least in the top ten."

He barks out a laugh. "At least." He moves around me, trapping me by laying his hands on the counter by my hips. "You all set for tomorrow? Need anything from me?"

I shake my head. "All good, don't you worry. Unless you have insider information of what to expect from the bridal party."

He grimaces. "Keep your purse by you. One of them, Jennifer, is a kleptomaniac."

"Excuse me?" I blink. "Maybe I shouldn't assume this, but I figured Valerie's friends would be, I guess, in a similar financial situation as she?"

He nods. "You'd be correct, but that did not stop Jennifer from stealing one of my Rolexes and Aunt Bethany's pearl earrings."

"One" of my Rolexes is a hefty reminder of our vastly different tax brackets, and I try not to flinch. No matter what I pretend, I'm not *really* a part of this life. Maybe my life's puzzle piece fits perfectly beside Anders's, but we're in different shades, presenting different pictures.

"And she keeps her around because?"

"She's actually a really nice person," he promises. "Just, use a bag with a zipper."

"Noted," I say, though if she saw what little I have, she'd probably deposit a couple of dollars into my purse.

"Hey"—Olive appears beside us, narrows her gaze between us—"are you guys in a fight?"

"Huh?" I say, as Anders asks, "What makes you say that?"

She looks to me. "All your stuff is in the guest room and in the bathroom."

"Oh." Anders looks to me, wide eyed, for help.

"Of course not," I assure her. "That's all my sister's. She came to visit." An easy thing to say since, technically, most of the clothes are hand-me-downs.

"Really?" Olive says, looking around as if Taina will suddenly appear. "I didn't know that, where is she?"

"Out with her husband," I lie. "She came to stay for a bit, now they're having a little TLC away. She'll get her things when they're back."

"I want to meet your sister," Olive says, as Anders grabs her shoulders again and starts pushing her to the hall. "Let me meet your sister."

Unable to say another lie, I give her a thumbs-up as Anders takes her away. When they leave, I begin to clean up, my stomach starting a slow descent.

Olive is such a cute kid, and it's clear she likes me. And I do her. It's a lie that they'll meet, but I know if she has any affection for me, she'd adore Taina. It would be cute to see them interact, but it seems I keep forgetting my time here comes with an expiration date.

"Lucinda," Anders says, in a tone that says it's not the first time he called my name.

"Sorry." I put down the glass I just dried. "I think I need a shower. Can I use yours?"

"Of course."

I move to his room and feel his presence shadowing me as I go. When I enter, there's a light scent of lavender.

"Thank you for cleaning the sheets," Anders says, as if the scent reminds him to. "You absolutely didn't have to do that."

"I know," I say, heading to his attached bath, "but I like to clean. Helps me clear my mind."

As I open the door, he grips the edge of it. "And what are you clearing your mind of?"

You, obviously.

Instead of voicing the thoughts, I gently shove him away. "If I don't get this layer of grime off my skin in the next sixty seconds, I'm going to puke."

He nods, then reveals my vanilla-scented bodywash from behind him like a magician. "I snagged this when Olive was searching through the drawers. Figured you wouldn't want to smell like sandalwood."

"Sandalwood and mango," I say, then immediately burn when he cocks his head as I admit not only do I like the way he smells, I know exactly what he smells like. "Okay, thanks, bye." I snatch the wash and shut the door in his face.

I take the world's coldest shower, and when it feels like my skin is going to harden into ice, I remain for another five minutes. The cold steals all thoughts. All I can focus on is the feel of it on my skin, and my teeth grinding while they chatter.

When I step out of it, the thoughts slowly make their way back to me. The first, I realize as I wrap myself in a towel, is that my clothes are all in the room I claimed to be my sister's. Would it be too suspicious to go in and sort through my suitcases when I should have my own drawer here, in Anders's room?

I open the door slowly so it doesn't creak, and peek out to see Anders hunched over his desk, swiping on a tablet with an Apple pen. There's another smaller tablet beside him, propped up on a stand, displaying text in a font that's thin on the top, thicker on the bottom, with wider space—a special font to help him read because of his dyslexia.

Curious, I tiptoe over. As I suspected, he's working on a book cover. He's on the sketching phase, so it's just two plain doodles of bodies, and on the side, a bunch of colors in dots like a digital paint palette.

I lean in to read the text when he says, "Is this your attempt at being sneaky?"

"Oh no," I say, "just nosy. If I wanted to, I could sort through all your things, and you'd never realize."

He chuckles as he finishes the curve of someone's leg. "Good to know."

"Is that the book?" I point at the propped tablet.

"Yes," he explains. "It's nice to have it as a reference when I'm working on a cover."

"Do you read the entire thing?"

"If it's interesting enough."

"Oh," I tease, "so selective."

He chuckles, then turns to face me. He stills, giving me a once-over before his gaze locks on to my face. His Adam's apple bobs. My neck warms. He clears his throat.

"My clothes are in the other room," I say.

"Right." He gets up, carefully, so that our bodies don't touch—a stark contrast from the normally easygoing way he reacts around me, and shuffles through his drawers. He pulls out a pale blue shirt and sweats. "Will this work?" His voice is this strained, polite, single tone.

"Perfectly." My own voice sounds perky, airy, and I grab the clothes from him and change in the bathroom, slowly, trying to even out my breathing. I have to roll up the pants twice so I don't trip on them, and the sleeves that probably stop just above Anders's biceps fall midway down my arm.

When I come out, Anders is pulling out the thin sheet from under the comforter. He hears the door open and gathers it to his chest.

"Olive fell asleep in your room," he says. "I'll take the couch."

"So much for movie night," I say, plopping down on the side of the bed. "What will you say you're doing if she walks out in the middle of the night and catches you on the couch?" The girl is too observant for her own good. It'll raise another red flag if she catches us sleeping separately. It's not a big deal if she knows, but if she relays that to Valerie or Bethany, it could bring too much suspicion on us. Or at least make it seem like we're in a fight when I'm trying to get close to the family.

"Okay"—he grabs a pillow and tosses it on the carpet—"I'll take the floor."

"Don't be ridiculous." I gesture to the mattress. "There's plenty of space for both of us. And we've already slept together here."

"Right," he says. "When I was delirious with a fever."

"Are you saying that the only way you'd share a bed with me is if you're delirious?" Not to mention, he didn't seem delirious when he wrapped himself around me. But adding that will feel way too angry-girlfriend-like, and I am just a phony.

"Of course not," he says, looking from the floor to the bed. I can see the wheels turning as he tries to navigate this conversation.

"Unless," I add, "you're uncomfortable. Then I can take the floor. This is your house."

Anders pinches the bridge of his nose, letting out a frustrated sigh. I'm not sure what I've done to warrant it, seeing as I'm offering to sleep on the solid floor instead of him.

When I get up, I move to where he drops the pillow, and he grips my arm as I kneel. "Lucinda," he says, "the reason I am trying not to share a bed with you is because I can barely control myself now. You're in my clothes, still wet from your shower, and in my bedroom. I am a man." The last part is said so deadpan, I can't help but laugh despite the dots of warmth sprouting throughout my body.

"You Tarzan, me Jane."

He laughs, though there is still some frustration leaking into it. "Just get in the damn bed."

I do, dropping a few pillows in the center as Anders moves to turn off the light, leaving only a sliver of moonlight to creep in from behind the sheer curtains of the windows. My eyes are adjusting, so I can't see him well when we're flooded with darkness, but I feel the mattress shift, and it steals some of my air from me as it does, like the room just lost half its oxygen supply.

"Good night," he says.

"Night."

We've been alone plenty of times, but this time, it's a little hard to breathe. We're both sober, there's nobody around watching us, and we're cloaked by the darkness while lying inches apart.

Of course I knew why Anders didn't want to share a bed, but I was trying to be nonchalant. If we're not going to acknowledge this blooming attraction between us, then I certainly am not going to be the first to say anything about it.

I link my fingers over my stomach, shutting my eyes and begging sleep to just take me. I remain like that for a few minutes before shifting, and shifting, and shifting. No matter how much I toss and turn, no position is comfortable enough for exhaustion even to pretend it's ready to blanket over me.

After what feels like hours of turning, Anders says, "Are you okay?"

I pause mid-shift. "Yup, just . . . not tired, I guess."

"Me either," he says.

I chew on my bottom lip. Now that I know he's up with me, I'm too self-conscious to keep obviously struggling to sleep. I fill the silence with, "Can I ask you a question?"

"Of course."

"Why do you work?" I ask. "Your stock makes you plenty to live off of. Why do you keep doing art?"

He hums, and I like the way it sounds, like the start of a ballad. "I love art," he starts, "and I like that people like my art enough to want it."

"Is it fun?"

"Most of the time," he says. "If I have a block, it's a little agitating, but usually it feels like relief. For me, it's like there's a bottle inside me, and when I'm not working on anything, it starts to fill up. It's an uncomfortable feeling, and it only goes away when I start to work on something. I have to keep pouring it out, so it feels light. Does that sound pretentious?"

"Not at all." I smile at the thoughtful answer, at the hint of insecurity at the end of it. Anders can feel a little perfect, and that can be intimidating, but really, I'm learning, even if I think he's without flaws, he doesn't feel the same. It makes him more human, more relatable instead of this rich, handsome, perfect man who always seems to know what to say.

Whenever I learn something about Anders, I'm eager to dig for even more. Like one taste makes me crave his whole life story. "How did you start getting into art?" I ask. "What's your favorite way to work?" I sit up, lean on my arm, and face his blurry silhouette. "I found your website with your pseudonym, well, my sister did, and I looked through your stuff. I like your paintings, the landscape collection."

He's quiet for so long, and panic seeps into me. Was that too far? Maybe I should have kept it to myself, but when lying so much to other people, it's nice to speak honestly. With Anders, there's really no need to lie, not when it's just us.

"Or," I say, "we can just go to sleep now."

There's a rustle of movement, and my eyes adjust to see his silhouette mirror my stance, leaning his head on his hand, facing me. "It's just a little embarrassing."

My mouth hangs open for a moment before I say, "I'm literally a jobless, houseless, twenty-eight-year-old two-time divorcée, and you're worried about being embarrassed in front of me?"

"I hate when you talk about yourself that way," Anders says. "Like those facts are these permanent identifiers for who you are, like it's all you are. They're not."

It stuns me briefly, has my heart racing, and my stomach doing somersaults. I'm guilty of self-deprecating here and there, and speaking to myself that way doesn't feel like too big of a deal, at least to me.

But I'd be lying if I said it didn't feel good to have someone defend me, even if it's from myself.

"Anyway." I shift gears. "We're talking about you."

"And I'd much rather talk about you."

"Just answer the damn question, Anders," I snap.

He chuckles, and it feels like the noise brushes over my skin, tickling where it touches. When he finishes, he makes a small sigh. "When I was a kid, before I realized what was really going on, I used to think my mom was coming to get me. That one day she'd open up Aunt Bethany's door and bring me home with her."

"Oh, Anders."

"It's okay, all in the past," he says. "Back then, Aunt Bethany would take me with her everywhere, to try to distract me from the fact that my mom had left me. Whenever we'd go somewhere really nice, I tried to draw it as best as I could, to impress my mom. I'd give it to Aunt Bethany to mail to her, wishing she'd see one and hurry home to me. When she didn't, I thought maybe I didn't show how beautiful the places were, so I tried better the next time. Aunt Bethany would supply charcoal, or paint, or pencils, anything that I wanted. My mother never came, but I found that creating something helped fill the void she left behind. At least, temporarily.

"Aunt Bethany is a voracious reader, and we used to do this thing where she'd explain to me the setting of some fantasy book she was reading, or gush about her favorite character, and then she'd ask me to try and create it for her. So, that's where the book illustrations came in."

When I'm silent, Anders adds, "I told you it was embarrassing."

"No, no, not at all." The words come rapidly. "I just got so incredibly sad that I had to think of really angry things to keep from crying."

He offers me a warm laugh. "Lucinda, no, I'm fine."

"I know," I say, then add, "But are you? Do you ever still wish for your mom to knock on your door? I do . . ." I hold out a hand he can barely see, probably. "I know our situations are entirely different, though."

"At this point in my life, I'm pretty content with the understanding that Aunt Bethany is the closest thing I have to a mom."

"You never refer to her as your mom," I point out. "But you've only known Bethany. Is that something you've ever considered?"

"I-I," he stutters, then says, "I wouldn't want to burden her with that, especially now when she has an actual child."

It would absolutely break Bethany's heart to hear that. To know that her worries and heartaches, stemming from watching Anders continually make himself as small as possible because he views himself as a burden, still have a hold on Anders even now.

And it's currently breaking mine, to see that someone so kind, and so lovely, and so generous, views himself in this way, and it makes me realize why Anders was offended with how I speak about myself.

"I know that I'm overstepping by saying this, but you're the only one who thinks you're a burden. Nobody else sees you that way," I say. "And if I can't speak badly about myself, then neither can you." I lie on my back, letting my hands lie on my side.

Anders doesn't respond right away. I hear him shift and then feel his fingers linking through mine.

After more silence, he says, "Thank you for showing me Sora."

I laugh. "Thanks for showing you a dog?"

"Yes," he says. "It makes me feel closer to you. When you share things you're passionate about, you light up. You get this look like the whole world makes sense for a second. You care so much," he says. "About dogs and people and everything. It's nice to see someone care that deeply."

For a second, I can't say anything. Maybe because the compliment isn't about how I look or how I sound or how I make someone else feel. It's about what I care about, and that feels more meaningful.

I let out a slow breath. "That's nice of you to say."

He stays quiet, giving me space I'm not sure I want. This urge to let out some of my worries within me climbs to the surface in this quiet, comfortable moment we lie in.

"Honestly," I say, my voice suddenly softer, "I'm scared about my life, about the future. I've been working toward this idea for so long. But what if I fail? What if I pour everything into it and it just doesn't work out? What happens then?"

I clear my throat and go on. "This dream is the last one I've got left. If I lose this, I don't know what's left for me to want."

He's quiet for so long, embarrassment spreads through my bloodstream. I force a laugh. "That sounds pathetic, doesn't it?"

He shifts closer, enough that I can feel the warmth of him beside me even if I can't see his face clearly.

"It's not pathetic," he says.

My chest stings. He sounds so sure. "I've already lost so much. My parents. My marriages. Years of my life to things that weren't for me. And I know people say it's never too late to start again, but I feel like I'm always starting over. What if, after this, there are no more beginnings? No new place to start from?"

It's too much, probably. So I try to wave it away with a weak smile he can't see. "Sorry, again, pathetic. You can cut some of my pay for emotional labor."

Anders squeezes my hand again, more firmly this time. "You're allowed to be scared. But Lucinda, you're going to be okay. You haven't lost everything, you've *survived* everything. That's different. And the fact that you still care enough to want something good, after all that? That's not pathetic. That's a strength I've never seen anyone else ever wear."

My heart skips and speeds. I press the back of my hand against my mouth, trying not to let anything spill out that I can't take back.

He adds, softer now, "I believe in you. I believe in this dream you're chasing. But even if the impossible happens, and you don't get what you want—"

I cut in, voice tight, "Then what?"

"Then you'll still be okay. You'll still find yourself, and you'll find new dreams. Dreams that fit the person you've become along the way."

His words don't erase the fear, but they don't let it swallow me whole either. And I feel every fragile wall I've tried to build between us start to crumble.

Not because of some grand gesture—but because he notices. The small things, the big things, most things. Because he pays attention—not out of obligation, but because he wants to. Because his care is quiet and genuine, like everything else about him.

And I'm not entirely sure what to do with all this affection blooming in my chest.

20.

With Olive being the flower girl in the wedding, Anders drops the both of us off at the boutique after a quick stop at a bakery where we loaded ourselves up with coffee and pastries.

The place is modestly sized, but it feels somewhat fragile. Countless glass centerpieces stand on thin displays, and even the rack holding the array of colorful dresses is this slim golden band closer to a necklace chain than a clothing bar. The employee stands by a curved desk with a thin, oversized monitor.

She leads us to a separate room with high ceilings and three beautiful and incredibly stiff-looking couches clustered around a three-way mirror on a tiny stage I assume is meant for brides to show off their gowns.

"Champagne?" the woman asks us. "We also have nonalcoholic for the little one."

The "little one" comment earns a glare from Olive. "I'll take a champagne with alcohol."

"We'll just have water," I say, trying to stifle a laugh.

Just as she leaves, Valerie enters in a tiny white silk minidress, barely covering her thighs. I suddenly feel like I should start waking up at five for long runs. And go on a diet.

"Wow, so prompt," Valerie says by way of greeting. "You'll be the only ones. I told everyone else we started thirty minutes earlier, and they've yet to arrive."

"Wouldn't miss a minute," I say. "I take my job as a stand-in dress placeholder incredibly seriously."

"Good," Valerie says, "because I've picked out seventeen dresses that will look good on Cierra." When I laugh, she gives me a look of sympathy. "Oh, that's not a dramatization."

"Well," I say, "let's get started."

The woman assigned to help us, Mimi, returns with drinks, a dress-fitting kit, and endless patience.

At first, Olive and I have a little fashion show. Our fitting rooms are beside each other, and with each try-on, we strut down our pretend runway, making a show of twirling for Valerie as she downs her wine and cheers.

Seven dresses in, Olive and Valerie mutually decide that a pale-pink dress with a flowing skirt is her best and cutest option. I-as-Cierra, unfortunately, am on my tenth dress and still not impressing Valerie.

Only two of Valerie's four other friends have arrived—one of them, Jennifer, whom I see reaching into a bag I'm not entirely sure is hers at least three times. We all keep removing and pulling on clothes for Valerie, who has very detailed criteria on what looks good and what doesn't.

I'm not entirely sure what the criteria is, since she only says, "So cute . . . but no," or "Are you trying to outdo the bride?" depending on the dress. While our try-on continues, all Valerie's friends eventually join.

The final one is a woman, Ashley, in a miniskirt and slicked-back ponytail with a girl around Olive's age beside her. "Sorry," she says, irritation marring her unnaturally smooth features. "My brother had an appointment and dropped my niece off with me. He's still not back. You know Erin, right, Olive? You have art together."

Erin, in the same slicked-back ponytail and a mirror of Ashley's irritation, smiles as she sits beside Olive, who stiffens. I recognize the look of an asshole kid—when you grow up wearing only hand-me-down off-brand clothes, you become familiar with it. I clock it, but move on.

Not your place, Lucy. Olive isn't mine to protect, no matter how much I want to.

I need to draw my lines. Not just with Anders, but with all of this. His family. His world. Because when I go—when, not if—I don't want to leave too much hurt behind. Especially for a young Olive, who is growing attached to me easily.

Valerie appears, holding up another dress for me to try.

I've lost count after seventeen dresses, and automatically just swap my outfit and head back out. Another dud. Ashley and I are the only ones still on the hunt for the perfect dress, until an off-the-shoulder lightweight gown for her gets Valerie's approval, and she forces me to try on a spaghetti-strapped number.

My arms ache as I lift, this time needing assistance from Mimi to remove the previous dress, and she gives me a thumbs-up when I pull down the newest option.

I grip her arm as I leave the fitting room. "Pray for me," I say, causing her to laugh.

When I make my reveal, Valerie's thin brows pull together. She joins me on the stage, observing me, circling me, tapping her lips. "Stand up straight," she orders.

I do as she says, and she moves back to get a full-length view. "Can you spin?"

I do.

"Slower."

I do.

She hums, and it reminds me of how Anders does the same, and both of them sound so musical when they do.

"I love it," Valerie says.

She barely gets the words out before I say, "Thank God."

She laughs, then slaps my shoulder. "That's it, girlies, we've all got our dresses."

Some of the girls do a cheer, and I watch Olive smile but shift away from Erin after she whispers something in her ear.

Mimi appears, clapping her hands. "Shall I take a commemorative photo?"

All the girls remain in their dresses for it, and line up on the stage. I try to hang back, since I'm not officially in the party, and Valerie yanks me up with her. "Don't be ridiculous," she says. "It's just a photo."

After we take a few shots before we all change back into our clothes, one of the girls says, "Wait, we haven't seen you in your dress."

Valerie sweeps her hair behind her. She, Bethany, and Olive did the wedding dress shopping privately. Valerie showed me a picture of every angle of her dress when we were drunk at the park.

"Can we see you try it on?" Jennifer asks.

Valerie pretends to act modest and shy as the girls start to chant. "See the dress! See the dress!" At last she gives in, and Mimi takes her to the larger, single, bridal changing room.

We all rush to the fitting rooms to remove our clothes. I'm too late, and all the rooms are taken, so I pace. Then I realize Olive isn't with me.

I head out back to the main room and find her with Erin.

"Is this why you've been ignoring my calls?" Erin pokes at Olive's shoulder.

Olive, my precious girl, has her head facing the floor as she says, "I've just been busy."

Erin snorts. "Right, it isn't because you've got even fatter? Please, that's why you have to wear this gross dress. But, whatever, I'll forgive you for ignoring me if you take Ashley and me with you to Valerie's salon. My stupid aunt still hasn't got an invite, and we want to cut our hair there."

My jaw drops. I move forward, but someone—Jennifer—grabs my shoulder and says, "Room is free if you want it."

When I turn back to the girls, Erin is smiling sweetly at us, while Olive, head still down, hurries to the fitting room. As she goes, all I can think is *My baby*, and the visceral, all-consuming protectiveness that floods me so quickly almost takes me off my feet.

I breathe through my nose as I follow after Olive, but she shuts herself in a room. As soon as the next one opens, I yank off the dress so fast I rip out some of my hair. Once I'm out, one of the girls grabs my arm and rushes me back to the room. She joins all the girls on the couches. Erin has placed herself between her aunt and Olive.

Valerie stands on the stage, and her beauty is so staggering, I nearly forget that I'm angry. It's more modest in person, the sleeveless number tight across her waist, then cascading down her length in tiny ripples. The back is low and accentuates her muscles there.

Aside from my sister, she is the most beautiful bride I have ever seen.

I open my mouth to say so when one of the girls asks, "That's what you're wearing? Are you pranking us?"

"Please tell me you haven't bought it yet?" another says. "The one hanging on the mannequin by the window is better than this."

"My aunt picked this for me," Valerie says, and for the first time since I've met her, the way her hands attempt to straighten the already ironed gown, I see her insecurity.

"Isn't she like sixty?" someone says. "Let us pick it out for you."

"She's literally fifty," Jennifer cuts in—as Anders said, she's an actual nice person. "I think it's nice."

"Who asked you, klepto?"

For the second time in ten minutes, my jaw drops. Valerie says, "You know what, it's because my hair and makeup aren't done. Once you see me with everything, you'll see how good it looks."

"Unlikely," someone says.

Mimi steps toward Valerie. "Let's go change."

Valerie follows her out, and I stand there, feeling crazy for several reasons. For Olive. For Valerie. And, genuinely, I can't tell if they're just being mean for the sake of it, or if they actually think Valerie doesn't look good. Either way, they should have kept their negative thoughts to themselves.

All the girls are talking among themselves, laughing, and someone grimaces. Erin, when she thinks nobody is looking, flicks the center of Olive's head.

Fuck the lines.

My feet propel me forward. I grab a jug of water and dump it over Erin.

Everyone goes quiet for a moment.

"What the hell?" Erin stands, and Ashley follows suit immediately.

I make a fist and jerk it back like I'm about to hit Erin. "You're lucky this is all I'm doing." I make her flinch again—though for the record, deserving or not, I would not hit a preteen. "You're worrying about someone's weight when you should be worrying about your own appearance. Clearly, early-onset wrinkles run in your family, so instead of a haircut"—I point to her aunt—"why don't you get her to book an appointment for Botox? I can already see the crow's-feet around her eyes."

"Excuse me, bitch—"

"Watch your mouth in front of Olive," I interrupt Ashley. "And if anyone is to blame, it's the people who don't know how to raise a child not to make fun of someone else's appearance."

"Speaking of." I step back and address the entire room. "I don't know who raised you all to be such horrible people—not to mention liars—because Valerie looks stunning. And if the next words out of your mouths aren't 'Sorry, Valerie, we were just kidding, you look beautiful,' then I will personally"—I lean forward and cover Olive's ears—"shove a bottle of champagne up every single one of your asses."

Ashley scoffs, stepping forward. "Calling someone fat is a fact. If it's a problem, maybe you shouldn't feed a kid until they get overweight."

Never mind Olive isn't my child, because the anger coursing through me feels like she is. Like the fury I'd feel if someone tried to hurt Taina. It's like my parents taught me from when I was a child—you *always* protect your family, no questions asked, no consequence too great. Family comes first, and you don't let anyone disrespect those you love.

I wonder if they knew I'd consider that for a found family too.

Before I can react, I see Valerie enter the room, still in her beautiful wedding dress. Without hesitation, she grabs a nearby glass and throws its contents all over Ashley. The liquid soaks Ashley's clothes, and Valerie, teeth clenched, says, "You and your bratty-ass niece can get the hell out. And don't bother taking the dress—you won't be needing it."

"Excuse me?" Ashley snaps, glaring. "What does that mean?"

"It means I'm not going to have some bitch who makes my cousin feel bad about herself in my bridal party," Valerie says. "Now get out."

Ashley smirks. "Then you're down a bridesmaid. Who is going to walk with Jeremy?"

Valerie wraps an arm around me. "Why, my new best friend is. The girl who shows up on time, defends my cousin and me without being prompted, and who is thirty seconds away from shoving a wine bottle up your ass."

"Whatever." Ashley snatches Erin by the collar. "I was doing you a favor coming, and I've never liked your prissy little attitude anyway."

Valerie waves, and I point to the corner of my eye. "Botox," I say to her, "don't forget."

They storm off, and Olive stands up, grabs Valerie and me by the arm.

Worry strikes me in the chest. "Olive, are you—"

"That," Olive interrupts me, "was so badass!"

21.

Valerie drops me off at Anders's right as the sun begins to set. I wave, open the door, and head up the stairs.

"Wait," she calls to me.

I turn and she jogs over, remaining on the bottom step. "What's up?"

"Two things," she says, hands on her hips. "First, thanks for defending Olive. And me."

"Truly, no thanks necessary."

"I know you mean that, which leads me to my second point," she says, and I raise my brows when she struggles to speak, switching between hitting her nails together and twisting her hair. "Look, I don't have a lot of friends. And the ones I do have, well, you can see they're not the best."

I purse my lips. "Well, Jennifer seems okay."

She snorts, then nods. "She can be. Anyway, my point is, you've already been a good friend to me, better than what I'm used to. I know you're Anders's girlfriend, but I meant it back there. If you want to be a bridesmaid, I'd have you. If you want."

My smile forms instantly. "If I want?"

She rolls her eyes. "Fine, I want you to be one. Now, will you agree? Asking is so humiliating."

"I'd love to," I answer.

She fights it, but a smile plays on her lips. "Great, because I already bought your dress—dress number thirteen."

"I thought you didn't like that one."

"For Cierra," she says, "but you look beautiful in it. So, it's yours."

"Thank you," I say.

"For what?" Valerie asks back. "You're the one doing me a favor."

"For trusting me," I say.

"Oh, don't get all sentimental on me." Valerie steps away. "I'll text you more details. Just know I'm forcing you into more wedding planning. You can't take it back."

"I won't," I say, and wave her off.

I keep waving at her until she drives away, then turn to the door. When I reach for the doorknob, I pause, my smile slipping away.

For a moment, no, for hours, I hadn't thought about ruining Valerie's marriage. I was totally immersed in dress shopping, in hyping up Valerie, reassuring Olive, and trying not to strangle the girls when I felt they weren't doing the same.

I'd done such a good job at this, at being good to Valerie in general, that she invited me to be a part of her wedding party. For Valerie, I've become someone she values enough to call a friend, to be a part of what she thinks is the biggest moment of her life. But for me, this is all a means to an end.

This is exactly what I'm supposed to do, worm my way into her life. The more involved I am, the easier it will be to wreck from within. This is my job.

But now, it feels like there are shards of rock floating around the pit of my stomach.

This has never happened. No matter how rough it was, getting involved in someone's relationship, ruining a pairing, I've never felt this . . . guilt before, clawing into every organ in my body and pulling them down.

My own fault. I'm getting too emotionally attached. I've never stuck around to see the wreckage left over. I didn't care, because it wasn't my job to care.

But I care now.

That's the difference between this job and the others. In this one, I've fallen for Olive, and Bethany, and Valerie.

And most of all, Anders.

It's a disservice to him, not focusing correctly, doing what he hired me to do. Because we are employer and client. I need to get my head on straight. I can't afford to slip up here. Because I care and I want Valerie to be with someone perfect for her.

Because I care about myself and my life, and I need the money for Save a Paw, and I need the money to move for Taina's marriage, I need this to go well.

No more distractions. No more flirting with Anders outside of the facade. No stolen touches, no wandering glances, nothing romantic, no messy lines.

Maybe I skipped over these boundaries for Olive, but I couldn't help it. Couldn't stop myself from watching out for her. It's the caretaker in me. And she's so sweet and smart. So bright eyed and curious and endearing.

And I hate bullies.

But that's the last time. That's where I draw the line.

From now on, it's about the job, and the job alone.

I take a fortifying breath and let myself in. I kick off my shoes beside Anders's and pause.

How nice would it be to always see them beside each other like this?

I turn around, walk out, then step back in.

There. Fresh start. Starting *now*.

When I walk through the hall that spits me out to the kitchen, Anders is there cutting up an avocado. I don't make a sound with my bare feet, but he looks up as soon as I step in.

"You're back," he says, pushing a plate toward me as I join him.

"Smells good in here," I comment.

"Hopefully it tastes as good too," he says, dropping slices of avocado on a plate of rice, beans, and tofu. "I read a recipe on how to make Puerto Rican rice and beans. If it's horrible, then we can order out."

"Are you kidding me?" I snap. I need to go outside and let myself back in again.

"Um, no?" He does his cute little head-cock thing. "If you don't want to try, there are plenty of delivery options."

"I'm not hungry," I snap again, though my heart threatens to burst from its cage. It's like it and my brain can't get on the same page, and the contradicting emotions are going to drive me insane. "I mean, I don't feel that well."

"Did I get you sick?" He immediately approaches me, hand on my forehead. "You don't feel warm. What's wrong?"

Out of all the things my brain can think of, I say, "I just got my period."

"Oh." He blinks, then recovers instantly. "Can I get you anything? I can go to the store."

"Nope." I step away from him. "I'm all prepared. I'm just going to shower and go to sleep, okay?"

"Lucinda—"

"Good night!"

I practically fling myself into my room. No, the guest room. Not *my*—nothing here is *my* anything. It's something I repeat when I shower, washing the day away, a needed reminder.

It was way too easy to fall for everyone involved in this, but I should have been better at keeping a distance. Of course, I know that my situation is difficult. I am in a very emotional stage of my life, and I have a lot on the line. Can I keep blaming myself for making very human errors?

Yes, but all I can think about is the way Anders says he hates the way I speak about myself—a sentiment now that's not only helping me be easy on myself, but driving me up the wall that he would be so kind to me.

When I exit the bathroom, Anders is hunched over the bedside table. When he rights himself, he drops the heating pad he plugged in on the side of the bed.

Are you kidding me?

"Hey." He notices me and gestures to a bottle of pain medicine on the table. "These should help with the pain. Val left them here a while ago. Are you sure you don't want anything to eat?"

"I'm sure," I say, heading for the bed. I immediately pull the sheets to my chest. "I just want to sleep."

"Okay," he says, then pauses by my feet. "Is there a reason you won't look me in the eyes?"

"Maybe I'm too busy focusing on my uterus being ripped apart?" I counter.

He blows out a breath, paces by the foot of the bed, until I say, "Is something wrong?"

"Not wrong," he says.

"Well, that sounded like a lie."

He chuckles. "If you're still feeling bad tomorrow, let me know."

"Tell me now, Anders," I say, since it's clear he's waiting to ask something.

"With Valerie planning on getting married and everything," he says, "my father wants us all to have dinner together. He wants to sit down with John and the rest of us tomorrow. Valerie mentioned you to him, and he asked if you'd join."

"Ah," I say. A very different request from usual. One that sends an uncomfortable array of nerves through me. "When's the last time you had a meal with him?"

"Me?" He makes a face as he thinks back. "Not for a couple of years now. Valerie, though, a couple of months ago. She has a bit of a soft spot for him. Keeps hoping he's developed the emotions a father should have."

Instantly, I feel this protectiveness start to flood me. I want to go, be a support system for Anders, be ready to step in if he hurts Valerie's feelings.

But that has nothing to do with wrecking Valerie's wedding, and is exactly the kind of blurred line Anders and I have been dancing along.

"I'm sorry," I say. Truly, I am. "But my period is the worst on the second day. I usually just take some medicine and sleep the entire time."

He nods. "Okay, no worries, of course." He moves toward the door. "I'm sorry for bringing it up."

"Anders—"

"Sleep well," he says, and I feel like the worst person on the planet.

Anders has repeatedly shown up for me, outside of the job, without question. I know that. But if I don't draw a line now, neither of us ever will.

I don't get more than an hour of sleep.

The next morning, Anders comes in with more medicine and water and asks if I'm feeling any better. I'm so emotional about abandoning him when he needs me that when I say "No," he presses a kiss on my forehead and returns with some soup and crackers and Vicks, which he rubs into the heels of my feet.

I very nearly say, *I'm feeling better, I'll join for dinner*. Even if he isn't mentioning it—of course it's not like him to say anything—I know this meeting will be hard. To have to sit around someone who is supposed to love you no matter what but you only see once a year. I know he'd like support. I want him to have it.

But I keep my mouth shut.

I don't sleep the whole time he's away, and at night, I shut my eyes, knowing he would peek into my room to see if I was okay. I hear his footsteps, feel his fingers as he brushes my hair from my face, then drops something weighted on my stomach.

When I hear the door click shut, I see he's placed the heating pad back on my belly.

And I feel like the worst person in the world.

22.

I managed to get a couple of hours of sleep by the next morning. When I leave the room, I don't hear a single sound. Anders isn't in his room or anywhere else in the house. When I get to the kitchen, I read the tiny note he left for me.

Working at a coffee shop. Text me if you need anything.

I blow out a sigh of relief. For a little while, I can be completely by myself. Being around Anders is fun, easy, and that's exactly why it's better if he stays away for now. As soon as I think it's best to keep some professional distance, he skips over the boundary—unbeknownst to him—and I risk it being erased before it's already fully formed.

I text Valerie, asking if she needs any help with wedding planning, then call Taina for a catch-up, but surprisingly, it goes straight to voicemail.

In case Anders comes home, I get ready for the day, then head out back to the shelter to see if Dainese needs any help. When I get there, she's delighted, as am I by her welcoming reaction.

Dainese says there's nothing much to do today other than give the dogs lots of love, and lucky for them, I have so much to offer. I try to spread the love equally, and we open up the cages and let them all have fun, but I can't help but gravitate to Sora, who keeps trying to play with the other dogs, then gets scared when they approach him too fast from behind.

Eventually, I sit with him against a wall, and we roll a small ball back and forth between us.

Dainese joins us. "Any news on the adoption?"

I shake my head. "I haven't had the chance to talk to him. It's been a little busy."

"You should make the time," she says, kneeling by Sora, giving him a stomach rub. "We're getting a couple more dogs in, and I won't be able to give Sora the attention he deserves."

I narrow my eyes at her. "How dare you?"

She laughs. "You know how it is," she says. "Willing to do anything for the dogs, including manipulating with guilt."

"I respect that."

"So," Dainese says after a while, when the dogs all get tired and just lie in the middle of the floor, "what's so special about Save a Paw?"

"Why?" I tease. "You want me to stay here with you? Already attached?"

She sticks her tongue out. "I got nosy and looked it up, and it's great. I'm not going to dog out another shelter—"

"Ha, dog out."

"But," she continues, unimpressed, "it's so big, how can you have the time to care for all of the animals?"

"You know, I think you may have forgotten since your sister and mom went away, but there is a thing called staff."

"Ha ha," she counters. "I'm just thinking about you specifically. I mean, you're just visiting, but you fell in love with Sora instantly at the market, then came all the way here, did free labor, and you're back again. You just feel like the kind of person who, when doing a job, wants to dedicate herself to it fully. Don't you wish you had more time to be with all the dogs?"

I tilt my head back against the wall. "Well, sure. There's never enough time in the day."

"There is here."

I laugh. My phone vibrates, so I pull it from my pocket. It's Anders.

"On that note," I say, pocketing the phone, "I should probably get back home."

"To talk about adoption?"

"Yes." I laugh, because even if I'm drawing lines between Anders and me, I'm willing to scribble them out for Sora.

"Good luck." She salutes.

When I get back to Anders's home, instantly something feels off. I sense it even before I open the door, and when I kick off my shoes and spot the designer heels beside Anders's, it skyrockets into overdrive.

I consider turning my ass around and going straight back to Sora.

But if Anders brought a woman to the house—his house—I should see it. It would be beneficial to engrave that image in my head. I shouldn't be having any romantic thoughts about Anders and vice versa.

Good. This is great.

I drag myself down the hallway, enter the living room, and my eyes widen so much I blink before they feel like they'll slip from the sockets.

Anders is the first to stand when I enter, like his Lucy radar rang in his head.

Then, my sister gets up and holds out her arms. "My favorite person in the world!"

Shock fills me to the brim, replacing the jealousy I'm pretending was never there, but somehow I manage to storm over and grab her ear. "What are you doing here?"

"Ow, ow, ow," she squeaks, trying to reach out to Anders for help. "You monster! This is how you greet your sister after weeks?"

I let her go, then turn to Anders, trying to keep from boiling. "Why did you let her in?"

"She said she was your sister." He looks between us.

"And what if she wasn't? What if she was some psycho murderer you let into your house?"

"I am a little psycho," Taina mutters.

"Is she?" Anders asks. "Your sister, not psycho."

"Quiet, both of you." I rub my forehead, then my eyes, making sure they're working just fine.

"I'll deal with you first." I grab Taina, then pull her to my—no, Anders's—guest room. I slam the door shut behind us and hiss, "What are you doing here?"

"Obviously I'm here to see you." She plops onto the edge of the bed, unfazed. "Sad to see this bed is used. Guess you and Anders haven't slept together yet."

I pinch the bridge of my nose. "Taina—"

"I told you I wanted to visit."

"And I told you I'd think about it. And you came here, without telling me, to Anders's home. You don't think that's crossing a line?" Of course she stored away his address when she did her deep dive on him.

Taina gives me a look. "Since when do we have lines between us?"

"Maybe we should!" I shout. "I've been too cheap with the lines; I haven't drawn as many as I need." I draw an imaginary one between us. "There, there's another one."

"Ah." She nods. "I see, you've lost your mind. This is what happens when you go too long without me."

"What did you tell Mathew?" I snap. "Please don't tell him you came to see me."

She blinks. "Why wouldn't I tell him the truth?"

I place my hands over my mouth and scream.

"Jesus," Taina says, "what is happening to you right now? You want one of my Xanax?"

I open my mouth to curse, then say, "Actually? Yes."

Taina rushes out the door, presumably to the luggage sitting in the living room. When she comes back, she practically shoves it into my mouth. After I take it, I sit on the bed, and Taina joins me.

"Okay," she says after a while, "are you going to explain what's happening right now?"

"What *was* happening," I begin, "is I was trying to drive some distance between Anders and me. And then my little sister shows up at his home, unannounced, and made me cross the lines I've been drawing."

Taina smirks. "Oh, so that means you've drawn close enough to him that you're freaking out and trying to pull back? Interesting."

I groan, dropping back on the bed.

Taina does the same, faces me. "I can't believe you've been keeping secrets from me."

"It's not a secret."

"Oh, so Anders knows you like him."

I slap a hand over her mouth and apply pressure as she squirms. "Say it louder; I don't think he heard you."

She mumbles into my hand, repeating the words, and I practically choke her until she licks me. I peel my hand back, and she whips up. "You're so far gone. You're freaking out so bad."

"This is so inappropriate of you," I snap.

She cackles. "Oh, Lucy, you're adorable. Let me get my phone, you have to see how red you are."

"Taina, go back home. Mathew is probably so upset that you left him."

She frowns. "Why would he be upset?" Then, "And if you ever listened to what I tell you, you'd remember he's away this week. Or are you too lost in Anders to remember things about your poor little sister?"

There's a light knock on the door. I open my mouth to say go away, but Taina covers my mouth and shouts, "Come in."

Just as Anders lets himself in, Taina yells as I bite her hand.

She mutters, "You're not being very attractive right now."

"Sorry to interrupt," Anders says, his gaze traveling between us, then falling on Taina. "The sushi you ordered is here."

"You ordered delivery?" I yell, just as Taina runs off and leaves Anders and me by ourselves.

"I'm so sorry." I stand. "She did not tell me she was coming. And I didn't tell her to come. She wanted to come, sure, but she said she'd stay at a hotel, and I said I would see if I would even have time."

"It's okay."

"It's most definitely not." I rub a hand over my face. "But I'll deal with it."

"Really, it's okay," he says, then pulls out his phone. "This is my aunt. She wants me over for dinner. I told her you weren't feeling well."

I'm very clearly feeling better, seeing as I just wrestled with my sister.

But not only is Taina something I need to deal with at this moment, she's a reminder of why I need to finish this job well. I need to get my money, leave her place, leave her and her husband alone, and focus on building my career—the real one outside of this one.

So I say, "I'll pass on joining today."

Anders's shoulders stiffen as he smiles and nods. "Okay."

And he leaves.

I wait until I hear the front door shut before joining Taina in the kitchen. She's spread out her food on the counter and has already cleared out a box of California rolls.

"There's some vegan ones," she says, mouth full. "Take a bite, then take a breath."

"You can't stay here."

She rolls her eyes. "Duh, I'm not a cockblock. I got a place. I just wanted to see Anders in person, check for signs of life. Sue me for caring."

I rub a hand over my face. "I'm having an incredibly stressful day, and you're making it so much worse."

She drops the two rolls in her hands. "What's wrong?" She looks around, like she's just realizing Anders isn't here. "Did he upset you? I'll kill him. The bastard."

"No, he didn't do anything wrong," I say. "It feels like I am, though." It feels like any choice I make isn't a good one. Being there for Anders is crossing a line. Not being there for him is causing him pain when he's been nothing but good to me. It's too frustrating.

"Talk to me."

"I don't really want to talk about it," I say. "I just, I need this to go well. So please don't show up unannounced again. Or track my location when I'm out and show up there to spy, either."

She pouts. "You're being so secretive with me."

"Taina."

"I won't show up unannounced," she grumbles. "Are you just going to abandon me even though I'm here?"

"Of course not," I say. "I'm going to pack my things and stay with you."

Taina follows me to the guest room, where I immediately start shoving everything of mine into my luggage. Her gaze is warm at the back of my head as I move, but she doesn't speak until I'm halfway done.

"I'd love for you to stay with me," she begins. "We can stay up all night watching reruns of *The Nanny*."

"Just like the good old days." I shove the rest of my shorts into the sloppy mess of clothes.

"But."

"No buts," I counter.

"However—"

"No synonyms of buts."

"You're very obviously stressed out." She ignores me. "I haven't seen you like this since, forever, really." She pauses, then adds, "Well, not since you had to bail me out of jail."

"A happy memory," I say. "Thank you."

"What could have Miss Keep It Together Even When the World Is Ending in a frenzy like this?" Before I can tell her to shut up, she says, "You *like* Anders! It's not just attraction."

Always the observant little brat.

When I don't say anything, she pounces.

"You like Anders, you're freaking out because you're trying to ruin his sister's wedding, and you're already telling yourself every single reason why it will go wrong, and how you have to focus on working on what you know for sure isn't risky—money. Getting paid."

I slam my hand on the suitcase when the zipper gets caught. "What am I? Some teenager nervous to ask a boy to prom?" I stand. "I like Anders? I think I'm too old for a crush."

Taina rolls her eyes. "Because your heart shrivels up and rots after the age of sixteen?"

"Because I'm an adult doing a job, who lives in an entirely different state, with no ties to Anders or this place. And I'm about to make his entire family hate me." When she approaches me, I hold up a hand. "I swear to God, Taina, I'm not in the mood. Help me close this suitcase before I shove you in it."

"Yes, ma'am," Taina says, and helps yank the zipper into place with both hands and a little grunt.

We sit in silence for a moment, side by side on the edge of the bed, catching our breath like we just fought the suitcase into submission. Which, honestly, we did.

Then she says, more gently now, "Don't get mad, but I'm serious. You can talk to me. Unload whatever thoughts are ping-ponging in that pretty little head of yours."

And maybe it's the fact that the room feels too quiet, or that her tone has softened just enough to slip through my defenses, but something in me gives. Would it be so bad to share some of my worries?

Anders and his family rely on each other so easily, like it's second nature. I watch it happen between them all the time—silent support, unspoken understanding—and I realize I've never really let that happen between me and Taina. Not really.

Taina never held back her troubles; it's been me all along. But maybe letting someone else hold a piece of it, just for a moment, won't be the end of the world, especially because Taina loves me in a way nobody else does. Wouldn't her comfort mean more?

I lean forward, resting my elbows on my knees. "I don't know what I'm doing."

"With Anders?"

"With a lot, but especially with him."

She waits, like she knows I'm not done.

I sigh. "It's not just that I like him. It's that *if*, keyword *if*, I did want something more with him, I know it wouldn't work. Not because he's done anything wrong, but because I haven't got my shit together. I mean, look at me. I'm floating from couch to couch, trying to scrape together enough money to finally start the life I've been planning for years. Meanwhile, he's already living his. He's stable. He's good. He knows what he wants."

Taina leans back on her hands. "*And?* You think people only fall in love once they've got health insurance and a 401(k)?"

I shoot her a glare.

"I'm serious," she goes on. "You think Anders is gonna look at your credit score and think 'Wow, deal-breaker.' That's not what love is."

"You're using a pretty strong word that I never said."

She rolls her eyes. "Don't be dense. Love. Like. Crushes. It's all the same. And you shouldn't look at them like they come with prerequisites."

"I don't know; it feels like they should."

Taina frowns. "You keep waiting for this perfect version of yourself before you let anyone in, and I'm telling you, you'll be waiting forever. You don't have to be fully healed, or fully successful, or fully anything to be loved."

I stare at the floor. My throat tight.

Taina lowers her voice. "People love each other at their messiest, their ugliest, their lowest. You don't have to earn that. It just comes with the territory."

"I don't know how to believe that."

"You don't have to yet," she says. "You just, I don't know, have to stop running from the chance that it might be true. Just let things run their course. Stop cockblocking your own life."

I laugh. "Wow, you sound filled with wisdom right now."

Taina grimaces. "I know, don't get used to it."

Another laugh tears from me, and I feel just the tiniest bit lighter.

23.

Taina has been doing an almost good job the past week. I've stayed at her waterfront rental, overlooking a long, peaceful creek. It's been home base while I spent time visiting Sora, joining Valerie for some wedding planning, and narrowly avoiding questions about Anders while dodging his calls.

Taina hasn't brought up Anders again, but has given me lots of raised eyebrows, asked "Who keeps texting you?" when my phone vibrates, and when we're watching a show with any kind of romantic element, her gaze is pinned on me for some sort of reaction.

The first day I left, that's when Anders called the most. I only texted that I was staying with my sister after Taina mentioned how often the phone was ringing. The next days the calls were fewer, but that's because he knew Valerie and I were out picking the floral arrangements with Bethany and Olive in tow, or finalizing centerpieces, or having tea.

Today, nothing.

It's already three, and Anders hasn't messaged at all. Granted, I left, so of course, it would be entirely hypocritical and unreasonable to care at all about that. I'm the one ignoring his questions on why I left, why I'm being so cold. Me. I'm the cause of it.

Yet I feel a vibration in my shorts pocket for the twelfth time and check the screen only to find a picture Taina sent of the beach, glistening under the sun.

"Earth to Lucy." Valerie holds up the barcode scanner to my face so the red light momentarily steals my vision. "Are you even paying attention here? You almost scanned the red plate set. I'd rather see my own red blood in the kitchen cabinets than red dishware."

"Graphic"—I bring myself back to attention—"and noted."

"Come on." She nudges me. "Let's look at some machines. Scan anything that does the work for me. Rice cookers, egg cookers, anything that cooks so I don't have to."

When Valerie called me painfully cheerful at six in the morning, telling me, not asking, to come join her shopping as she picks out gifts for her wedding registry, I thought we'd be finished by early afternoon. Instead, we've been at several stores, hours at each, and my stomach is gnawing.

We've been in this store for just fifteen minutes, and she's already scanned an ungodly amount of overpriced goods.

All items are set on the thinnest glass shelves, and I keep my shoulders straight the way my mother would demand when walking down aisles. *Don't touch anything you can't buy.* Which in this store would be legitimately everything.

"You could have done this online," I say, as she scans through a new aisle, "but I'm learning you're more hands-on than you seem."

"Meaning what? You think I would have paid some planner to pick out everything that will be in my house?"

"More like, you'd do this online, add things to a cart immediately instead of going to a bunch of stores."

Valerie nods. "True, it would be easier. But I wanted to get out of the house a bit. Get my steps in."

"Just a couple more months to the wedding," I say, and hearing it aloud makes my nerves avalanche. Though I've been asking calculated questions, pointed out very obvious differences between her and John, played up her desire for fun and expression, the progress isn't where it should be—even with this tight deadline. "Will people have time to buy everything?"

"They better." Valerie scans some machine I can't recognize, but mimics a tiny washing machine. A high-speed microwave? I have no clue. "I need this."

The quick addition of desperation at the end of the sentence captures my interest. "You need what? Gifts?" When she stiffens, I know this is a good thread to pull. "Valerie, respectfully, you're rich. I didn't think you'd even have a registry." I pause a moment, then add, "You didn't, did you? This is a last-minute idea."

"Don't be nosy, Lucy, it's gross." I know she's nervous because she scans a red blender instead of the stainless steel one beside it.

I match her quickened pace. "Is something wrong?" Why would Valerie, a proud nepo baby, be frantic to add a bunch of gifts to a last-minute registry? Wouldn't she be able to just buy anything and everything she wants? Didn't she offhandedly mention to me once that she had a family credit card with no limit?

She snorts. "I have no idea what you're talking about."

"You're being evasive."

"You're being aggravating."

I give her a moment to crack, scan a few more items, before we reach the end of the store. We return our scanners to the front desk, and the employee helps Valerie review her list of items on the monitor to ensure she got everything. (She deletes the red blender.)

We leave the store, and I point to a couple of benches on the sidewalk overlooking Queen Street, the long road filled with endless shops, restaurants, bars, and activities. The most active part of Charleston. Before she can disagree, I loop my arm through hers and drag her to sit.

After a few minutes of watching cars and people go by, the silence eats at us like I knew it would.

She snaps, "Are you going to make a big deal out of nothing?"

"Hm." I hum. "Depends on what it is, but, Valerie, you can trust me," I say, and my throat feels itchy as the words come out because she can, in the sense that I'm doing what's best for her, but she can't, in that whatever she says I'll have to use to separate her from John. "That's why you asked me to be a bridesmaid. I know I'm not the closest person to you, and I know you're worried I'll talk to Anders about whatever you say, but I can be a good friend to you if you let me."

She looks at me through unusually thin lashes—she forgot that step she has always remembered every other time I've seen her. She removes her arm from mine, then places her hands on her thighs below her pale miniskirt. A couple of her manicured gel nails are missing.

"You swear you won't tell Anders?"

I hold out my pinkie so it feels less like a lie when I nod. She wraps her pinkie around mine, tightening her grip.

"I mean it," Valerie says. "Anders cannot find out about this."

I reach for her hand, keep it pressed between both of mine. "Valerie, I'm here for you." The words slip out easily, because I mean them. Every syllable.

"Okay." She takes a breath. "I got scammed out of a million dollars."

I blink. "Excuse me?"

"Calm down," she says quickly. "And I know, my father is loaded, my brother even more. But as much as I can get away with spending thousands on my card without raising any flags, me taking over a million from our accounts is not going to go over well."

"A million?" My eyes nearly bug out of my skull.

Valerie slaps a hand over my mouth and glances around like one of her relatives might spring out from behind a bush. "Calm down, you're not the one down the money."

"How in the world did this happen?" I ask. "What is going on?"

She rubs a hand over her face. "Ugh, it's a mess. I should have paid more attention. Should've asked John to show me the paperwork."

"Okay. Slow down. Explain it to me."

"John found this house," she starts. "This cute, boring thing overlooking a creek. Not my style at all, but it was his dream home, so I agreed. I figured I could decorate it, make it mine. That was the compromise. Even if it meant gutting the place—because I swear, the '70s died in there. It had orange shag carpet and lemon-yellow tile in the shower. Who does that?"

"Valerie," I say. "Focus."

"Right, right." She nods. "So John's credit score isn't great, and we used my name for everything. But instead of going with the family's tried-and-true realtor, he insisted on using his friend's friend's friend. Total stranger. No reputation. Said it would be quicker and cheaper."

"Okay, that's already a lot of red flags."

"I know," she mutters. "Anyway, this sketchy realtor tells us there's another buyer. Supposedly offered an extra fifty grand, but was applying for a mortgage. He said if we went in all cash and added another fifty on top, the seller would go with us."

"Oh no."

"Right? So we wired the money. The full amount." She exhales. "And then, poof. The guy disappears. Just had his license suspended for mortgage fraud, and we're out a million."

"And you haven't told anyone?"

"How can I?" she asks. "Everyone already thinks I'm a bratty airhead with an attitude problem. And they're not wrong. But my dad already put me on a spending limit. He says I'm wasteful and wouldn't survive in any other family. If he finds out I lost that much money? Game over. My cards go dead for a year, minimum."

"You have to get help. Legal help. You have to try to recover it."

"I know." She waves her hand, like we're talking about losing her keys. "I used to sleep with this guy who interned at my dad's law firm. He's got a new job now, but said he'll help if I convince my dad to hire him full time. So I'm working on that."

"Okay, but—" I hesitate, then push, "What about John? What's he doing to fix this?"

She stiffens just slightly. "What can he do?"

"I don't know. Something. He picked the realtor. He pushed for this house. Shouldn't he be making calls? Talking to lawyers? Taking responsibility?"

Valerie crosses her arms. "He's devastated, too, okay? He knows it's bad. I don't need him to fix it—I just need him not to spiral. He's not great with stress."

"That's not the same as being helpful."

Her gaze sharpens. "He's trying. He's calling around. He's upset. But he doesn't have connections like I do. He doesn't have a rich dad with lawyers on call. It's different for him."

I hold back from pushing harder, but I can feel the words trying to claw their way out. Different doesn't mean he gets to screw up and let you carry the fallout. If there's already trouble like this *before* marriage, imagine what could happen after.

Instead, I say, "You made the registry to have other people buy what you need while you try to recover."

"Yeah." She sighs. "And being poor sucks. No offense."

"Hard to be offended if it's true." I pause. "But seriously. If John's this bad with money, how are you two planning to handle joint finances?"

Valerie shrugs like it's too heavy to think about. "Anders warned me he was bad with money. Said every time someone asked for help back in college, John gave them whatever he had. That the rest he lost playing cards." She leans her head back and closes her eyes. "And now I've just proven to Anders that I'm just as irresponsible. If he finds out, he'll never let it go."

If Anders finds out his suspicions were right—that John hasn't changed, that he's still reckless with money and now has direct access to Valerie's—he'll picture a future of joint accounts, shared debt, and the tears and stress of his sister, and walk into the wilderness never to be seen again.

"So," Valerie says, like she's trying to reset the tone, "tonight, when we're out, you can't act weird about this. Process it, then remove it from your memory."

I open my mouth, shut it again. "We're?" I ask. "Where are we going?"

She frowns. "What do you mean?"

"What do *you* mean?"

"It's Anders's birthday party tonight."

My eyes go wide for a second before I force myself to play it cool.

"Ah." I slap her arm playfully. "I thought you meant earlier, before that. I'm taking Anders out for a little stroll before the party. Private time. You know, romantic prelude." I'm rambling. "I thought you were inviting yourself to our pre-date."

She snorts. "Yeah, right, I don't need to third-wheel you and my brother."

"Right."

She checks her phone. "When's your date? You should probably head out soon—the party's in a couple hours."

"Right, right," I say, rising. "Let's get moving, then."

Valerie grabs my arm before I go. "And remember—this stays between us."

"I gave you my pinkie," I say, like that means anything.

24.

Valerie drops me off in front of Anders's home. Shortly after she drives off, Taina pulls up in her rental car.

"Going to explain what's going on?" Taina says when I throw myself into the passenger side.

"Yeah, later," I say, "but now, I need you to dress me up for a party."

Easily distracted, Taina smiles. "Oh, amazing, you'll look so good in this black slip-on I just got."

When we get back to the rental, I hurriedly shower and straighten my hair. When I'm on my last strand, my phone lights up with a call from Anders.

"Finally," I say into the speaker, "where have you been? Why haven't you answered any of my calls?"

The line is quiet, then, "I was busy."

Which is at least a more polite response than *Oh, you can ignore all my calls and messages, but when I do it, it's a problem?*

"I almost blew it today," I say. "Valerie brought up your party, and I had no idea."

"I tried calling you before," he points out. "I wasn't sure what else to do. I was going to say you were sick if anyone asked."

"I already played that card," I say, slapping a hand over my face. I just admitted that playing sick when he needed me for his family dinner was a lie. Sloppy. "Anyway, missing this is too obvious. I'm getting ready now."

"Okay."

I hate how clipped his voice is, and the lack of words he uses instead of speaking to me with drawn-out sentences. And I hate that I hate it.

"I'll be ready in an hour. I'll drop the address where I'm staying. Pick me up."

"Okay."

"Okay," I snap, hanging up, ridiculously annoyed, even though I have zero right to be. I'm just a little frazzled. I was taken off guard. And the pressure of the wedding coming up is getting to me.

And it's Anders's birthday today.

Taina knocks on the door. "Hurry up," she calls out. "I'm dying of boredom here."

It's been silent during the ride, from the moment Anders opened the passenger door and let me in. He only nodded to greet me, and he didn't even turn the music on. The tension is heavy and thick; the air is hard to breathe. So, I push the window down, despite the thick humidity from the night air, which is sure to frizz up my hair.

Still, frizzy hair or not, my skin looks flawless and dewy thanks to Taina, and my spaghetti-strapped black dress pairs well with Anders's black trousers and white button-up. We look good together.

He looks good alone. His sleeves aren't at their usual rolled-up positions, but the veins on his hands protrude under his skin as he grips the steering wheel, his watch reflecting the lights of oncoming cars every so often. Even with the window open, his aftershave reaches me, and the scent of it brings me this blend of comfort and desire so suddenly I have to cross my legs and look away.

When we get to the vineyard, Anders parks at the end of the full lot. After this, I'm going to Taina's, so I grab the tiny bag sitting by my feet and hand it over.

He looks at it like it's holding a mousetrap.

"For you." At that, his brows go up, and he stills, like he's never been given a gift in his life. "It's not much. It's kind of cheesy."

Anders reaches into it, pulls out the miniature golden frame with a replica of his favorite painting in it. "What is this?"

"I remember at the gallery, Valerie said it was your favorite painting. The artist was at the market when I went with Bethany and Olive, with tiny prints of his other works. I got it then and forgot to give it to you."

Then, because I'm not sure if he remembers how words work, I add, "Happy birthday."

He shoves the gift in the bag, then gets out of the car. Seconds later, my side opens up, and he pulls me out with him. "What is this?" he asks.

I frown. "You can throw it out if you want."

"Not that." He shoves a rough hand through his hair. "This. Disappearing without telling me. Then showing up again with a gift. You've been different. Distant."

A flash of headlights pours over him as another car pulls up.

"I'm still working on the wedding." I look at my feet, already sore in these heels. "And I'm making progress, don't worry. I can give you more updates later."

"You know I'm not talking about that," he snaps.

My gaze flickers to his heated one. "You should be, though."

Then I hear doors slamming shut, footsteps—close, deliberate—approaching fast.

He narrows his eyes. "I'm a reasonable man, Lucinda, but even I have my limits." He steps closer to me. "If I did something wrong, I'll apologize, but I'm clueless if you don't tell me. And if you're putting distance between us—"

"Stop, stop, stop!" I hold up my hands as the footsteps grow louder.

"You can't keep avoiding—" Anders starts, and then, without thinking, desperate to stop him before anyone overhears, I fling my arms around him and press my mouth to his. The shock of it steals any response from him other than his body going stiff.

I pull away, my arm snaking around him as a couple approaches us.

"Anders," the woman says, and my heart sinks to my stomach.

Long blond hair, a perfect pointed nose, and smooth tan skin. Anna, the woman whose wedding I wrecked, and her husband, Lucas, beside her.

She opens her arms for a full hug. He pulls away from me slightly, gives her a half hug, and does the same to Lucas. I was in a half-assed disguise when I saw them and caused enough chaos they shouldn't recognize me—hopefully—but nerves fill my stomach anyway.

Despite everything, Anders still keeps in touch with them. Weekly catch-ups, the occasional coffee, enough shared history to keep them tethered. So naturally, they know about me. Maybe not everything—but enough. Anna narrows her gaze my way, giving me a once-over. "So, you're the secret girlfriend," she says.

"That's me."

"Nice to finally meet you." Lucas holds out a hand, and I match his firm handshake. Unlike his wife, his smile seems harmlessly curious.

"Likewise."

"You're different than what I imagined," Anna says in a small but firm voice.

I cock my head to the side. "What did you imagine?"

"Someone more reserved," she says, giving me a once-over.

My dress stops midway up my thigh and exposes a lot of shoulder, but is loose-fitting outside the chest area. Her dress is also sleeveless, with a deep plunge, but stops below her thigh.

I'm not sure if it's a subtle insult, separating us when she knows she was with Anders longer, so I say, "Well"—I give her the same once-over—"looks like Anders has a type."

Anders snorts, and Lucas wraps an arm around Anna. "Before this gets more awkward, maybe we should all get some liquor in our systems."

"Great idea." I tighten my grip on Anders until he puts his arm around me as we walk.

He and Lucas exchange pleasantries while Anna and I keep glancing at each other. Neither of us is giving the other dirty looks, and it's not like I need to be territorial since Anders isn't really mine and Anna is married, but there is this tension that travels with us as we move through the indoor entrance of the vineyard.

When people notice Anders, they all cheer and rush over to give their birthday wishes. Some hang back and wave, taking a more patient approach. I try to pull away so he can greet them all properly, but he snakes a hand around my waist, pressing me against him.

Right. There are more eyes on us than ever. If there was ever a time to play up the role of doting girlfriend, it's now. Especially when we step through the French doors at the back of the building, leading outside to the endless rows of vines, and his favorite people are standing around under hundreds, maybe thousands, of string lights woven throughout thin apple trees that stretch farther than my vision allows.

Olive rushes toward Anders and gives us both a hug. "Happy birthday!" she says, then to me, "You look so pretty."

I blink. "Oh, I thought you were reading my mind—that's exactly what I thought when I saw you."

She smiles widely as Bethany joins, gives us separate hugs, then pats my shoulder. "A shame you didn't make the family dinner. Anders spoke so sweetly of you; he actually made his father twitch, which is his form of a smile."

Guilt and nerves pinch the sides of my stomach, but I force a smile. I place my arm on Anders's chest. "I'm aware of how lucky I am."

He grabs my hand, lifts it up to his lips, and leaves it there for a long, warm kiss. New, sweeter nerves swarm my stomach and replace the anxiety there.

"Gross," Valerie says as she joins, John hanging behind her. She hugs her brother, then me. It may be my imagination, but she squeezes me extra tight before pulling away.

"Shall we grab a table?" Bethany says, already walking to a long one on the cobblestones. I try to follow, but my heel gets caught and sinks into the grass.

Anders's hands grip my waist, yanking me so my back presses against him. The memory of us at the billiards table, our bodies pressed tightly against each other, flashes through my mind. It sends a hot shot of heat straight between my legs so suddenly that, if not for Anders wrapped around me, I'd buckle.

"Careful." His mouth presses against my ear.

"Thanks." The word is pathetically breathless.

And the sound of it floods my mind with memories—and Anders, too, with the way he begins to harden against me. As much as my body's instinct wants to press back against his length, I maneuver myself away.

He clears his throat, then holds a hand at my back as he leads us to join the table.

We sit across from Valerie and John, with Bethany and Olive on opposite ends of the table.

"So, Anders," Bethany says, "how are you feeling? How has the day part of the birthday been treating you?" She looks at me. "I hope you made it special."

I chew on my bottom lip just as Anders's arm wraps around me, pulling me close against him. "She gave me a very thoughtful gift." He ends the sentence with a kiss on the side of my head.

My hand falls on his thigh, and I give him a light squeeze as I lean into him. He presses another kiss, this time under my ear.

"Ugh, get a room," Valerie says.

"Why don't you and John ever kiss?" Olive says.

John stiffens, and Valerie scoffs. "They're barely kissing."

In answer, Anders grips my chin and presses a quick kiss on my lips.

"Okay, show-off," Valerie says, "some of us are less PDA and more behind closed doors."

"Anyway," Bethany interrupts, "thank you for taking care of my boy. It's nice to see him smitten."

My lips pull into a smile. Tonight, I can't waver or think about what's real. Right now, I have to believe it is, to play my part.

I pinch Anders's cheek. "Is that it? Are you smitten by me?"

"Endlessly," he answers.

Valerie gags before pointing at me. "I forgot to tell you, we moved up the Jack and Jill party to this week. I hear your sister is visiting. You should invite her."

I smile like I'm thinking about the possibility, but it's impossible. The wedding is fast approaching, and I'm not making the progress I need. I've decided to go forward with my most creative, and insane, wedding-wrecking plan.

Unfortunately, it involves my sister, so Valerie can't see her outside of what I have planned in two days—Taina playing a psychic, guiding Valerie to the understanding that this wedding isn't meant to be.

"I'll bring it up to her," I lie, shifting in my seat.

"What about you?" Valerie asks Anders. "Are you still going to make it? You're cutting it close."

When I give Anders a perplexed look, he tells me, "I forgot to mention, I have to travel to New York for just a couple days. I'll be back early morning before the Jack and Jill."

Anders presses another kiss to the side of my head.

And Bethany claps her hands. "You two are so damn cute; let me get a photo." When she whips out her phone, Anders and I lean into each other, cheek to cheek.

We take a few shots, and then Anders asks, "Can you send me those?"

And my heart doubles its pulses.

Bethany asks about Anders's newest book cover, and Olive busies herself with a game on her mom's phone. Valerie joins the conversation now and then, and I keep my eyes on John, who barely joins in but is paying attention. Whenever Valerie fidgets with her hands, he covers them with his. If she twirls her hair, he pulls her fingers away.

"This is a vineyard," I interrupt them all, standing up. "Shall I grab us drinks?"

"Sure," Bethany agrees. "Get us the house wine."

"I'll help with the cups." Anders starts to get up.

I press my hands on his shoulders and shove him down. "John," I say, "let's let them continue their conversation. Come help me."

There's no weapon in my hand, but John looks as if I'm pointing a gun his way. "Me?"

"Yes, you."

Valerie's eyes widen, and I give her a slight head shake. Of course I'm not mentioning what happened with the scammer. For a plethora of reasons. Also, thinking of even having a million dollars makes my head spin, let alone losing it.

He follows me at a slower pace than necessary as we make our way inside to the curved bar overlooking the hefty guest list. I order the house wine and a Shirley Temple for Olive.

"So," I say, "heard I'm a bridesmaid now?"

John shoves his hands in his jeans pockets. "I did."

I frown. "You don't sound excited."

"No," he says, then brings his hands back out in a frantic wave. "I mean, yes, I am."

"You're incredibly hard to read. Has anyone ever told you that?"

"No," he says, but if that's true, that doesn't mean other people don't agree; it's just that they're not saying it to his face.

"You and Valerie are vastly different," I point out. "She can light up a room and talk up a storm." I don't say the rest, but let him hear the implication that he's far from those things.

"I know."

"Does it make you nervous?" I ask. "You seem so. Even Olive can see how awkward you two can be." When he stammers, I add, "In a sweet way, of course. I mean no offense."

"Yes, it does," he answers, and even when he does, I still can't get a read on him. I want to feel him out more. Gather more information. And, really, the more I care for Valerie, the more genuinely I want what's best for her. Unfortunately, the little I've learned about John isn't reassuring.

They come from different lifestyles, and they barely so much as glance at each other when in the same room; he got her scammed out of a million goddamn dollars. Her family is already hesitant about the pair.

I just don't see this working.

"So why ask her to marry you?" I say. "I know that's blunt—I know I'm a new addition to the family dynamic—but I really adore Valerie, and I want her to be happy."

He avoids my gaze. "Maybe we don't look perfect to you, but Valerie thinks we are."

"And what about you?" I counter.

He opens his mouth, then shuts it, then opens it again.

The bartender returns with our glasses, and John gathers all he can and scurries away. Running away from me, from the question, and now I can't help but wonder if this pairing is more one sided than I thought.

I grab the remaining drink—the Shirley Temple—and head out. Anders is walking toward me, and nobody is at the table anymore. A quick scan shows John and Valerie walking toward the small fountain, and Bethany laughing incredibly hard at something a handsome man is saying.

"Party's already over?" I say as Anders approaches.

"They want me to mingle more," he answers. "They say the birthday boy needs to get a lot of kisses and touches and—"

I press a hand to his chest before he wraps his arms around me. "Somehow, I don't think anyone at the table mentioned that."

"In my head, they did." He moves back, and because, behind him, I see his ex-girlfriend watching, I lean into him, sipping the drink.

"While we're alone," I say, "let me update you on some things."

A screech pierces through the air. I jerk back, scanning for the culprit and find a man with a microphone beside a guitarist and a keyboard player, just beside the fountain. "Sorry about that," the singer says into the mic.

Then they start playing a cover of a song I can't remember exactly but heard recently on the radio.

"Can you talk and dance?" Anders says, already pulling me by my waist to the center of the patio.

"Growing up in a Puerto Rican household," I say, letting him sway us to the pop melody, "I can dance and cook and clean all at the same time."

He smiles in his easy way, and I shake my head when my lips try to mirror it.

"Anyway," I go on, "there are a lot of eyes on us, so I need you to put on your best acting facade because what I have to tell you is going to piss you off an unbelievable amount."

His hand stills for just a second before he recovers.

I update him on exactly what went down and how I became a bridesmaid. On how I've been speaking with Valerie, texting her, chatting with her, trying to plant subtle seeds of doubt. I tell him what he's missed and, finally, tell him about the million dollars as the band goes through their set.

My stomach knots the moment I say it. My voice lowers, my breath shortens, and guilt settles somewhere heavy in my chest. I pinkie-swore I wouldn't say anything. Valerie trusted me. But I also watched her dig herself deeper into a hole, and I couldn't let Anders stay in the dark—not when he's technically my employer.

And not when I genuinely believe this isn't something that Valerie should keep a secret.

His face furrows together, anger pulling at every muscle.

I finish explaining. The moment stretches as a new, slower song drifts through the air. Anders goes still.

His jaw tightens. His hand—still resting on my waist from when we were dancing—clenches slightly. His eyes drop to the ground like he's trying to process the weight of everything I just dropped on him. His sister. A million dollars. Gone.

"She didn't tell me," he finally says. His voice is low, like he's afraid of how loud his anger might be if he gives it any more breath. "She lost a million dollars, and she didn't tell me."

I shift closer. "She was scared, Anders."

"She should be," he snaps, then instantly shakes his head. "No. No, that's not fair. It's not even about the money. It's him. John. I knew he was reckless. I *told* her he was reckless. And now it'll be her problem, forever."

"It won't, we'll stop them."

"She listens to everyone but me," he says, on a tangent. "And I don't even care about being right. I just . . . I care. And she makes it impossible to protect her."

"You're doing all you can."

"It hasn't been enough."

He sounds defeated. And I hate that.

"I know," I say gently. "I know you feel like she's slipping away from you. But she still listens to you, Anders. She still loves you. She just doesn't want to disappoint you."

"I'm not even mad at her. I'm mad at him. And I'm mad that I can't trust him. Not with her, not with her future, and definitely not with her money."

He takes another step away from me, then turns back, his face unreadable now. "Anders—"

His mouth presses on mine. If not for his fingers gripping the sides of my waist, pulling me closer to him, I'd fall over. All the wires in my head short-circuit, and I feel the bolts ricocheting throughout my body in hot, sudden flares.

My hands grab his neck, to pull him away, to bring him closer, to feel his skin under the pads of my fingers. Only when my head starts to spin—faster than it already does—do I press my hands on his chest.

Right before I lose my very last breath, he pulls away.

I'm trying to compose myself, and Anders, the bastard, simply wipes my lip stain from the side of his mouth, the most out-of-place thing about him, including the stray hairs falling at the side of his face.

"Sorry," he says, his thumb caressing my lips, presumably to remove the smudged lip stain. "You wanted me to act, and that was the only way to hide."

"It's okay." I step back.

"Actually." He grabs my arm. "I'm not sorry. At all." To prove his point, he presses another kiss to my lips, and I can feel my body heating at the speed of a kettle on a flame.

It's way too easy to kiss Anders, to lose where the line between reality and acting lies. My heart shouldn't beat at a thunderous pace; my body shouldn't plead with me to look for him in every room and glue itself to his, and my brain should know better than to fall for someone who absolutely won't stay with me.

"I need to go to the bathroom," I lie, shoving him off me.

I think someone calls my name, but I hurry through the vineyard, speed through bodies lining up for drinks, and throw myself out the exit. I'm not sure where to go, only that I need to get my traitorous heart and body as far away from Anders as possible.

I spot a lantern hanging at the opening of a trail—I'm not sure where it leads. Trying to keep my balance on the pebbled lot, I make my way to it. Then move to the next lantern that leads me to a path lined by hundreds of tiny lit bulbs, their yellow light pouring over the meticulously cared-for landscaping of fruit bushes and flowers.

Like a fairy garden come to life.

"Lucinda!" Anders, of course, grabs my hand and pulls me to a stop.

"Don't start with me." I yank my hand away.

The glow of the lights makes his skin a warm tan, and his hair is a shade lighter here. He looks perfect, as always, but now I feel the urge to shove his head through the bushes for it.

"What's wrong?" he asks, undeterred.

"What's wrong?" My eyes widen. "You. Me. Us. There's no us, see? There's the problem."

"You're not making any sense."

"Oh, please." I shove him with my finger. "You know what I mean."

"Pretend I don't," he says, "spell it out for me."

"I shouldn't be buying you gifts," I tell him.

"Well, you can't have it back," he answers bluntly.

The fact that that's his first worry almost makes me smile, but the nerves simmering in my stomach remind me to be serious. I take a breath, calm myself. This conversation is long overdue. Instead of drawing lines between us in my head, I need to tell him they're there.

"I just mean, I'm a temporary addition to your life. I'm here for a limited amount of time. I'm going to keep your sister from getting married, which is going to leave some hurt people for you to deal with when I'm gone. You're paying me to do the job. I will do it well. But that's the extent of this relationship between us."

He crosses his arms against his chest. "Says who?"

"Excuse me?" I almost laugh. "Who needs to say it? These are all facts."

"Not to me," he says. "I understand if us, the way we are, how we were at the bar, if you think that's all a mistake. I'd rather you say that directly to me than speak for me."

"It's not a mistake—wait, don't you think it was a mistake?"

"When did I say that?"

"Well, the day after we—" Even thinking about what we did at the bar makes my cheeks flare. "After the bar, you avoided me. I remember. I figured you wanted to act like it didn't happen."

"I avoided you, Lucinda, because it was painfully obvious you were listing every single reason why that night was a bad idea, and I didn't want to have the conversation where you give voice to those thoughts."

I press my fingers into my temples. "Okay, so I was wrong about that. But I'm not wrong about the rest."

"Why did you get me the gift?" he asks.

"What?"

He repeats the question, but I'm not entirely sure of my answer. "I don't know; I didn't really think about it. I saw it, thought you'd think it was funny, and got it."

"Because you like me."

"Well, yeah, you're a pretty likable guy. Who doesn't like you?"

"You like me as more than a friend. You know exactly what I mean."

Of course I do, but the point of this conversation is to draw very necessary lines between us. "I'm not sure why that matters here."

"It matters because I like you too."

"You don't know what you're talking about. You don't know everything about me. You don't know if you'll be bored of me in a couple of weeks."

"I know enough to know you're wrong," he counters, "and I can learn more too. I'm not asking you to fall in love with me at this moment. But you're here, right now, and for a while. I want to explore you, and if you want to stay with me, even when this is all over, is that so bad?"

"I—" This is not at all how I pictured this conversation would go. Especially after talking with Bethany. I thought he'd agree just to appease me, and we'd move on. Easy, if a little awkward, and then normal. Like two roommates who work together. "How would this ever work?"

"How wouldn't it?"

"How would you explain me to your family?"

"I don't have to tell them how we actually met, what's happening with Valerie. There wouldn't be a problem. They all like you already."

"Valerie would find out eventually."

"She won't," he says, firm. "And even if she did, we'd deal with it. *I'll* deal with it. I'll take all the blame. I'd handle the brunt of it all."

I shake my head. "And what about when it's been long enough that your family starts to notice I don't actually have the job you told them I did?"

"By then," he says, "you'll be working at the shelter. We can tell them the truth about that."

"We live in different states," I remind him.

"I like to travel."

"Anders," I say.

"Lucinda," he says.

"I'm being serious here."

"As am I." He pulls me closer to him. "Tell me you don't want to explore whatever this connection between us is, and I won't pursue you. I'll be polite, help you when you need it, and we won't speak at all outside of work, I promise. Tell me now, and I'll do it."

I stare at him. "You told me you thought love was fleeting. That people don't know how to stay in it."

"I did." Anders nods.

"So why are you saying all this now?"

"Because I've never felt this before. I've never wanted someone the way I want you. Your company. Your laugh. Your body. Even when we're silent or awkward, I crave it. I crave you," he says firmly. "And I know I won't stop."

"I have nothing to offer you," I say, the words scraping out like a confession. "I can't take care of you. I'm a mess. You're so put together. What am I supposed to do with that?"

"You do take care of me," he says softly. "God, Lucinda . . . you make me *feel*. Everything with you feels better—warmer, softer, brighter. You're not a mess. And if you get into one, let me be the one to take care of you."

When I start to shake my head, Anders adds, "Why won't you accept that people care about you too? If you think it's so important, then let me take care of you. Let me be with you."

His words steal my automatic denial.

A small, hopeful voice in my head wonders if it wouldn't be so bad to be cared for. To be held together by someone who doesn't expect me to earn it first.

And maybe I'm not so broken that I have to keep proving I'm worth something. Maybe I already am, just by being a person. Haven't I done enough good in my life that it would be okay?

And yet, the hope fights with fear. "You're not seeing the bigger picture here," I say, trying to find a straw to grasp, wondering why I can't just tell him no, he shouldn't pursue me. All the reasons I had seem to go hazy when he brings me closer to his chest.

"Give me this month to be with you," he says. "Let me take you on real dates, treat this like a real relationship. Give me a real chance, and we'll see if it's worth continuing. That's reasonable, right?"

"No," I say, finding another straw. "Anders, we live entirely different lives. You're established, well off, so incredibly put together, and I'm basically a homeless, broke mess of a woman. Why in the world would you want to date me?"

"I can think of several reasons."

When I roll my eyes, he grips my chin to face him. "You make me laugh in a single conversation more than I've laughed in months. And when you make someone else laugh, you smile like hearing them feel joy is a reward." My heart pounds. "Every time you see something you think your sister will like or find amusing, you take a photo and send it to her. Because you like making people feel like they matter in your world, even when you're apart." My palms grow hot and sweaty. "And maybe I haven't seen all of it, but I know enough to see how you've built the beginning of your life around helping your sister. And you don't complain, because the love in your heart is this endless gift that can move past any unfairness that it comes across." My breathing comes rapidly. "You don't have enough money to pay for a round of shots, but you went out of your way to get me a gift just because you thought it'd make me laugh for a brief moment, because tiny instants like that feel like big ones to you. And you appreciate even the smallest of things, and make them feel big. You're always looking to help, but there's more to you than that. I think it's just where you've learned to put all your love, so you don't have to risk handing any of it to someone who might not hold it carefully."

"Anders," I whisper, my heart stuttering, butterflies fluttering in the pit of my stomach.

"Say yes," Anders pleads with me, "and I'll keep giving you reasons to believe me. Let me hold some of your love. We can figure out the rest as it comes. I'll figure it out for you. Just say yes."

Never in my life have I ever had a man confess to me this way. His words feel like they're bandaging tiny paper cuts in my heart, small wounds I thought healed long ago. And not a single thing he said had to do with how I look, yet I've never felt so seen in my life.

Anders is a genuinely good man, and for some reason is interested in me.

Every part of me wants to say yes. How could I not? He isn't wrong; we could try—we could see if whatever's between us can be great. Cross the messy bridge when we get to it. When will I ever meet a man like Anders?

Never, because there is no other man like Anders.

I suck in a breath and give him my answer.

25.

We trip over each other from the car to the front door, our mouths at a more desperate pace to reach each other, faster than our legs can carry us inside. Anders slams the door shut, and I kick my heels off, the ache of wearing them for too long making me flinch and buckle.

"You okay?" Anders pauses mid-kiss.

"Yeah," I say, "just my feet."

In answer, he grabs my ass with both hands and lifts me in a swift move.

Instinctively, I wrap my legs around him, grinding my body closer to his. My dress hikes up, and his fingers dig into my skin, bare from the thong I wore to prevent any lines.

"Jesus, Lucinda," he says, feeling all the exposed skin there, his mouth traveling down to my neck.

There's a small clattering approaching us. I turn my gaze, and my heart nearly bursts from its chest.

Sora turns the corner, head tilted as he inspects us.

"You got Sora?" I say, my voice thick with sudden emotion.

"It's why I was busy," he explains. "Dainese was helping me with the adoption papers."

I love you. I love you. I'm pretty sure I'm hopelessly in love with you.

The words are stuck in my throat, so I move to get off Anders and greet Sora.

He tightens his grip on me. "Please, Lucinda, give him a wave, but I need you now."

"Then take me now."

He carries me swiftly to his room, shutting the door with his foot.

Ribbons of light from the moon glow over us as he slowly takes me to the edge of his bed, dropping me softly.

I grip his neck, try to pull him to my mouth.

Anders pulls away, his hands on my thighs as he goes on his knees. His mouth presses against my inner thigh, his fingers gliding up it, slowly, up and up as he brings his tongue to follow before he reaches the curve of me.

He looks up at me through thick lashes, a desperate, devoted heat burning in his gaze. "I have wanted to taste you from the moment I met you."

Before I can think of a response, he presses a kiss over my panties. He starts from the bottom, skips the middle, and comes down from the top, and ends up below where I need him again.

When I shift, try to maneuver so he presses where I need him most, he chuckles.

"So impatient," he says softly into my skin, before pressing a kiss at my center.

The pressure of it has heat branching off into every other part of me. He digs his finger under the fabric, yanks it to the side while sucking my clit into his mouth in a swift, hard pull.

Stars burst throughout my vision.

My head tilts back, my body arches into his mouth. He presses his thumb against my skin, pressing down so that my clit is entirely exposed as he licks and sucks the very tip of it.

My eyes drift shut. I bite my lip so hard I taste my own blood, but it's nothing, *nothing* compared to Anders devouring me.

He pauses. "Look at me."

Even his voice adds to the growing heat flooding me. I lean my head down, my fingers reaching to dig into his hair. His gaze is piercing, intent, as he grips my thighs and spreads them farther before feasting at my center again.

The pleasure skyrockets through me, my legs overwhelmed by all the sensations, and I try instinctively to shut them, to bury him farther into me, trap him between my thighs. He keeps a tight grip as he devours me, and small, needy whimpers begin to rip through me like a desperate chant.

The possession continues until they become loud, desperate pleas of Anders's name.

The explosion comes so suddenly and quickly, my heart stalls as I moan out his name—scream it when he doesn't let up, when he digs himself deeper into my thighs, and I grind on his face, finish on his tongue.

My heart pounds in my chest, in my ears.

Anders pulls away, slowly getting up from his knees so he can reach my mouth. His fingers sweep the side of my face. "Taste how sweet you are, Lucinda."

I open my mouth, and he slips his tongue inside. My eyes roll to the back of my head as he kisses me, my body molten hot, my skin tingling in ways it's never before. As desperate as the rest of me, my fingers graze his shirt, pull and pull till he gets the cue and lifts it off.

The shadows of his abs are thicker in the dark, and I want to lick every crevice of them, of him. I want my mouth on every possible part of him until I have explored the entirety of the map that is Anders.

I grab my dress that's crumpled around my waist and pull it off, exposing my bare breasts.

Anders reaches over, pressing a hot kiss to me before pulling away and moving toward the nightstand. He turns on the lamp and returns to me.

"Good," he says, tensing as his gaze snags on my breasts. "I want to be able to see you while I'm inside you."

In answer, I yank the string of my thong so hard it rips, the scraps falling uselessly to the floor. My legs spread as wide as they can. Anders wants a full view of me, and I could not deny him anything he could possibly want, ever.

Not like this, now, when his gaze is trained on me like I'm all he has desired, that this is what he's worked for his whole life. To take me, in every way he can.

"I've thought of you like this," I say, my hand sliding down my chest. "So many times, right next door, stopping myself from coming into this room and filling myself with you."

He sucks in a breath before unbuttoning his pants, and my gaze is trapped on the movement. His long, hard, artist's hands remove his pants, his underwear, and I watch with rapt attention as his hardened cock pulses before me.

"Did you touch yourself when you thought of me?" he asks, squeezing his length.

My gaze goes hazy as I watch his fingers close in around himself. I nod as I follow the movement, see the veins all along his length.

"Show me," he says, "how you touched yourself."

My fingers move across my chest, until I cup my breast, squeeze it in my palm, then reach down to my center. It's soaked from Anders already, and my fingers slip trying to find my most tender area to press down.

My mouth pops open at the pressure, the spot already too sensitive from what's been done to it. I squirm against my fingers, pinching my nipple.

Like he can no longer handle being a spectator, Anders yanks me to the center of the bed, his knee spreading my thighs open, before his body presses against mine, his mouth enveloping my breast.

His teeth take a small bite of my nipple, and I let out a whimper. Anders answers with a slight rumble of a growl, a pulse of hardness where his length pushes against my thighs. His mouth presses hot kisses from my breast all along my collarbones.

When he reaches the space below my ears and I gasp, he spends extra time there, his tongue tracing small circles before he sucks the skin there, his hand reaching down my stomach until his fingers rub into my center and I buck into him.

"It feels so good," I manage to get out between whispers.

The praise makes him work harder. His mouth moves to the other side of my neck, giving it equal attention as I grind onto his fingers, faster and faster, wetter and wetter.

"You're so goddamn beautiful," Anders says, fingering me, his face hovering over me. "I want to watch you come over and over again."

Another needy whimper escapes me as the heat builds and builds. I writhe against his hand, my heart hammering against my rib cage. It's more pleasure than a human should feel; it's torturous and overwhelming, and I need more of it, endlessly.

"Anders," I plead. "I need you inside me. Now."

"Anything you want, beautiful."

I watch as he positions himself. He grabs his cock, then guides it between my folds, moving it up and down, drenching himself in me.

"I'm so wet," I say, my words no longer able to reach a decibel above gasps. "I've never been this wet before."

He grits his teeth as I arch myself up, letting myself feel every inch of his length.

"I'll do this for you, always," he says, the tip of him finally, *finally* pressing inside me. He takes it slow, maybe to not hurt me with his size, maybe to slow down what we've built up for so long.

A strangled cry escapes me, and Anders groans as my legs wrap around his waist, and I pull myself up until he is buried inside me. I tighten myself around his cock, and heat burns through my center, throughout my body.

His jaw is tense as he slides in and out of me, all of my slickness coating him, making soft, wet sounds as he takes me faster now.

"I've thought about this," Anders says, "imagined the feel of you, imagining the way you'd look with me inside you."

"And?" I pant. "Is it what you imagined?"

"Nowhere near." He rocks into me. "Not at all as good as you feel, Lucinda."

"I love the way you say my name." I match his pace, slamming into him in desperate, fast knocks. "Like a prayer."

"I'd gladly worship you." He rhythmically pounds into me, enough to steal any ability to speak.

The sensation of Anders inside me is better than any touch thus far. I squeeze his cock as much as I can, relishing in the sounds of his almost pained groans.

He grips my waist, pulls me up until we're sitting upright, and I'm able to fully ride him, my hands digging into his shoulders, using him to stabilize myself as I jump, pounding myself into him, filling myself with as much of Anders as physically possible.

His mouth travels from my mouth, my ear, my neck, sucking and kissing every available surface as we press into each other, our bodies equally desperate to rejoin each time we separate.

"I'm going to come," I manage to get out, my breath ragged.

"Come," Anders says, "again, and again."

"You too," I plead. "Inside me. I need to feel you. Please."

He slams his mouth over mine, slipping his hand between us, his thumb circling my clit without losing the rhythm of sliding inside me. Now, instead of needy whimpers, ragged shouts echo out of me between kisses, incoherent sounds of pleasure, Anders's name said like a prayer, my center pulsing as euphoria sweeps over me like a tide.

My body racks itself with sobs, my eyes burning with tears as I scream his name. Hot liquid pools inside me, and I squeeze, getting out as much as I can from Anders. Pleasure pulses through me, Anders jerks inside me, and a final cry rips from me as I come along with him.

My vision is freckled with white spots, my breath comes in rapid gasps, and my legs grow limp and useless. He drops his head into the curve of my neck before moving up to my mouth, taking his time, laying soft, sweet kisses like dozens of thank-yous.

When he pulls out of me, I cry out, a sudden burst of pleasure hitting me in an aftershock. If I could move my legs, I'd want to get on my knees and start all over, tasting him.

For now, I push my fingers inside me, feeling the mix of my and Anders's come, and bring it up to my mouth and suck.

Anders's jaw tenses, and he grabs my wrist, pulling my fingers from my mouth to his, sucking before leaning down and kissing me until I'm dizzy. He pulls away, presses another kiss on my temple, then walks to his en suite bathroom.

He returns with a small, wet hand towel and cleans me off with gentle, slow movements, pressing kisses where he wipes along the way.

Heat flushes through my cheeks initially. I nearly tell him I'll do it myself. When I think about it, no other lover has ever cleaned me up after we've had sex. Not even my ex-husbands.

Anders must see something on my face because he asks, "What's wrong?"

"Not wrong," I say, then, with even hotter cheeks from the admission, tell him what I was thinking.

He drops the towel beside me, leans down and holds my face in his hands. "Lucinda, I'm going to treat you like you deserve; I promise you."

"Do you mean it?" I ask, humiliated at how small my voice sounds, at the sudden fear of it not being true, and worse, the hope that it will be.

He pulls my hand to his mouth, presses a kiss on my palm. "I'll prove it to you."

26.

"I can't believe you actually flew out your sister's psychic." Valerie squeezes my arm as we walk through Anders's house—he's missing, of course, because he claimed he wouldn't be able to keep a straight face at everything planned—out to the backyard.

"No worries," I say. "Anders paid for everything. I'm just the idea girl."

"Still," Valerie says, adjusting her Libra necklace, "everyone else always rolls their eyes when I talk about this stuff. You're the only person who doesn't make me feel like an idiot for believing in astrology."

Knowing this is all a ruse makes the statement sting, but I smile as we step onto the deck.

Anders helped me drag a circular table out of his basement. It's now sitting on the pale wood deck overlooking his meticulously trimmed lawn—mostly bare, except for a tiny patch in the corner where a younger Olive and Anders built a fairy garden.

My heart pounds—just thinking his name turns me into a puddle of affection.

I shake it off. This is the final push. The biggest pressure yet between Valerie and John.

Just then the "psychic"—Taina, of course—emerges onto the deck. "Greetings," she says in a thick Spanish accent.

A snort escapes before I can stop it. I cover it with a cough, but Valerie doesn't notice. She's wide eyed, watching as Taina circles the table and stops in front of her—coincidentally both wearing white dresses—to inspect her with a dramatic flair. She moves her hand, each finger heavy with rings, and waves them as if pulling Valerie's scent toward her.

She hums deeply before sitting across from a hopeful Valerie.

"You're confused," Taina says, placing her hands in a prayer shape on the table covered in a white tablecloth. Everything but Taina's rings, layered necklaces, and hair is without color—purposefully plain, so she could "easily read the colors of Valerie's aura," she'd said, after "extensive research" on Spanish psychics she found on a Reddit thread. She took notes all night.

"Your soul is splattered with emotion," Taina continues. "So much so that your inner self has become a shadow lost in a dark room, unable to find itself."

Valerie stiffens.

"I'll give you privacy," I say, phone secretly recording under the table.

Valerie grabs my hand. "Stay," she whispers. "Let me know how you feel about her when we're done."

I drag over a cushioned chair and sit beside her.

Valerie rests her hand on the table. "How long have you been doing this?"

Taina impressively lifts a single brow. "How long have you known how to breathe? My gift was passed down to me by my mother at birth. Our seer ability has traveled through generations, given to the next in line, taken from the one who births."

I focus on the gold chains on her neck to keep from laughing. But then I see Valerie's face—how much she believes this—and guilt digs into my ribs. If she knew this was all fake, would she lump me in with everyone else who dismisses her?

I've always cared. But now that Anders and I have decided to be together—really together—everything feels heavier. My head scrambles, my heart falters, and guilt gnaws through my chest as violently as an energized woodpecker, first thing in the morning, on a brand-new tree.

"A honey psychic," Valerie says—a term I've never heard before. "My last psychic was the same. I didn't tell anyone that."

"Fate binds you to the familiar. The familiar shall guide you."

I should've never let her binge-watch a marathon of low-budget Lifetime magical movies last night. Taina might be pulling from all of them at once.

"You have the biggest decision of your life to make," Taina says. "Figuring out if you want to say 'I do.'"

I snort. "Yeah, that's not exactly brand-new, top-secret information."

Taina holds a finger to her nose. "The universe whispers to me about you. It says you need a cleansing."

"Focus on Valerie, please," I mutter.

"You're wavering." Taina presses her fingers into her temples. "You see a name that is not the one you're meant to wed."

Valerie freezes. Panic flickers before she smooths her expression. "What name?"

Taina closes her eyes, tapping her nails on the table. A long pause. Then she opens them. "Nick."

Valerie glares at me. "You told her."

"I did not." I totally did. But I thought she was too drunk to remember telling me about him in the first place.

Valerie leans toward Taina. "Tell me something only I would know. Something no one else could guess."

Taina closes her eyes, humming something familiar—until I realize it's a Bad Bunny song. I discreetly kick her under the table, and she switches melodies.

Her brows furrow in mock pain. Then, right on cue, clouds gather and thunder rolls faintly in the distance.

Or maybe our mom is rolling in her grave, ready to claw out of her coffin and strangle us both for this brujería. I can picture her making the sign of the cross with her fingers and whispering a prayer to ward off whatever spirits she thought this would invite.

She believed even saying "Oh my God" was a sin to confess before entering heaven. I say her signature forgiveness prayer in my head. Just in case.

Thunderclaps. Taina opens her eyes. "When you were a child, you wanted to be a ghost hunter."

Valerie grips my arm. "I've never told anyone that."

"The universe hears you anyway."

No way that was a lucky guess. If I had to bet, Taina's late-night drive was to Bethany's house to hack Valerie's search history and take notes on her niche interests. Taina once told me she could track a cheating boyfriend's incognito tabs. In another life, she'd be recruited by the NSA.

"Okay, okay," Valerie says, mostly to herself. "I have been thinking about Nick. A lot. Why am I doing that? What does that mean?"

"Often when we think we're happy," Taina says, "our memories echo truths in our souls."

"I think I'm happy?" Valerie echoes. "I am happy."

"Then why are you here?"

Valerie hesitates. "Clarity."

"And what clarity will you gain from one not of your heart?"

"What do you mean?"

"Perhaps," I interrupt, "the universe could explain itself less cryptically."

Taina raises a silencing finger, then clasps Valerie's hand. "If your heart teeters, you must place it on the scales and see to which side it breaks."

Valerie pulls back. "I can't see Nick again. My family would kill me. I promised I'd never see him again."

Taina doesn't flinch. "Then why does he still visit your thoughts?"

Valerie wavers. I can see the answer forming, her eyes flicking toward the tablecloth like the answer might be embroidered into the hem.

"Valerie," I ask gently, "why do you think you keep remembering him? Is there something John lacks that Nick didn't?"

Her brows knit. I've hit something.

She groans, tossing her head back. "It's my stupid brother. He got in my head. Don't tell him I said that."

"What did he say?"

"That John's terrible with money. And to be careful with mine. I brushed it off, but now, I don't know, it's messing with my head."

"And Nick wasn't?"

She shakes her head. "He came from money, so it wasn't even a factor. But he had his own issues."

"What kind of issues?" I press, softly.

She hesitates, then gives a small shake of her head. "I don't want to get into it. It doesn't matter."

Taina drums her palms against the table again. "The more you speak of him, the more the universe screams. The voices are loud."

Valerie's eyes widen slightly. Then narrow. "What voices?"

"They are yours," Taina says calmly. "They just sound different when you try not to listen."

Valerie flinches.

For a second, I think she's going to settle down. Ask more questions. Stay in this a little longer. But then—

"No." Valerie stands abruptly. "I can't. I won't see Nick again. I'm sorry. I have to go."

"Valerie—" I call, but she's already halfway across the garden.

Taina sighs, sagging in her seat like she's winded. I slump into my chair and groan.

Taina grabs my hand and rubs my palm. "I see a great deal of back pain in your future."

I yank it back. "Please break character."

"I don't know." Taina wiggles her brows. "Think I found a new hobby."

"How about we focus on the hobby you *are* good at," I say. "How fast can you find Nick's contact info?"

"How fast can you make your signature mofongo?"

"An hour and a half?"

"Make it tasty." Taina grins. "All right, plan time."

I raise a brow. "You thinking what I'm thinking?"

"Oh, absolutely," Taina says, pulling out her phone. "The universe speaks to me."

"I'll kill you."

"Just tell me what you need from me. You're going to invite him down, right? Set up a meet-cute?"

"I don't know what that means."

"God, Lucy, read a book, will you?"

"Anyway," I go on, "if you mean getting him down for the Jack and Jill party this week, then sure." I sort through blurred, drunk memories of our night of venue hunting. "I think he lives in North Carolina."

"Not at all too far; doesn't even warrant a flight."

"Can you get me his contact info?" I ask. "Some general info on him?"

"Can a dog bark?"

I give her an exasperated stare.

"Okay, I'm on it. How are you going to get him down?"

"I'm pretty sure Valerie changed her number when she moved on to her next boyfriend. I can pretend I'm her with mine."

"All right, we're doing this."

"*I'm* doing this. And then after this," I add, folding my arms, "you'll book a flight home, right?"

Taina freezes. "What?"

"I appreciate your help, and it's been nice seeing you, but I have to finish this up on my own." *And you have to go back home before Mathew realizes you've been helping me all along.*

She shakes her head. "No way, it's getting good. I'm not leaving yet. What if you need me again?"

"I won't," I promise, "but thanks."

She crosses her arms against her chest. "No."

"Taina, I'm serious." My brows pull together. "This is my mess; you've done enough to help."

"Why can't I stick around the whole time? I'm your sister," she snaps, eyes flashing. "It felt like you were finally relying on me. You don't just cut that thread now because you feel like it. Why can't I be around, just in case?"

"I'm not pushing you out," I say, even though I absolutely am. "I'm just letting you off the hook."

Taina's voice sharpens. "I want to be on the hook."

"That doesn't make any sense."

"It does, and you know it," Taina says. "Besides, you *do* need me. Not just for wedding wrecking, but God, you need a reminder to lighten up a bit. Not freak out after you overthink about what you and Anders have fallen into. Live a little."

I open my mouth, shut it, then snap back, "I think I'll be fine. The wisdom you showed before seems to be missing now."

Taina scoffs. "Wow. Just like that, you view me as the fragile little sister not able to help out when it matters."

I blink. "Taina—"

"No, don't backpedal now," she says, quieter. "You're always going to be this way, Lucy, aren't you? Always going to dip one toe into trusting me, then yank it back the second it feels uncomfortable. Always going to share a little, hide a lot more, and push me away when you think you're showing too much."

I run a hand through my hair. "That's not fair."

"It's not"—Taina gets up—"and I'm getting a little sick of it."

She leaves me there, guilt rising in my chest and something heavier under it—something embarrassingly close to shame.

27.

Anders and I aren't exactly a couple, so I'm trying not to get prematurely girlfriend-crazy at him for being unreachable all day. He's been gone for three days already. The first day, we talked several times. The second, I was busy with Valerie and Taina for the whole psychic thing. And today, he's supposed to be flying back here to make it in time for the Jack and Jill party tonight.

Maybe I'm more sensitive now because Taina hasn't answered a single one of my calls and texts, and it would be nice to speak to another human being rather than sit in silence.

He said he was heading for the airport at seven in the morning, which was three hours ago, and he still hasn't called me like he said he would. I need to update him on my plans for Valerie.

Sora walks up to me and lays his face on my lap.

"You want to go outside, cutie?"

He wags his tail, so I take him out back to run around. As he lays out, displaying his stomach to the sun, I sit on the rocking chair. My screen lights up. I answer before the first ring finishes.

"Anders," I say into the phone before I hear the chaos of the early morning airport in the background.

"Hey, Lucinda," he says, warmth with a hint of aggravation clipped at the edge.

"TSA beat you down?"

He snorts. "It's insane here. A thunderstorm delayed most flights, including mine."

Extra nerves begin to pinch my insides. "Will you make it in time for the party?"

"I'm not sure," he answers. "Even if they get us on the plane, it's pretty bad out there."

I pause. "They won't fly unless it's safe to do so."

A longer, more interesting pause. "Right."

I sit up. "Anders, are you afraid of flying?"

"I don't like your tone."

I can't hold back my laugh. "Aw, Anders, I didn't know."

"Let the record state I have made no such confession."

"There's nothing to be scared of," I assure him. "Turbulence is like you're in Jell-O. Just a fun little ride."

"I've seen that video, and it brought me no comfort."

"So, you admit you're scared."

He sighs. "You know, my great-great-grandfather died in a plane crash. I look just like him. Could be him reincarnated. Wouldn't want to tempt fate."

"Really?"

"No," Anders admits, and I laugh. "But I don't want you to think I'm some coward."

"Coward, no," I tease. "Scaredy-cat, on the other hand . . ."

"Anyway," he says, "how is my dog?"

My dog. Already attached enough to claim Sora as his own. I knew he'd be a good owner.

"Good. Currently sunbathing."

"And how's my girl?"

My heart stutters. "Good. Watching your dog sunbathing, waiting for you."

"I guess I'd better get on the plane if I can."

Though his words are laced with warmth and sincerity, there's still a hint of edge to them. If he's stressed about even the thought of flying, I won't add to it by telling him what I have planned. If he doesn't make it, he'll be freaking out about missing it. If he does, he'll be trying to calm his ass down on the plane.

I'll just check his flight info. We still have plenty of time for him to make it; the flight is just under three hours. Plenty of time before the party. Once he touches down, I'll tell him in person—less stress for the anxious man.

"I hope so." I inspect my nails. "I'm tan, my skin is glowing, and I've never been prettier. It would be a waste if you didn't get to see me in all my glory." Then, feeling a little cocky and wanting to ease some of Anders's anxiety, I add, "In more ways than one."

"Lucinda," he calls my name softly.

"I don't want to be a cliché 'guess what I'm wearing tonight,' so I'll just tell you: With how tight my dress is, nothing at all underneath it."

Anders sucks in a breath. "Need I remind you I'm in a very public place?"

"Just thought I'd remind you that I miss you," I say. "Especially at night."

"Lucinda." This time, my name is a warning.

"But I've made do," I add, "in your clothes, in your bed, thinking about you while I touch myself."

There's a rustle of movement, then, "Jesus Christ, Lucinda."

"Talking about it is making me needy," I go on. "Maybe I'll head back to your room now."

"I'm honest to God about to grab a plane and pilot it myself," Anders says, and I cackle.

"Oh," I say mid-laugh, "I'll be late if I don't leave soon. I should go now."

"You are a menace," he says, exasperated.

I end the call on a chuckle and a bundle of satisfaction in the pit of my stomach.

Time to focus—wedding ruining D-Day is here. The Hail Mary.

It's time to put the nail in the coffin.

It's weird being without Anders as I enter Bethany's home. I've grown used to the comfort of his presence, his body, and the feel of his arm wrapped around my waist, the ease with which we slip our fingers through each other's.

Still, I keep my chin up as I move through people, dressed in all white as Valerie requested to match with the white balloons, white centerpieces, white gift bags; all white for the bride, who is standing by Olive, speaking with her fingers pinching her nose.

As I get closer, I spot the orange stain on the side of Valerie's dress, matching the color of the half-empty glass Olive holds. I hold in a laugh as I approach, just as Bethany appears and starts blotting the stain.

"I told you to stay in your room and read your book," Bethany says while rubbing the stain furiously. "Nothing at this party is interesting enough for a kid to join."

"I finished my book already." Olive crosses her arms against her *Iron Man* T-shirt. "I'm bored, and you're the one who doesn't allow TVs in bedrooms."

Valerie gestures to the living room occupied by friends and family, drinking, chatting, and laughing. "Did you really think you could watch a show right now?"

I join them, hand in my tote bag. "I have stain remover," I say, holding it out to Bethany. "I knew an all-white party was a risk."

"Thank you." Bethany snatches it.

Olive grips the side of my dress. "The new Marvel show is out, and I need to watch before I see any spoilers."

I smile and suggest, "Try watching it on your iPad?"

Valerie groans. "The little brat dropped it down the stairs today. The entire screen is cracked."

I scan the room. "Where's John?" Clearly Valerie is stressed and the groom-to-be is nowhere to be found.

"Late," she answers, anger coating the word, "and I'm already agitated enough about that as it is. And half my bridal party still hasn't arrived. The caterers sent the wrong order. The florist sent lilies instead of daisies, and I'm about to lose my goddamn mind."

I keep my face as unbiased as possible, ignoring the guilt flooding me since Taina and I spent hours meddling, calling vendors, giving wrong times, and changing orders. The bridesmaids, though—they suck all on their own.

This on-edge Valerie is only going to get worse, so I pull out my phone. "Use mine." I hand it to Olive. "Why don't you head to your room?"

She snatches it from me. "You're the best," she says as she runs off.

"Stain's out," Bethany says. "Let's get you under a blow dryer."

"I'll be nicer later," Valerie promises as Bethany, who probably has dealt with her wrath all day as things went wrong, pushes her along. I wave and smile, help myself to a glass of wine, then remember I drove here and replace it with a bottle of water.

My gaze keeps lingering on the front door. Nick said he would come. He lives just a few hours away, but what if he got cold feet? It was easy to guess Valerie still had lingering feelings for him.

But what if Nick isn't as stuck on Valerie as she him? What's my next step? Do I just crash the wedding? That'll implicate me, taint me for the family forever, and won't stop anything permanently. It's not even a plan.

I could do an intervention—straight-up sit down with Valerie and tell her I know from experience how to tell when something isn't going to work out. Try to save her heart in an honest, plain way—but every time I try to pry too deep, she runs away.

It's like the more Valerie's family tells her something isn't good for her, the more she wants it.

Maybe when John arrives, I can snatch his phone, have Taina hack into it, and find something incriminating. But I don't think he's cheating, unless we find messages that say he's using her for money.

That's more of a possibility.

Now I'm scanning the room for Nick *and* John.

My bag nearly falls off my shoulder, and I jerk back. Jennifer, her hair tied in a ponytail, is inches from my face. I grab my compact mirror from her hand, put it back in my bag.

"Jennifer, good to see you, I think."

She grins at me. "Hey, fellow bridesmaid." She crosses her arms. "I'm glad you're in. Some of the other girls are just nasty. I mean, they're not even here yet. Would it kill them to be on time?"

I step an arm's length away and rezip my bag. "It's good she has you," I say hesitantly. "How did you two become friends?"

Her eyes widen with excitement, and she starts telling me the story of how they met in high school, when they both were dating someone on the football team, learned it was the same guy, and hatched a plan of revenge rather than hating each other.

I listen to her tell me the rest of the story animatedly, backing away whenever she closes the distance between us. I don't have any valuables in my bag, but I still prefer my items to remain mine, thank you very much.

"Excuse me?" A deep voice joins us. "Have either of you seen Valerie?"

Jennifer's eyes widen in recognition first. Then, since I've never met him in person, only saw photos from his Instagram that haven't been updated in a decade, I recognize him, sort of. His blond hair has gray streaks throughout it, and a gathering of wrinkles pulls at the sides of his thin lips.

"Nick?" I can't help but ask. Taina found his home address and info, but he's supposed to be twenty-eight, and he doesn't look *old* but he looks old*er*.

He blinks. "You know me?"

"What the hell are you doing here?" Bethany shouts, storming over. She grabs the bouquet of flowers in his hands, slaps his face with them, then tosses them to the side.

Valerie hesitates behind her aunt, her eyes wide, her body moving like weights hold down every muscle.

"Valerie—" He tries to approach, but Bethany blocks his path.

"What the hell are you doing in my house?"

He looks Bethany up and down in a way that makes me inch closer to them. "I was invited."

"The hell you were," Bethany says.

Valerie finally moves at a normal speed, grabbing Bethany and pushing her to the side. Her expression is unreadable as she looks up at him. "You brought flowers," she points out. "I'm getting married soon. This is my Jack and Jill. What are you trying to do here?"

"I want you back," he says. "I don't care that you're getting married. I don't care about the age difference. I don't care what your family thinks. We should have never broken up."

A hush settles in the room as every single person stops what they're doing to watch.

I cannot help but insert myself. "How old are you?"

He glares at me, probably wondering who the hell I am and why I would ask that during his confession, then brings his attention back to Valerie.

Jennifer whispers beside me. "He's pushing fifty."

"Fifty." I've lost all sense of control. "Isn't he in his twenties?"

Jennifer frowns at me. "Do you mean his son? They have the same name. Are you confused?"

There's a sudden pounding behind my eyes. A hammering of different bundles of information bouncing around in my head, trying to make sense of things, but the nails loosen as soon as they are pounded into a board. Taina is so thorough when checking someone's info; I'm not sure how she could have messed this up.

She must have seen the younger Nick and assumed that was Valerie's ex. Not the man who could have been her father. Daddy issues or not, that age gap is something I'm not entirely sure I can get behind.

This is who Valerie keeps thinking about?

"Get out"—Valerie shoves him—"and don't ever show your face here again."

Olive, who apparently has a sixth sense for too-adult conversations, appears dragging something behind her. When she tries to pass Valerie, I see she's holding a bat.

"Jesus." I hurry over and snatch it before she takes one of us out.

"Yeah, you're stronger," Olive notes. "You hit him."

I pry the bat from her and toss it away from anyone's reach. "I think we all need to regroup here."

Nick steps forward. "How are you going to invite me, then take it back now that I'm here?"

"I didn't invite you," Valerie snaps, looking back at Bethany with wide eyes. "I swear I didn't!"

Nick snatches his phone from his pocket and holds out the screen, showing the messages Taina and I sent back and forth with him. My cheeks burn. This is not at all how I envisioned this happening. This was supposed to be a warm reunion between two age-appropriate adults who were meant to find their way back to each other.

Valerie jerks back. "That is not me."

"What?" he stammers, then he types into the phone and holds it to his ear.

I take a step back, ready to leave. I'm too slow to realize before it's too late. Before Olive pulls my phone from her pocket, the screen lit up with Nick's phone call.

"Olive?" Valerie shouts.

"It's not my phone." She drops it from her hand like it shocked her.

I hurriedly bend for it, snatch it, and back away. All eyes are on me now. More importantly, Valerie's are. I see it on her face, the rapid calculating, trying to understand what's happening. Sorting through bits and pieces of information that don't make sense, no matter where they're placed.

"Lucy?" she says my name like a question, like it's the only one she can think of at the moment.

I haven't had a chance to figure out what to do, what to say, when this moment happened, if it happened, and I'd really hoped it wouldn't.

My first scenario is that I would simply go back to New York, and everyone I met here would be a memory. Then, after Anders, after our promises, I thought I could have Valerie end the wedding herself, and there wouldn't be any fingers pointing my way, and anger, or questions at all.

I was foolishly wrong.

Bethany manages a full question. "Why is Nick calling you?"

Olive looks up at me with wide eyes. "What's going on, Lucy?"

I want to shrink myself into a size so insignificant that I can hide between one of the cracks of the floorboards. At least until I can formulate a response that will explain myself while managing to keep Anders's family from hating me, while not throwing Anders under the bus, but also explaining my reasoning for all I've done.

But I just don't have the time.

I'm so sorry is all I can think to say. I gesture to Nick. "He isn't who I thought. This isn't what I thought—what I wanted. I'm so sorry."

"What is happening?" Bethany snaps. "Explain yourself."

"I'm sorry," I say again, and run as fast as possible to Anders's car. I throw myself in, lock the door, and rush back to Anders before I can face the fire of questions I'm not equipped to defend myself from.

This wasn't supposed to happen like this. This wasn't supposed to happen at all.

When I pull up to the house, an unfamiliar car is parked in the driveway behind Taina's rental. Not an Uber, since there's nobody in the car. I'd think it's Anders, but he wouldn't get a rental just to get back home.

Then I get out, spot a man talking with his hands on the porch, and my sister in front of the door, shouting.

My stomach free-falls.

I rush over and call out her name. Then he turns—Mathew. I stop so fast my knees can't keep up, and I trip on the stairs. Pain ricochets up my body as I grip the railing for support.

"I knew it," Mathew spits out. "Of course you're here. Bailing your sister out of whatever trouble she's gotten into. Again. Always."

"What trouble?" Taina rushes over to my side, still in her sweats. "Sorry, I came unannounced again. I wanted to finish our fight." Then, she faces Mathew. "We're having a little vacation together. I told you I was coming here."

"This isn't the address of the rental you booked," Mathew says. "Why are you here?"

"Why are you tracking my exact location? What have I ever done to warrant that?"

"You're helping out with one of her ridiculous jobs, aren't you?" He looks to me. "You really can't do anything on your own."

I look down as Taina says, "Who the hell are you speaking to like that?"

"I told you I was sick of this!" he tells Taina. "I told you to let your sister clean up her own messes for once. You said this was a vacation. I knew you lied."

"And you didn't?" Taina shoots back as I try to step away, but she tightens her hold on my waist. "You're supposed to be on a work trip, not stalking me."

"You're my *wife*."

"And she's my *sister*."

"I'm your *husband*."

"I should go." I pry Taina's fingers off me. To fling myself into the ocean, if it meant getting away from anyone and everything right now. It's all too much.

"You should have gone a long time ago," Mathew says. "Your time limit is almost up. I warned you. I don't care if you don't have the money. You promised you'd leave my house."

Taina grips my shoulder with her nails. I'm sure she'll draw blood. She pins me in place, looks up at Mathew with a flat expression, her voice a single, leveled tone. "Excuse me? What time limit?" Then she turns to me. "What promise?"

"You coddle your sister," Mathew says, "and it's exactly why she doesn't grow up. So, I stepped in."

Taina takes a measured breath, looks to me. "And you didn't tell me about this conversation?"

My brows pull together. "I don't want to ruin your relationship."

"Yet you do an amazing job at it," Mathew shoots out.

Taina lets me go. I see it in her, the lack of emotion, the fists at her sides, the straightening of her shoulders. I wrap my arms around her. "Taina, no."

"Wife?" Taina struggles to free herself from my grasp. "I'll be a widow from this point on."

"Taina!"

"I'll kill you," she says to Mathew. She turns and elbows me. "You, too, for keeping this from me." She nearly slips out of my grasp, but the extra weight I have on her helps me yank her down the steps.

Instead of using the space as a barrier, Mathew storms down to us.

Before he reaches the center of the stairs, someone bullets past us. Anders grabs a fistful of Mathew's shirt and throws him down with force.

Anders is larger, but barely. Mathew doesn't roll down the stairs, but the impact sends him stumbling down, gripping the railing to keep from hitting the pavement.

Anders is in an all-black sweatsuit, his hair a windswept mess, and his brows are knitted together; a long wrinkle dents the center of his forehead. When he approaches us, reaches out to touch a hand to my face, his hand is a gentle contrast to the anger radiating off his body.

"You okay?" he asks so softly, my eyes burn with tears from the only person tonight who has spoken to me without a hint of anger.

I nod, and he caresses my cheek.

Mathew barks out a cruel laugh. "What's this?" he asks. "Are you sleeping with him? You really will use anyone for your own benefit, won't you?"

Both Taina and Anders whirl on him, and I somehow am able to run in front of them both, placing a hand on each chest.

"Please stop."

Anders firmly grips my wrist, pulls me away. "That's the bastard who threatened you, isn't it?" Anders asks. "He wanted to kick you out even with nowhere to go."

Taina shoves a finger at Anders. "You told him and not me? Are you kidding me?"

A screeching of tires tears through the air, and we all turn to the sound. Valerie is storming toward us, barefoot, with a wild look in her eyes. Oh no.

"She knows," I warn Anders. "She knows what I've been doing."

His expression remains impassive as he faces Valerie. He stands in my path so that her fury lands on him first. "Was it all a lie?" she asks him. "You never really got behind the wedding. She never convinced you."

"It's true," Anders says.

Valerie laughs harshly. "I knew you hated the idea of us marrying, but I thought you hated Nick more. I can't believe you tried to use him to manipulate me."

Anders falters. "What?" He glances at me. "What is she talking about?"

"I was going to tell you today," I hurriedly get in, "but you were so stressed about the plane, about missing the party, I thought I'd catch you up later."

Anders digs the bottom of his palms into his eyes. "Lucinda, *no*. You should have run this by me. I would have never let this happen."

"I didn't know!" I get out, the words a desperate plea nobody cares for, words that hold no meaning. "I didn't know he was a father, the age difference."

"You didn't know that he tried to control my whole life?" Valerie shouts. "You didn't know that he managed my day, what I ate, who I spent time with, what I was allowed to do, wear, say. You didn't know he was a manipulative bastard that ruined my life? I didn't tell you because I didn't *want* to."

"You wanted to get married where he took you on your first date," I explain, try to see the reasoning behind this, find the lost communication. "You said it's where you realized true love exists."

"Because of *John*." Veins pop out of her neck. "Anywhere Nick took me, all my favorite places, felt tainted, felt unreachable. John spent months and months bringing me to all the places I loved and hated, and showed me that I could form new, better memories. *That's* what I meant."

Panic blooms from every pore. "He tracks your location when you're out."

"Because I have a tendency to wander off on my own, and he wants to make sure I'm somewhere safe."

"You guys barely show any affection."

"Oh my God, Lucy. He's shy, is that a crime? Is it so horrible that he's this awkward, weird, quiet, foolish man? I love him anyway! I love the way he makes me feel like me. No matter what he is, he's *never* a bad person. That's all that matters to me. You had no right to try and ruin that. I thought we were friends." She shoots out the last word like venom before turning on her brother. "And we're blood."

Mathew says, "You really ruin everything you touch." Turning to Anders, he sneers, "You really think she cares about you? She only attaches herself to established, wealthy people—people who can take care of her, because she doesn't know how to do it herself. She wouldn't give you an ounce of attention otherwise."

"Not true." I can barely get it out, and the sound of the words feels like a lie anyway.

"Lucinda," Anders says, like a plea.

"She ruins weddings for a living," Mathew says. "You think she believes in love? That doesn't matter to her. Save yourself the mess she brings wherever she goes."

Not true, not true. It's not true. Right?

But if it wasn't, then the weight of everything I've done, everything I've done wrong, shouldn't squeeze into my bones like they're in the process of being smashed by a handpress. I can take a lot, but not this. Not the eyes of people I love and care about watching me like I'm a stranger, waiting to hear words they deem empty.

Rightly so. They owe me nothing. Not anymore.

If I reach out a hand, if I try to defend myself, everyone will recoil. And witnessing that, feeling the cold of rejection so firmly, is something I can't bear.

There's only one person, a single human, who, no matter what I've done, no matter who they're against, will forgive me and save me from any pain if they could.

My sister.

I meet her gaze, and I see her register every thought and emotion running through me. See her own counter it—the betrayal, the anger, the sympathy, and understanding.

And what overwhelms it the most is the loyalty of love.

In a blur of motion, she grabs my hand and pulls me away. Gripping her keys, she shoves me in a car, and we drive away. Together.

And my sister's presence, no, her very existence, is the only thing that keeps me from breaking entirely.

28.

Days have passed since everything imploded.

I haven't turned on my phone once since we left Charleston. I've been taking comfort in a small cottage on the coast of Connecticut, away from Anders, Mathew, or anyone else—just Taina and the lake surrounding us.

It felt wrong to leave everything so messy, without a word, but I'm too much of a coward to face anyone—especially Anders. All I could do was leave him a handwritten letter, filled with apologies and my wish to have done better, to have been better, to be better. I told him Mathew was right: everything I touch shatters into something horrible. It's better this way—before I break everything beyond repair.

I left another letter for Valerie, explaining it was entirely my fault, my plan, and that Anders had nothing to do with it. (I gave Anders a heads-up in his letter, so he'd know he could throw all the blame my way and repair his relationship with his sister.) I told them I was sorry, and I wrote the same to Bethany and Olive, telling them they deserved better.

A coward's way out—leaving it to Taina to put the letters in their mailbox. Proving Mathew's point that I rely on her too much. But I'm so incredibly fragile that any conversation puts me at risk of spiraling.

That's not why Taina has barely spoken to me all these days, though I pretend it is. I know it's because she has so much she wants to say, she can't process it all at once, at least not in the beginning. Now, she waits for an opening—one where she feels I won't break.

And I'm not sure when that will ever happen again.

Instead of facing anything, I rock on a wooden chair overlooking the lake, surrounded by thick trees and untamed grass. The soft night wind sends ripples through the water, the setting sun dipping into the center of it.

There's only one chair out here, on the dock at the foot of the cottage.

That's probably why Taina—who catches my attention with the sound of wood scraping against concrete—is dragging a dining room chair. When she reaches the dock, the scratching sound eases.

She places the chair directly in front of me, blocking my peaceful view.

"We need to talk."

"Okay."

She narrows her eyes. With the glow of the sunset behind her, her hair uncharacteristically pinned into a bun, she looks so naturally beautiful it steals my breath.

"Don't sound so defeatist already," she says. "We're talking, not arguing."

"Then why is the vein at the side of your forehead making an appearance?"

Her eye twitches. "Maybe because my wonderful, agitating sister somehow still manages to be a smart-ass even while being depressed."

"A truly useless talent."

"You know I'm mad at you," Taina says, getting straight to it. "I've never been angrier with you than I am now. You know that, right?"

My gaze drops to her bare feet as I nod.

"Good. So let's skip to the point." She grabs my ear, pinching until I lift my head to face her. "You should've told me as soon as Mathew approached you." She shakes her head. "No—if he felt comfortable threatening you, he's already spoken to you before. He's already made you feel bad about yourself. You should've told me the second he so much as gave you a dirty look."

"He's not entirely wrong," I say, hating to defend him—and hating that I mean it. "Recently, I've been ruining everything. And I've been a thorn in your marriage. He told me about the therapy. About your nightmares."

Both her eyes twitch this time. "Those are things he never should've told you."

"So you can keep secrets, but I can't?"

"My secrets were to protect you."

"So were mine!" I jump at the sound of my voice skyrocketing. I've been in this numb, leveled, faded calmness for days—just letting time pass without feeling too much. But now, heat and emotion rise to the surface too quickly to suppress; an unexpected tsunami after an earthquake.

"If someone hurt me, and I didn't tell you," Taina says, "you'd kill me."

"Isn't that what I've been doing? Hurting you? Should I fling myself into this lake?"

"Be serious, Lucy."

"I am," I say, my feet tingling. "I'm supposed to be the older sister. I'm supposed to take care of you. I shouldn't be the reason for your stress or anxiety. I shouldn't be a nuisance in your marriage. I should be able to take care of myself."

"Lucy—" She tries to grab my hand, but I stand and rush to the edge of the dock.

"Lucy," she repeats, standing beside me, gazing out at the water. "The only reason I can take care of myself is because of you. You think I don't know everything you've sacrificed? You're my sister—not my mom."

I open my mouth, but she holds up a hand.

"You shouldn't have had to work multiple jobs as a teenager. You should've been able to go to school without a single worry beyond picking out an outfit. Our parents should've taken out loans so you could go to college without having to do anything but study. They should've helped you find an apartment so you could get internships and find a job through them. They should've been around to tell you your exes were trash and forced you to break up. They should've called you over for family dinners and vacations with all the free time you should've had."

She grabs my hand and makes me face her. The tears in her eyes tighten something in my chest like a frayed rope pulling taut.

"*I* got to do all that because of *you.* Your life should be vastly different. But you gave up everything to take care of me, and you never complained. I am who I am because of you. And I could never—will never—be happy if you feel like your presence in my life has been anything less than the best gift I've ever received. This world has been cruel to us both, but I can forgive it for one reason: It gave me you as my sister."

"Taina . . ." My voice breaks, and she tightens her grip on my hands. The pain of it finally pushes the tears out.

"Do I think Mathew is an evil, vile man who deserves to die?" she says. "No, I don't. But could I love a man who casts aside the person who made me who I am—the person who's the reason I even met him—without resentment? No. Lucy, I love you more than anyone. Ever. Period."

"That's not fair to you," I start.

"You don't get a say in what's fair to me—or anyone," Taina says. "It might pain you to remember this, but I am an adult. You helped me grow, but now I am my own person. I make my own decisions. I decide what's important to me. I decide what's fair. I decide what I can tolerate. You always want to fix things before they break, so you don't know this—but sometimes, breaking isn't the end. Breaking lets people learn they can pick up the pieces, no matter how jagged, and put them back together in any way they want. Let people break, Lucy." She places her hands on my cheeks. "Let yourself break."

A small cry escapes me before my not-so-little-anymore sister wraps her arms around me. She rubs my back, hushing me as I cry—until the sun fully sinks into the lake and the moon takes its shift in the sky.

I'm not sure if I can put my jagged pieces back together—at least not in a beautiful, bright way like Taina can. There are so many pieces, shattered and reflecting back at me, looking like nothing more than failures.

But if I move them around, will it be less painful?

Where do I even begin?

When my breathing finally evens out, Taina sits me down and takes the seat beside me. It's a little embarrassing, crying like this in front of her. But now that I've done it, my shoulders feel a little lighter.

The silence embraces us until Taina says, "So . . ." She stretches the word. "What's your next move? Are you going to talk to Anders? Are you going to tell Joshua you're buying his share of Save a Paw? Are you going to go AWOL and send me postcards from around the world while I search for you?"

"What's *your* next move?" I counter. "Mathew's probably trying to find you. Did you turn your location off? Otherwise he would've shown up by now, wouldn't he?"

"I know exactly what my next move is, and he's lucky it isn't murder," she says. "But I'm asking you, Lucy. What's next? You can't hide forever."

I blow out a breath. "I didn't ruin the wedding. I'm not getting paid. And I'm not sure Anders—after everything—should give me a dime."

Taina purses her lips. "He already did. He paid you everything he said he would."

I freeze. "Excuse me?"

"I turned on your phone." She shrugs. "We weren't talking, and the Wi-Fi sucks here. I was bored. And nosy. He's been trying to reach you, but I haven't answered his calls or anything."

"Just looked through all his messages?"

She smiles, unashamed. "He's upset about a lot, but he thinks you still deserve the money. The chance for your dream to come true. Even mad, he still sees good in you. I'm not sure that's a man you should ignore, Lucy."

"I—" The words catch in my throat as another wave of tears comes.

"That's okay," Taina says, patting my back. "Get them all out."

Anders thinks I still deserve a good life. But I'm not sure if I deserve kindness. Did I do enough to earn it? Was what we had enough to sustain some kind of fondness between us?

For me, of course. Absolutely. But for Anders?

This gift is both heavy and painful—but I'm so grateful.

And it hurts too. It's only been a couple of days, but I miss Anders—his easy way, the comfort he brings, the way he makes me feel confident and funny and adored and loved.

Love? Is that why this hurts so much?

Knowing I messed things up in such a humiliating way that it will never look the same again?

And now that everything's blown up, is Anders seeing me in a different light? In shades of color he hadn't seen before?

Does he like what he sees with all of them together?

I'm not sure I'm ready to find out.

"I think," I say between tears. "I think I need some time to myself."

"Then take it. As much as you need."

"But not from you," I say, leaning on my sister—without guilt, without shame. "If that's okay with you."

"Oh, big sis." Taina pinches my cheek. "You'd have to kill me to get rid of me."

I laugh—and some of the pain eases at the sound. At the reminder that I am more than one color, more than just broken pieces.

29.

Two weeks later, I sit on one side of a tiny green table at a coffee shop in Charleston. My iced latte remains filled to the brim, condensation pooling in the morning sun. The chai across from me is half empty, held by manicured hands digging into its sides—tiny half-moons denting the plastic.

Though Valerie agreed to meet me when I called two days ago, she didn't technically agree to speak, which might be why she hasn't even offered a greeting. She just sat down, took her drink, and glared at me while I worked up the courage to say what we both know I'm here for.

When I open my mouth—almost like she doesn't want me to get the jump on her—she speaks first.

"You reached out to me before Anders? Why?"

The mention of Anders steals some of the moisture from my throat. I haven't responded to a single message or call, and they dwindled until he finally stopped trying.

"I hurt you the most," I answer, trying to sound like my heart doesn't feel bruised. "So I wanted to see you, to say that I'm sorry—and to let you rip into me, because you deserve the outlet."

She narrows her eyes. "Is this reverse psychology? You want me to feel bad for you so I don't tear you a new one?"

I shake my head. "I want you to do whatever you want. Whatever will make you feel better."

She tilts her cup back and forth. "And if spilling this all over your head would help?"

I push my coffee toward her. "This one's full—use it instead."

Valerie slams her cup down. "I don't get you. You do something horrible, but you look like I just killed your childhood pet. You could have stayed the hell away from me, knowing how pissed I am, but instead, you're sitting here, willing to let me humiliate you? Anders hired you to ruin my wedding, yet you tried to shoulder all the blame and make it seem like you manipulated him into it?"

At my wide eyes, she gives me a look.

"Did you really think Anders would let that slide? He told us the truth. All of it. Start to finish. I don't get you, Lucy. Are you a good person or a bad one?"

"I don't know." I look down at my lap. "I'm just a person."

She rolls her eyes, downs the rest of her chai, and glares at me. "If you think just because you're sorry I'm going to forgive you, you're embarrassingly mistaken."

"I'm not sorry because I think you'll forgive me. I'm sorry because I misunderstood, and I did a horrible thing to you."

She looks me up and down. "So you don't care if I forgive you?"

"I'd like you to. But I understand if you can't."

Her bottom lip trembles. She bites down on it before snatching my coffee out of my hands.

"I thought we were friends," she says. "I knew you were Anders's girlfriend"—she uses air quotes—"and that came first. But you made me feel like you were a safe space. That was a lie."

"I lied a lot," I admit. "But if you needed me—if you still need me—I'm here for you. That part was never a lie."

She looks away, sips from my drink, but her hand is shakier than she probably wants it to appear.

"I really like you, Valerie. I like that you don't care if you're being snobby, because you're still kind. I like how you defend your family and yourself. I think you're brave, and funny, and a little careless with your words in the way only a self-proclaimed nepo baby can be. I like that no matter if you're in a good mood or a bad one, you own it fully. I like so much about you."

She pulls back like I've insulted her. "What the hell is this?"

"A confession," I say. "A real one. Maybe a few months—or a few years—down the line, you're bored and think of me. I can still be a friend. If you need it." I shake my head. "Not need. You don't. You stand on your own. But if you want."

She traces circles on the table with her curved nail, eyeing me, inspecting my face like she's trying to peek into my brain and decode my thoughts. Figure out if I mean it. Figure out if she even cares if I do.

"You came all the way to Charleston for this?"

"No," I admit. "This was part of it. But I've got other things to see to as well. Still, this was one of the most important."

"You had me—all of us—fooled," Valerie says. "It's hard to tell if this is real, because you've already proven to be a good actress."

"I wish I could prove it to you in a way you'd believe," I tell her.

She shuts her eyes, tilts her head in a stretch, and then opens them again. "John isn't who you or Anders thought he was." She looks down, swirls my latte, looks up at me. "And Anders finally admitted that," she adds. "He came over after everything, said he was wrong about trying to intervene. I know he projected all his own stuff onto John because he didn't want me to get hurt again. But he gets it now. He sees that we love each other deeply."

My chest tightens. "That's good. I'm glad."

"I know he's not what anyone saw for me," she says. "And yeah, John made that mistake with the money. But it wasn't anything like what Nick did. Everyone screws up. John just does it while meaning well. And that counts for something. He's naive, but it just makes me want to protect him more. And I'm emotionally all over the place, and he is always patient with his care. It's a messy love, but it's both our lives to sloppily go through together. I don't need a perfect partner. I just need genuine love."

She goes on. "I know he makes mistakes, but when Nick hurt me, it was on purpose. And there's so much more to John that his mistakes feel like nothing, in the grand scheme of things."

My years in a lower tax bracket will never let me dismiss a million dollars lost as "nothing," but it's not my relationship. It's not my broken piece to put back together.

"You're right."

"I am," she says. "And you and Anders were wrong." She cocks her head. "You're alike, but different. Anders wants to take care of everyone, but acts like he isn't trying to. He wants to be invisible—on the sidelines, watching the people he loves be happy. You're similar, but you want to be visible. You don't mind getting involved, getting your hands dirty, being seen trying. You're both pains in the ass."

I laugh, then slap a hand over my mouth. I'm not sure it's something I'm allowed to do right now.

Valerie laughs too—then frowns, like she hates that she let it slip.

"Look, you saw my shitty bridesmaids. You know I don't have too many good friends. And unfortunately, I like you too."

The present tense makes hope perk up in my bones. I sit up straighter, leaning forward.

"You said you wish you could prove you're telling the truth. Do you mean that?"

"I do. Yes. Of course."

"Okay." She links her fingers together. "I've postponed the wedding. Not because I don't love John—or vice versa—but if everyone around me is nervous, everyone who's seen me through some dark times, then I want to ease some of the worry. This fall—I'm getting married. For real this time."

"Okay."

"Will you help plan it?" she asks, and it's the last thing I expected. "If you want to prove you're a good friend, then repair what you broke. Do the opposite of what brought you here. Help me get married. For real."

"I've never planned a wedding before," I stammer.

"But you've planned how to ruin one," Valerie points out. "So you know the ins and outs. You've been trying to wreck weddings every which way—you probably know more than you think."

I chew my bottom lip, trying to formulate a response—trying to process my workload—when she adds, "Is it Anders? Do you not want to be in Charleston?"

I don't respond. I haven't nailed down what my future looks like. I have a general idea, but I don't want to get my hopes up.

She takes my silence as an admission.

"He's not even going to be here much. He's going back to the office in New York for a while—thinks he wants to get away from us, or give us a break from him, not sure. You'll barely see him. Honestly, we've seen him more with you here. He usually works, travels—this is the longest he's let us have him."

"That's not it," I finally say, a flood of emotions rushing through me. "He's not the problem. I—I actually have plans that'll keep me here. In Charleston. But nothing's for sure yet."

"What is this, hide and seek?" Valerie asks. "You come here. He goes there. Are you purposely avoiding him?"

I shake my head. "I don't want to avoid Anders."

"But you won't see him?"

"I'm not sure how."

"I'm offended you found me more approachable than him," she says. "But, Lucy, Anders is doing what he always does—putting himself on the sidelines. I don't think he belongs there. I think you should pull him onstage, because he doesn't know how to get there himself."

I open my mouth, then shut it. I agree. I think Anders should be happy out in the open. I don't want him to feel like he has to pull away—like he isn't wanted.

But I'm nervous I'm not the one who can make him as happy as he deserves. Every relationship I've been in has failed. Even if his family forgives me, who's to say our relationship can ever be healed? Shouldn't he be with someone with less baggage?

"Can we revisit this conversation?" I finally ask.

Valerie rolls her eyes. "I've barely forgiven you, and you're already taking advantage."

"Sorry," I say.

"Yeah, yeah." She waves a hand. "What are these plans? If you're not staying for Anders, why the hell would you stay in Charleston?"

"I'm going to buy K9 Friends," I say. "I think. It's actually not up for sale."

"The place Anders adopted Sora?"

My heart stutters at the thought of Anders traveling so much, but between him and Olive, I know Sora is well loved and taken care of.

"Yeah. It needs a lot of repairs, a lot of funding, a new staff member—maybe more. Just an overall facelift. I think it deserves it. It lacks a lot, but not love. It's loved so much, and I want it to have everything it needs. I want it to be better."

"So"—Valerie frowns—"you're going to buy a shelter that's not for sale."

"I don't know if you know this about me," I say before I can stop myself, "but I'm pretty good at convincing people to do things."

When Valerie glares at me, I add, "Too soon?"

She frowns for a second, then tilts her head in a laugh. "I hate that I like you."

"I love that I like you."

She smiles—and I feel the pieces of our friendship click back into place. When they do, it's brighter and warmer than it was before.

30.

My hands ache from gripping the metal wrench—slick with the sweat from my palms—trying to turn the screw, under the water valve, to the left. At this point I'm sure, when I pull away, some of my flesh will remain on the tool.

Dainese, behind me, says, "I told you we should just call a plumber."

"Do *you* have plumber money?" I say through gritted teeth, trying to turn the damn screw for the millionth time. We have three new dogs to groom, and the pipes decided this was the perfect time to stop working.

"I might if someone hadn't purchased brand-new monitors for the cages," Dainese counters.

"You can't live without falling asleep to TV," I shoot back. "The dogs deserve the same."

"Touché."

I suck in a breath and twist.

In a violent burst, the screw completely loosens, the pipes buckle, and water shoots from them, smacking into me. Dainese yelps, and we scramble to shove them back into place on the walls.

"Find the screw!" Dainese shouts, and I drop to the floor, feeling around for it.

We're drenched by the time I find it, and nearly drowned by the time I position it back where it belongs and screw it shut. The water eases but still leaks from sporadic areas of the pipes.

Dainese, hair so matted it looks like a second skin, deadpans, "Should I call the plumber now?"

"I think that's a great idea. I wish you had thought of it before." She shakes her fist at me, then leaves me at the grooming station.

It was the only place we haven't renovated since I purchased a share three months ago. Partly because it was the most expensive quote, and partly because I wanted to focus on the dogs' living areas—extending the walls for more space, clear glass so it felt less like a prison and more like shared area, grade-A cushions for dogs with arthritis—then getting a new POS system, hiring a permanent assistant for when I wasn't around, buying the supplies to onboard more dogs, and gathering quotes for potentially building an addition for private vet visits for dogs who don't do well traveling, so we could have vet techs do what they needed here.

Business ownership is exactly what I thought it'd be: challenging, scary, overwhelming, and entirely rewarding. Though the rewarding part is the animals outside or watching HD dog TV, and not housekeeping work that tends to pop up each time I think we're finally settled.

My phone buzzes in my overalls pocket.

I answer Valerie's FaceTime, and she grimaces in rollers and an unfinished face of makeup. Taina peeks her head in and waves, then grimaces too. "Gross."

"Thanks, you're both so sweet," I say to the girls, who have become incredibly close since Taina began visiting every other week in between traveling around, trying to find "what place calls to her; what place feels like home." Close enough that Taina's doing her wedding makeup tomorrow.

"You better get your ass dried and presentable, rehearsal starts in three hours."

"Do you really need me there?" I ask.

Valerie narrows her eyes. "You'd have to see Anders at the wedding anyway, wouldn't it be better to get it over with before then?"

I scoff. "That's not what I meant."

Taina snorts. "Sure it's not."

"Wow, betrayed by my own flesh and blood."

"Be honest," Valerie says, "have you really not heard from him all this time? Is this going to be your first time seeing him in months?"

"It is," Taina answers. "Lucy, don't forget to pluck your eyebrows. You can't see him looking like that. Have some dignity."

I slap the phone to my forehead.

It's true, I haven't spoken to Anders in months. Stalked online? Searching his social media every single day, waiting for a new post (he never posts), watching to see if he uploaded any stories? (He only did three times, all covers he was working on.) I typed up his name to call, then immediately turned off my phone, then immediately turned it on, and dialed from a private number to hear him say "Hello?" enough times that he thought it was spam and stopped answering. Drove by his house a couple of times trying to see if his car was there, pretending I had the courage to go up and knock on the door and say hello and sorry and bring up all the unresolved emotions that keep me up at night and raise my water bill when I'm in the shower for way too long—stuck on an endless cycle as permanent as day turning to night and night turning to day.

Yes, humiliating. Yes to all the above.

Has my heart stuttered every time my phone rang, hoping it was him, feeling endlessly disappointed when it wasn't?

Also, embarrassingly, yes, of course.

So the thought of having to see him again is invigorating and terrifying and embarrassing because, even though I was the one who pulled away first, I can't help but feel like he's completely finished with whatever we were building. Which is totally fine, for him.

And yet I spend so much time thinking of ways to reach out, then finding reasons to pull away instead, and cycling these useless thoughts over and over again instead of facing it head-on.

"Earth to Lucy," Valerie says.

"I'll go," I mumble. "See you later."

I hang up and head out to the entryway, larger now, with new, easier-to-clean floorboards and a fresh coat of light-blue paint on the smooth walls. Dainese frowns as she hangs up the phone from behind the desk.

"No luck?" I ask her.

"Too much luck," she says. "Ever since you moved here, everyone is . . . nicer when I call?" She shakes her head. "That's not the right word; it's not that they weren't nice, but they're almost too eager to help. And their quotes are way lower than they used to be."

"Are you sure?" I frown. "I don't know anybody, so I wouldn't warrant any special treatment. Maybe they like you and you don't realize it."

She counts off her fingers. "The vet charges way less for visits. Our bulk orders have been discounted fifteen percent each time, the carpenter didn't even charge us for the floorboard changes, and this plumber just quoted me two thousand less than when the pipes first broke."

"Well"—I point to my drenched appearance—"I'm not often lucky, so whatever is happening, I say we don't question it."

"I guess," Dainese says. "But if you're sleeping with any of the vendors, you can be honest, I won't judge you for it."

"Excuse me? Most of them are, like, sixty years old."

"Nuh-uh," Dainese says. "The plumber is our age, and he's genuinely the sexiest man I've ever seen in my life."

"No way!" I say. "I've never seen him."

"Please hold." She brings up her phone, types for a bit, then pulls up a photo of him. "Sexy, right?"

Blond isn't normally my type, but he's got sharp, defined features and a movie-star smile. Not at all what comes to mind when I think plumber. I usually pull up a *Super Mario Bros.* visual.

"Sexy, but still, not sleeping with him."

"Then it's not too late for me."

"On that note," I say. "I have to head out early."

"Rehearsal," she remembers, grabs the towel she used on herself, and tosses it over my face. "Hope you clean up beforehand."

"Is this a roast?" I snap, grabbing it and drying my face off, leaving her to her laughter.

The air is crisp and sharp as the light autumn wind slices into my skin, made worse by the water still clinging to my hair and clothes. It's been an abnormally warm fall, but being wet in the wind makes my teeth chatter as I walk home.

My route is familiar now from all the times I've walked back and forth from the shelter to my condo. It's a fifteen-minute walk, longer before I found a shortcut through a cemetery that shortened the time by ten minutes.

Creepy sometimes, but also safe, knowing nobody here cares at all about me. And since my condo overlooks it, the price is significantly lower than any other place so close to the beaches.

As I walk, I think about what Dainese said. About the weird luck. The way things have somehow fallen into place here, even when I was too busy to notice.

And I think about Save a Paw.

For years, that was the dream. The only dream. The thing I worked toward every second. And when it began slipping out of reach, all I could feel was this dread of inevitable failure.

But I didn't love the shelter because of the name on the building.

I loved it because of the dogs I cared for. The ones I cleaned, and fed, and sang off-key to. I loved it because I loved what *I* was able to do for *them.*

That's what I've found here, accidentally.

Maybe because I stopped trying to force things. Or maybe because I finally looked up and realized this life—this business, this place, and the people that I've fallen in love with—wasn't a backup plan.

It was an evolution of a dream I've always had.

I quicken my pace as the cold starts to seep into my bones, and a few too many sneezes rack through my body. If I get sick the day before her wedding, I'm pretty sure Valerie will remove the nails from my fingers and toes.

My teeth are chattering by the time I make it out of the cemetery, turn the corner to my house, and hurry up the path. Then I see someone leaning by the front door, arms crossed over his chest.

I trip over my own feet, save myself from a complete face-plant with my sore hands, and right myself just in time for Anders to look up and notice me.

He's in dark jeans and a black sweater that makes his hair even darker, his eyes even brighter, even at this distance. He's got a little five o'clock shadow and a tiny wrinkle between his slightly furrowed brows. The wind has swept up stray strands of hair that fall on his forehead, his cheek, and it's slightly longer—just a couple of centimeters—than the last time I saw him.

My heart pounds as he pushes himself from the door and approaches me with long, purposeful strides. His scent hits me first—sandalwood and mango and pure comfort. He stops an arm's length away, and I tilt my neck to meet his gaze.

His is without heat or coolness. Unreadable.

"Lucinda," he says, and hearing his voice in person, instead of a generic greeting from the phone speaker, makes my stomach flip.

I open my mouth, feel a sneeze coming on, and then hold a hand to my lips. He looks handsome and sexy and amazing, and I look like a drowned rat that got resurrected only to be drowned again.

"Why are you here?" I shout without meaning to, then suffer three sneezes back-to-back.

"Why are you so wet?" he asks, moving forward, then immediately moving back. "You're going to get a cold; you should go inside."

"But you're outside," I point out, "at my place—how did you know it was my place? What are you doing here? Why are you here? You have the worst timing ever."

"Will you get inside and change?" he snaps.

"Will you answer any of my questions?"

"Once you're dry."

"What if I like being wet?"

At that, we both pause, and his expression wavers as his eyes flicker, and I slam a hand to my mouth twice in punishment for being the most idiotic thing about me.

"Oh my God." I move around him, fumble with my keys, and take three tries before being able to actually unlock the door. "Pretend you never saw me," I call out to him, gripping the door. "Erase this from your memory. I don't look like this. And I didn't say that."

He opens his mouth, and I slam the door and lock it.

I've wanted to see Anders again so badly, it's ruined my critical thinking skills. I've lost track of thoughts, dozed off mid-conversations, because I thought of him somehow and have had to actively reposition myself into reality.

And, of course, he sees me looking insane, saying insane things, while being vastly underprepared.

Too much luck.

Yeah, right.

I take over an hour to get ready. I shower twice. Shave three times. Drench myself in lotion and body oils. I start my makeup, hate the base, wash it all off, and start again. I flatten my hair too perfectly, then curl the roots for volume, but it gives it a weird lump at the top, so I straighten it all over again.

I exhaust myself until I become an annoyingly beautiful version of myself and make it to the museum with only five minutes to spare.

This is how I wanted to see Anders again. I make my way into the venue, hurry past the entryway and into the largest hall with enough room to fill the fifty guests coming tomorrow along with the bridal party and groomsmen.

And somehow, I'm still earlier than everyone aside from Bethany, Olive, Taina, John, and Valerie.

"There she is," Bethany says when she hears my heels clicking on the floor.

Olive waves at me. "I knew you weren't going to chicken out." She points a thumb toward the group sitting on one of the benches wound with flowers and hand painted by Anders with floral designs Valerie picked out. "They bet one hundred dollars you'd pretend to be sick to get out of it."

I hold out a hand as I approach. "Well, I hope I get a hundred dollars for the embarrassment."

Taina stands. "Great timing, I have to use the bathroom." She links her arm through mine and leads me away.

"You needed my company to go potty?" I ask as we move. "This brings me back to the good old days."

When we exit the hall, she lets me go and blocks my path, her arms crossed against her chest. "I overheard—"

"You snooped."

"—Valerie on the phone with Anders. He said he had a migraine and wasn't coming to the rehearsal. What happened?"

I keep my features blank. "What do you mean? You answered your own question. He has a migraine." Then something clicks into place. "You little rat, you gave him my address."

"Duh." She shoves me. "He asked me for it months ago, and I've been waiting for him to do something about it forever. Valerie said he mentioned trying to see you before the wedding, that it might make you feel less awkward."

I rub my eyes. "And now he didn't come because I shouted at him to erase me from his memory."

"What?"

"A misunderstanding." I slap a hand on her mouth to quiet her down. "I wanted him to erase the way I looked then. And restart now. Not that I didn't want to see him at all."

"I really can't stand you sometimes."

"You and me both." I sigh.

"Well"—Taina links her arm with mine again—"let's go out tonight. Can't waste how hot you look on nobody."

"Me drinking before a wedding?" I ask. "Bad omen. Let's keep it sober."

"Booo." She thumbs me down.

And that's the image I play in my head all night. The sound of a sitcom's booing track echoing in my skull over and over.

Hopefully, I find my luck again.

31.

As much as my gaze travels to Anders throughout the wedding, and how much he always takes up space in my head, I finally have enough of a distraction to think of something else.

Valerie, as she promised, with her makeup and hair done—half up, half down—looks radiant as she listens to John's shaky, nervous but genuine vows. Even when she cries at them and her cheeks become speckled with mascara, the happiness in her eyes—made brighter when John wipes the tears away—makes her an ethereal being.

I pat my own cheeks dry as the officiant, Bethany, pronounces them wife and husband, and I let out a half sob when they kiss.

Officially married.

How it was meant to be, always, even when I thought differently.

We cheer for them as they walk out of the hall hand in hand, and the party follows them down the aisle before the rest of the guests clear out for the reception. Somehow, I get paired with Anders as we walk, and our arms bump each other twice as we make our way out.

He apologizes swiftly, and I shrug it off, pretending each physical touch doesn't make my heart pound and my head spin.

Like we promised, when we make it out the doors, the bridal party steals Valerie away to a separate room and helps her change into a sexier minidress that shows enough cleavage to make John pass out.

She keeps the veil on when we're done, and during their first dance. She tosses it to the ground as soon as it's over, turns to the crowd, and screams, "Let's party!"

And the night really begins.

As soon as I'm clear of any bridal party duties, I grab the nearest wineglass and chug it. Nerves have killed my appetite, and the liquid burns as it slides down my throat, settling at the pit of my stomach.

I'm seated between Jennifer and Taina—Taina already up and flirting with one of the guests—and I don't care that Jennifer is reaching into my clutch, because while she steals my second-best lipstick, I steal her wineglass and down that too.

My gaze scans the room and immediately lights on Anders, who is standing by the round tables, talking to a woman I don't recognize. It's not exactly jealousy that runs through me, but it's too unpleasant to be anything close to neutral, so I take Taina's left-behind glass and drink that too.

In my head, I was going to approach Anders immediately, clear things up, strike up a conversation, ask him how he's been, tell him how I've been, mention, I don't know, that I think about him way too much to keep to myself, and I'm regretful for ignoring him and leaving, not trying harder to stay when he's spent his whole life worried people will leave so he makes himself as small as possible to prevent that in the first place.

Easy, light stuff.

I groan and slam my head on the table. Where is the courage that brought me back to Charleston? That let me face everyone I feared, leaving behind New York and what I thought I wanted, and start something different—similar, but different.

Does my courage apply to everything but love?

No, I'm in a different place now. I have a job I love and my own space, and I'm not exactly where I want to be, but I'm on the way. I love where I live. I love having an honest start. I love my life here, my friends, my sister, and I'm happy.

Nearly perfectly happy, too—but that's impossible right now, anyway. Not when I'm missing one thing, one person.

I suck in a breath, fortify myself, and stand. I move forward toward Anders, and his head turns slightly toward me.

And I whirl around and bump into another table. Amazing start, honestly.

After a few minutes, I try again, and as soon as Anders makes a move to turn in my direction, I pivot. It happens enough times that Anders and the woman finish their conversation, and he walks away talking to a man with blond hair.

Instead of trying again, I find an empty table and sit down for a quick time-out. I need to get it together. There's no need to be nervous. I told myself weeks ago I was going to face Anders head-on when I saw him. It's not like I'm doing anything difficult. It's a conversation, for God's sake.

I get up, my knees buckle, and I immediately sit back down.

"You're the worst," I mutter to myself, dropping my forehead onto the table once, twice, several times in punishment.

Something soft blocks my headbutt, and his words make my body pulse with warmth as he says, "Are the tables here upsetting you? I've seen you bump into several."

I move my face back from his palm, and when I turn, my nose is pressed against his; he's so close. Every part of me stills, and my heart races hard enough that the vibration reverberates throughout my rib cage.

"You've seen me all this time?"

"I, well, yes," he admits, pulling away to stand, and my body instinctively misses his proximity. "I wasn't sure if you wanted to talk to me or if I kept catching you trying to avoid me, so I thought I'd just ask you directly."

Too desperate to have dignity, the words tumble out of me. "I don't want to avoid you."

Finally, a glimpse of Anders appears. His dimples press into his cheeks as his smile slowly takes over his face. "That's good to know."

"I also didn't want to avoid you yesterday," I explain, "but I was—you caught me at an inopportune time—I wanted to, I don't know, not look ridiculous."

"You were as beautiful then as you are now."

I frown at him. "You've become a better liar."

His smile falters—maybe the reminder of the time we spent apart upsets him as much as it upsets me.

"Can we talk?" We ask at the same time, mirroring each other's smiles.

Anders holds out a hand as the band plays a slow couples' dance. I take it, and he leads me to the dance floor. His hands snake around my waist, and I press my palms to his chest, let my hand feel his heartbeat, and notice its rhythm speeding to match mine.

He leads me through the first half of the song, and I lay my head on his chest, letting myself get lost in the moment without any baggage or hurt or anything in between. Just the comfort of Anders, of us.

Anders breaks the silence. "Why did you leave?" he asks. "And why did you ignore me when I reached out?"

I tilt my head back to face him. "I wanted to stay with you, but I didn't want to either," I answer. "That doesn't make any sense."

"Then make it," he says softly.

I suck in a breath. "I think I was worried that what Mathew said was right. That everything I touch gets ruined. That somewhere deep in my subconscious, there was someone who used people, and if I was using you, then I couldn't do it anymore. I didn't want to. But then I wanted to be with you so much, so badly, and wished that it was all real, of course, but if it was and I ruined it, how could I forgive myself? And after what I did, I wondered if you could forgive me at all anyway?"

He doesn't falter as the melody changes to another slow ballad, but his hand travels to my face as he cups my cheek. The act is sweet, tender, but his words are hot. "That pisses me off," he says, "that you thought he was right, that you assumed how I would feel without coming to me first."

I try to look down, but he pulls my face toward his.

"I thought," I explain, "it was better not to know than to risk finding out that you couldn't forgive me. That it would hurt less if I left it all open instead of letting you shut the door between us."

"But that's not everything," he notes.

"No. I needed some time to try to figure myself out. To try to heal a little of what I didn't even know was broken. Honestly, I'm not sure if I fully have. I'm probably still a little broken right now. So maybe it's wrong to be here with you, like this. You're supposed to love yourself first before anyone can love you, right?"

"Even if you haven't figured out how to love yourself fully," Anders says, "I have fallen in love with you easily and fully, so no, you don't have to love yourself for someone to love you. I already do." When my legs buckle, he wraps his arms around me and leans down. "But I'd like for you to see yourself the way I do."

"Anders, wait"—I hold out my hands—"this is not what I was planning. This is not my vision. We're skipping steps. I need to say sorry, and then also make a humiliating mention of how many times I stopped myself from reaching out to you, how I called you to hear your voice. Then I was hoping, you know, you had some equally, if not worse, embarrassing moments for me, so that way I don't feel like such a moron for not just reaching out. We can equally just realize that—"

"Please"—Anders grips my face with both hands—"take a breath, Lucinda."

He's so focused on me that we bump into a couple of dancers nearby. Anders pulls away, one hand remaining on my waist as he apologizes.

This close, I see it's the blond man Anders was talking to earlier. Then, a bulb flickers so bright in my head it burns. I hold out a finger toward him. "You're the sexy plumber!"

"Excuse me?" both he and Anders say at the same time, the latter very much annoyed by the statement.

I wave him off, then push the finger to Anders's chest. "You know him?"

"Yeah," he says, then immediately shakes his head. "I mean, not well. We went to high school together. We haven't spoken in a while."

He's not looking me in the eyes. "So you're actually *not* a better liar."

When his lips twitch and he pulls away so I can't examine him closely, I know he's lying.

"You're my luck," I say, more and more pieces forming into warm, jagged, sweet pictures. "You told him to give the shelter a discount."

"Lucinda, I don't know—"

"I bet if I called all our vendors, they'd say they know you, like you, and have spoken to you about K9 Friends."

"Listen, I don't know what you're talking about." He fully steps away, looking around like someone can save him.

"Anders."

He sighs, rubbing the back of his neck. "I don't want you to feel like I was overstepping, or taking anything away from all you worked for. I just thought, you know, even if I couldn't help directly, I wanted to try and ease some burdens for you. It's a lot, owning a business, and you moved down to a new place on your own, and you barely have any staff."

"Anders"—I hold my hands to his chest—"you have been keeping tabs on me this whole time? It hasn't been just me?"

"Of course, Lucinda, how could I ever get you out of my head?"

I grip his face, pull him down to me, and press my mouth to his. As soon as I feel the softness of his lips, the warmth of his touch as his hands wrap around me and press me closer to his body—harder and harder until there's no space between us—my heart races so fast I'm sure it's leaving tire marks in my chest.

The feel of him, his very presence, fills every gap of happiness that has been left open since he's been gone.

I pull away, my chest pounding, heat rushing through every muscle in my body. "Anders, I've missed you."

He presses a hungry kiss over my lips in answer.

I pull away again, and he groans.

"Anders," I say, "I love you."

"Lucinda." Anders presses a kiss on my cheek, my neck, my chin, my mouth, like he's trying to kiss every exposed inch of skin as he speaks. "I love you too." More kisses, more fingers clinging into my skin, pulling me closer. "Stay with me. Don't leave again."

"Wasn't planning on it," I answer with my own spread of kisses. "This is my home."

His gaze softens, and his lips move to the side of my head. At that, a round of applause thunders around us. Anders's family, my family, smile our way, and Valerie and Taina make kissy faces as they do.

No glaring, no lies, no baggage.

Just love, all around, for everyone.

Acknowledgments

I'd like to tell you about my greatest love: my pit bull, Storm (Stormy, Stormy Wormy, Storm-Storm). She is mentioned in the novel as Lucy's dog and her inspiration for working at Save a Paw. Storm is my forever puppy, an old girl diagnosed with Cushing's disease, which is treatable but incurable. I give her all my love all the time, and I would appreciate it if, in her honor, you'd donate to an organization like Grey Muzzle, a place that helps senior dogs in so many amazing ways—www.greymuzzle.org/about-us/who-we-help. Storm is the sweetest, kindest, most innocent and beautiful angel, and was my companion throughout writing this book (and all my books).

"Woof." —Storm on *How to Ruin a Wedding*

I am incredibly lucky in life to have so many people to thank. I fear I may miss someone here, with all the abundance of support I've received. So if I miss you, know it is my forgetful brain typing this out in the middle of the night. I promise I love you as well!

Emily Annie, my life is great for an endless number of reasons, and most of them are because of you. Thank you to Selena James for believing in this story from the moment it hit your inbox—I am eternally grateful. Abby Zidle, thanks for your amazing feedback and help on this novel. To Pippa White and the rest of the team of editors who helped get this story into book form—thank you.

Thank you to Mindy Kaling for picking my book for your imprint! I cannot believe you like this story. Part of me has a God complex that understands why—it's an amazing book! And the other part of me, the one battling imposter syndrome, cannot believe someone as cool as you even knows I exist.

Thank you to my sister, Jessica, whom I love with all of my being—thank you for always being at my side and always ready to play *Super Mario* with me. Thank you to all my family for always bragging about me.

Thank you to my light, Michelle, for never letting me be negative toward myself. Hearing your voice, seeing your name flash on my screen, thinking of your very existence, fills me with happiness.

Thank you to Aylin for always showing up, posting, and trying to make me famous so you can quit your job and steal my money. I'm really trying. I'm currently writing this in your living room, and you're yelling at me that it better be good. Is this enough to ease your pesky, cute self? Thank you to Jeremy for all the game nights when my brain is rotting. Mimi, I love you. Cheska, my life would be significantly less exciting without your joyful presence. Chris Rosa, I have a concerning amount of affection for you (let's watch *Demon Slayer* five million more times). Hiba—my Hiba—what did I do to deserve a friend like you? (Let me know so I can do it again and have you in another life.) My friend Teresa—who eats rare meat and rides horses—you're so cool.

Thank you, Em. You were the first person to read the very first draft of this book (and look how different it's become!). You are such an uplifting soul to me and to the book community. Thank you to Anthony N., mi primo Gabriel, and all the bookish friends I've made online who have supported me and shown me kindness. Thank you to my dear friend Kamilah Cole, who always lends a hand and fights my thanks because "this is just what friends do!"

My Harper people are so dear to me! I have made such genuine friendships, and you've all been supportive in a way I am deeply grateful and honored by. Matt and Ryan—my power couple—I look forward to every moment together, even on that damn commute. Abby, Emily, Lexie, Michael, Sophie, social, all my friends there—thank you! I love my team: Lauren, Sari, Lisa, Danielle, and Emma (thank you for letting me crash at your place and analyze *Avatar: The Last Airbender* because it is very serious to us).

I'm unable to write anything at all without music. It's such an integral part of who I am and my process. So I thank Ryuichi Sakamoto—rest in peace—Nobuo Uematsu, and Yoko Shimomura, my all-time favorite composers, whose music always guides me through my stories.

When editing, I always pick a comfort show to fixate on during breaks, so thank you to Kōhei Horikoshi, the author of *My Hero Academia*, whose story brought me so much peace (and panic) throughout editing this book.

Lastly, thank you to the readers who picked up this story. Your support means more than these words could ever accomplish in relaying. I am so grateful.

About the Author

Photo © 2025 Liv D Photography

Elba Luz is a lover of stories, whether in the form of anime, manga, video games, or books. A failed astrophysicist turned publishing professional in New York City, she can be found annoying people with facts about space or lounging about with her adorable pit bull Stormy. She writes romance for adults and teens.